To My Da... u

CW00983441

The Forgotten Fort

Thank you for inspiring me to write this story. Hope you enjoy reading it!

Lots of love

ARIBA PARTI

N notionpress
.com

LEGEND OF THE HIDDEN TEMPLE SERIES

The Forgotten Fort

KRIPA DEVAR

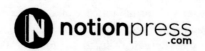

Notion Press

Old No. 38, New No. 6
McNichols Road, Chetpet
Chennai - 600 031

First Published by Notion Press 2017
Copyright © Kripa Devar 2017
All Rights Reserved.

ISBN 978-1-947202-94-8

This book has been published with all reasonable efforts taken to make the material error-free after the consent of the author. No part of this book shall be used, reproduced in any manner whatsoever without written permission from the author, except in the case of brief quotations embodied in critical articles and reviews.

The Author of this book is solely responsible and liable for its content including but not limited to the views, representations, descriptions, statements, information, opinions and references ["Content"]. The Content of this book shall not constitute or be construed or deemed to reflect the opinion or expression of the Publisher or Editor. Neither the Publisher nor Editor endorse or approve the Content of this book or guarantee the reliability, accuracy or completeness of the Content published herein and do not make any representations or warranties of any kind, express or implied, including but not limited to the implied warranties of merchantability, fitness for a particular purpose. The Publisher and Editor shall not be liable whatsoever for any errors, omissions, whether such errors or omissions result from negligence, accident, or any other cause or claims for loss or damages of any kind, including without limitation, indirect or consequential loss or damage arising out of use, inability to use, or about the reliability, accuracy or sufficiency of the information contained in this book.

To My Parents,

Mrs. & the late Mr. Jugadheesan Devar

Acknowledgements

- My beloved Divine Master, Bhagawan Sri Satya Sai Baba through whose grace and guidance inspired me to create this story.

- To my loving parents: So much of me is made up of what I've learned from you. As proud South Africans, we never got to find your family in India, yet a deep-seated love for Indian culture always existed in our home. From a young girl, you inspired me to understand the deeper mysteries of life and trusted me to follow my destiny. This enthused in me a passion to write this story about India - a beautiful, colourful, vibrant and great spiritual hub of the world.

- To my beautiful daughters, Dharani and Nandini: In this journey together, we took a road less travelled. And in doing so, you grew up having the courage never to be afraid, and the confidence to seek and live your dreams. I am so proud of you!

- Grateful thanks to my publishers, Notion Press, for designing a remarkable book to inspire everyone to read.

- To my editorial team – Lorna King and Nandini Parshotam – who worked endlessly with great patience and encouragement, feeding me honest comments and supporting my dream to complete my first book!

Acknowledgements

- My soul family in Bangalore – Srinivas and Seeta, Nidhi and Teja - In the joy and sweetness of our friendship a unique story unfolded. Thank you for your never-ending support and love.

- Lastly, to my gorgeous grand-daughters – Ananda Sai, Jhanavi and Puja: Thank you for inspiring me with your beautiful love and innocence to create the most magical, fun-loving story for YOU and all the other young people in the world. I love you to the stars!

Chapter 1

Dear Diary,

My name is Pooja. I am 12 years old and live in Bangalore, India. We live in a really posh apartment called Emerald Cascades.

Generally, I am a happy girl who loves school. Some kids call me a nerd because I get the highest results, wear glasses and have long braids. But I'm not!

I think I'm cool. I love junk food, listen to pop music – especially my favourite band One Direction – and have some crazy friends. Of course, shopping at our famous malls, watching movies or meeting my besties for pizza is normal stuff for me. But after today, my life is not as simple as I thought.

You may wonder what I'm talking about. OK! If you're a teenager (and I nearly am) living in my times, you'll understand and feel my pain. Let me tell you my sad and pathetic story...

I made ONE stupid mistake. *ONE!*

And guess what? I'm grounded!

You'll get over it, I hear you say. Sure, I will. But in my life it's *not* that simple!

My wonderful parents decided to take punishment to a totally new level. And the result? A ruined life – a life I have barely started! (Tears roll down my cheeks...)

A young and innocent life over! I am so angry, perhaps livid is a better description of how I feel.

I want to know which moron came up with the word "grounded" so often used by parents. We learn about people who invented the light-bulb, telephone, airplanes, computers, mobiles, television – the list is endless, but no one bothered to check this crazy person who created a form of punishment called "grounded."

I grab a dictionary from the bookshelf, and scanning through hastily, I stop...

Grounded means 'to prevent or prohibit a child to go out socially as a punishment'.

I sit up and frown annoyingly.

"My parents must be really stupid not to understand the meaning," I mumble to myself.

It does not state:

Mobile phone taken away...

Banned from watching TV and using the computer...

No friends, no movies, no visiting malls.

Most parents don't understand that the techno-age is the teenage-age. It is our drug, our survival kit! My mobile phone is my precious possession. This tiny gadget is my life-support machine. Now it means no Facebook, no Instagram, no Twitter, and no WhatsApp. Basically, NO LIFE!

They simply added all these extra "punishments" and couldn't be bothered about my feelings. Do they realise I may be psychologically damaged for life? No wonder school counsellors always have long queues outside their office.

How damn annoying are these adults? They come up with strange things to suit themselves:

Eat your vegetables they're good for you. Hello! I'm a vegetarian!

Or, going to bed at 9.00 pm is too late on a school night. But how will I obtain good results if I only study until 8.30 pm?

Or, getting 75% in exams is not good enough. My marks are always over 90%, so why the lecture?

Or, being a doctor or an engineer is the best career ever especially if you are an Indian! Anything else is not acceptable. But I want to be a vet?

I rest my case! The problem is parents don't listen to themselves. Crazy people!

But punishment tactics is probably the most annoying thing about parents. I think there's a secret code given to parents when their babies are born, which allows them to log on to a "parents only" website.

I flip through the Thesaurus for the word "angry" and scribble "furious, fuming, outraged, annoyed," underlining each word twice as tears roll down my cheeks and fall on to the page.

I stare at Eros, my baby pet turtle who can actually float upside down on his shell. This is what I call a cool, simple life. Not a care in the world. With his teeny-weeny legs, he wriggles happily in his bowl of water.

"I wish I was like Eros – carefree, happy with no parents," I say to myself. I continue to scribble. In big bold letters I write the words, I REALLY HATE MY PARENTS, and highlight each word in bright orange, pink, green and blue.

Suddenly I stop writing and burst into tears.

Grabbing my pillow, I clutch it tightly to my chest, weeping loudly until my sobs slowly subside. I lay back staring at the ceiling and whimper like Anjali from *Kuch Kuch Hota Hai* (an ancient movie, but really cool!).

The air is stifling. The lilac and pink curtains are pushed open, but still there's not a breeze. It's November and way past our sweltering summer days, yet it is so sultry. Even my tears dry quickly on my puffy face.

My room is a mess, as if an earthquake has just hit it. The purple Indian cotton quilt is rolled up like a lopsided crocodile and thrown on the floor. Books are untidily stacked on my desk. Pictures of my friends framed in woven batik cloth and decorations of colourful knick-knacks droop lifelessly on the shelves. There is a big gap in the middle of my desk where my computer used to be.

Scowling, I stare at the closed door. After this afternoon's hungama, you would think we would still hear guns blasting like we were in a war zone – but all seems unusually quiet.

I kick off my slippers and one of them bangs loudly against the bathroom door.

"Who cares?" I mumble to myself.

I grab tissue paper, scrunch it up and one at a time throw them furiously into the bin. Within minutes, the floor is covered with white blotches, forming shadows of blurry, nimbus clouds obscuring dark grey marble tiles.

Ignoring the mess, I straighten my pink T-shirt over my grey track pants and pull my dishevelled, long black hair away from my face. Grabbing my journal, I step out on to the balcony. As usual, the oppressive, scorching heat of our motherland aggravates my bad mood.

I stare angrily down into the street. Our ever famous black and yellow auto rickshaws weave skilfully through the busy, narrow street like giant bumble bees, almost toppling over sleeping oxen lying peacefully in the chaos around them.

4

By now the sun has changed into a deep reddish-ochre, like a ripened nectarine gliding gracefully across the horizon. I plonk myself on the rocking chair, scraping it loudly against the pale brown tiles and watch it hedge dangerously towards pots of green plants that languish limply against the wall.

Removing my glasses, I wipe my misty eyes again with the sleeve of my T-shirt and open my journal. The words dance on the blotchy paper making smiley faces as they twirl mockingly into the light.

Pushing it aside, I stare around thinking how badly my parents handled the recent events in my life. I thought the new trend in child development was all about having an open relationship. If they used their "exclusive" website to gain tips on how to raise a normal child, then surely one of the rules should be: "Don't use force or corporal punishment like your parents or grandparents! Always talk to your children!" After all, the new word for parents is "negotiate."

My parents talk. They love to talk, but always in the form of... LECTURE, LECTURE AND MORE LECTURES!

They never listen, and the weird thing is they actually ask questions! For that I must give them some credit.

But here's the tricky part...

They ask the question, but before you can respond, they've either answered it for you, moved on to the next question, or left you utterly confused. How nutty and crazy?

We have no chance in hell with modern parents. And what makes me even more nervous is their strategy. During confrontation they become aliens... their faces distort, their eyebrows grow thicker and look gross - my father's moustache even twirls as he speaks, and his lips curl into strange, animal-like smirks.

As for me, I become a nervous, agitated wreck who may end up in some mental hospital or start taking drugs by the age of 16, or perhaps consider taking a gap year to disappear into the Inca Trail in Peru (something I saw on the *National Geographic* channel).

They fire question after question without giving me a chance to respond. My mind goes blank. I am brain dead, desperately trying to untangle my muddled thoughts. By the time I open my mouth to answer, they're on to the next question. I don't know if they're on a quest to win the 30-Second Game and use me as their bait, but all I know is that my eyes dart from one to the other, looking utterly stupid and confused.

And they keep staring directly into my face – never blinking. Is that even possible?

They don't pause, nor do they take time to breathe.

Feeling totally agitated, all I can hear is a strange, wheezy, grotesque sound coming from somewhere deep inside of me. Instead of sympathy, they immediately dismiss it as snorting, shout out "WIN," and fire the next question, followed by another and another! Where is compassion? Hello, I could be dying from an asthmatic attack!

I know it's heading towards death row or life imprisonment because they look at each other smugly as if to say, "I knew it, I told you so!"

Whatever happened to innocent until proven guilty? Certainly not happening in my house or in my life. I am ruined, which is why I am scarred for life.

They are sly, manipulative people. They plotted my failure, their minds made up way before this interrogation, and they're simply providing evidence for themselves.

As for me, I am exhausted! I give up! I can't fight them any longer. They are cute and smart. Yippee PARENTZRULE!

To top it all, they stand up and do a strange jig to the song, *I like to Move it! Move it!* I stare at them fuming mad! That is *my* favourite music from *my* favourite movie, *Madagascar*.

I am positive my parents are members of a secret agency – working for Criminal Minds for Children. They operate so smoothly, as though they've been specially trained not to save a child but to catch them out!

They give each other the secret victory look above my head before adding their victorious words, "You are grounded for a month. Give me your mobile phone, you are banned from using it for a month."

Staggering from these words, I push my chair back and shout loudly, "I made one small mistake. I didn't burn down the apartment, so why my phone?"

Of course, they hit back with their second famous words, "Pooja, it is not negotiable!"

By now I am so desperate I try using begging tactics.

"Ground me, I have no problem with that, but let me keep my phone."

Then the third most famous words, "Pooja, we are the adults and you will listen to us as long as you live under this roof."

Hello! You brought me into this world. So where do you want me to live?

But the punishment didn't end there.

"I will decide your proper punishment within the month," growled my dad that fateful night.

"What punishment? You just grounded me!" I retorted angrily and bewildered. What does he want? My life? My blood? Agggg!

"Pooja," he shouted back contemptuously, "you are the child in this house, don't question me! After your behaviour this afternoon, you lost all your privileges! So accept my decision!"

Infuriatingly he stared at me before marching off.

What did I tell you – some parents enjoy making their children's life an absolute hell. Well, mine do. Who are these people? I no longer recognise my parents.

Closing my diary, I push my damp tendrils away from my face, stand up and lean against the balcony railing staring grimly at the tall walls of our apartment. Emerald Cascades is one of the most prestigious apartments in Battersea Colony, Bangalore, made up of four huge buildings inside the complex, each with its own name and playground for children. We live in Jasmine Block, which has a garden as big as a park filled with kaleidoscopic flowers and smooth green grass as soft as a carpet that flows over small sand banks. Bees and butterflies dance between colourful flower petals, intermittently stopping to smell the fragrance, and then twirl up into the air. Baskets of multi-coloured flowers cascade from tall marble pillars forming enchanting archways along the paved driveway. Nearby, a waterfall gently bathes the sacred deep pink lotus perched on its broad, green leaf as it proudly sits amongst small goldfish and white pebbles.

"How did I get into this mess?" I moan dejectedly to myself as my mind drifts back to the events that took place after school.

Earlier that afternoon I rushed out to play. It is my daily ritual after school to play with Reet, my friend from Azalea Block. I found a small garden table under a shady tree and set up the pieces on the chessboard. Feeling the strong Indian sun burn my tender skin, I quickly removed my sandals and sunk down into the velvety grass.

I hear footsteps behind me and turn my head to greet my best friend. Reet is a 10-year-old Punjabi girl with a small thin face, large brown eyes, and really strange alien ways. Her eyes glow with excitement as she pushes her pram towards me.

Even though she is tiny, she is bossy and has a loud voice which scares most of the boys in our apartment.

She has created her own style of weird fashionable outfits to suit her mood. Today a bright red shawl hangs loosely over her jeans, and around her short, curly hair is a striped bandana proudly showing off the Indian national colours. An orange cloth sticks out from underneath the bandana swinging like a long braid, and on her feet are two different coloured trainers with a colourful bracelet around one ankle.

"Hi Pooja," she greets me breathlessly as she marches along the short pathway.

I smile and count to five.

"Hare, hare," Reet shouts in annoyance, as she pushes her pram under the tree, dumps her overstuffed, multi-coloured bag on the board game and smacks her hand on her head. The pieces from the chessboard go flying across the small table. The tiny mirrors on her bag twinkle and dance in the afternoon sun like bright little rainbow lights.

Ignoring the mess, she turns to me in her whiny, high-pitched, Punjabi accent. "Pooja, I can't cope with Mama?" Her huge eyes roll upwards in total exasperation.

I knew it would take less than five seconds for Reet to begin her conversation about her mother.

"Now what happened?" I ask quietly knowing full well it's going to be another sob story.

Still breathing heavily and wiping her forehead with the sleeve of her T-shirt, Reet plonks down on the soft grass and unties her trainers. She kicks them off – the Nike white and pink trainer flies across the grass, over the pond and hangs from a branch in a small tree like an unused lantern on a hot summer's evening. The black and orange trainer shoots straight into a nearby hedge. Reet doesn't bother to go and fetch them, but instead pulls off her socks and stuffs them into the bottom of her pram.

"You know, she nags me daily to eat my lunch and only then am I allowed to play outside. Heh! Is that fair? You tell me," complains Reet as she folds her jeans up to her knees.

"What's the big deal? We all do!" I shake my head in annoyance. Reet is such a drama queen who exaggerates the same stories every single day.

She changes to the next bit of news.

"Pooja, by now these parents should know I can't stand dolls. What is wrong with them?" she whines loudly grabbing the dolls from her pram and shoving them into my arms. "Are they crazy?"

Reet's parents come from Chandigarh, and being an only child, her parents always spoil her with beautiful toys, especially dolls. But she hates dolls.

I smile to myself. Reet is a tomboy, and would rather spend time riding bikes, flying kites or bullying boys in the apartment than wear dresses and do girly stuff.

"I am 10 years old, Pooja, hasn't my mother learnt anything about me?"

Her mother, Aunty Jolly, misses her family from Chandigarh. She has very few interests – and Reet is not one of them. She hates cooking, but loves reading every woman's magazine she can get her hands on or watching her favourite TV soapies.

Reet stares down at her bare feet and continues her tragic story, "My room is filled with these stuffed animals and dolls. I simply hate it! You know Pooja, at night I am sure these things change into monsters. I keep having nightmares that they're trying to choke me!"

I swing around and stare at her in disbelief.

"I swear Pooja, if I don't die from those dolls and teddy bears strangling me, then I will die of food poisoning."

"Reet, why do you make up these stories?"

"I'm not lying," interrupts Reet quickly, "those parathas are like flying saucers. I chew them like bubble gum."

"Stop exaggerating, Reet. Your problem is you are too lazy to eat."

Reet laughs loudly and once again smacks her hand on her head.

Standing up, she puts her hand into her bulging pockets and pulls out small pieces of paratha.

Laughing, I shout in disbelief, "No wonder your mother gets fed up with you."

"Oh, don't worry. I learnt a new trick to keep everyone happy," giggles Reet as she skips towards the pond and quickly throws her left-over lunch to the goldfish.

"There, you see," she sniggers loudly as she runs back. Her eyes roll up towards the sky, and wiping her hands on her jeans, she playfully shouts, "Even the Gods will be happy I am not wasting food."

"You are better off than me," I console her. "I have only one hour to play and already you have wasted so much of my time."

Reet stops in her tracks, stares at me for a moment, then grabs the rest of her doll things and dumps them on my lap. I excitedly hug them tightly to my chest. Reet looks at me sadly.

"You may think I am crazy to still be playing with dolls at my age – but I love them. They are so cute and cuddly."

Two weeks after my ninth birthday, I returned from school to find all my dolls and teddy bears missing. My mother insisted I was too big to keep them, so she donated them to an orphanage.

I cried for a week – and will never forgive her for taking away my beloved toys without my permission.

But, my dear friend Reet loves me too much and every single day brings all her dolls for me to play with before I go home to complete my homework. My mother thinks I am happily playing board games. If she only knew!

Pretty little clothes lay on the garden bench. I grab a white dress with a shimmery white veil, "Wow Reet, this is so cool," I scream excitedly.

Reet – who is fixing the wheel of her pram – turns around, "Oh," she says disinterestedly, "that is a new gift. I think there is some silver jewellery packed somewhere."

"This is awesome!" I say excitedly as I clip silver bows on to Barbie's long, soft golden hair.

With the pram upside down and Reet lying on her tummy, she explains, "Mama bought it to keep me quiet so she can prepare for the kitty party. You know, all she has to do is plan the party games," continues Reet. "You would think she was inviting the Minister of Women's Affairs or something. The servant has been cleaning every nook and cranny as if the guests are going to look inside our cupboards. Even the food and snacks have been ordered. So why stress me? What's the big fuss?" she scowls angrily, her big eyes rolling backwards and her head shaking from side to side.

"It's at my house next month," I say clasping the doll's hair with red and silver hairclips. "My father told my mother to stop this kitty party nonsense and to do some charity work instead."

"Huh! And?" Reet looks up startled, her eyes growing larger with curiosity.

"I never saw my mother so angry," I giggle.

"Pooja, it's such a waste of time, all this eating and playing like children. Even Papa gets irritated. But he would never dare say a word."

Both of us laugh loudly. I love spending time with Reet because she's a real madcap, with crazy stories about school and home.

My life is so serious – and there's just my elder brother Teja. He is always busy with so many interests, I don't know how he finds the time to study – playing sport or music or surfing the net on environmental topics. All I love to do is read every book I can lay my hands on, chat to my friends or simply study.

He even finds the time to help my mother in the kitchen, making a salad, or cutting up fruit or something. I never go into the kitchen unless I'm called to set the table. And how long does that take? Two minutes! That's the sum total of my contribution to family bonding.

However, I must confess, I did try baking a chocolate cake last year – and it was such a flop I think I'm permanently traumatised. The inside of the cake was a dark, gooey liquid with the top hard like the shell of a tortoise. I stood at the oven for the whole 45 minutes the cake had to bake and still it burned. Well, thank you very much, but that will be the last time I tackle cooking!

Teja laughed so much, tears rolled down his cheeks. My father did reassure me that the second time it would be better!

"Fat hope," I thought to myself. Why bake when you can buy cakes. It's less stressful and far more practical.

Getting back to my story in the garden, we were so busy having fun with dolls and crazy stories we didn't realise someone else was also in the garden, close by and watching.

Reet, of course has another problem with her mother.

"Hare, I keep saying 'Please, Mummy, take me out of that school'. Do you think she listens? Never, never, all she does is switch TV channels. Is she deaf, Pooja, tell me, is she deaf?"

Then she smacks her hand against her head shaking furiously.

"Maybe talk to your father. Teachers are not supposed to hit children."

In a dejected voice, Reet says loudly, "I really hope and pray Mr. Vijay Singh leaves this school. Between him and my mother, my life is sooo miserable." Her big eyes grow sad.

Meanwhile, the stranger remains hidden behind the hedge, listening to our chatter.

"You know," continues Reet, "I told fat Karan we should do some special prayer to get rid of Mr. Vijay Singh. Tomorrow Karan is bringing jalebis as offering to the school temple."

"But you don't pray, Reet," I said looking up.

Smacking her hand on her head again, she explains, "Don't worry, Karan will pray for both of us. Fat Karan eats six jalebis daily for breakfast with two glasses of warm milk. This time, he will add some to his tiffin. We have it all organised." Reet laughed loudly.

Then suddenly her voice grows serious. "And he's bringing a small lime and a piece of camphor. I heard you must light the camphor on the lime, turn it around Ganesh (Hindu God – known as the remover of obstacles) and if the camphor falls off, then your prayers will not be answered. So I told Karan to practice today."

Flabbergasted I stare at my friend. "You're nuts! Never play games with God!"

But Reet ignores me and cries desperately, "Pooja, I wish I was in your school. That would be so cool, you know. At least I could travel with you in the auto. My life is so hard. Every day I have to go with *her* (referring to her mother) in the car. You know what her daily mantra in the car is?"

Smacking her hand on her head yet again, she looks up to the sky and raises her voice to imitate her mother. "Please be good, don't fight with the boys, Reet. Don't let that Vijay Singh call me to school again, I can't take so much stress and tension, please beta." Then she places her hand on her forehead like she is fainting.

I stare at this madcap friend, a real drama queen.

Then Reet jumps up and with her false plait swinging from side to side she pleads, "Really Pooja, does she know my stress with her, heh!"

"Stop exaggerating! Reet, you are a spoilt girl."

"No, Pooja, seriously, I hate my life. I don't know why we left Chandigarh. There I was so happy, yaar. My school was really good. Mama had so many friends around her, especially her sisters, Aunty Lolly and Aunty Molly. Even when Papa was away, she was busy everyday shopping or eating out." Reet pauses, shaking her head from side to side, "Hare, here she only screams at the servant to clean and clean and shouts at me for everything."

Reet moves her hips from side to side swaying like her mother. Suddenly her smile fades from her face and looking dumbstruck, she stops talking and her eyes grow big with fear. A large blue head with green and black antennas is jutting out of the nearby hedge.

"Pooja," she whispers in the softest, strangest voice ever. "I think there is an alien in the garden."

"What!" I shout out, looking around irritably. Why does Reet say such ludicrous things?

"I just saw a strange, blue head bobbing over that hedge. It must have landed here somehow."

Within a second Reet falls to her knees, crouches behind the tree and scans the garden. One would think she was in combat training.

"You talk nonsense sometimes, Reet."

"Really Pooja, it has antennas popping up and down from a big, big, blue head. I saw it over there," she says pointing to the hedge.

"You watch too many late movies," I snap back impatiently, "and your imagination runs away with you."

Fed up with Reet's stories, I get up and straighten my clothes. "I have to go inside before Teja comes looking for me."

"Please, Pooja, just one minute... I never saw such a big bald head with round eyes," whispers Reet, her hands stretching wide open and her eyes darting from side to side.

Half listening to Reet, I start packing up.

"You know, I saw something on TV the other day about aliens landing on earth. They watch how we live, and then abduct a few of us to experiment on."

"You're so stupid! No wonder your mother gets fed up with you," I retort crossly as I stuff things into my bag. Reet's fantasy stories are beginning to irritate me. I turn around to Reet and laughingly say, "In fact, they should abduct you."

Suddenly – out of the corner of my eye – I see a blue head popping up over the hedge. For a second I stop, then shake my head annoyingly. I'm becoming like Reet with my stupid imagination.

As I look around, I turn to Reet and whisper with great relief, "Idiot that is Amug spying on us."

Amug is one of the bullies in the apartment who hates Reet because she beats him in the cycle race every year. This year he wants to be the champion at our annual Emerald Cascades' sports day.

Reet stands up bravely, her hands firmly on her hips shaking from side to side. "Shall I tackle him?" she whispers threateningly.

"No, I think we should ignore him."

Reet throws her hands in the air in exasperation, and, grinding her teeth in annoyance, yells impatiently, "Why do you always take Gandhiji's teachings so seriously, yaar?"

"What's the big deal?" I protest angrily. "I don't think we should bother about idiots in this apartment."

"Pleasssssssssse! Yaar," she retorts. "Gandhiji didn't say everything in life should be about peace and non-violence. It's time we taught this idiot a lesson. Simple!"

I pause, look around the garden momentarily before I smile, "OK, but I have a better idea."

Chapter 2

Before you judge me, listen to the remainder of my story. It gets worse...

Loud screams echo through Emerald Cascades. Doors fling open and women rush from their apartments, shawls flung over their creased saris or salwars, as they tidy their hair neatly with their hands before rushing into the elevator. Some stumble while shuffling their feet into slippers, others look annoyed at being disturbed from their afternoon nap. Grabbing their children, they dash through the quiet corridors and run across the garden.

From the east wing of the complex a siren goes off and security guards sprint across the vast lawns. Even the music blaring from the shops outside the apartment stops. Residents and guards swarm towards the loud cries and stare in bewilderment at the utter confusion in front of them.

There are dolls and toys strewn all over the grass, and a blue cap wobbling precariously on the bougainvillea hedge.

The thick, green border dividing the pond and park shudders violently as startled residents watch in horror. Three pairs of legs can be seen sticking out, and muffled screeches emanate from inside the wobbly hedge.

"What is happening? Hare, someone is stuck there," the women scream hysterically.

"Hey, there's more than one person inside the hedge," shouts the security guard. The women rush forward but stop immediately as the hedge begins to shake violently.

Suddenly, a black and orange object flies out, up into the air and straight towards the startled guards. The residents quickly scatter aside as it hits a guard on his head, his cap falls off and the Nike trainer gets wedged between his foot and a broken branch. Rubbing his head with one hand, he bends forward to retrieve his cap, when suddenly a sandal drops directly on to him... followed by another.

Now trying to hide his face, the guard steps stealthily towards the wobbly hedge but suddenly slips on the chess pieces which are coated with cooking oil Reet had used to fix the wheel of her pram. The poor guard loses his balance and rolls down the bank, knocking over two other guards who were running up to help. For a moment everyone forgot about the children stuck in the hedge, and couldn't help laughing loudly as the guards roll down the bank.

Through the crowd, a short lady in a bright yellow and green salwar pushes forward and grabs the orange and black Nike trainer. Turning around, she spots the other trainer hanging from a branch nearby.

For a second she stares around her... at the trainer in her hand... the upside down pram... and the toys strewn all over the grass. Almost instantly her pretty face changes to crimson red.

Deep rage echoes through Emerald Cascades as she charges towards the hedge like an enraged bull. Spectators jump aside knowing the full wrath of Aunty Jolly's anger.

Like a scene from a Hindi movie, Aunty Jolly screams piercingly "Reet Sarabji. Get out of there now! I am waiting and counting to three."

She pulls her shawl from her shoulder and ties it around her thick waist. Her face turns blood red, blending with the henna dye on her hair.

Immediately, the hedge stops moving. Aunty Jolly taps her feet impatiently, then storms off towards a tree and breaks off a thin branch. Tearing away the leaves, she marches back towards the broken hedge and in a tirade of Hindi words not suitable for young children, screeches like a lunatic who has just escaped from a mental home.

Panicking, we push and shove each other trying to scramble out of the wreckage. The first pair of legs to touch the steady ground is, of course, yours truly!

Burning with embarrassment, I collapse on to the soft grass.

Can you imagine the sight I looked as I got up? It was so awful! My long braids tangled with broken leaves and red flowers. One lens missing from my glasses... the ruined frame hanging carelessly from my right ear. I try to straighten my shirt, and notice my skin covered in scratches with blood speckles on the torn sleeves.

Children give me funny looks, as if I have just landed from Mars. They snigger and hide their pretty faces behind their mothers' chudidars. At this moment, I hate children!

I did nothing wrong – it was a plan that went horribly wrong, I want to scream to the spectators.

"Stop looking at me as though I am India's worst child criminal." Stupid people!

Of course, tears flow shamelessly down my cheeks. Then I spot Teja marching towards me.

"Come inside quickly," he says abruptly, "you are in big trouble."

I was so embarrassed and humiliated. I nod without raising my head to look at him. As I turn away, I hear Aunty Jolly still screaming at the top of her voice.

I quickly disappear up the garden path, desperate to get as far away as possible. Not to our apartment, but anywhere else on this planet. I know how this will become the "news" of Emerald Cascades for the next week. Gosh! I hate my stupid plan.

Meanwhile, Reet is set free, held upside down by her ankles as her mother shakes her from side to side. Grass mixed with sweet papers and pieces of paratha drop out from her torn pockets. Tears stream down her dirty face as she wriggles and screams louder than her mother.

"Sorry Mama! I'm really sorry. I thought she was an alien. It was her hair colour."

"Reet, be very careful what you say," screams her mother, "I told you to play outside the bedroom window so I could keep an eye on you. But you don't listen, Reet. Why?"

Turning to the crowd searching frantically for at least one sympathetic onlooker, she continues, "You know I must have my afternoon sleep, but how can I when she doesn't listen to me?"

Aunty Jolly drops her on the hard ground, and Reet falls over coughing and spluttering. Aunty Jolly – still screaming as she dramatically flings her hands in the air – is not finished with her tragic story. "I don't know what I did in my past life to have a child like this. Thank God, He only gave me one child," she continues smacking her hand on her head and shaking herself.

"You know," she said enjoying her small audience of women who had gathered around her, "without the afternoon nap, I get such a migraine, and hare, look, look," pointing her finger at her dishevelled daughter, "what I have to put up with."

Meanwhile, Reet sits on the ground holding her bruised leg close to her chest. She wipes her face with her dirty bandana.

Her eyes narrow against the afternoon sun's rays as she stares at the strange "alien" emerging from the broken hedge.

"Who is this idiot?" Reet glares angrily.

Two security guards pull the stranger from the mangled wreck. The blue head seemed to have disappeared, replaced with bunches of leaves and twigs jutting out from her untidy hair like a dried overused Christmas wreath with half an earphone hanging from one ear.

Natalie is the new girl on the block. She is also 12-years old. After school this afternoon, she had rushed into their empty apartment, threw her bag on to her bed, and changed into a pair of cargo trousers and a bright orange T-shirt with a picture of *The Lion King* – her favourite movie – then stepped out on to her balcony. As usual, there's a buzz of people rushing around the busy street below, and loud blaring hooters everywhere as countless vehicles zigzag through the congested traffic.

Turning around, Natalie looks sadly at their luxurious apartment. They had recently arrived from America and her parents had already started work. Tears spill down her cheeks. How she misses her friends and home in Los Angeles.

She thinks of wide open spaces in LA where the streets are quiet, and trees line the pavements spilling over their white picket fence.

She hates India. She is always alone. And it is always busy and hot here.

Shoving a blue Lakers baseball cap over her short, black hair, she puts on her trainers, grabs a can of 7UP cool drink and lets herself out of the apartment. She sighs sadly. The beautiful garden looks peaceful and tranquil, yet lonely like her. Seeking refuge from the intense heat, Natalie finds herself underneath the shade of the huge hibiscus tree, puts on her earphones and switches on her music. Forgetting her loneliness for a moment, she closes her eyes and sways to the beat of Justin Bieber.

Her first day in Mumbai was a nightmare. She had been standing outside their hotel watching the fruit and vegetable vendors park their carts along the pavement. At first she gazed in amazement as they carved the orange papaya, red watermelon and sun-gold pineapple into intricate and skilful artistic designs.

Suddenly, an army of black flies took siege and with immense brutality, venomously sucked into the richness of the juicy, ripe fruit. Natalie stared in disgust.

"Yuck," she shouted in horror, "that is so gross!"

Praying her new life in India would get better, she didn't expect her arrival in Bangalore to be even more shocking!

The congestion on the streets gave new meaning to the word chaos. Drivers drove like maniacs winding and twisting their cars through the bustling crowds. The hooting and honking was deafening. In the centre of the street was a sweaty traffic cop standing inside a small white box – just big enough for him to fit into – blowing his whistle tunelessly, whilst waving his hands agitatedly around him. No one really paid any attention to him.

"Guess what, Mum!" she shouted loudly, "there are no demarcations on the road and people drive like crazy lunatics."

Her dad, sitting in front with the driver, laughed loudly and teasingly winked, "Natalie, get used to this."

Turning to his wife, Niru, he chuckled, "We didn't miss this chaos, did we?" Then they both started giggling like little children on a tour bus excitedly chatting in their home language, Kannada.

Irritated by their lack of alarm, Natalie ignored them for the rest of the trip and pushed her hot face against the closed, cool window.

There was a constant flow of taxis and black and yellow auto rickshaws blasting their hooters incessantly as they wrestled through the narrow streets. Suddenly her eyes grew large with panic. She grabbed her mother and began screaming hysterically as she watched their taxi head directly towards two huge, grey oxen lying at the side of the street. Her parents laughed as the driver expertly steered his car around them.

"I thought the driver was going to kill them," she screamed angrily as her mother wiped her eyes with her red shawl.

Natalie was horrified her parents found her hysteria so amusing. Her dad, of course, tried to keep a straight face as he stared out the window. Thankfully her parents found this apartment, its high walls offering "protection" from the hustle and bustle of the streets.

For a moment Natalie's thoughts turn to the appearance of multi-coloured butterflies which seem to dance in the afternoon sun, pausing every now and then to smell the perfumed fragrances from the many flowers. Natalie's eyes follow the butterflies as they disappear into the glistening hot sun.

Taking out her mobile, she looks sadly at the pictures of her friends in LA, and recalls how she cried when her father broke the news that his company was transferring him to India to oversee a project. Her mother – working for an international children's charity – was tasked with setting up a new office in Bangalore. Both her parents were excited at their new prospects – this was their dream come true. They spoke with such joy about their childhood days in India, and going back would mean the world to them.

Natalie, on the other hand was less than happy. "What about me and my life?" she cried, "What am I going to do in that poor, overpopulated country?"

Her parents were upset that she didn't want to move, but hoped she would change her mind once she arrived in India.

And, of course, all the angry outbursts and fights with her parents didn't matter to them.

Looking around her now, their plush apartment or the beautiful, lush gardens of Emerald Cascades, she was lonelier than ever.

"Why can't children come out to play?" she thinks to herself. But she knew it was too hot for anyone to be outside.

Suddenly, her thoughts are interrupted by loud shrieks of laughter. Curiously she looks around and walks towards the play area. Peeping over the hedge, Natalie spots two girls under a tree, one lying on the floor fixing a pram and the other playing with her dolls.

Chapter 3

Dear Diary,

How my botched plan went horribly wrong!

I learnt a huge lesson here. I broke a hedge.

OK, I heard the entire border around the block had to be removed. So what! It's only a plant. And plants grow.

But, with my parents this meant consequences to my actions.

With Hindus, it's called KARMA!

On that fateful day, my karma started. I made ONE stupid mistake.

1. Social embarrassment to my parents – *grounded!*
2. Dolls banned for life – *my childhood lost forever!*
3. Board games to be played indoors – *stunted growth!*

But what about children's rights? *No one interested!*

It is Saturday afternoon and I'm sitting on my balcony trying to complete my Maths homework. It's been three weeks since I broke that stupid hedge – and life hasn't been easy for me.

You would have noticed that I haven't bothered to write anything. And all this time I have prayed that residents in our apartment would forget that stupid incident.

But of course, people here don't forget. Did I know it would turn out all wrong? NO! Where did my plan go wrong? No idea. So why am I still the laughing stock of Emerald Cascades?

Annoying, annoying people who simply have no life!

Every morning when I leave for school, I sneak through the back gate like a criminal. I hate the way everyone sniggers behind my back, whispering "the crazy kids." At home, there is an air of quietness and tension. No one speaks to me, ignoring me as if I committed murder. I don't understand why my mother even tiptoes on her precious porcelain tiles. Only Eros is my ever-faithful friend.

Last Friday Reet and Natalie's parents visited our home and I was told to remain in my room. Like I really care! Nodding my head with irritation, I grabbed my schoolbooks and stormed down the passage, grumbling that I might as well be room arrested instead of house arrested.

So I kept to my side of the punishment and got on with life. The three weeks passed by slowly and painfully. I missed my mobile – especially WhatsApp! But the best part of my day was school, especially my friends. They were hysterical when they first heard my crazy story. Bhavana screamed so loudly we were sent to the office for disturbing the assembly.

And then it was forgotten. No big deal. Life was normal. No one ever made fun of me or treated me as if I had set fire to the apartment. Now that's what you call friends.

I'm still waiting for the final verdict from the "chief," AKA my dad, who said he would make a decision within the month.

My KARMA!

Just then Teja opens the door and whispers quietly, "Daddy wants to see you!"

OMG! My father arrived early! Verdict! Punishment! Karma!

Pushing my new glasses backwards on to my nose, I take a deep breath. Remaining still for a moment, I feel a light breeze wash over my flushed cheeks and the bowed branches of the coconut trees gently fan my frayed nerves. Why couldn't my father put this stupid incident behind him as a childish prank? Or have memory loss – with age, one forgets things!

"Pooja!" screamed my brother from the doorway.

Pushing my hair away from my face, I walk to the dining-room. My father is sitting at the table drinking a cup of chai. My mother, wearing a lime green cotton sari, rushes in from the kitchen with a plateful of hot pakodas. Teja follows me with Rihanna blasting from his mobile.

"Show off!" I grimace as I stand nervously in front of my father, who points towards the chair in front of him. One cold stare from my father and Teja comes out of his trance-like stupor and instantly switches off his "hot babe" music.

I notice a huge red folder on the table with several colourful pages sticking out. Without smiling, my father offers us savouries. I refuse, but Teja grabs a few. At this moment I'm having one of my spasho attacks (combined symptoms of hot flushes and coiled knots down my spine caused by parent issues, eating spicy foods and drinking hot chai at the same time.)

My palms are clammy and shaky. There is a strange hot sensation creeping from the roots on my head going all the way down to my toes. Anxiously I shift my feet from side to side staring impatiently at my curled fingers on my lap.

My father drinks his chai slowly, dipping hot pakodas into green chilli sauce, munching loudly and unhurriedly as he reads the newspaper. Gosh, this man really knows how to build up tension.

For just a moment I pray he would blurt out the punishment, so we can get on with our lives. That stupid wall clock in the hallway ticks so loudly. Tick! Tock! Tick! Tock! It's like a thabla drumming inside my head.

At last my father begins. "Pooja, hmm!" turning to me and in his deep, firm tone, he starts, "I heard your behaviour has improved in the last few weeks."

I sigh with relief, and lift up my eyes to smile with joy. Wow! I scored points!

My mother nods her head with a half-smile.

Waiting breathlessly for the best news ever, he clears his throat, takes another sip of tea, and looks directly at me, "Good! But that does not mean I accept what you did in the garden. That behaviour was disgraceful. I expect better things from you."

I shamefully bow my head again, wondering why he has to give me this speech all over again, as if he is replacing Amitabh Bachchan in *Khabi Khushi, Khabie Gham.*

"Parents teach children how to behave respectfully, and girls..." I hear his voice slowly fade.

My mind drifts off, trying hard to recall the songs from that movie. I imagine myself getting to school and breaking into song and dance when I tell Bhavana I am now free! *Deewana Hai Dekho.* That's it. That's the song.

But of course my daydream is rudely interrupted by my stupid brother poking his thumb into my side.

I jerk up. Everyone is staring at me waiting for some answer. Blankly, I glare back.

Why can't I be like Harry Potter and use a wand to make my parents disappear to some faraway remote island? Instead I use my next best magic. Tears!

This is my greatest weakness. Tears and more tears well up! We are Indians after all. We love to cry. And yet I promised myself no matter what the punishment, I would not cry. I have no idea what the question is, but I am ready to weep bucket loads.

Ignoring me, he continues, "In light of what happened, your mother and I have decided to change a few things in this house."

I quickly interrupt with a soft, whimpering noise, hoping to make my case sound most apologetic and dramatic. "I'm sorry, Daddy. It was just a silly mistake."

"No, it was outrageous and embarrassing," his stern voice cuts across at a loud thunderous pitch.

"You have damaged the property and we are now responsible for the repairs."

"But it was just a small mistake," I whimper nervously.

"That is not an excuse," he growls back, then quickly adds, "we have decided to send both you and Teja to an international boarding school."

Silence reigns.

Nothing moves in the room. I can't even hear my own breathing. Startled, both of us look up almost immediately, speechless and shocked.

My mother chips in and coos like a nightingale, "Shraddha International School is the best school in India." Both of us simply ignore her.

Teja jumps up protesting loudly, "Why me? I didn't do anything wrong."

"Teja, sit down," my father says calmly.

Teja turns angrily to me and screams, "You do stupid things and I get punished."

Of course, my tears are now flooding the banks of the Ganges River as they shamelessly spill down my cheeks.

I feel sorry for Teja and want to say something, anything – but I find my mouth dry. I try to swallow and can't – my throat goes into some sort of spasm and shuts down.

Kaput! Finito!

I sit stunned like a half-witted moron. Now more than ever, I need my big mouth.

I must be having an out of body experience. Suddenly my mind starts in first gear, and races up into fourth gear. My body seems to be stuck to the chair in this strange house with two weird people staring angrily at me. Then my brain goes into turbocharge. I can see their faces grow larger and larger... they're looming in front of me... I'm sure it's a dream... a nightmare. There's this strange sensation rushing through my body. At first I smile, then I laugh softly, then louder. This is a dream. Their distorted faces are laughing back at me, goading me to say something – but I continue to stare blankly, dazed and stupefied.

The only thought going through my mind right now is, *"who on earth makes such a life threatening decision without consulting their children?"*

Once again, the answer is MY PARENTS!

KARMA!

Remind me when I get to meet God I want to ask him two questions.

1. Why was I born a Hindu and lessons of Karma pushed down my throat so early in my life?
2. Why didn't I get to choose my parents before I was born?

These two crazy people sitting in front of me would never have been my first choice, or second, or for that matter even considered on my list. That's an important issue I have to tackle with God.

But right now, I have bigger problems. I blink quickly to stop the tears from spilling down my cheeks. This cannot be happening!

Then I hear my father's voice. "Start packing. We leave early tomorrow morning so you can settle in before your Monday class."

With disbelief, I turn to Teja. His face is red with anger as he slumps against the chair pushing away his plate of cold, half-eaten pakodas. I watch Teja's fingers shake uncontrollably as he tries to pour a glass of water, but spills it all over the white tablecloth.

"Teja," my father's voice thunders crossly.

Almost immediately I awaken from my dazed state, and stand up in slow motion with an unusual sensation of outrage, like bile rising from deep inside me. Biting my lip to stop myself from screaming, I look directly at my father and calmly ask, "Why did you make all these arrangements without talking to us?"

"We are your parents and we decide what is best for you," interrupted my father brusquely as he puts down his cup with such force that the tea spills on to the saucer. His brown eyes grow darker as he glares at me.

"I refuse to leave tomorrow! Are you going to take me by force?" I challenge him.

Before he catches his breath, I quickly add, "I do not want to change my school nor leave my friends. My results are always outstanding. You *are* ruining my life."

I am so livid with my parents. Unabashed hot tears brazenly sting my eyes and pour down my cheeks as if the Ganges River has broken its banks and merged with all the rivers from the Himalayan Mountain cascading ferociously across the entire land of Bharat.

I can't be bothered to even wipe my face. There's no stopping my tears from overflowing and flooding the universe. I don't care.

But my parents stare blankly across the table as if they are part of the grand jury – passing judgement for one stupid, meaningless, foolish act.

"I accidently broke the hedge. Pay it out of my allowance for the rest of my life for all I care," I scream at them. "Your punishment is simply ridiculous!"

My mother interrupts grimly, "Pooja, your father and I made the decision. You need to pack your things."

I look at her resentfully and shout back cheekily, "No, I want to talk first. I don't want to go and you cannot force me. I am not going to some stupid boarding school because I damaged one small part of your precious apartment. And why is Teja punished for what I did? It's not fair, both of you are not fair!" I cry hysterically.

Teja pulls my hand but I hold firmly on to the table.

"No Teja," I sob uncontrollably, "This is 2012 not 1960! In their generation, they were only seen and never participated in any family matters. They had no life. This is my life, my future! I am not accepting their decision."

"Pooja," screams my mother. "I said sit down now! We had to pay for damages to the garden and hire the landscape people to redo the entire boundary. Your father's business is important and that behaviour was really embarrassing."

"So you're more worried about your status than your children?" I retort angrily, "I did something stupid and foolish. Can't children make mistakes?"

"Pooja!" barked my father ferociously like a lion. "Watch how you speak!"

I ignore him. Right now my punishment can't get any worse.

Instead I continue to stare defiantly at my mother. "Why did you agree to this? Why? How can you let us go?"

"You still want to play childish games with Reet," my mother replies loudly, "but this school will help you grow into a responsible adult."

"I am only 12-years old, not 20!" I scream even louder stressing on my age.

"Pooja," my father cuts in angrily, "did you not hear your mother?"

He stands up, pushes the red folder in front of me and says calmly, "My decision is final. We have the transfer papers here. Have a look at your new school. It's excellent and expensive!"

My mother quickly boasts, "It is the best in the country."

I glare at both of them in total horror. I cannot believe what has just happened. I realise they have made up their minds, and nothing I say will change their decision. Defeated and frustrated, I scream at both of them, "I will never forgive you."

I remain rooted to the spot, staring dismally as they walk away without a care in the world, leaving me seething with resentment for all parents of the human race born in this universe.

Pushing my chair back angrily, I scream at the top of my voice, "You are the worst parents ever!" I storm out of the room, down the corridor stamping my feet noisily against the tiles and slam my room door. Then silence!

Hours later I return to the balcony to retrieve my journal. My face is swollen from crying, and my head throbs with pain. I stare glumly over the tall walls. My life cannot get any worse. The final punishment – and it's like they hammered the last nail into my coffin. I just want to crawl somewhere else and die.

It is already sunset, only a soft glow of the rising golden moon peeps playfully through the opaque, whimsy clouds. Hordes of black crows sit perched on broad, green branches of the coconut trees, cawing loudly and swaying against the evening breeze. They too are protesting against my punishment. I smile as tears once again scorch my hot cheeks.

The street comes alive with bright lights and the latest Bollywood music blasts loudly from every shop. Street vendors sit along the uneven pavement threading garlands of fresh, colourful flowers, while others artistically decorate their fruit and vegetables on small, wooden carts to attract people passing by.

The noise is deafening. Turning away from the pandemonium of a typical Indian street, I stare across at Reet's apartment. I wonder what punishment she got. I bet it's not worse than mine! I'm really going to miss my friend, my crazy friend! I smile sadly through my tears, turn around and enter my room to pack for my journey.

Chapter 4

Dear Diary,

It is late afternoon when we arrive at Shraddha International School. The school is built on top of a hill surrounded by acres of manicured gardens and historical buildings. I am exhausted and totally depressed. Who wouldn't be? Stress overload. Sleep deprived. And don't forget we had to leave Bangalore at the crack of dawn. I am in a bad mood. And just to remind you, throughout the trip I refused to speak to my parents. I closed my eyes and pretended to sleep.

As we pull in, smartly dressed security guards stand upright as if they are royal guards at Buckingham Palace. I peep curiously through half-closed eyes as my father fills his details into the logbook.

My mother turns to smile at me. I totally ignore her and stare out of the window.

"Traitor!" I think as I slump against the window. What does she expect? A smiley face? No ways! She conspired with my father! And right now I am a traumatised girl!

My dad drives down a long driveway flanked by rows of towering trees. Branches bend and sway in the breeze as if in a welcome dance.

Everyone is quiet except Teja who shouts excitedly when he spots the massive sports auditorium across the lawn. I show no interest – just stare outside blankly.

Teja, on the other hand, has this sudden enthusiasm for his new school.

"Why can't he just shut up?" I say to myself, glaring angrily at him.

We stop in front of an enormous architectural building, and as we get out of the car, I stare around in amazement.

The landscape seems to blend between the school and the surroundings like an idyllic picture from a faraway resort in a travel brochure. In front of the administration building stands a tall pillar. We climb up the marble stairs into the hallway, which opens into a vista of peace and tranquillity.

"Wow! This doesn't look like a school," my father whispers to my mother as they stand mesmerised in the reception area. At the far end of the room is a huge marble statue of the elephant-head deity, Lord Ganesh. A row of jasmine flowers bedecks his neck and its sweet smell mingles with the sandalwood incense burning nearby.

Large golden framed pictures of India's leaders hang proudly around the room. Soft instrumental music filters through the air from afar. A well-dressed lady rushes down the stairs to meet us.

Mrs. de Souza, personal secretary to the Head of Shraddha International School, Dr. Raj Malhotra, is dressed in an orange sari with her hair in a low bun. We are escorted into his private reception area. Through the slightly ajar door, I can see

Dr. Malhotra sitting behind a massive mahogany desk, talking earnestly on the phone.

As soon as he finishes his call, he gets up from his huge chair and walks around his desk to greet my parents. Dr. Raj Malhotra's smile is quite charismatic as he invites us in. My mother puts her two hands together and bows her head as if she is greeting the Prince of Gujarat.

Sitting down, he begins to speak with a distinguished English accent, "This school was originally an old disused building found hundreds of years ago. There were different owners until Dr. Clanis, our current director, bought this building and decided to convert it into an international boarding school."

Turning to my father, he continues, "We have an exceptional education programme here, one which gives our students opportunities to explore and experience the world... where children learn to respect tradition and culture and integrate strong social, moral and spiritual values into their daily lives."

Sitting quietly between my parents, I listen carefully as Dr. Malhotra explains the general rules and international standards they maintain. My parents find all this education jargon very interesting.

At that precise moment we are interrupted by the house-lady who enters with a tray of coffee for the adults and mosambi juice for Teja and me.

My father has the largest grin on his face. I haven't seen him this happy for a long time. After all the hungama in our lives these past few weeks, I'm amazed he can smile, let alone speak so much. Highly impressed with the school and the Head, he scans the documents in front of him, and without any hesitation, signs the admission papers.

I stare at his million-dollar signature and think to myself, *"Yup, there goes my life!"*

A school rubber stamp seals my fate for the next few years. At this very moment I want to do a Reet act – in other words, act sick and fall down like I've fainted. How will my mother react? Will she leave a sick daughter in a foreign school, with foreign people in a foreign place? I stare at her. She's giving me the biggest smile ever! Tears well up so I stand up and walk towards a huge bay window that looks out on to the picturesque gardens.

I will *not* let myself down. Nor will I give my parents another chance to humiliate me. No thanks! These two people who call themselves parents have just messed up my life!

The next moment I hear a voice behind me. "That pillar is called Sarva Dharma," says Dr. Malhotra standing next to me. "It was first sighted by archaeologists who discovered this fort buried in a jungle. At the base there are symbols of the world's main religions – Christianity, Hinduism, Judaism, Islam, Zoroastrianism and Buddhism."

My parents walk across to the window, and stare at the impressive pillar which towers over the central courtyard.

"We promote and practice all religions of the world," he says proudly, turning to chat to my parents. By now I am bored and totally disinterested in any more social studies talk.

Meanwhile, Teja is busy finishing his juice and rudely interrupts, "Where are the hostels? How many sporting activities can we choose?"

Dr. Malhotra turns and smiles patiently. He immediately speaks into the intercom, and seconds later Mrs. de Souza enters with a pen and notebook.

My dad smiles proudly at Teja, then looks across at my mother and winks. I know Teja loves sports, but his behaviour today is quite weird compared to his outbursts last night. This sudden interest confuses me. When did he have a change of heart about this school?

"Show Teja and Pooja their rooms," Dr. Malhotra instructs, then turning to my parents, he hands them a copy of the school brochure and rule book, and shakes hands with my father.

"Don't hesitate to call us if you have any questions, Mr. Narayan."

Teja jumps up and heads for the door.

"Students stay in different buildings, separate for boys and girls," explains Mrs. de Souza as we walk downstairs and away from the administration building.

"Teja will stay in Gandhi House. It is the boys' hostel with large rooms, fully fitted with a desk, bed and cupboard for each student," says the secretary. "Each house accommodates 40 students, and each room is occupied by two students. Teja will share his room with Colin from America."

We enter a beautiful red stone building, and Mrs. de Souza introduces us to the house mother, Mrs. Lutchmee. I grudgingly follow, noting that this is like "going on a grand tour."

Inside the room, are two single beds, both covered with bright blue striped duvets made from handwoven Indian cotton fabric. Nearby stands a desk and chair with a desk light attached to the desk.

On the other side of the room, clothes are thrown across a chair, toiletries left open on the desk, and a wet towel lies on the unmade bed.

Mrs. Lutchmee quickly says, "Oh, not again. Rooms are not to be kept this way, but Colin is really an untidy boy who needs constant reminding. We follow strict house rules," she continues, "and Colin is not going to earn any bonus points with his untidiness."

She quickly writes something in her notebook, and turning to Teja adds, "Teja, your uniform, bag and other sports wear is already in your cupboard."

Teja drops his bags on the floor and excitedly rushes around the room, opening his cupboard, checking out his desk, and switching the desk light on and off as if he's a kid with his first Christmas gift. How stupidly embarrassing.

"Sudden change of heart, I see," I say glaring at my brother irritably as he stuffs his bag into the cupboard.

"Oh, last night I checked out their website. It's really cool here."

"Traitor," I hiss back angrily.

The tour continues around Gandhi House. The common room is very cosy, painted lime green and blue, and tastefully furnished with large sofas scattered with bright, colourful cushions. A TV and music centre stand at the far end of the room.

"This room is supervised for one hour daily after dinner and all music is monitored by the senior students," explains Mrs. de Souza then leading us to an enclosure room says, "This is the reading room, where students spend their evenings reading or playing board games."

Bookcases built from wall to wall are filled with various books for boys, and rows of shelves are piled with board games and audio visuals.

The next room is a kitchenette. "Each house has its own little kitchen, where students are allowed to make hot drinks in the evenings. This is also supervised by senior students and prefects. They play a very active role in each house, taking charge of various duties, such as behaviour, neatness, and assisting students with homework, or duties in the common room. These students can be identified by their different colour blazer or jersey."

Teja stands proudly next to my parents. All smiles – their golden boy.

I frown angrily. Idiot! Deserter!

My father asks, "Where are the meals served?"

"All meals are served in the school dining hall and all students have to be dressed in their full school uniform," responds the secretary.

Mum enquires, "What time does school start?"

"What is this?" I grumble to myself, "question and answer time?" Irritating people!

Hello! I am here! Does anyone care about how I feel right now? Don't even bother to reply! I'm sure I'm adopted because I have absolutely nothing in common with these people. What if there had been a swop in hospital when I was born? I stare at my family!

A sudden bolt of reality is snapped when my mother nudges me in my side and whispers crossly, "Stop dreaming and listen carefully!"

I stand quietly next to her pretending to listen. But my mind wanders off again. Do these people know that the school daily timetable is pasted behind each door? I can read! So why bother to listen. And do I look like a sports mad fan, or horticulturist? No thanks! Yes, this is the land of yoga, but hey, I'm NOT interested! Give me a book anytime! And right now nothing interests me. My own crisis is major. So please let me sulk! It's the first time I'm going to be in a boarding school far away from my parents... in the state of Gujarat with a different culture... and Bangalore now seems to be so very, very far away.

What about my friends? Especially Bhavana and Sejal? We won't be able to hang out at McDonald's or Pizza Hut together. I'm so tempted to ask if they have a therapist here. Can you imagine my mother's face? She may faint!

I giggle to myself as I walk across the grounds to meet Mrs. Roy, my house mother.

Meera House is designed the same as Teja's house, except the walls are painted pale lemon, with orange and green duvets. I get to share my room with another new student who has yet to arrive.

My parents try to settle me in as quickly as possible. With an awkward hug, they disappear through the door. I'm sure they're afraid I'll have a tantrum. Feeling abandoned and alone, I sit on my bed staring out the window at the beautifully manicured gardens.

Chapter 5

Dear Diary,

Cannot believe, I've spent my first night in a boarding school, miles away from home. For the next few days, I manage to find my way to classes but hate the new routine. It is so different from living at home. Each morning is a manic stress – we are awakened by the deafening sound of the hostel alarm bell, then rush off to yoga and after the quickest shower ever, I run over to the dining hall to make it on time for breakfast before school begins! The first Thursday morning I was still asleep when I heard the bell thunder in the corridor. I pulled the duvet over my head and shut my eyes tightly. No 12- year-old in the world gets up at the crack of dawn unless there's a fire. The next moment someone pulls the duvet away from my head. Irritably I open one eye. Mrs. Roy, our humongous house mother is grinning like a Cheshire cat.

"Pooja, get up! Get up! Get up beta, your meditation class is about to start."

"This is crazy! Really!" I grumble to myself as I make my way to the bathroom.

Waiting outside the prayer room, the students are dressed in white tracksuit pants and long white kurtas. With half-closed eyes I join the queue.

This is so annoying. I can't imagine doing yoga at this ridiculous, unearthly hour trying to look peaceful and calm.

My brain is dead. My eyelids are still heavy with sleep. At that moment, soft music permeates through the corridor. I feel a nudge, and opening my eyes, Miss Hegde says softly, "Go inside please."

We jostle each other as we sleepwalk into the room. My eyes grow huge with surprise as I take in the dim, serene scented room. Colourful cushions lay around the floor and the smell of incense chokes me, awakening my lifeless brain and lethargic body. Help! I splutter and cough.

This is truly a heavy dose of serenity for a young person like myself. It is old people who get up early and exercise to keep fit. Not a 12-year-old! So why am I being forced to wake up this early and pretend to be calm and happy? I protest! I need my beauty sleep.

I have two choices – I can either grab one of those inviting cushions, claim to have a spinal problem, or pretend I'm meditating and simply sleep while sitting in the lotus pose. Of course, I don't have any luck!

"Namaste and good morning!" says Miss Hegde sweetly as she smiles at us. She is dressed in a white kurta suit with a peach band around her waist. Slim and tall, her hair is as golden as the sun and tied into a high ponytail. Her voice is as soft as a nightingale, and her piercing jade blue eyes match her charismatic smile. This is the famous Miss Hegde whom every girl in the school loves. Besides her beauty, I've heard rave reviews of her music and dance productions from Mrs. de Souza.

That's what I'm interested in. I promised myself to be included in all those musical productions. How cool!

I listen as she speaks, "Ladies, you know the drill on a Thursday. It is chilly but a lovely morning, and we don't want to miss the sunrise."

Sanam, whom I met the night before, pushes herself next to me and whispers, "I hate exercise, let alone getting up so early."

Her cousin, Diya, standing on the other side of me, gives her a disapproving look and says calmly, "But this is an important part of our lives, so we can be healthy, fit and keep our minds alert and peaceful." With that she turns her nose up and makes her way to the front to pick up a cushion.

I chuckle softly, "Sounds like she's quoting from a Deepak Chopra book."

I quickly follow her to grab a cushion and sit in Padmasana (lotus pose). I need to be a gymnast to keep my back straight and cross my legs at the same time. Of course, I fall over several times. Somehow my long limbs seem to be sticking out from places I don't recognise. I peep through half-closed eyes and everyone seems so flexible and skilled. I wait for the minutes to pass, but I soon feel pins and needles in both legs and I'm already cramping from head to toe.

By the time we finish this first session I am exhausted, bent over and panting like a rhino. We then line up and walk out to the gardens.

"It is our school policy to practice Surya Namaskar every Thursday morning outside," Miss Hegde explains to me as I walk alongside her down the corridor towards the garden, "it is the second session of exercise that refreshes our mind and fills us with intense energy."

As I step outside, I find girls from different houses dressed like the rest of us, already standing in long rows to perform the sublime movement of this ancient tradition. Across the vast green lawn, boys also dressed in similar white kurtas wait silently with the school staff to begin the morning ritual.

Just then the golden sun appears through the clouds and across the soft orange sky. The sound of the school bell is heard. Even before the celestial rays of the sun could touch the ground, students in total unison perform the Surya Namaskar, paying obeisance at the feet of the Sun God, for providing light, warmth, and life to the universe. The students bend their supple bodies to touch the ground and stretch high up to the sky in total harmony and poise. They move in subtle synchronised movement as man, sun and earth become one with nature and God.

As for me, I fumbled around with some strange bends and turns, but I managed to survive this exercise regime. By late afternoon, every limb is aching and I spend the remainder of the day waddling around like a duck!

A few weeks later

How time flies. It's already three weeks since I started at this school. Can you believe I'm doing horticulture? Actually it's another name for gardening. At first I didn't want to dirty my hands. Yuck, dirt under my fingernails – that's not for me!

At home I play in the garden, not dig in the garden or pick up worms or make compost.

Once again, do I have any choice? No! I just think the Gods are after me. A young girl with such charisma like myself, why would my life change so drastically? It's like the universe has a mind of its own. It gives me opportunities to do things I don't like or want. Somehow I seem to have lost all control and power over my own life. There's no free time – it's all taken up by school activities.

Like the others, I was also given a small patch of land under a tunnel made from mesh built at the far end of the vast grounds. At first I moaned, whinged and grumbled to Teja.

"Teja, I can't dig. I hate shoving dirt! Look!" showing him my painful blisters that hurt my tender fingers.

As usual Teja ignores my dilemma! Staring at me straight in my face, he explains sternly, "Pooja, do you know this school provides free lunches for five schools in a nearby rural area? You are responsible for growing the fruit and vegetables which contribute to the school's feeding scheme. Stop whining!"

"Teja," I moan loudly, "my nails never get clean after those horrible garden visits."

"Oh Pooja, get over yourself. Grow up and start taking responsibility. And wear gloves for goodness sake."

Hello! Who is this boy? A few weeks ago he was my irritating brother, who always annoyed me with his MP3 music blasting in his room. Now he's excited about a stupid subject like horticulture or permaculture or gardening or whatever! Same difference!

Whenever we meet he is always happy and bragging about being one of the students selected for the "Food for India" project. How cool is that, he would say?

I don't show an inch of interest.

Then he begins to preach as if he is the Minister of Environmental Issues.

"Pooja, did you know, children from slums leave home before sunrise to get to school? They don't eat any food unless the school provides them with a meal. That means our school has to donate fruit and vegetables. Please show some interest and help out!"

After that lecture from my environmentalist-horticulturist brother, I dared not slump on to my bed after school. Instead, I learnt to turn the soil, weed, plant seeds in rows down the length of the garden bed and water my vegetable patch.

My new friend, ▬▬▬ from England, taught me about mulching. "Once you plant the seeds," informs ▬▬ in her strong British accent, "grab dry grass and spread it over the seedlings."

"What does it do?" I ask curiously as I carry bales of dry grass.

"It's good for water retention and prevents weeds," explains ▬▬ like a science teacher, "it forms a blanket for the soil to stay cool and moist."

Her two cousins who are also from England, ▬▬ and ▬▬ work side by side nearby. I like my new friends, especially their accent. I laughed when ▬▬ whispered, "I find your accent really hard to understand."

And we get to share the same hostel and sit together in the dining hall.

In the beginning, Teja explained my school programme. "Listen carefully, it is compulsory to participate in two extra activities after school and one volunteer programme. So what have you decided on?"

As usual I am really confused. But thankfully ▬▬ and her cousins convinced me to take up pottery, which they have enjoyed since the beginning of the term. The pottery room is huge – and has so many kilns, wheels and tables to work on.

"This looks easy," I whisper to myself as I watch the teacher at the wheel. But each time I rolled the ball of clay and placed it on the platform of the wheel, it slumped to one side and the clay flew everywhere.

"Don't worry, you'll get the gist of this," ▬▬ consoles me. The girls laughed loudly as each of them explained their first few experiences in the pottery class.

"At least you don't have to wash this room each time you work," shouts ▬▬ "I used to hate this lesson, but look at my work now," and proudly shows off a hand-painted pottery lampshade.

My friends are cool!

Before dinner, we have an hour to complete homework. ▮▮▮▮ who is slim with beautiful long, straight hair, loves telling me stories about England.

"I don't like India, it's too dirty," she grumbles as she slumps back on her chair. "The school itself is clean, but outside it's horribly dirty with people sleeping on the pavements and slums everywhere."

Kash, with her beautiful black eyes and the best smile ever showing sparkling white teeth, laughs loudly, "Our breakfast is so different. I love honey coated cornflakes and muffins."

"Then why are you living in India," I ask inquisitively, "I thought your country has such good education."

"Well," mumbled ▮▮▮▮ "my parents don't like the teenage lifestyle there."

▮▮▮▮, listening to her cousin, quickly interrupts, "But you lied to your parents and went to a club with friends."

"What is wrong with clubbing?" snaps ▮▮▮▮.

"You are only 12-years old," retorts her cousin.

Before the argument gets more heated, I quickly change the subject, "I'm afraid of the underground trains there," I say laughing loudly.

Forgetting her anger, ▮▮▮▮ turns to me, "It's the best and so quick!"

Relieved to change the topic, ▮▮▮▮ adds, "Well it is if you compare it to the overloaded trains in this country, especially when they sit on the roofs!"

Agreeing with ▮▮▮▮ nods her head, "I think that is by far the craziest and scariest thing ever."

" ███ shouts ███ "what about in the movies, when they dance in the aisles of the movie theatre. That is like real madness!" They both get up almost instantly and begin a bhangra dance, humming a Hindi song as they swing their hips, swaying around our table, roaring with laughter.

I enjoy my evenings. We chat about movies, fashion, living in India and sometimes when we are really bored, we end up playing board games.

Tonight after my shower, I sit in front of my desk with my journal open. I read what I have just written, and look out through the window and smile.

The words dance in front of me, "I am enjoying my new school!"

I cannot believe I just wrote that. But it's true. I even miss my parents, and send my mother pictures of some of the activities I enjoy, especially my pottery classes. I no longer miss my old school friends, or teachers – in fact I can't imagine my old school life. I wonder what Reet is up to? Is she still under house arrest? I add a smiley next to her name.

Sitting back in the chair, I think about yesterday. It was Saturday, and I had the best time ever. It was our social welfare activities programme. In the morning we distributed food parcels to nearby villages. As I got off the school bus, the stench of sewer was unbearable.

With ███ and ███ next to me, we held our noses as we carried bags filled with food parcels and ran along dirty, narrow pathways. ███ suddenly screeches hysterically as she stumbles across a dead rat on a heap of garbage. Squeamish and ready to vomit, we grab each other's hand and race through the filth, our white trainers squeaking and squelching in the muddy water.

We hear some of the boys laughing as they throw stones at dogs scavenging through the garbage.

At last we are inside a cramped, dark hut. Only a piece of colourful cloth covers a small makeshift window that gives this family some privacy. Little children peep from inside their mother's saris, with huge bright eyes, and black bindi showing off their pretty faces. Living in absolute poverty and squalor, these poor people receive our food parcels with tears of joy and happiness. Bags of blankets and clothing are handed over by the boys, and some of the girls have brought in packets of sweets for the little kids.

By now ▓▓▓▓ refused to go further down the street – especially after finding rats running around the garbage, and naked children playing in dirty water in the hot, blazing sun. She burst into tears and rushed back to the bus.

When we finished an hour later, we found ▓▓▓▓ stretched out on the back seat with a cold compress on her forehead. Mrs. Shilpa was quite relieved to see ▓▓▓, as ▓▓▓▓ wouldn't stop crying. As we began our trip back to school, everyone was quiet. Even the driver didn't put on his loud music as he usually does on all our trips.

Most Saturday evenings we watch a movie on the big TV screen, and once a month, on a Sunday, I am allowed to have lunch with Teja – and because he is a senior, he is allowed to take me out of school for a meal.

I now love this time with Teja. OMG! Who am I?

Thinking about it, I do miss him and his stupid pranks. But I get really excited when I see him – he somehow looks so much happier at this school.

I must be growing up. I squiggle tall legs and hands on a smiley face which resembles Teja and then close my diary.

I sit at the window and watch the moon disappear slowly behind the translucent clouds. I smile to myself as the yellow and orange speckles of stars emerge and teasingly twinkle at me. At last I am happily settled into this new school.

Chapter 6

Dear Diary,

I am not sure if I should thank myself for destroying the gardens at Emerald Cascades, or thank my parents for their punishment. But whatever, right now I like my life!

Our formal assembly is held once a week in a massive auditorium with boys and girls seated in separate sections of the hall. It's like sitting in parliament. The silence is nerve-racking. There's not a sound – no fidgeting or whispering.

I almost jumped out of my skin when the school bell sounded. The main door opened softly and Dr. Malhotra entered and walked down the aisle followed by teachers dressed in long black gowns. They walked slowly towards the stage, and with Dr. Malhotra standing in front of the podium, the teachers sat in rows behind him.

I was too afraid to even breathe. Absolute silence!

The quietness was suddenly interrupted by the booming voices of 10 boys chanting *Vedic Mantras* as they walked down the aisle. They were dressed in crisp white dhotis and kurtas. Just as they ended the chants, Dr. Malhotra took the microphone and greeted the assembly. Standing aside, the head student walked up to the podium and read out the morning prayer, which the entire assembly repeated. Then the Christian prayer was read aloud by another student, then the Muslim prayer, a Jain prayer, followed by Sikh, Jewish, Buddhist, Hindu and Zoroastrian prayer.

OMG... we just prayed for the entire world! A one-minute silence followed. By this time I was exhausted and fidgety... but ~~████~~ grabbed my hand tightly. Heads bowed. Again silence! Not a sound could be heard in the hall, just the soft twitter of birds outside. I smiled, listening to their melodious banter like a cheerful choir.

Dr. Malhotra returned to the podium and in unison with the assembly, recited the universal prayer.

ASATHO MAA SATH GAMAYA

THAMASO MAA JYTIR GAMAYA

MR.ITHYOR MAA AMR.ITHAM GAMAYA

OM SHANTHI SHANTHI SHANTHI

Lead me from untruth to truth

Lead me from darkness to light

Lead me from death to immortality

Let there be peace, peace, peace.

"Good morning students," he greets.

"Good morning Sir," greets the assembly.

We all sit quietly. Dr. Malhotra begins. "There are many announcements this morning but before I comment on those, let me reiterate our unique learning programme. Always know that your school is unique. It is an institution that inculcates values of truth, peace, non-violence, love, respect, compassion and academic development. We are here to inspire and motivate you to become the best ambassadors of a new age. Mahatma Gandhi said, *'Your character must be above suspicion, and you must be*

54

truthful and self-controlled. The truest test of civilisation, culture, and dignity is character...'

"This is why Shraddha International School has been chosen as the best school in the country, because our education programme has never been seen anywhere else in the world. It empowers you to become successful leaders, leaders who can change the world to become a better place for all to live in harmony. That is why our learning is not only about obtaining book knowledge. We are here to mould you into great human beings with the best character exposing you to charity, selfless service, humility, passion and commitment. We are here to develop your aspirations, to build your dreams and to pursue your goals for tomorrow."

"Looking at the world today, you will learn that violence against each other, violence against women and children, and hatred against humanity is unacceptable."

He pauses, looks up at the assembly and very slowly says, "I want our school to create its own tapestry of a distinct, new age of education. Our education must ignite a light of knowledge to spread globally so that you grow into great individuals, better citizens and an empowered nation."

Students and teachers clap loudly when Dr. Raj Malhotra stops. He looks around and then quietly quotes the famous words, "We must be the change we wish to see."

Looking at his notes in front of him, he continues, "There are a number of new students and staff who have arrived this term and we welcome them. Our new deputy principal is expected shortly, unfortunately he has been delayed due to some unforeseen circumstances."

Turning to his staff he nods his head and addresses us again, "Now special awards will be given to students for their Grama Seva project completed in the last term. Congratulations to the 10 senior students who coordinated a social care programme for a village nearby. A slide show will be shown later this week highlighting their work, from distributing food hampers to clean-up operations of the village. We also had students start organic farming programmes in five nearby villages. These programmes are part of our sustainable development action plan, which teaches people how to survive and support themselves."

As he reads out the rest of the announcements, I watch students walk up to the stage to receive their certificates and medals.

We applaud loudly, and for the first time I see a different school with different ideas of learning. This is the day I am truly proud to be a student in this amazing school.

When Dr. Malhotra finishes speaking, he and the staff leave the auditorium accompanied by the sounds of soft instrumental music.

Now you tell me, is this not a truly unique school run with such precision and style?

Chapter 7

Dear Diary,

Just when I was starting to think life was getter much better than I expected, the universe changes its plans for me. I am sure God gets bored with life and decides to add some fun to His life. And of course, He chooses me to be His joker! When you read what's to come, you will certainly understand why.

It's Thursday morning. I'm minding my own business working quietly in my history lesson, when Mrs. de Souza enters the class and speaks to Mrs. Jyothi, the history teacher. Both turn towards the door and beckon someone standing outside.

"Students," smiles Mrs. de Souza, "we have a new student, Natalie, who is joining your class. She is from America. Please make her feel at home."

And then in slow motion, the only Natalie I ever met for 30 seconds, suddenly emerges through the doorway like a mirage from a horror story. I stop writing, almost toppling off my chair.

The alien from our apartment!

Biting my lip in anger, my fingers curl tightly around my pen, and I unconsciously stab a deep hole on my page. I screech hysterically – then realise I'm screaming inside my head. No! My brain goes into rewind.

Emerald Cascades! The day my innocent life came to an end.

I watch Natalie stand in front of the class looking nervously around her. You know when someone has pushed you into the deep end of the swimming pool and you simply cannot swim? That is how I felt.

My lungs seem to be expanding like a giant balloon. I gag for air, my face turning a bright shade of indigo. Thankfully I am sitting at the far end of the class, so I grab the biggest book on my desk to cover my face.

Curiously, I peep! Antennas have disappeared from her big fat head. In fact, she looks like an ordinary girl, dressed in our school uniform with a maroon tie, white shirt, and a maroon and navy check skirt.

Mrs. Jyothi smiles and calls out, "Sonalika, please take Natalie to your group and show her what we are researching."

My mouth drops wide open. I am sure I look like a frog, with eyeballs ogling like flashlights, and my tongue hanging out like a giant tentacle.

I am angry. No! That's TOO simple a word to describe how I feel. I grab the Thesaurus lying on the desk and search frantically for other words. Yes! I smile as I read "enrage, infuriate, incense." Now that sounds more like how I feel. I wish she could just disappear into the thick, black clouds never to be seen again.

PING! Of course, that doesn't happen. The universe does its own thing – and never considers my feelings. So I decide to call God – "He whose name I shall not mention" – very Harry Potter moment, I know! However, He never comes to my aid, and here I am having another CRISIS!

Getting back to my own dilemma, I glare with daggers, wondering what the hell she is doing in my school, let alone in my class! Hasn't she caused enough trouble in my life? I can feel my teeth grinding loudly as I watch her walk towards Sonalika, another irritating student in the school. The famous "Miss Perfect and teachers' pet Sonalika"! Just then Kash kicks me under the desk. We stare at Sonalika as she hugs Natalie and introduces her to the students sharing her table.

I remember how ▓▓▓▓ and ▓▓▓▓ complained about the famous, Miss Goody-too-shoes, Sonalika, the one and only Miss Shraddha International. If given half a chance, ▓▓▓▓ and ▓▓▓▓ would vote for her to win the Oscar for being the most pompous, conceited and pretentious student.

"She participates in every activity. Her room is the cleanest, her project the best and she is every teacher's pet. She just gets on my nerves," complained ▓▓▓▓ one evening as we sipped chai in the common room.

"She has been chosen head prefect of Meera House for the last two years," added ▓▓▓▓

It seemed most of the girls in our dorm hate her. At this moment, I am not interested in Sonalika. She is the least of my concerns. Hello! We have an alien here... who totally destroyed my life... and all within a few seconds!

My flushed face is burning hot. I look away quickly as I feel tears welling up.

"She is the reason I am here, the reason I had to leave home, my school and friends in Bangalore. This is the girl who caused so much havoc in my life in such a short time."

I remove my glasses to quickly wipe my eyes. She's living in Bangalore, so why come all the way to the north of India to study? There are hundreds of schools in Bangalore or any other part of India for that matter.

I remember that a few days after "the incident," Teja tried to give me details about Natalie. But I barely heard what he was regurgitating from the gossips in our building. I hate her and that is all. This stranger simply destroyed my life, and that is unforgivable!

For the remainder of the day, I stay far away from my enemy. That afternoon I rush to my room to change for cycling. Now this is one of the very few sports I like, and back home I used to love cycling around the vast grounds of our apartment.

Nearing my room I slow my pace as I think of home. I miss home, now more than ever. And it's because of this insufferable Natalie. I miss the lovely restaurants and shopping malls built inside our massive apartment grounds with a gym, swimming pool, two supermarkets, and the coolest game centre where bigger kids would hang around. I sigh miserably as I brush these thoughts aside and open my room door.

I stop! The most outrageous sight greets me.

"What the hell has happened here?" There are bags scattered all over the floor, teddy bears and dozens of trainers on *my* bed.

Stunned, I scan the room and spot clothes thrown everywhere, with books, make-up and colourful beads spread all over the other bed. With the door slightly ajar, I slowly tiptoe in. The first thought in my head is that someone has broken into my room. Scandalous!

I look at the mess on my bed. It is unrecognisable!

"How did someone enter my room and what would they steal?" I ask myself hysterically as I glance around. Angrily I push the trainers off my bed.

"Tch! Tch!" I mumble loudly to myself. Shoes on a bed is unacceptable. Idiots!

I pause when I hear music coming from the bathroom. The shower is on. I am flabbergasted! Disgusted! Horrified! Who in their right mind would break into a room and have the nerve to take a shower? Burglars generally steal and run for their lives, not take a shower and play Justin Bieber music. The cheeky bugger!

With my head against the bathroom door, I bang loudly and shout, "Whoever you are, get out of my bathroom now!"

The sound of water stops. A muffled voice replies, "Coming out now."

I feel my blood pressure rising as a hot sensation fills the roots of my hair and runs down my spine.

OMG! I cannot stop my spasho attack... (my ever worrisome symptoms of hot flushes and coiled knots run down my spine).

Standing astride in front of the door, fuming like a bull ready to charge, I wait for my criminal to emerge. He even has the guts to respond. I would have thought he would jump through the bathroom window to escape – NOT answer back! This really infuriates me even further.

I've never met a burglar before. What if he is stronger and bigger than me? I have no game plan. I start to panic. I don't know how to tackle or fight. OMG! This is the one time I really need Reet. She knows how to tackle any girl or boy.

Looking around my chaotic, messy room, I quickly grab a huge bath towel and confidently get ready to pounce on my intruder.

I will smother him and pin him to the ground. At that moment the door slowly opens. With steam clouding my vision, I watch the strangest creature emerge pushing a small trolley. Then I spot a colourful head.

I am haunted by yet another alien. I scream!

This time it is a huge underwater animal, a combination of a blue-ringed octopus and a multi-coloured mandarin fish. And since when does a burglar – or alien or whatever creature has taken over my room – dress in a brightly coloured robe wearing purple and pink slippers? What is this world coming to?

Immediately I pounce on this creature, wrapping my towel around his psychedelic head. Muffled screams come from within as I push him down on the ground. I ignore the blubbering, monstrous sounds beneath me, and quickly sit on the intruder, pinning his hands down. Staring down at my victim I smile proudly. I must tell Reet about this. How I wish I had my mobile – this really is a Kodak moment!

Getting back to my problem I shout, "What are you doing in my room? And how did you get in here?"

Hands keep thrashing around and muffled incoherent sounds come from the shaking head, but I don't ease off. My grip gets tighter. I am not about to lose this fight.

Out of the blue I hear the words, "I am your roommate! Please get off me."

"*Hmmm! He has a high pitched voice!*"

"You have the wrong hostel, idiot. Boys are in Gandhi House."

The wriggling creature shakes like a jelly fish, gasping for air as the voice echoes through the towel, "I am a girl!"

"What?"

What if he is lying and trying to trick me? Hmmm! Clever move. Of course I don't budge. I still need to interrogate this creature with some rules of *my* own.

"If we are to share this room, then let's talk about some house rules," I shout loudly. "The first rule is to keep it clean and tidy. You are so untidy that you have just lost your rights to be anything else in this room but my roommate! Do you understand?"

62

The jellyfish-cum-octopus-cum-sea monster twists and writhes on the floor.

I know I am not the neatest person, but for Pete's sake, have some pride.

I am happily sitting on her, ready to add more rules to my speech, when there's a knock on the door. It flings open, and there stands Mrs. de Souza in her neatly pressed blue sari, holding a huge folder in her hands. Mrs. Roy stands next to her with Sonalika and her loyal followers.

"Pooja, where is your roommate?" she enquires, "I need to introduce you and have her sign our rules register?"

Quickly looking around the room, her eyes fall on the squirming sight on the floor. I roll off and splutter guiltily, "I thought she was an intruder," staring at the crowd that had now gathered.

Meanwhile, the purple-striped sea creature slowly pushes the wet towel from her head and looks up.

There sits Natalie! My nightmare! Natalie stares sheepishly at me. With a look of disgust, Sonalika pushes the door wide open and rushes forward towards the heap on the floor.

"Nats, are you OK?" she asks with such sweet concern that I want to throttle her. Natalie pulls her gown tightly around her waist and grabs Sonalika's hand to stand up.

"I'm fine, really I'm fine!" she smiles at everyone without looking at me.

"What happened here?" asks Mrs. Roy, clearing some space on the desk.

"I thought, I thought..." I stammer like a moron, totally humiliated, "she was an intruder."

Mrs. de Souza laughs, "No, silly girl! Natalie is your new roommate. Now that you have met, I'm sure you will make her feel comfortable."

I hear sniggers and feel cold stares coming from everyone in the room, especially Sonalika and her stooges.

Idiot! I am such an idiot! I stare angrily at the floor as Natalie signs the register and the staff leave. Sonalika and her friends help Natalie tidy the room and pack away her belongings.

In the meantime, I lock myself in the bathroom. Rocking myself on the floor, I hold my head and moan quietly. "What is my karma?"

Cycling is forgotten. I sulk in the overheated, steam-filled bathroom wishing the ground could open and swallow me up.

One week later

Just an update! It's been a week since Natalie, the alien, arrived. We share the room in silence. My new rule is IGNORE my new roommate. I spend my evenings doing homework or playing board games in the common room with Kashmira and Sanam.

The day "she" arrived, I sent a text to Teja.

I couldn't wait to meet Teja for lunch the following Sunday.

"Tell me again. How did this happen that you end up sharing a room with your worst enemy?" Teja shouts loudly over the blaring music in Pizza Corner. Usually Teja loves pizza and would not talk until he had finished an entire one.

But this was breaking news – Nataliegate!

He actually stopped eating and listened to every word I said. Rudely and most irritatingly, he constantly interrupts in his newly acquitted American accent, "OMG! Who would have thought that she, of all people, would arrive from Bangalore to be in the same school as you? And share the same room?" he says incredulously.

Then he begins to laugh hysterically, shaking from side to side. Of course, I don't find any of this funny and glare at him in horror.

Gulping his Coke, he grabs a slice of his chicken and mushroom pizza and munches merrily. He looks at me and starts to laugh again, shouting even louder, "What's your karma? To get into trouble twice in such a short time?"

I ignore his stupid question and stress emphatically, "I don't even like her."

I look down at the crumbs of pizza and slices of dry tomatoes lying limply on my plate. I hate tomatoes and Teja always orders my vegetarian pizza with tomato, mushroom and olive topping. I really think this is to irritate me! I lift my head as a black olive hits me on my face. Angrily I look across at my stupid brother.

"Pooja!" shouts Teja over the loud music. "I'm talking to you. Did you make a request to change your room?"

"Yes, but Mrs. Roy said that Natalie hasn't even settled in yet and I seem to have a problem. She also saw me sitting on Natalie 'with her own eyes,' and thinks I am making up a story."

"Hmm," he replies, slurping a spoonful of ice-cream into his mouth.

He looks up with a frown, as if he has some lifesaving plan, then says flatly, "She does have a point, you know! Maybe you should give her a chance, and if you still have a problem, then gather enough evidence to support your case."

Well, that sounds like a more practical way of handling this problem. I nod my head. Of course, my stupid idiotic brother chuckles again. More like snorting like a hyena!

"There's nothing you have now except your garden story," he says, recalling the stupid incident which I would prefer to forget.

Thankfully we are interrupted by Teja's friends, Michael, a British student, and Colin from America. Listening to them chatting, I realise why Teja has developed this new mixed British-American accent.

He's such a confused wannabe British-American idiot. I smile to myself as I sit quietly sipping my chocolate milkshake.

So much for my sad life!

Chapter 8

Dear Diary,

The Nataliegate saga continues...

It is two weeks since Natalie, the unknown alien, arrived. Zero communication!

NO TALK! I give her the silent treatment. In my spare time I sit cross-legged in meditation. Of course, I have become an expert at this particular lotus pose! He! He! He! Even Miss Hegde is most impressed at my progress. But my meditation is really an excuse to swear in silence and not be seen in the same room as my "alien" roommate.

I don't want, I don't need, and I can simply do without her in my life. However, I am forced to share a room. And so I watch her like a hawk. Thankfully she tidies up after using the bathroom and keeps her side of the room quite neat.

If I find anything out of place, like her stupid colourful trainers thrown near my bed, I write on bright coloured sticky notes and place it on her pillow. After many notes and scribbles reminding her of the rules in our room, she eventually got the message.

Today I am sitting in the hall watching the slide show of the Grama Seva project. It's simply amazing how good students feel to go out into the village and help the poor.

"All these rich children getting their hands dirty!" whispers Sanam to me.

"Good. At least they're learning that life is not only about themselves and their designer clothes," giggles Kash.

"Like someone we know around here!" I whisper as all three of us stare at Sonalika at the same time. The prefect sitting at the end of the row bends forward and gives us a "dagger stare" as though to say, "Shut up, you idiots!"

Saved by the hall lights coming on, we ignore her and look straight ahead as Dr. Raj Malhotra walks to the podium.

"We have some important announcements today," he begins.

"Firstly, we welcome visiting researchers from England who will be in our school for a few months."

"Mrs. Selina Haskey is in India to research curriculum planning for private and public schools. Her research will take her across many parts of our country, but we are honoured to have her use our school as her research centre. She will stay in staff quarters and have access to all our school facilities.

"She is also the assistant research director of the British Commonwealth Countries for Education. She is widely travelled and has a good understanding of education in many countries around the world."

He turns to the side of the stage, and nods his head with a smile.

Mrs. Haskey greets us in the traditional Indian way with her hands clasped together. Her blonde hair hangs loosely over her shoulders, but she looks terribly awkward in her short black pencil skirt standing next to Dr. Malhotra, who is dressed in his long white kurta and black Indian-cut jacket with black trousers. A tight pink blouse exposes her tanned arms, and black stiletto shoes make her look taller than she really is.

Her husband, hovering behind the curtain, comes forward as Dr. Malhotra introduces him as Neal Haskey. Smiling nervously, he looks around and his mouth opens into a wide smile with white teeth sparkling against his pale skin.

Suddenly loud screeches from outside the hall interrupt the assembly. Everyone turns around and looks towards the door. Because we are sitting at the front of the hall, we can barely see over the heads of the other students.

"Get me out of here someone! Help!"

Stunned, Dr. Malhotra pauses for a moment before a few teachers jump up from their seats and rush down the aisle towards the exit. Sharp, piercing screams echo throughout the hall.

"Please Mama, I don't want to go to boarding school. I don't want to stay here!"

Somewhere a door slams shut, and immediately there is absolute silence in the hall. Then like an explosion, students burst out laughing, prodding their friends, others holding their tummies as they laugh and talk at the same time about the comic interruption they've just heard.

Suddenly the deep booming voice of Dr. Raj Malhotra thunders across the hall. "SILENCE!"

Staring angrily at the unnecessary interruption from outside the hall and the rowdiness of his assembly, he bellows loudly, "Bad behaviour is not tolerated in this school!"

Selina and her husband walk hurriedly off the stage, looking just as alarmed as us. Immediately everyone stops laughing and silence reigns once again. In the distance we could still hear the loud screams of the girl, still protesting.

Dr. Malhotra looks around before saying in his deep voice, "We pride ourselves to respect the rules of this school. I don't want anyone to ever behave in such a riotous manner again."

Turning to his staff, he announces softly, "Dismiss the assembly please." Without looking at us, he marches off the stage through the side exit.

I never gave that incident another thought until that evening when Kash and I arrived late for dinner.

During prep time we decided to help our art teacher, Mrs. Suhana to put all the completed pieces of ceramic work into the kiln. That took us longer than we thought.

Having no time to run up to our rooms to clean up, we dashed into the washroom before rushing into the noisy dining hall.

Grabbing my plate, I whisper to Kash, "My favourite," as I pile noodles and vegetables on to my plate and quickly add a kulfi ice-cream for dessert.

"Wow! I didn't realise I was this hungry!" laughs Kash as we stare at our overflowing plates. We look around for a table, but most of them are already full. As I glance around the room, I suddenly stop and stare dumbfounded.

"This cannot be happening." I feel the blood drain from my face as I catch a glimpse of the one and only Reet Sarabji cushioned between a prefect and a house mother. With bulging eyes she looks around dejectedly.

Kash pushes me forward, and laughs as I stare shell-shocked at the sight in front of me.

"Oh, that's the girl who caused history in our school," giggles Kash.

"What do you mean?" I ask gaping at neurotic Reet. She was busy playing with her fork, teasing the noodles by twirling them up and then curling them into strange patterns on her plate. Reet has a strange artistic flair for destroying good food.

"Well, she was the one screaming outside the hall during assembly," reminded Kash. "Apparently, she was arguing with her mother to take her far away from this school."

I hastily edge towards the far end of the room, out of sight from Reet. The last thing I need right now is for Reet to spot me.

After the Nataliegate, I don't need any more drama – especially with people from my past. I know Reet, and today she has blown it big time by acting like a circus idiot.

I raise my eyebrows upwards, *"He whose name I shall not mention, why me? Why am I caught between Natalie and Reet again? My life is over,"* I silently cry to myself.

I look down at my delicious meal, and immediately my appetite disappears. I was starving, but who can eat when chaos is sitting right in front of me?

My life is an absolute mess. What did I tell you about the universe and my karma? It keeps slapping me with things I don't want. Please! He whose name I shall not mention, have some mercy!

Tonight I am sitting on my bed angry and dejected. I am stuck with an alien as a roommate, and now the universe sends me another problem. Do I look like the United Nations who always seems to have the answers for children's rights? I am FED UP with God, the universe, and the world. Now I have to figure out how to avoid Reet.

I draw a light-bulb on my page. I need a game plan. Life is becoming impossible and unpredictable. Dejectedly, I close my book and switch off my lamp.

This night I have the best dream ever. I am the CEO of Teen GPS, and only students between the ages of 12 and 16 can be members. The rules are simple. You download the app on your tablet or smartphone. If you don't want certain people in your life, all you do is colour code them according to priority using the colours of Holi powders and fill in all their details. Then the minute your enemy is within close range, the GPS beeps, the colour comes up and it immediately gives you an alternate route to avoid them. One can update, add new names or delete old names. If they really annoy or bully you, instead of getting verbal or becoming a victim of bullying, you just paintball them. You also select different pictures for each person. This is great for all those dreadful people you want out of your life forever. You don't fight them or be terrified of them. It becomes the best therapy ever. No violence! No bullying! No punishment. Simple elimination! And guess what? The more you visualise it, the more the universe will make it happen – and you feel great!

I wake up the next morning feeling pretty good about life. I had the best sleep ever. Besides being a successful CEO in my dream, I also chose pictures from the house of horrors for Natalie and Reet, and enjoyed paintballing them until they fell down unconscious. The Dungeon of Mercy – an underground team of aliens who lurk in the sewer and darkness – capture them for a collection of experiments, and once finished, each person is put into a small time capsule and discarded into outer space.

I am no longer angry with Reet or Natalie. In fact, I don't scream in the shower any more. My therapy is working. All I do is paintball them and hand them over to the Dungeon of Mercy, and thankfully they disappear into the darkness. My confidence still intact!

One week later

Dear Diary,

Nothing has changed in my personal life! My problem still exists, so I have decided to make contact with Reet. This is for my own peace! I managed to avoid her in the first week. I believe she has been staying in the dormitory with two younger girls and a house mother.

Earlier this afternoon she moved into a room downstairs in Meera House. Knowing I have to accept her in the same school and in the same hostel – and considering she was my best friend at Emerald Cascades – I thought it best to get it over with.

This morning I sent her a note telling her that I am in the same school and staying in the same hostel.

I am really enjoying this school. Reet, I hope you make it work for you. Please stay out of trouble. Your entrance was a nightmare!

Thank God, I didn't hear about any further antics regarding Reet.

This evening I met her in our common lounge. As usual Reet is in high spirits, excitedly shouting and rolling her big eyes as she grabs me tightly.

"Guess what Pooja, I don't miss my Mama," Reet laughs loudly, "but I do miss Papa."

I quickly intervene and sit her down to read her the riot act. This is one girl who does not understand the consequences of bad behaviour or getting into trouble. You have to spell it out clearly and directly.

"Reet, this is a good school. Please, I beg you, DO NOT blow it for yourself." I begin to talk seriously, "Thankfully the boys are not close by for you to pick a fight with. And your Papa warned you about your temper. Listen to your teachers. They are really nice. I thought I wouldn't like it here, but it is far better than my old school."

"Hare," slapping her hand on her head, "this is heaven compared to my old school. That dragon, Mr. Vijay Singh was the worst. So yes, yes Pooja, I promise. I will make this work."

"So what was all that screaming and performance about when you arrived?" I ask angrily. "The entire school thinks you are an idiot, a real idiot."

Guiltily Reet looks away as she answers, "Pooja, I didn't know this school was so good, and when Papa told me that I was coming to a boarding school, and Mama had such a big smile on her face, I already hated the thought of staying here."

"But you always wanted to change your school, yaar, so what's the fuss?" I ask.

"I know, and when I saw you in the yoga class, I knew that God answered Karan's prayers," she said shaking her head and smiling proudly at her dearest friend.

Quickly Reet changes the topic before her friend continues to scold her,

"At least Mama will be happy now," she laughs, "all her stress will have disappeared."

She pauses, and then whispers seriously, "Pooja I have a secret."

Alarmed, I ask suspiciously, "What! Now what have you done?"

She quickly interrupts, sensing my annoyance as I stand up and glare at her. "Nothing. Come with me."

Before I could resist, she grabs my hand and drags me down the long corridor, down two flights of stairs until she reaches her room. It is a small room, just a single bed with the same lemon and green furnishings.

Forgetting the secret for a moment, I ask curiously, "How come you have a single room?"

"Because we registered so late, and there were no boarding facilities available, the registration officer decided they could fit one single room in this little corner. They got Papa to pay much more fees for late registration, and they had to furnish this room," explains Reet.

Nervously scanning her room, she goes into the bathroom and returns with a little bundle wrapped in a bath towel. She carefully places it on her bed, then checks the door is locked. With a big grin, she opens the bath towel. Wriggling out of the warm, green towel appears a little white terrier, sniffing at me as he rolls over like a ball of cotton wool.

I jump up immediately, shouting, "What is this?"

My eyes pop out of my sockets as I glare at Reet. "Are you out of your mind? Do you want to get caught and thrown out of school?"

The dog wags his tail as he licks Reet's fingers.

"And where did this new arrival come from?" I demand, knowing full well that pets are not allowed. I am so angry my hands are shaking. I check the door is locked, and hope no one hears us, otherwise this idiot would get us into a lot of trouble. I can't blow it for myself.

Turning to Reet, I say quietly yet in a seething voice, "Why do you always bring problems into your life and mine?"

My eyes flash angrily at my friend cuddling the dog. Reet is nervously rambling on about a stray dog, but I refuse to listen. I swing around, open the door and storm out of the room. Rushing along the corridor I can feel my heart pounding. I stop for a second to take a deep breath. I sit on the cold tiles ready to burst into tears. Reet is already breaking the school rules. This is one time I will not support Reet – too many times I have protected her, and now she must take responsibility for her own actions.

How many more secrets can I keep? I am so fed up. Slowly I get up and walk back to my room.

"I will not be responsible for Reet's problems. I cannot afford any more muck-ups in my life," I think to myself as I get into bed and fall asleep.

Chapter 9

Dear Diary,

As promised to myself, I stay far away from Reet, and even when I see her jumping like a monkey to attract my attention, I ignore her. Besides paintballing her each night on my GPS, I am truly too busy with projects and my own life to be bothered about her or her stray dog.

Two weeks have now passed and I am thrilled with my avoidance tactics. Kash, Sanam and I joined the dance and drama programme. We were so crazily excited when we auditioned, it felt like we were auditioning for "*Dance India Dance.*" Sanam looked like a Bollywood star. She's really beautiful and more stylish than anyone I have ever known.

This afternoon I rush to my room to change for rehearsals, only to find Natalie sitting inside her cupboard. She didn't hear me enter and was both crying and singing loudly at the same time to some Katy Perry music.

Shocked, I yank the door open. Her eyes are blood red and swollen and her pathetic, tear-stained face stares at me in disbelief. It reminds me of Po from *Kung Fu Panda*, especially when he was depressingly miserable.

She crawls out and sobs hysterically. Looking flabbergasted, I hold her as she confesses. "I haven't been Sonalika's friend for two weeks. She's a bully and insists we do all her dirty work. And because I refused, she's been harassing me."

"So I've been hiding here for the last few days. I just miss my home and friends in LA."

This is all too moving for me. Yes, I don't like Sonalika, but now I actually feel sorry for Natalie. She's not the alien I thought she was. In fact, over the weeks I have noticed that she's intelligent, loves music and reading, gets on with everyone in class, but keeps away from me. Maybe it's time I made some amends. After all, I only knew her for a few minutes when we wrestled in that stupid hedge. But I did blame her for my parents' punishment and everything else that followed.

I smile at her and quickly say, "Well, you can join me instead. After all we are in the same class."

Bells suddenly ring loudly inside my head. Did I really just say that? Even I am surprised at myself. As usual, my weakness, I always feel sorry for any stray or helpless person or animal.

Ping! Like Reet of course! Taken aback by my own strange behaviour, I hastily add, "You like music, come join the dance class. It is fun and you'll enjoy it as much as I do though I have two left feet." Minutes later we're both running down the corridor, giggling loudly as we approach the dance studio.

That was the beginning of my new friendship with Natalie. And I have to confess, I am pleased. No more horror stories or dramatic trouble like Reet.

A few days later, there's an announcement requesting all students to assemble in the hall. It's still very hot but we grab our blazers as it's compulsory to wear full school uniform to assembly and rush out of class.

Dr. Raj Malhotra is already seated on the stage, so as soon as the students settle, he walks to the podium.

"Students, I'm sorry for interrupting your lessons, but felt it important to have an assembly before lunchtime. Before I begin, let us bow our heads for a minute's silence for the tragedy in Varanasi. A bomb blast went off in a local market this morning, killing many people and leaving hundreds of people injured."

We bow silently. I hold Kash's hand tightly.

Dr. Malhotra clears his throat, looks around the hall and continues in a solemn and serious tone, "This morning I attended an important meeting for heads of schools. It was decided that all international and private schools will amalgamate to form an International and Private School Social Development Board. The aim is to work together to help eradicate poverty in our areas. We don't have enough schools built for children living in surrounding rural villages. Our plan is to provide some form of educational programme in these areas."

"Schools like Shraddha International is fortunate to have one of the best facilities in education, and this project will give you the opportunity to contribute to the service of humanity."

I listen attentively. It is the first time I have ever heard of a school take on so many welfare projects. Most of the schools in India focus merely on academic results. Yet Dr. Malhotra is spearheading a social-welfare programme that is really unique, while at the same time is giving us opportunities to learn about life, opening the locked cages for us to fly and see the real world around us.

"This would mean further fund-raising projects, with monies collected going towards purchasing school books, furniture and resources for these rural schools."

Looking up, he continues, "We have selected a senior team of students who will coordinate various projects. The 'winter warmer' project will begin immediately where we will be collecting blankets and clothes to help people keep warm during winter."

"Classes must work together on these projects. Our market garden will continue. The dance and music festival is one of our biggest fund-raising projects."

Kash pinches me and we do a quick shake of the hip as we smile. Thank the Lord we are already in the dance programme.

Dr. Malhotra pauses. Turning to the side of the stage, he nods and continues, "The second important announcement this morning is to welcome Mr. Vijay Singh, our deputy principal. He has worked with children for over 30 years and is very excited about our unique education programme. Students, please welcome Mr. Vijay Singh."

Students clap loudly, and from the side of the stage comes a short man, wearing a brown jacket and black trousers. His peppery hair is greasy, curls at the edge of his collar, and is flattened to his scalp with a side sweep making him look like an old weird character from a mystery story. He splutters as he makes his way on to the stage, and with glasses crookedly placed on his nose, he greets the students with his two hands held together. Immediately he sneezes, and quickly shoves his hand into his pocket to grab a handkerchief. Too late, his specs fall off and as he bends to retrieve it, he accidentally bumps his head on the podium.

Suddenly someone at the back of the hall gasps loudly. "Hare."

"Shh!" Prefects can be heard. We don't even bother to look at who is disturbing the assembly. Everyone is giggling, amused with the new deputy.

"That I don't find funny!" thunders Dr. Raj Malhotra in his deep voice. "Be quiet!"

Mr. Vijay Singh straightens himself and quickly fumbles at the microphone. He pushes his hand into his trouser pocket and out comes the hanky, then a piece of crumpled paper which he feebly attempts to unfold.

There is absolute silence in the hall as we stare at this clumsy man beside the distinguished Dr. Malhotra.

At last in a wheezy tone Mr. Vijay Singh mutters, "Namaste, good morning to one and all." Looking down at his paper, then over his glasses which are perched on his nose, he continues, "I am looking forward to working in this prestigious school. Your school is well known throughout India as the model school of the 21st century. It has taken education to a new level of integration – academic, spiritual and life skill components created into one powerful tool so you can reach your greatest achievement – that is, your character. You are exposed to the best education possible, nurtured and trained to become great leaders of our world. The government is now looking at ways of using this school programme as a blueprint to implement its ideologies into all schools around the country."

He pauses, takes out his handkerchief, and sneezes.

He clumsily tries to straighten his glasses as he wipes his nose, and his greasy curly tendrils fall over his face.

"I'm sure the oil from his hair is dripping down his neck," whispers Kash.

Trying not to smile, we watch the comedy show on stage.

"And choking him as it seeps into his nose and mouth," I whisper.

"Yuck!" shudders Kash.

One of the other teachers on the stage goes to help him, but poor Mr. Vijay Singh suddenly has a bout of coughing which doesn't stop.

Once again, someone shouts, "Hare! Hare! Why!"

Dr. Malhotra strides across the stage, whispers something to Mr. Vijay Singh, and turns towards us looking stern and angry.

"As you can see, Mr. Vijay Singh is not well. Please return to your class to continue with your lessons. Reet Sarabji, please remain behind," he says glaring at Reet somewhere at the back of the hall. Shaking my head in dismay, we walk quietly towards the exit.

"Pooja! Pooja!"

I look up to see Reet standing with two prefects, staring at me, rolling her huge eyes. She gestures her left hand across her throat while shouting loudly, "Vijay Singh!" The prefects drag her towards the administration offices.

"I wonder what she's trying to tell you?" whispers Natalie. "I feel sorry for her, you know!"

"OMG! It suddenly dawns on me like a bolt of lightning! This is none other than Reet's Vijay Singh!"

Sonalika walks towards me with one eyebrow raised. "I see your friend loves trouble. Does she think she is still in some village school?"

Glaring at Natalie and Kash, she smiles smugly, "Are all your friends as stupid and idiotic as that troublemaker?"

Kash replies sweetly in her strong British accent, "Yes, but certainly we are not pretentious!"

"Or a hypocrite!" adds Natalie.

We giggle loudly, but Sonalika flicks her hair with her well-manicured fingers and struts off, her minions rushing behind her like sheep following their leader.

As for Reet, if she could faint, she would. Still reeling from shock, she enters the reception area. Mrs. de Souza looks up from her computer. "Reet, sit quietly and wait until Dr. Malhotra calls you."

Her poker face dazed and unsmiling, she is on the verge of crying. She looks around the room anxiously digging her heels into the soft, blue carpet. Disturbing the assembly is not the problem right now. Her problem is facing the demon of all demons! Evil, vile Mr. Vijay Singh! Her worst and nastiest nightmare!

"What is my karma?"

She shifts to the edge of her chair and wonders how she is going to cope. Her heart beats rapidly, she feels sick as she recalls how he tormented her in her last school. Agitated, she nervously stands up, and walking around the coffee table deep in thought, she suddenly kicks the table and shouts hysterically, "Why, why, why, did he come to this school?"

Mrs. de Souza looks up angrily, "Reet, please sit down and be quiet."

Reet quickly plonks herself down and picks up a magazine.

"I wish Miss Shilpa was here," Reet thinks, staring at Mrs. de Souza with irritation, *"she is so friendly. This one is a dragon. She thinks she is the head of the school."*

Staring at the magazine she quietly moans to herself, "I am about to die right now, and she thinks she has problems! I can't seem to get rid of this man. I'm going to die! I know it, I know it, I know it," hitting her hand on her head and stamping her feet on the carpet.

Mrs. de Souza once again looks up from her typing and glares at Reet. Reet quickly picks up the magazine that has fallen on to the floor, and the centre page catches her eye. It is the horoscopes. Reet scans her birth sign, Aries, and reads, *Someone from your past will return. Trouble brews all around you. Tread carefully as you will see double-trouble in one day.*

"*What!*" she thinks to herself. "*How did they know what to say?*" She reads it again. Now I know why mama buys these magazines. These astrologers know what they are talking about. I always thought they wrote rubbish."

Her mother, obsessed with astrology, would grab the newspaper before her father every morning and quickly read her stars. Then she would call Aunty Lolly and Aunty Molly all the way in Chandigarh to discuss them. Nothing interested her more. If the stars predicted an accident, forget it, she would never leave the house.

Now Reet stares at the paper. Maybe her mother was right after all.

"*What am I going to do? Even the stars predict the truth. I have to speak to Pooja before Dr. Malhotra calls me in,*" Reet thinks to herself.

She looks around desperately, then walks towards Mrs. de Souza, and in her sweetest voice says, "Miss, may I please go to the bathroom."

Mrs. de Souza looks up from the computer, walks around her desk, and holding Reet's arm tightly guides her back to the chair.

"No, you will sit here and wait for Dr. Malhotra."

"But Miss, I really need to go," says Reet, squeezing her legs together and shaking from side to side.

"No! This trick I know too well."

She marches back to her desk and continues with her work ignoring Reet.

Reet sits glumly, fuming with anger and frustration. "No one will ever understand my problem besides Pooja. What do these idiots know of my life and my past with this man?" mumbles Reet under her breath. "Idiot! Moron! Madcap!"

A few minutes later, Reet notices the artwork hanging on the walls. Getting up she reads the subtitles on the painting hanging behind her seat, *Lady with the Lamp* by Raja Ravi Varma. Forgetting her problems for a moment, Reet spots more paintings down the long passage – *Lady with Flower Garland, Sakunthala,* and *In Contemplation.* Standing in front of a dazzling painting of *The Milkmaid* she suddenly hears voices.

Then she realises she is standing right next to Dr. Malhotra's office. Getting panicky is not going to help, so she anxiously turns back when a voice from inside the room makes her stop in her tracks.

"Dr. Raj, you are such a wonderful and kind man. It is impossible for me to stay in cottage No 16? It's too damp and draughty. Neal and I think No 23 is far bigger and far more accessible to the library and school facilities."

It is the shrill voice of Selina Haskey.

"Who can ignore that strong British accent," Reet thinks to herself as she starts to backtrack. Suddenly a deep but monotonous voice is heard.

"Raj, give Miss Selina the house No 23. She is right. It's more comfortable for them."

Reet has never heard that voice before. Quietly she steps closer to the office door.

"Dr. Clanis, I told you we have staff already living there and it's not fair to ask them to move out now. Miss Selina is with us temporarily, and our guest cottages are fully furnished to international standards," answers Dr. Malhotra irritatingly.

"Dr. Raj," comes the sweet and husky voice of Mrs. Haskey, "this will certainly add mileage to our report. You know this is the most impressive school in the country, and I'm sure you can make alternative arrangements for your staff."

"Mrs. Haskey, you are making a very difficult request," interrupts Dr. Malhotra impatiently. "Arrangements were made six months ago for you to stay in our guest lodge, with all the luxury furnishings of international standards, whereas staff houses are equipped with basic amenities."

Meanwhile, Reet peeps through the slightly ajar door. A short gentleman with a huge smile on his face is sitting in Dr. Malhotra's chair. He is busy talking to someone on his mobile phone. She watches Mrs. Haskey brush aside her blonde hair with her red painted nails as she bends towards the Head. Looking directly into his eyes, she whispers softly, "I will give you the best media coverage in the UK if you make this change for me."

Mrs. Haskey then walks around the huge mahogany desk and stands close to the stranger sitting in the big, leather seat. Her perfume wafts through the air and into his nostrils as she whispers, "Tell him, Dr. Clanis that we have important research to complete."

Reet gawks in surprise as she watches Selina place her hand on Dr. Clanis' shoulders, and while fluttering her eyelashes at Dr. Malhotra, she continues, "I promise this school would double the student population in the next three months if you agree."

Dr. Clanis pushes his chair back and turns to Dr. Malhotra. Selina steps away immediately, her dark eyes flashing angrily. "Raj, as Chairman of the Board, I don't have time for all this. Just make the changes, please."

Selina looks at Dr. Malhotra with a strange smile. Not a good pleasant smile – a sneer, sly and unpleasant smile, her thin lips twisting sideways like a cat.

A cold shiver runs down Reet's spine as she gapes in horror at Selina and Dr. Clanis.

So this is the chairman! Poor Dr. Malhotra stands up, looks at both people angrily as he removes his handkerchief from his top pocket to wipe his brow. He is not a happy man!

Mrs. Haskey smiles seductively, standing way too close to Dr. Clanis.

"Now that is strange!" Reet ponders gaping at Selina. *"Why is she touching this man?"*

At that precise moment, Reet's nose tickles. Quickly she shoves her hand into her pocket to grab her hanky, but too late. She sneezes – and so loudly that she loses her balance and falls forward. *"Oh oh! Double-trouble!"* she thinks to herself as she falls forward and lies sprawled out on the carpet inside the office, staring at a pair of polished black shoes. Almost instantly, she looks up at the stern face of Dr. Malhotra towering over her.

"Oh hi! Good morning Mr.....Mr.....M...," she stammers, as she feels another sneeze coming on. Achioooooooooo!

"Miss Shilpa, Mrs. de Souza," the booming voice shouts loudly.

Reet remains frozen on the floor. Please God! Let me disappear right now!

The old dragon charges down the passage. Dreading the onslaught of her wrath, Reet quickly gets up and straightens her uniform. She glances around the office and catches sight of Dr. Clanis sitting back on his seat, staring at some documents as he talks on the phone. He seems totally disinterested in her problems.

But Mrs. Haskey stares directly at Reet. With eyes slanted and piercing, she looks elegant and poised seated on the big brown leather chair.

Mrs. de Souza grabs Reet's arm.

"Miss Sarabji," roars Dr. Malhotra as loud as a lion, "explain to me what you are doing in my office."

His nostrils flare up like a swollen fish, and his eyes dart between her and Mrs. de Souza. Looking angry and agitatedly at Reet, the dragon shakes her while digging her long nails into Reet's arm.

"Sir, I am really sorry, Sir," she whispers quickly, "Reet was waiting for you at the reception. I can't understand how she got here."

Dr. Malhotra interrupts abruptly, "Mrs. de Souza, get Reet to report to her house mother. She will help in the kitchen every day."

Turning to Reet, he bellows, "You will peel potatoes until I get a report stating that your behaviour has improved."

He turns, marches into his office and slams the door loudly.

"But Sir," interrupts Reet staring at the closed door, "it's my hay fever." But no one is listening.

Looking utterly defeated, Reet mutters loudly, "This woman should work in the army, not in a school! Horrible, horrible, woman," as the dragon pulls her roughly back to her office.

Chapter 10

Dear Diary,

Tonight I notice Reet is not at dinner. I can't stand her stupid pranks but somehow I do feel sorry for her. Natalie and I go to her room, and as soon as she sees me, she bursts into tears.

"Pooja, Vijay Singh is back in my life. I can't stay here."

"Don't cry!" exclaims Natalie startled to see Reet so hysterical.

Reet sobs louder.

I quietly hold her, "Shhh! Reet, stop crying!"

Turning to Natalie, she wails dramatically, "You don't know the misery this man put me through in my last school."

Grabbing me tightly, she breaks into another round of sobs, "Tell her Pooja! My life is over! What will Mama say? Tell her plezzzzzzzzzzzzzzzzeee!"

Like a Bollywood movie star, she tragically falls on her knees and holds her head crying, "I wanna go home, I can never stay at this school."

I really feel for my friend, but right now she is nuts. I don't know whether to be angry or laugh at this drama. Don't get me wrong, I do feel sorry for her, but more often than not she does stupid things – like being over dramatic or over-exaggerating everything!

Alarmed at how Reet is affected by Mr. VJS's presence, Natalie sits next to her on her bed and says patiently, "Listen Reet, it can't be that bad. I had worse teachers than him, but that didn't stop me from working hard and becoming a star pupil."

I, on the other hand, have no time for calm, loving words. I simply butt in, "Reet, just don't get into any more trouble! It is that simple!"

Reet nods her head, and wiping her tears with a tissue explains, "This morning I was really shocked Pooja. I just couldn't help myself. It was the worstest nightmare ever to see that nasty man on stage."

"You mean 'worst nightmare,'" Natalie corrects her patiently.

"Huh!"

"But that is not a good enough reason for you to disturb the assembly," I interrupt angrily. "Your voice echoed throughout the hall. Do you have a microphone stuck inside your throat?"

"Pooja, my whole body was shaking... like shivering!"

"What nonsense is that?" I retort impatiently. "You exaggerate everything, which only gets you into deeper trouble."

Turning to Natalie, Reet tries to justify her story, "Natalie, you know when you are shuddering? Mama and I have the same problem when we are in shock!"

Natalie looks at her blankly, "No, what nonsense are you talking?"

"What I mean is, my hands and legs simply wobble like jelly, yaar!"

She stretches her small, thin hands out and shakes them vigorously. "See like this. Like a leaf. I can't stop it."

"OK! OK!" replies Natalie soothingly. "We get the message. Reet, listen to me, the more trouble you get into, the more reason you give Mr. VJS to punish you."

"Do you want to become a target for his entertainment again?" I ask seriously, my eyes bulging in anger.

"No, I really like this school."

"Then do yourself a favour. Behave. How hard is that?" I snap back angrily.

Cuddling Pudding, her puppy, closer to her chest, she nods her head.

Natalie quickly decides to change the subject. "Why is your dog called Pudding?"

Reet immediately forgets about Vijay Singh and chats happily. "When I found him, I had to hide him in the bathroom. There was nothing for me to feed him, so each day I saved food. Pudding was his favourite."

"How cool is that?" chuckles Natalie, "and he is a vegetarian."

"Oh yeah!" shouts Reet as she jumps up and takes a box of Maltese sweets from her cupboard. All three of us sit on the bed munching and slurping thick, gooey chocolate, telling stories about horrible teachers in our old schools. It is at this moment that Reet decides to tell us one more piece of her story of how she got caught eavesdropping at Dr. Malhotra's office.

You should see my face. Blood red! Horrified! Simply mortified! I give up! No comment! How many more times must I tell this idiot to behave? Turning quickly to Natalie, she continues her story, too afraid to look at me. To put an end to all this nonsense, I stand up, "Natalie, let's go!"

Natalie quickly steps in and with a little firmer voice says, "Reet, promise us you will finish all your work tomorrow without any more trouble?"

Looking at me nervously, she makes a cross with her finger on my heart. That used to be our cue when we made promises, but for now I am not interested. Ignoring her, I walk towards the door.

My midnight discovery

Later that night, I am fast asleep when a sudden crashing sound awakens me. I pop my head out of my duvet and look around nervously. CRASH! BANG! THUD! THUD!

OMG! Where is that coming from? I turn to Natalie, but she's sleeping peacefully.

It grows louder. Terrified, I pull the duvet over my head, and wrap myself into a tight ball. Holding my breath, I listen. Weird noises are definitely coming from somewhere.

Sounds like a train rumbling in the dead of night.

I remain still – suffocating under the duvet. It stops! Then silence. I shut my eyes tightly and try hard to sleep. Suddenly I hear loud wailing cries. Beads of perspiration form on my forehead. I try hard to hold my breath, but within seconds my lungs get tighter and tighter. They're ready to burst.

I shove my head out of the duvet, choking, spluttering, and gasping for air. Of course, Madame Natalie is still asleep. I stare in irritation. Even if I am dying I cannot trust this girl to save my life. Forget it, her sleep is far tooooo precious!

I pull the duvet right up to my face with only my eyes peeping out, darting from the window to the door. I'm sure someone is in the corridor. I can hear muffled sounds.

Turning to my new BF, I whisper, "Natalie, Natalie, get up! Someone is outside our room."

I watch Natalie stir, turn on to her tummy and go back to sleep.

"OK, who in their right mind sleeps through a crisis?" I glower at her crossly. I push the duvet aside and sit up on the edge of the bed. Silently my toes touch the floor. Praying I don't make any noise, I quickly tiptoe across to Natalie's bed.

Shaking her I whisper, "Natalie, wake up, wake up!"

Natalie stirs as she opens her eyes, "What?"

"There are strange sounds outside our door!"

Natalie listens for a few seconds.

"Maybe it's the fan in the corridor?" replies Natalie irritably.

Relieved, I jump as quickly as a fox back into my bed. Almost immediately I turn back to Natalie and blurt out crossly, "That's not the fan."

A strange, eerie, rustling sound swishes against the window. But Natalie is already snoring loudly.

I immediately spring into action. Grinding my teeth to stop myself from swearing, I march back to Miss Sleepyhead, Miss Know-it-all, and shove my fingers into her back. I couldn't care if the burglars rush through the door right now, I am so angry.

"Ouch," shouts my friend turning to find me right in her face.

"How can you snore when there may be someone outside our room?" I screeched loudly.

At this moment I don't care about disturbing the ghosts in this building. Natalie looks at me for a few seconds – four, perhaps five at the most – and like an expert on noises, replies smugly, "Pooja, it may be just a dream. There's no noise. Go back to sleep."

She turns, closes her eyes and starts snoring again. Standing over her, fuming mad, I stare at her sleeping peacefully without a care in the world. Right now, I would like to thump her with something.

I tuck myself into bed and lie wide awake staring at the ceiling. My eyes vigilantly examine every scratch on the wall as shadows dance fuzzily. I am on high alert. Those noises came from somewhere! It wasn't a dream!

Then the single worst thought ever. GHOSTS! What if there are real ghosts in this school? After all, this building is ancient. What if ghosts prowl at night? My eyes grow bigger, ready to pop out of their sockets. OMG! Not good! Not good! My BP has gone through the ceiling.

"Calm down Pooja!" I tell myself. Think good thoughts. Positive thoughts. My brain is in overdrive. But there is not a single joyful thought. Brain dead as usual. What's new?

Any damn thought, but not ghosts. Nothing! OMG! There must be something I know that sounds happy! In desperation I start humming, *I love you! You love me, we are one big family!* Then I stop. What the hell am I humming? OMG! Why would a 12-year-old be singing a nursery rhyme from *Barney* at midnight? I feel like I'm losing my mind. I am nuts! All I want is one positive thought. But the only thing that comes to mind is:

Vijay Singh – suspicion/dirty/greasy; Reet – annoying/troublemaker; Natalie – snoring; Selina – false; parents – punishment.

This is all too much. I am such a young girl yet cannot find anything happy to think about. How serious a problem do I have? And so I softly sing to myself my favourite song from the movie *Titanic*.

Every night in my dreams

I see you, I feel you

That is how I know you go on...

Just as I am swinging and swaying to this great love song and imagining myself standing at the bow of the ship with arms outstretched, cool breeze blowing through my hair – PING!

Abruptly I stop singing! A revelation. Those stupid shuffling, swishing noises outside are branches hitting against the window. I am such a dope!

But my question right now is, why must a huge tree be right next to my room? As if someone is going to answer that question. OK, environmentalists are all for going green, and I'm all for saving the planet, but not when it affects my sleep and stress levels. Chop off those damn branches! Relieved, I tuck myself back into bed and shut my eyes.

But then a cold shiver slowly runs down my spine. What if someone is climbing the tree? Wide awake again, I can hear a strange humming, like a power tool. I strain my ears. This cannot be my imagination. Who could be cutting wood this time of the night? I shiver again, like someone has just walked over my grave.

Grave? OK! Not good! Reminds me of death, murder, cemetery, blood. My eyes bulge until they nearly pop out of their sockets. Last week on the news there was an announcement of a chainsaw attacker on the prowl – an escaped prisoner who was on the run. OMG! What if he is in our building, in our corridor? I jump out of my bed and scramble into Natalie's bed.

"What now!" Natalie shouts angrily pushing my icy cold feet away from her.

"I'm scared," I whisper nudging her slightly and grabbing the duvet to cover my head. Natalie sits up and rubs her sleepy eyes. Then listens to the soft stirring sound.

"Pooja, that's the generator, you stupid! Sometimes it makes that droning sound. Please go back to your bed?"

At first I resist, but swearing under my breath I tiptoe back to my bed, and curl up into a ball under the duvet. The weird, rumbling sound drones on.

"And don't get me up again. Your trouble is you read too many mystery books," Natalie snaps crossly rolling back on to her stomach, turning her face away from me.

But of course, I simply cannot sleep nor lie like a statue fretting the night away. I watch the tree branches sway from side to side, sometimes brushing against the window, making swishy, hissing sounds that send spasms of panic into the pit of my stomach.

My mind races with various versions of things that could happen to us. With social media, just imagine the stories. Serial killer enters girl's hostel... or, Alien abduction... or, Mystery on a dark night... or, Chainsaw killer spotted at top international school. OMG! That's it. The chainsaw killer is here, on our floor, outside our door, drilling, sawing, and chopping!

I start to think crazy thoughts, and realise I simply cannot lie here, knowing full well there are murders taking place in my school. I have to do something, anything and right now!

Even though I am trembling with fear, I have to warn someone. I get out of my warm bed, slip on my shoes and tiptoe to the door. I pause, turn and look at Miss Sleepyhead. Terrified, I lean against the door to listen. THUD! BANG! THUD! BANG!

This time it seems to be coming from downstairs. Perhaps I will go to Mrs. Roy...

Quietly I open the door and slightly pop my head out. It is mysteriously dark and empty. Even the corridor lights have gone off – how convenient for the attacker.

I slowly step out, and hugging the wall, I anxiously make my way along the corridor to the top of the stairs. With trepidation, I pause and wait until my eyes have grown accustomed to the dark. I pray the chainsaw attacker is not nearby. I nervously step on to the first stair, and slowly creep down the stairs one at a time until I reach the bottom. A cold draught sweeps through the darkness, and I pull my pyjama coat tighter.

Suddenly I spot something moving in the dark shadows. I stop dead in my tracks – frozen to the spot. OMG! I am an open target for the killer. *"Please don't let me die by the chainsaw killer,"* I think as I frantically look around. Then I hear a soft growl.

I try to scream, but my throat closes up. I am now in danger and there's nowhere to hide. I hastily sprint back up the stairs to the first floor and hide behind the wooden stairway.

Breathing heavily, I peep through the balustrade. To my horror I see not one, but two black monsters climbing up the stairs. "OMG! Please Lord Venkateswara! Or any God right now! Please help me!" I whisper to myself. (FYI – meaning Him whose name I shall not mention). I try to scream again, but all I can do is croak like a stupid frog. At this moment I wish I could at least hop like a frog. That may save my butt.

Fear retching from the pit of my stomach, I quickly crawl along the corridor. Which is the fastest crawling insect or animal? Right now I am sure I can beat that track record.

Of course, my karma surfaces again, and once again it's not the good karma. I find myself at end of the corridor, barricaded by walls. Nowhere to go. Defeated, I slowly turn, and see two of the strangest-shaped monsters I have ever seen in my life moving towards me, with red eyes glowing in the dark. Just as I am about to scream, a huge, yellow hand clasps over my mouth. I faint!

"Pooja, Pooja! Wake up!" I slowly open my eyes only to find myself staring at Reet.

"Are you alright?"

"What am I doing in your bed," I whisper softly as I try to get up, but fall back immediately as my head starts to spin. Pudding is licking my face as if welcoming me into his little safe haven.

"Take it easy!" she says in a concerned voice as she places a cold facecloth on my forehead.

With bulging, fearful eyes, I whisper, "I had this horrible dream – strange noises and men with chainsaws coming to kill us. I was going downstairs to tell Mrs. Roy when two monsters attacked me. And now I have a terrible headache."

"Hare! The monster was me!" laughs Reet proudly. "I also heard strange noises, and went downstairs to check it out."

Looking absolutely baffled, I look up at Reet, "What! No! This monster was wearing a black robe and had a huge yellow hand. That was not you, was it?"

"Oh, it was my sports glove." Reet laughs proudly and continues, "You know the one with the huge finger?"

Pulling it from under her bed, she shows me the massive psychedelic yellow glove, and slips it on to her small dainty hand. Then she picks up the black robe. "This is my disguise at night in case someone sees me. In this way, I can escape without anyone identifying the night prowler. How is that for detective work?" boasts Reet.

Of course, I am not impressed. Sitting up slowly I cuddle Pudding as he wags his tail. I hold him close rubbing his back, then turn to Reet, "What did you see?"

"Vijay Singh was talking to three men near the library. Then they all headed towards the main hall."

"Hmm! That's odd! Why would Mr. VJS meet people so late at night?" I ask out aloud.

"I know, does seem odd, but he gave one man a huge envelope. I saw him counting loads of money while another man was holding a torch. I tried to follow them, but it was too dark. That's when I decided to come back for a torch, which is when you arrived."

"You fool! What if you got caught?" I ask angrily.

"I know! I know! But I can't sleep. In the last week there have been strange noises coming from downstairs, and every night when I go down to investigate, it's always quiet. Tonight is the first time I saw Mr. VJS. I heard him say something about 'not enough time,'" says Reet looking at me strangely.

"I think there is something fishy going on." Getting up from the bed, I stand up unsteadily, and holding the door handle I say quietly, "Let's go back to see what we can find."

"What, hare?" smacking her head with her hand. "You of all people, do you want to get caught when you cannot afford to let your parents down yet again?"

"No, I won't," I reply impatiently as I straighten my pyjamas, "but this time we take the torch and check out the hall."

Looking stunned, Reet stands rooted to the spot. "Are you sure Pooja? I don't want you to get into trouble with Mr. VJS."

"Yes, yes!" I retort hastily.

Reluctantly Reet locks Pudding in the bathroom and follows me quietly down the stairway towards the main doorway. There is a hushed silence in the building as we step into the large, dark entrance.

The dining hall is open, with everything ready for breakfast. There's no noise, no shuffling or dragging sounds coming from anywhere. All we can hear are the sounds of our breathing in the empty room. I look around in the darkness, vigilantly checking that we are not missing anything, when suddenly Reet nudges me.

"Shall we go back to our rooms?"

"No, let's go and check out the main auditorium," I reply, "you said you saw Mr. VJS heading towards the library."

"I think it's too late, Pooja, and we will get into trouble," murmurs Reet in a trembling voice. "Maybe we will come out again tomorrow night?"

"No!" I say sharply and walk towards the main door. "I know this may sound crazy, but there is something strange happening here tonight. It may not be a chainsaw murderer or an escaped convict, but there is definitely something mysterious going on."

Call me foolish or daft, but I am not leaving until I find out what these strange sounds are. And who better to have as an accomplice than Reet. In fact, I have become crazier than her these past few days. But this is what happens when parents send you to a boarding school. When curfews are pointless! And the word "grounded" is meaningless.

Reet follows me as I open the door and she stands outside in the shadows. The wind bellows like ghosts whizzing through the darkness. Bewildered she whispers quietly, "There's no one here, Pooja, maybe the men have left? Please, let's go back."

"No! You can go back to your room if you want. I'm checking this out tonight," I snap.

Leaving her standing alone, I run out into the dark path. A frosty, cold draught sweeps through my pyjamas. Tree branches sway from side to side as icy, blustery winds blow through the dark, cloudless night. Trembling with cold and fear, I push open the heavy wooden door of the auditorium. It creaks loudly. I jump aside and remain still in the dark. Now that I am here, I am petrified of getting caught. I feel my heart pounding.

The next moment I feel cold fingers curl into mine. I turn around and there is my loyal bestie standing right next to me, with a half-smile of dread and terror on her face. Together we enter the empty hall. It is dark and silent like a cemetery. The thick maroon curtains are drawn, and the chairs are neatly arranged for assembly.

From behind the curtains, a faint flicker of light can be seen. Placing my finger to my lips I whisper, "There's someone using a torch," pointing my finger towards the stage.

"Look, it's moving again!" Reet murmurs, her voice trembling with fear. We stand in the shadows against the brick wall watching the flickering light move from side to side.

"I'm really scared!" whispers Reet. I grab her hand and bend down, edging our way closer to the stage. We crawl between rows of chairs, hoping to get as close as possible to the stage.

Reet's voice quivers softly, "I think we should leave," staring petrified at the dark shadows making monstrous, sinister shapes against the windows.

Before I can reply, the torch light goes off. It is pitch black – just an eerie silence surrounds us. Then it hits me. It's like another light-bulb moment.

I turn to Reet and smile, "What fools we are? That must be security checking around during his shift."

"Hare," laughs a relieved Reet. "Why didn't I think of that? Every night I get so scared to sleep, wondering what is going on down here. Instead of sleeping, I keep thinking someone is breaking into the building," as she slaps her hand against her head and looks at me.

"We are such nincompoops!" I giggle giving her a high five. "Enough of playing detective, let's get out of here!"

As I slowly get up Reet tugs at my sleeve roughly and pulls me down. The flash of light appears again. But this time someone pushes the curtain aside. We dive down, wedging ourselves between two rows of neatly packed chairs.

"Mr. Vijay Singh, as discussed, the truck must pick up the consignment tomorrow night. We have already wasted too much time."

Peeping through the chairs, we stare in disbelief as Selina Haskey and Mr. Vijay Singh walk down the stairs from the stage. Following them is Selina's husband, Neal, holding a briefcase and a torch. Selina is speaking rather loudly in her strong British accent.

For a moment Reet and I look at each other in confusion, then at the three musketeers. What in the world is Mr. VJS doing with the likes of Selina Haskey and her husband? And how does he know them?

Still in shock, we watch them step down from the stage and stand near the aisle. Freaking out in case we get caught, I push Reet's legs underneath the chairs. The last thing I want is for Reet or me to get caught. Terrified, I lie flat on my tummy, with my head slightly raised. I can barely see them but it's safer.

"This consignment must be completed quickly," echoes the husky voice of Selina, "this is the last meeting we have in the dressing room behind the stage. Thank God, Dr. Clanis was at the meeting with Dr. Malhotra and gave us permission to move into No 23. From now we schedule meetings at our house. That stupid Dr. Malhotra is a stubborn, arrogant man who thinks he is the chairman of this school."

Neal rushes forward to join his wife and pulling out a page from the side pocket of his bag, interrupts her quietly, "Mr. Vijay Singh, two things before we leave. Here is a map of the library. Remember we mentioned that the library is part of the original fort. The book we need is on the first floor where ancient books are kept. If you go up the spiral stairway, you will find an old oil painting hanging between two marble pillars."

Flashing his torch on to a second page, he continues, "And this is the code for our first consignment. Those drivers we met tonight have been paid in advance to complete our work. Can you check the cargo is loaded and ready for delivery?"

Looking bewildered, Mr. VJS stutters something inaudible.

"Mr. Vijay Singh, I don't have time for excuses," snaps Selina, "you came on board to work on this mission, so remain focused!"

"This project has taken years of research and planning, Mr. VJS. Now we have a deadline," Neal says patiently in his soft, gentle voice.

Shoving the paper into his pocket, Mr. VJS remains quiet and stares into the dark hall.

Selina walks forward slowly, each step threateningly loud. Suddenly she stops right next to the chairs where we are hiding. "Mr. Vijay Singh, let's work together and get this project completed. You are getting paid a very large sum of money and can retire soon. You can travel, buy a big house and enjoy your life. That sounds great, doesn't it?" Selina says sweetly.

Reet and I remain petrified and frozen on the floor. I'm sure Selina can hear my heart hammering loudly. She is standing so close that we can smell her floral perfume and hear her breathing as she leans against the chair.

Mr. Vijay Singh smiles in the dark and shakes his head, "Yes, I know."

Neal slaps him on his back and laughs softly, "Good, now get that book and cargo sorted for me urgently. We need to move quickly with the next consignment."

Without moving, we listen to their footsteps hurrying down the aisle as the two men follow Selina. The sound of a door closing behind them signals their departure and silence envelopes the dark hall. We wait with bated breath, remaining speechless as though hypnotised by the presence of a tall blond woman whose perfume still lingers in the darkness.

Massaging my cramped feet, I wonder what would happen if Selina returned to find us hiding? By now, Reet's eyes are bulging out of their sockets. We sit dumbstruck for a few minutes, listening to the wind howling loudly and the sound of an owl hooting somewhere in the distance. Looking around suspiciously, I whisper earnestly to Reet, "Let's get out of here quickly."

All Reet can do is nod. Holding her hand, we walk down the aisle towards the large door at the end of the hallway. We gasp and tremble as we inhale the cold air. Without hesitating for a second, we dart out into the darkness towards our hostel.

At last we are safe. We jump into bed, pull the single duvet to our chin, and sit wide awake waiting to get over the shock.

Through chattering teeth, I whisper, "There is something strange going on here."

"I told you Vijay Singh is evil... it's really true!"

"I think this is serious," then I add, "there's some project they keep talking about. I wonder what it is."

"And our Vijay Singh is involved big time," says Reet.

Jumping out of bed, I look at Reet intently and continue, "Listen, let's check this out tomorrow. For now, we have to sleep. Lock the door and keep Pudding close to you. I'll see you tomorrow evening after dinner, but please do not say a word to another person. Do you hear me?"

I glare at Reet, knowing full well how quickly she can talk if given a chance. Reet nods her head, too cold to talk.

Chapter 11

Dear Diary,

History, one of my favourite subjects, is my first lesson. However, this morning I can't be bothered to work. After last night's adventure, and with less than three hours sleep, I am shattered. Sitting in the library I look a mess – and my eyes burn. I just want to curl up under my desk and sleep.

Irritably I look at Natalie, and as usual she is bright, chatty and chirpy (don't forget she slept throughout the night without a care in the world). I refuse to engage in any meaningful conversation with her, and prefer to be grouchy and bad tempered. So beware!

As though I have no other problems to worry about, our history project is to research an historic hero who made an impact on the world – and we're only allowed to use history books, encyclopaedias and journals. No internet research is allowed.

I don't understand why teachers make life so unnecessarily difficult when everything can be found with a simple click of a button.

Exhausted, I blankly stare at the printed pages. My eyelids grow heavy, the pen slips from my hand as my head droops slowly down to the desk.

"Hmm! This is soooo good! Just a few minutes of shut eye...," I think to myself.

Just then, Mrs. Jyothi interrupts the class. "Students, all research must be completed today. And don't forget your project is due on Monday."

Grabbing my pen, I pretend to do some serious work, but within seconds I slide back into my comfy position. My body is switched off. My brain is dead. My legs are numb. Once again I am far away in slumber land.

I must have remained in that semi-conscious state for a few minutes when suddenly, through half-closed eyes I see the shadow of Mr. VJS enter the library. His untidy hair falling over his bushy eyebrows, he whispers something to Mrs. Jyothi, and in my trance-like state, I watch him smiling as she points towards the far end of the room. I close my eyes again – I don't need him in my dream – and within seconds I fall asleep.

PING! A light-bulb moment. *He is here in the library.* OMG! It's happening! Remembering last night, I immediately sit up, eyes wide open! He's here to find the secret book. I stare at his awkward figure suspiciously making his way into the shadows of the dark library.

Forgetting my exhaustion and the history project, I stretch my arms backwards. Ouch, I feel a painful tug under each arm. Yoga pains of course! I once heard Aunty Jolly tell my mother that all women are born to suffer but in life, there's no time for pain.

"Hare! You just have to put it aside and get on with life," she would say. So taking a lesson from good old Aunty Jolly, my brain changes gear and I spring into action.

Almost toppling backwards as I lean precariously on my chair, I watch him slink into the darkness of the library. He stops, leans against a bookshelf, and pulls out a piece of crumpled paper from his pocket.

"What can be so important in this library that they need urgently?" I wonder to myself as I tap my pen impatiently on my desk and watch his arched frame disappear up the winding spiral staircase, towards the Oval Gallery.

"Oh no! That's not good," I murmur to myself. I literally fall out of my chair. Kash and Natalie gasp loudly as they grab me and lift me up.

"What's wrong?" asks Kash in a soft, concerned voice, "Are you OK?"

I mumble something incoherent about finding more books and then grabbing a pen and notepad, I limp slowly towards the archive section.

Our library is really cool – a two-floor library is part of the ancient fort and the Oval Gallery, built on the top floor remains untouched through time with hundreds of books and journals of ancient history stacked against rows of tall wooden shelves. We were told that hundreds of scrolls of ancient writing were found on this site, but were removed by the British Raj and stored in museums in England.

Standing in the Oval Gallery, one could see the entire ground floor of the vast library where students are allowed to study and we have additional reading chambers found at the far end of this huge floor. Hiding in the dark shadows of overflowing bookshelves near the stairway, I watch Mr. VJS upstairs, leaning against the metal balustrade in deep contemplation. I quickly grab a book, open it, and pretend to be reading. He seems to be pacing around the room, disappearing between dusty old bookshelves and tall, marble pillars, stopping randomly to read book labels written in Sanskrit.

"I wonder what his plan is?" I think anxiously but terrified to go nearer.

Suddenly he stops and looks up at the ceiling. He is standing in the exact centre of an exquisitely sculptured lotus flower designed on the dome-shaped ceiling. In front of him is a huge bookshelf that stretches from wall to wall. Eagerly he looks around the room, and hurriedly picks up a wooden ladder lying against an old cupboard. I feel goosebumps tingling from head to toe as I watch him climb up the old rickety ladder. Immediately he starts removing books from the top shelf.

Within minutes, he stops and stares at something behind the shelf. Laughing to himself, he claps his hands excitedly as he pushes dusty, old books aside, grabbing a few and shoving them on the lower shelves. He seems to be in a sudden rush as he quickly climbs down the ladder. Breathing heavily, he pauses to remove his coat and climbs up again. Now I am very curious, so I crawl quietly closer. With his hand stretched out behind the shelf, Mr. VJS stands precariously on the rickety ladder reading something aloud from his page. The next moment there is a soft droning sound and the bookcase begins to turn. He jumps aside quickly. Lying like a panther across the first few steps. I watch him closely. Against the bare wall is a silver metal chest like a safe bolted to the wall. Mr. Vijay Singh climbs up again, but this time, he seems to be highly agitated. He glances at his page and slowly turns a dial on the metal chest. At first nothing happens. Wiping his brow with the sleeve of his shirt, he looks around nervously before mumbling some numbers aloud. Once again he turns the dial. There is a soft click as the door opens and Mr. VJS smiles to himself as he pulls out a thick red book.

He quickly shuts the door of the metal chest, the bookshelf slides back into its place and he hurriedly grabs some books and stuffs them on to the shelves. Silently I crawl back to my hiding place and sit on the floor waiting and watching. At this very moment, Dr. Malhotra enters the library.

Swearing under his breath and still standing on the ladder, Mr. VJS spots him and turns away quickly praying Dr. Malhotra will leave as soon as he has finished talking to Mrs. Jyothi.

But as luck would have it, Dr. Malhotra turns and heads towards the Oval Gallery, chatting to students on his way.

"Why, why?" he groans to himself.

"Ha, Mr. Vijay Singh," smiles Dr. Malhotra walking up the spiral stairway. "Mrs. Jyothi told me you were here. I was just making arrangements with her to leave this class early so that she can move into House 16. As you are aware, Mrs. Selina Haskey has requested to move into House 23. Will you please remain with this class until this lesson is over?"

Still frozen on the ladder and clutching the heavy book under his arm, Mr. Vijay Singh stares down at Dr. Malhotra. "Yes, Sir, no problem," he says, his thick lips curling into a pretentious smile.

With quick thinking, I discretely disappear behind a cupboard still remaining close to the staircase.

"No problem," repeats Mr. Vijay Singh loudly and overly enthusiastically wishing this man would vanish into thin air. Dr. Malhotra, of course, is in no hurry to leave and continues to talk about other school stuff.

At last, Dr. Malhotra turns to walk away, but pauses for a few seconds and in a mischievous tone whispers, "By the way, Mr.. Vijay Singh, be careful with that ladder. It is broken. I'll remind Raju from maintenance to replace it immediately."

At that precise moment, Dr. Malhotra spots me. My karma! What else can it be?

"Ah Pooja. What are you researching by yourself at this far end of the library?"

As usual I am dumbstruck, only this time, I croak as if a frog is stuck deep inside my throat.

He picks up my book and laughs loudly. "I didn't realise you were doing a project on the American Civil War?"

For the first time I look at the title and wonder which idiot would want to read about the American Civil War. My lips widen into the biggest smile ever, "No Sir, it's not my topic but I really love American history."

"Excellent! Good to see my students making use of such worthy books," he says before disappearing down the aisle.

As I turn around, I find Mr. VJS perched on the ladder staring down at me with the ugliest, most venomous eyes ever. I try to smile, but instead drop the book with a thud. Terrified to look him in the eye, I decide it's time to flee, but my legs become shaky and wobbly like jelly-fish.

At that very moment, as if in slow motion, the unsteady ladder begins to sway treacherously. I watch him topple and fall in a cloud of dust, rolling helplessly down the spiral stairway. Broken shelves and dusty books come crashing down after him.

The deafening noise brings Mrs. Jyothi sprinting across the library towards the Oval Gallery. She pushes away piles of books sitting on Mr. V's pudgy stomach.

"Are you OK, Sir? Sir, are you alright?" she splutters as the dust rises up like bellowing smoke. Mr. Vijay Singh is slumped on the floor, either unconscious or dead. I stare in shock – what if he really is dead?

Students run towards the pandemonium to see what is going on. Just then he jerks forwards coughing and sneezing. Mrs. Jyothi sighs with relief as she hands him a glass of water which he drinks in a single gulp. Dazed and irritated with the unnecessary commotion and interruption, he tries to stand up, but feeling light-headed, he holds his head and quickly sits down on a chair. "I'm fine, I'm fine," he mutters angrily and taking his glasses from Mrs. Jyothi, he looks around at the tons of books lying everywhere.

Turning to the students, "Please go back and continue with your work," says Mrs. Jyothi in a stern voice. Then she looks at Mr. VJS, and adds calmly, "Sir, I called Raju to come immediately and clean this mess. Are you sure you're alright?"

He rudely ignores her and stares in absolute anger at the heaps of books scattered around the floor.

"Where can it be?" he mumbles desperately. Flustered and angry, he searches for his prized book, but to his horror he cannot find it anywhere. Almost freaking out, he kicks away chunks of broken wood. Grabbing the iron balustrade tightly he searches through piles of books lying on the stairway.

Out the corner of his eye he sees Mrs. Jyothi approach him again.

"Mr. Vijay Singh, I'm leaving now. The students are busy with their research work."

He nods, and chewing his fingernails, mumbles under his breath, "This is a damn mess. Where is that book?"

The secret book has disappeared. *"What will I tell that woman?"* he thinks as he cringes with panic.

Raju arrives with help to remove the broken ladder, and clean up the mess. As soon as they begin to pick up the books, Mr. VJS growls, "Leave those books and folders on that table, I want to look at them."

He sits down on a large sofa chair to scan through every book, folder and paper. At last he comes across the red cover underneath a pile of large books. "Thank God!" he shouts excitedly, pushing the remaining books aside. Rubbing his sore leg with one hand and with the biggest grin ever, he grabs the book and strokes the cover.

Chapter 12

Dear Diary,

Breaking news! In the last few hours I have become a neurotic, crazy, nervous wreck. I thought I was a simple, uncomplicated girl. Oh no, things have changed! I am hiding in my room – inside the cupboard! The curtains are drawn, the room is dim and quiet.

Hugging my knees close to my chest, I wait for the formidable knock on the door. By now I have ulcers or palpitations or whatever, and I can even hear my heart hammering loudly against my chest – dum dadum... dum dadum... dadum dadum... I am dead! Expelled! Disgraced!

Just as expected, I hear footsteps rushing towards my room. I grow hot as though someone left heated hair irons on my hair. Knock! Knock! Bang! Bang!

Biting my fingernails, I peep through a crack in the cupboard door. Someone swears loudly in Hindi and kicks the door.

"Who is it?" I whisper cautiously.

"Hare, it's me man!" Reet screams loudly.

I open the door slightly and quickly pull her in.

"Hey! What's with the...?"

I cover her mouth, her eyes grow big with confusion. "Shh! Be quiet idiot," I whisper dragging her towards my cupboard.

Inside the cupboard, Natalie is sitting cross-legged grinning like a Cheshire cat, holding a huge torch with papers on her lap. Clothes from the hangers have been thrown on the bed.

"Did you see Mr. Vijay Singh as you came up?" I ask in my ever-famous squeaky high-pitched voice.

Let me pause for a moment. I have a horrible secret. Whenever I panic, my voice suddenly changes – sometimes it becomes squeaky and high, sometimes low or gruff or stops completely, but mainly it changes into cartoon characters. Seriously! Don't laugh! I do have a major problem.

This time I sound like Alvin from *Alvin and the Chipmunks*. All I need is a microphone to start singing *Everything's Gonna Be Alright*. But that is a totally different story, so let me get back to this major crisis.

In my sharp, high-pitched Alvin's voice, I repeat the question to Reet, "Did you see Mr. VJS anywhere?"

"No stupid! I saw Kash in the dining hall during tea, and she told me you were not well," she explains breathlessly with her hands flailing around like a crazed parrot. "Apparently Mrs. Roy sent you to your room. That's why I rushed here after that stupid abseiling session." Reet hates any sport that takes her away from land – swimming, mountain climbing and now abseiling – and admits she needs to be on same level as Mother Earth *at all times*.

I push Reet inside the cupboard and squeeze myself in. Barely breathing and packed like sardines, Reet grunts like a sore bear, while Natalie flashes the torch light from Reet to me, making strange, eerie sounds. Reet is not amused, and simply glares at us with daggers!

"Stop your stupid tricks," she shouts with exasperation, "and why are we sitting in the cupboard like morons?"

Natalie starts to giggle hysterically as Reet holds her hand against her face blocking the blinding light. I snatch the torch from Natalie and switch it off.

"That's enough!" I glare at Natalie. "The last thing I want is Mr. VJS coming in here!"

Reet immediately jumps up, and looking alarmed, whispers, "What? Why Mr. V?"

And so I relate my simple story to Reet.

"I had a tummy ache and told Miss Chitray, and she sent me immediately to the sick-room to see Nurse Geeta."

"Why? Did you eat something bad?" Reet interrupts with concern.

"No silly, I was pretending," I giggle softly in the dark, "I wanted to skip classes for the afternoon."

"Pooja Narayan! Are you becoming a rebel in this school?" Reet laughs loudly looking more relaxed.

"Last night in the hall and now bunking class. If only your parents knew!"

"Shh! be quiet." I put my finger to my lips.

"Why? What's the big deal?" she giggles. "So you missed your afternoon classes just to hide inside your cupboard."

"Stomach cramps!" Natalie guffaws loudly. "In this country when a girl our age has tummy pains the nurses think we are having our period."

"What?" Reet looks at both of us as if we are nuts. "But we haven't even had our first period."

Natalie giggles again, "Exactly!"

I nod, "That's why the staff panic. Nurse Geeta says the pain is unbearable the first time."

"Yuck! Too much information. I don't want to know!" cries Reet covering her ears.

"And guess what it is called in India?" giggles Natalie mischievously.

Reet stares blankly. Natalie and I shout together, "Menses!"

All three of us burst out laughing.

Reet asks seriously, "Why menses?"

Natalie opens her phone and Googles the word 'period'. "The correct word is menstruation. Not monthly, curses or menses."

We begin to laugh louder and louder, until we eventually push the door open and spill out on to the floor holding our tummies. But this time, it really does hurt.

Unbeknown to us, someone is outside the door. At first we do not hear the faint knocking, but then the handle of the door rattles. Jammed between my friends, with legs tangled over each other, we stop instantly and lie quietly on the floor. The knocking grows louder, and as fear grips me I feel myself break into a sweat. Nervously my eyes dart to Natalie, but before I can stop Reet, she jumps up and rushes towards the door.

Oops! I didn't get a chance to tell her my story of what happened in the library. Thankfully she peeps through the keyhole and her eyes grow large as if she's seen the devil. She opens her mouth and then shuts it. She turns around and stares at us, horror etched all over her face.

Like two crazy lunatics, I quickly grab my clothes and hang them back in the cupboard, while Natalie collects the pages scattered around the room and hides them underneath her mattress before straightening the duvet. All the while I am chanting the "Om Namah Shivaya" mantra as if it is the song of the year on *UK Idols.*

As for Reet, she is still standing at the door, motionless, her pale face turned white with eyes bulging like saucepans.

"Open the door now!" someone shouts banging on the door.

My face drains of all colour as I hear the familiar voice. Lord Shiva certainly didn't help! Karma again – what did I tell you about the universe? I am in BIG trouble.

Like a robot, Reet backs off one step at a time. Immediately Natalie pushes Reet on to the bed, grabs a book from the shelf and shoves it into her hands. Taking a deep breath I open the door. Standing outside is the fearful, yet expected Mr. Vijay Singh.

"Good afternoon Sir," I whisper guardedly. Just looking at this ugly, slimy man sends cold shivers down my spine. Ignoring me, he rudely pushes me aside and storms in. His sly and sneaky eyes quickly scan the room. Outside in the corridor are Sonalika and her three stooges. Why are these three idiots always around when I'm in a crisis?

Fuming mad I stare at them, "Don't you have anything better to do with your lives?"

Thankfully, Natalie steps in and jams her foot behind the door preventing it from opening further. "Do you want something? Sonalika?" she asks sweetly, putting on her best smile.

They stare back at her, shaking their hips like dumb mannequins. Sonalika's eyebrows rise slightly giving me one of her "Miss Know-it-all" looks. Through the corner of my eye I see Mr. VJS walk towards the bathroom. I follow him as he pulls the shower curtain aside. He opens the cabinet drawer and ruffles through our toiletries.

He steps back into our room and opens the cupboards, pushing hangers aside, throwing boxes, shoes and clothing on to the floor.

"Ahh! Sarabji, I knew I would find you here," he says turning to Reet with a strange twisted smile.

Reet's face turns pomegranate red, her eyes downcast, fixed on the book, too afraid even to blink. With one finger he lifts her chin up so that she is looking directly into his sinister eyes.

"Sarabji, have you lost your tongue?" he whispers coldly.

Reet remains silent, her bottom lip quivering.

"Let me warn you and your friends here. I am watching you and if there's one wrong move, you will all be expelled!" he says arrogantly.

Her eyes grow even larger with horror, but she remains quiet and still.

Natalie quickly interrupts, "Sir, do you want something else?"

"No!" he barks angrily. "It's just my routine check-up of all rooms."

"But Sir, I thought this was supposed to be done by Mrs. Roy?" I retort loudly.

"How dare he barge into our room and have the audacity to be rude as well," I think to myself as I glare back at him.

Slowly he walks towards me, and in a threatening voice whispers, "I have the right to inspect any room – if that is what you are insinuating?"

Thank the Lord I'm saved by Mrs. Roy who pushes her way into the room and looks intent on throwing Mr. VJS right out the door and down the stairs.

"Sir, our rule is no male staff may enter the girls' rooms."

He looks up and with a slow stride saunters towards the door. "I am completing a routine check for my report, Mrs. Roy."

Looking at the disarray around her, she reminds him in a stern, authoritative voice, "Then Sir, you have to inform me and I will escort you."

Mr. VJS glares at her for a moment, and without another word, marches out of the room.

Mrs. Roy angrily follows him. Sonalika and her friends trail after fat Mrs. Roy who is wobbling behind the arrogant Mr. Vijay Singh. Natalie immediately locks the door behind them and turns back to look at me.

"Pooja, Pooja, are you OK?" whispers Natalie. I don't think she has ever seen me look so shaken. Nodding my head, I look at Reet.

"What's going on Pooja?" Reet whispers nervously, her lips trembling with fear.

I explain about Vijay Singh's visit to the library and his lost book. Reet remains silent. Her small body stiffens as she digests my story. Of course, that doesn't last very long. Then like a person in a trance with drums beating loudly and needles pinned onto her tongue, she shouts angrily, "What? You mean you stole the book and now you're hiding the damn thing?"

"Shut up, idiot," I whisper agitatedly, "your loud mouth will get us into more trouble."

"Oh no! Not me. This time, *you* will get us into trouble! You stole a book. Are you nuts?" she jumps up, pointing her finger at me.

Hitting her hand on her head, she shouts frantically, "Do you realise how dangerous this man is? He just warned us that we will get expelled! You are such an idiot!"

Natalie quickly intervenes to try and calm the situation. "Listen Reet, I think Pooja wanted to check why it was so important for Neal to want the book."

Reet glares from Natalie to me, "I don't care if she stole the Kohinoor Diamond. Mr. V is the worst man ever to get on the wrong side of, and I don't trust him," she whispers, her eyes bulging with renewed fear.

"How desperate was he to actually break the school rule and enter our room?" Natalie says quickly trying to change the topic.

"Well, that is why I am so manic," retorts Reet staring at me, "you don't know him like I do. How are we going to return the book?"

"I don't know right now, but the book is not just a book. Come and see this!" I say excitely. Lifting up the mattress, I quickly gather piles of papers and place them on my desk. Then I push my bed aside, and tapping softly on the floor, I gently remove a huge marble tile. Pushing my hand into the wide gap, I pull out a black leather bag buried in the floor and remove a large red book.

"Hare! How did you find this hiding place?" whispers Reet breathlessly forgetting all about Mr. V.

"When I first got here I had the room to myself, and decided I had to find a secret hideout for some of my stuff. Walla!"

"How cool is that!" replies Natalie.

"Listen, it was so strange. As the ladder broke, Mr. VJS was trying to grab on to another bookshelf, but it also broke and he came tumbling down the huge stairway with all the books. And there, right in front of me, I found myself staring at the book Mr. VJS had under his arm. The book cover had slipped off, and before I knew it, I had grabbed the book and went back to my desk with the rest of the class."

"Is this what Mr. V was looking for?" Reet whispered.

"I hope so! I didn't realise there was another book inside this red book," I say excitedly, opening the book. "A book within a book!"

"What?" shouts Reet in confusion and immediately grabs it from me. She reads the title, *The Missing Treasure* written in faded gold paint. Inside the red book is a red velvet cloth lining with a thin layer of gold braiding stitched around the edges.

Natalie interrupts, "Look, we found this old frayed, thick brown leather book tucked inside. Sounds strange, but this red book is simply a cover for the brown leather book."

"FYI, this is a journal... it has a lock and maybe confidential information! Most diaries and journals have locks!" Reet interrupts rudely, turning it around and staring at the small tarnished lock.

"I have no idea, but this book must be very important if Selina wants it."

"Then let's break the lock!" suggests Reet.

"No! We can't damage anything." I grab the book and hold it to my chest.

"I'm not saying tear up the pages, idiot! But how do we read it if we cannot open it?"

As usual, Natalie interrupts with a logical explanation. "We found some loose pages tied together with string and attached to the leather book. This is what Pooja and I were trying to read before you got here. We were hoping it would give us some clue as to the key."

Totally disinterested, Reet cheekily butts in. "Why don't you get it? I am worried about two things. One, Pooja stole the book which has led Mr. V to this room. Two, we have to find out why this book is so important."

In her usual bossy way, she points her finger from Natalie to me, and demands loudly, "Tell me how to resolve both problems?"

"When I grabbed the book, I didn't know it was going to be this complicated, Reet," I reply keeping my cool. "I thought I would read the book, find some clues and return it. Simple!"

"Now how do you plan to do that?" quizzes Reet with her hands on her hips, staring at me as if she is Andy McNally from *Rookie Blue.*

"I didn't think that far," I mumble quietly trying hard not to show my irritation.

"Don't you think this may be too dangerous for us?" says Reet calmly. "If Selina is the leader, then I am more scared of her than Mr. V."

Just then Natalie interrupts, "Hey! Look. There's something written here."

She places the book under the lampshade and also switches on the light on her mobile.

With our heads close together, we see a title and a faded painting of an ancient fort.

And on the back cover, written in small black calligraphy handwriting, are the words, *Findings recorded until 1880 by archaeologist A.G.E.*

"That sounds ancient! Now we must find the key," whispers Reet curiously.

A light-bulb moment! "Perhaps it is stuck here," I say grabbing the book cover. Carefully placing my fingers inside, I touch the soft velvet cloth. "Nothing!"

"Oh, just tear the cloth," Reet says impatiently, shoving my fingers aside and prodding around with her tiny fingers.

"No!" I shout pushing her away.

"Idiot, I am not destroying any evidence, only tearing a teeny-weeny part!" she retorts rudely.

Natalie, fed up with our bickering, takes the journal, sits down at her desk and carefully feels through the soft velvety cloth. We all remain quiet, only the sound of our breathing can be heard. Suddenly she shouts, "Yes, there is something here. I can feel something under the cloth," she says looking up at me.

"What is it?" cries Reet curiously.

"We have to remove the velvet cloth first," she says seriously.

"Let me check it out first." I feel a wobbly knob shape and nod my head. In a flash Reet stands next to me with a pair of scissors in her hand. Natalie carefully cuts across the top edge of the lining and all along the sides. Very neatly she pushes the cloth back. For a few seconds we stand rooted to the spot – our jaws wide open!

"Hare, what is this?" whispers Reet.

Beneath the velvety lining is yet another lining – made from leather – which is sealed around the edges with embossed embroidery. Without hesitation, Natalie removes a penknife from her desk and carefully slits the material along one side of the book. The golden embroidery thread slips off easily, and within seconds the leather lining is removed. Tucked inside is a small, exquisitely carved crystal lotus flower. I remove it carefully and place it on my desk. It is deep pink in colour, embellished with tiny bits of sparkling stones.

Awestruck, Natalie whistles softly, "Are these real diamonds?" She touches the flat centre filled with shimmering stones that glitter brightly around the petals.

"OMG! What do we do now?" I keep repeating to myself.

The oval petals of the lotus flower are slightly opened. I don't know if they are real diamonds, but they seem to glitter extraordinarily and look expensive.

Totally disinterested, Reet pushes us aside and stares at the lotus flower for a few seconds, then looks up at me and asks irritably, "Is there a key?"

Natalie shines a torch directly into the gap, searching once again at each corner, "No key!"

"I wonder how Selina knows about this book!" I ask aloud, still staring at the exquisite crystal lotus.

"I think it came up in their research," replies Natalie softly, looking up, "there was no way they could just have this information."

"Hey guys, are these real? Have we found treasure?" asks Reet, suddenly realising the enormity of what is going on.

"I think so!" replies Natalie.

"We don't know yet," I reply seriously, touching the stones with the tips of my fingers.

Reet suddenly jumps on to the bed, her eyes bright with excitement, waving her hands around in typical bhangra dance style. "Wow! We're rich! We're rich!" Then she stops. "Guess what, we don't have to go to school... or see Mr. V's face or Selina. OMG! It's for real."

Natalie and I realise she may be right. We all start to laugh. I touch the crystal lotus again to make sure I'm not dreaming and almost instantly, I feel a tingling, burning sensation in my right hand. I pull my hand back immediately as if I got an electric shock and then notice a strange glow on my finger, only on my ring finger.

"*Oh no, this cannot be happening right now,*" I move away cautiously and lock myself inside the bathroom.

Sitting on the floor, I stare at a red light shining from my right hand ring finger.

OK... let me just backtrack here... when I was born my parents had taken me to a temple to perform a ceremony for newly born babies. There an old sage who was performing the final prayer told my mother to place me before the deity of Lord

Ganesh. He said that I was blessed with a special boon in the form of an invisible ring on my right ring finger. As I grew older, I wanted to know more about this boon, but I was told when the time is right, this special gift will appear. AND NOW, after all this time... it's suddenly happening... OMG!

Even though I am petrified, I want to test how powerful it is. And so I join my friends again and gently touch the lotus flower.

Suddenly the stones begin to twinkle brightly with flecks of light flashing against the wall and on to the ceiling. All three of us jump aside, and Reet grabs my arm. In slow motion, each pink and white crystal petal unfolds and becomes almost translucent as it spreads out. The light seems to fill the room. The centre pod gradually rises and begins to rotate three times clockwise – then stops.

"OMG!" we cry in unison.

"Hare!" cries Reet in confusion, smacking her hand on her head. "What is happening?"

A bright yellow and orange light shines from the centre like the early morning sun peeking over the horizon.

You should see us – standing like statues, shocked out of our wits. Everything seems crazy!

The light fades away until we see a small golden locket sitting in the centre of the pod. Reet nudges me, and I nervously take the locket. Without blinking and too frightened in case I drop it, I place it in the palm of my hand and carefully open it. A tiny bronze key is inside, which falls out on to my hand. Slowly the light from the centre pod begins to fade and magically seals together. Then the petals slowly close up. All three of us stand like idiots, gaping. Speechless!

Reet breaks the silence! "Hare, what just happened? It spooked me."

Natalie whispers impatiently, "Pooja, what are you waiting for? Open the lock!"

Slowly I insert the key. The tiny lock clicks. The journal soundlessly opens!

The yellow, stained pages are tightly compressed, tissue thin and very delicate, with some pages even torn at the edges. Strangely it does not smell damp or musty, but rather of jasmine. With some difficulty I turn over the first page and I'm surprised to see the most beautiful, calligraphy handwriting – written in black ink, faded and barely legible.

"My name is Arthur George Ealdwinne. As a senior archaeologist I was employed by the British Raj to lead a team of scientists to discover India's ancient civilisation. We know for a fact that for thousands of years, India was attacked by numerous foreign invasions and experienced countless natural calamities. This resulted in cities being buried deep beneath the land, most lost or forgotten and some untouched to date.

Long before spice trading began between Britain and India, the British knew that India held a wealth of treasure. From as early as the 1700s, sites were identified across India and scientists were deployed to excavate the buried treasures.

It seemed as though an unknown mystical power led us to this sacred and secretive land. Let me explain how we came across this mysterious fort...

We were on our way to our next site when we found ourselves lost, surrounded by tall trees with thick vegetation that stretched across the hills, covering rocks and stones and spreading down to the vast valley below.

To make matters worse, most of us contracted malaria. Hindered by high fever, disorientation, unbearable summer days and torrential rains, we wandered aimlessly through overgrown, wild forests. One afternoon, our world suddenly stopped. The sun disappeared, the air became oppressively suffocating, boughs of the tall trees no longer swayed but gathered as if conjuring something together. Everything faded into darkness. Blackness loomed around us. Huge boulders covered in thick foliage rose from everywhere.

Overflowing branches dipped into the ground to give birth to new saplings that swept across the damp, smelly earth. Their vines wound themselves around swollen barks like serpents gazing across the darkened forests.

We had to stop as we were too sick to move any further, so we set up camp under a strange looking tree whose roots seemed to hang upside down, rising high from its branches and then cascading downward to sink deep beneath the wet ground.

For now, we were grateful to be away from the torrential rains or scorching sun. I think we remained there for days, delirious with high fevers and chills, nausea, vomiting and diarrhoea. The local guides administered traditional concoctions of medicinal herbs and juices from roots, tree bark, bitter berries and leaves found around us.

While we slept, extraordinary things began to take place. The heart-shaped, leathery leaves from the tree under which we took shelter, covered us like a blanket, protecting us from the perils of hot winds and intermittent rain storms. At the end of each day the guides collected these leaves, muttering words of prayers as they hung them up to dry.

When we recovered from our illnesses, the sun began to shine brightly, the violent rains ceased and the tapering leaves from the tree fanned us as they swayed in the cool, gentle breeze.

Our guides explained excitedly that a miracle had happened. It seemed that the tree under which we had *sought shelter was called the peepal tree – one of the most sacred trees of India.*

Never before had they seen Sanskrit writings on these leaves. They were convinced that something great was about to descend, and so performed special prayers and circumambulation around the tree while we had slept.

All twenty of us scientists stared at the unblemished, calligraphy writing scripted beautifully on the dry, heart-shaped leaves. When asked to decipher the writings on the first leaf, we were told, "He who seeks the Truth shall find my resting place beneath the tree of Enlightenment."

Looking at the ancient Sanskrit writing, the guide looked very confused, and explained that every leaf had the same message. You have to understand that as learned scientists with a deep Western influence, we were sceptical about these strange writings.

We had also had enough of India, its miserable summers and monsoon rains, superstitions and all their mumbo jumbo nonsense. Exhausted and weak after our sickness and tired of living in unbearable conditions, we simply wanted to get out of this God-forsaken jungle and back to work.

Of course, this did not happen!

That night we packed our belongings to begin our trek back to our excavation site. We planned to leave at sunrise, but by midnight a storm had erupted. The wind began to wail, not just loudly, but shrieking and hollering angrily through the dark forest, thrashing and ripping trees apart with piercing cries of terrified animals running wildly around seeking shelter.

Streaks of lightning whizzed past us. And then the rains fell, not the soft pitter-patter of refreshing rain, but a torrential downpour, with huge hail stones, some the size of our fists, pounding and battering the ground with rage and fury.

Watching the overflowing deluge swell up around us, drowning the flora and fauna, we remained huddled together with fear and trepidation. The incensed thunder continued to roar and bellow from corner to corner of the dark skies, announcing its disapproval and anger for going against the grain of destiny.

The next morning we found ourselves stranded. Huge trees that had been ripped apart were thrown across our paths and debris from thick foliage floated past us in small rivulets. Of course, we were alarmed at the deluge and destruction before our eyes. Even though a faint glow of the sun could be seen peeping through the bent and broken trees, dark, thick clouds still hovered threateningly above us with silvery rains lashing down steadily. The local guides begged us not to leave, claiming there was a mystical power that had caused this destruction, and tragedy would once again prevail if we decide to leave.

After much discussion and arguments, and knowing it was absolutely impossible to find our way out of this jungle, we chose to remain and investigate the meaning of the strange message on the leaves of the peepal tree.

We waited many days for the storm to dissipate. Early one morning we were awakened by the guides who excitedly led us deeper into the jungle, through thick, green vegetation and across broken trees and debris until we found ourselves staring at an abandoned and derelict fort. It seemed as if some unknown power had lured us into this lost jungle and forced us to become stranded during the storm.

As researchers, we wanted to unearth the anonymity of this fort – however, a series of strange, unexplained happenings continued to take place. After many months *of clearing, digging and excavating, we were still unable to gain entrance into the abandoned fort. It was as though an invisible seal surrounded this mysterious building.*

Details of what we discovered inside the fort can be found in the pages that follow, but before we get there, I want to include some significant information regarding our findings.

As soon as we agreed to follow the cryptic messages written on the leaves of the peepal tree, we gained access through a hidden entrance which led us to find a treasure chest of gold and precious stones. Several hallways and rooms remained mysteriously undamaged. We examined many artefacts and medieval architecture, and found evidence that the fort had been built sometime during the Mughal period.

Even though we remained on this site for several years, we never discovered the original owner or what period of time this fort was built. Most baffling was that it remained untouched, forgotten and submerged in a jungle for a long, long time. We also found that some sections of the fort were carved into a huge mountain with a river running alongside the treacherous ravines – making it difficult for any form of invasion.

In time, the British took it upon themselves to claim ownership of the fort. We restored and renovated what we could salvage, and the treasures found inside this forgotten fort were eventually taken back to England."

"Hare!" interrupts Reet loudly and irritably, shaking her head and swinging her hands around, "I don't understand what is so secretive about this book."

Natalie and I nod our heads. Looking at the pages scattered on the bed and the mystery book, I have to agree with Reet. I am more confused than ever.

"This book is really, really old," exclaims Natalie as she picks it up from the desk, "and he's only describing facts about a fort."

Reet suddenly breaks the silence and rattles off dozens of questions as if we're Wikipedia. "If I want facts on the Mughal dynasty or forts in India, it is so easy to get information on the net. So what's the secrecy? How did Selina know it was in the library? How come this book is like hundreds of years old and never found?"

This is too stressful for me. How am I supposed to know the answers?

Reet grabs the book and exclaims irritably, "How can we read these pages? The ink is faded. Some pages are stuck together and have holes. I'm sure insects are eating it. Yuck!" She throws the book aside.

"Reet," says Natalie crossly, "what do you expect from an old book? The writing must fade. I'm sure there are missing pages as well, but we have to read what we can. Do you have a problem with that?"

Angrily Reet jumps on to my bed and with both feet tucked underneath her, stares moodily around the room.

Ignoring her, Natalie turns to me, "Look, Pooja, this book is filled with drawings and details of their findings. I am reading on the net about some of forts in India, such as Red Fort, Jama Masjid, Jahangir Mausoleum, Shalimar Gardens; Agra Fort... but there's none built in this area, Arathi Nagar. Nope, nothing! Not even in nearby places."

Looking totally confused, I add, "That's so strange. What if this was just an ordinary, old dilapidated building destroyed during one of the many invasions?"

"My parents were told this school was originally a fort," interrupts Reet joining me on the floor. "Are you sure we're not missing something?"

Nats shakes her head as she grabs some of the pages and sits down on her bed.

"This author says this journal details his experience about this unknown fort. Why can't it just be a simple story?" asks Reet, staring at me with her big eyes.

"Hey, why don't I read the introductory pages again to see if we're missing something," suggests Natalie taking the journal to her desk, "while you and Reet look at the loose pages?"

"What are we looking for again?" interrupts Reet as she grabs some pages from Natalie.

Without losing my cool, I suggest, "Maybe something familiar with our school. I don't know, but some clue we could relate to Arathi Nagar or surrounding areas."

Still looking baffled, Reet nods her head.

The invisible ring begins to glow again. This is so stressful because no one else can see the ring. And I cannot disclose it to anyone. I tremble nervously.

The room grows silent with only the soft glow of the lamp. All three of us begin to read quietly, scribbling with brightly coloured highlighters.

After a short while I interrupt the silence, "Listen girls, these pages were folded together with lots of designs. I don't understand a thing, but check out these drawings."

Both girls look up. Reet switches on the main light. I explain, "It says structural drawings." I place the page on the desk and point to a faded picture of a tall pillar in the shape of a lotus bud that looks taller than all the other buildings.

"Is that the Sarva Dharma?" whispers Natalie in astonishment.

"What? How sure are we it is *the* Sarva Dharma? It could be just any long structure," adds Reet loudly.

Ignoring her, we stare at the designs as if we are architects or land surveyors or something like that.

"And even if it is the Sarva Dharma, there may be other forts with that same structure," argues Reet smugly.

Reet is starting to get on my nerves. "Listen you idiot! How many forts do you know in this country with this structure? Tell me!" I ask cheekily.

Natalie the peacemaker quickly interrupts, "We don't know Pooja. Maybe we are just guessing."

I'm ready to slap someone here. I have a gut feeling about this finding, but right now, I am tired of fighting Reet. It is like arguing with my father. Taking a deep breath, I walk into the bathroom and wash my face with cold water.

Staring into the mirror, I say to myself, *"Stay calm Pooja. Strange things are happening. It is the first time I can see the invisible ring. Why did my ring glow when I touched the crystal? Why did the book fall at my feet? Why were precious stones hidden inside an old book? Why would Neal and his wife insist on finding this book? What are they searching for?"*

Back in the room I find Natalie reading aloud from the journal:

"After examining archaeological artefacts, we found this fort was built sometime during the Mughal period. It was built into a mountain, alongside treacherous ravines and a river that flowed nearby, making it impossible to invade. A large portion of this fort still remains buried beneath this land.

We spent years in this fort after discovering hallways, courtyards, spacious rooms and gardens. The greatest discovery was the emergence of a floating stupa found buried at the entrance of the building. As an expert archaeologist I had never seen a pillar grow from the depths of the earth and reach up towards the sky. According to the cryptic code found on the leaf, this floating stupa has no beginning, nor end. At the crown of the stupa sits a golden lotus flower.

We were never able to locate any records of the original owner nor the date the fort was built. This still remains a mystery. We were instructed by the British Raj that all research records, artefacts, precious gems and jewellery found on site were to be taken back to England. As soon as we began removing the treasures from the fort, strange and unexplained disasters occurred.

We started with a team of twenty British archaeologists and geologists, but very soon only five remained alive. Many men perished through accidents, diseases and unnatural causes. It was my decision as leader of this team to cancel further research and abandon this excavation. I know for a fact that what remains beneath the fort is far richer and more powerful than all the wealth found beneath the land, and hopefully one day will be discovered. But for now, we had to admit defeat and retreat from this holy land.

I take with me one precious lesson I learnt from this excavation: As man seeks the wealth of the land, he forgets the only priceless gift of all mankind lies deep within his own soul.

Only when it is unravelled by the wise and seekers of Truth, will Light fall upon this earth and darkness disappear forever.

With so many tragedies and unsolved mysteries linked to this unique experience, our team members chose to remain anonymous. The recordings in this book have never been published, for I believe when the time is right, when it is destined to happen, Truth will be celebrated."

I salute India! Namaste!

A sacred mystery lies deep within the fort!

The wealth untouched,

The spiritual knowledge rich and unparalleled

The magic lies in the TRUTH!

Truth is found in that Light!

Arthur George Ealdwinne

15th August, 1872

Looking confused, Reet asks, "Natalie, what is a floating stupa?"

"No idea!" she says softly, still reading from the book. "You know something, maybe these pages have nothing to do with our school. This school is too modern and this writing is way too old."

I suddenly jump up and shout, "Wait a minute, the floating stupa may be the Sarva Dharma. And what is on the top of the pillar?" I ask excitedly.

Natalie quickly shouts, "The lotus!"

I rummage through my desk to find a school brochure which has a clear picture of the Sarva Dharma. Walla! I open the brochure and the lotus flower sits proudly on top of the Sarva Dharma.

"The golden lotus!" the two girls shout in unison as they grab me and all three of us push our heads out the window to catch a glimpse of this beautiful stupa that stands proud and tall in our school.

Turning around excitedly, Natalie grabs her mobile phone and takes a selfie of us grinning like total nutcases with the pillar in the background.

"OMG! Our school is the ancient fort!" squeaks Reet excitedly.

"But I still don't understand what buried treasure Selina and her husband are looking for." I interrupt thoughtfully.

"Pooja, what about the gemstones inside the book?"

"OMG! This is soooo exciting!" We stare at each other as if we have just created the greatest app to avoid visiting a dentist.

Natalie and I stare out of the window as the deep orange sun glides behind the horizon.

"Hey guys, is the Taj Mahal part of the Mughal history?" interrupts Reet looking seriously at both of us.

"Gosh Reet, I am an American and know more about India's history than you," laughs Natalie.

"I hate history. Boring! Boring! Boring!" Reet giggles and smacks her hand on her head. "I wish this fort had a simple love story like the Taj Mahal."

"Madame Mumtaz, please Google it," Natalie says loudly handing her the iPad.

"Don't waste your time, Natalie, she would rather research every single gossipy detail of Bollywood stars than waste her time on this," I say.

"Now you're talking my friend," Reet screeches with laughter. Then like a crazed kid, she begins to babble, "When I grow up I'm going to produce the one-and-only love story, Shah Jahan!"

Smiling proudly, Reet earnestly explains, "Do you know, the emperor was devastated when his wife, Mumtaz Mahal, died. He had the Taj Mahal built as an expression of his love. That to me is the coolest love story ever! It is definitely far better than Shakespeare's *Romeo and Juliet* story."

"That poor wife died because she was giving birth to her 14th child. Who in their right mind wants to have so many kids? She was mad!" retorts Natalie.

Looking slightly hurt, Reet replies, "Whatever! But the Taj Mahal is one of the best architectural buildings in the world. It came from a man with great love. Show me another human being who built such a grand building for his beloved."

Laughing loudly, I swiftly interrupt, "Sorry Reet, but I agree with Natalie. The Shah built it only after his poor wife died. It wasn't as though she was alive and received this palace as a gift. I love India, but this story just doesn't appeal to me."

Now Natalie Googles the Taj Mahal history to add her bit. "Reet, did he enjoy the fort with his wife? No! She died – remember. It was a tomb, not a palace or fort, a tomb for a dead person. Where's the love story? Maybe between the Shah and a ghost?"

"You are so mean," Reet cries angrily, standing up with her hands on her hips looking as mad as a hatter.

"And so what happened to Shah Jahan after he built this world famous heritage site?" I enquire curiously.

"You mean after the Taj Mahal was built? Listen to me, you idiots, don't throw all your historical facts at me. I love the story and I will make a movie when I grow up," she says emphatically, turning around and storming off to the bathroom. We follow her screaming hysterically as she slams the door.

Leaning against the door, Natalie shouts sweetly, "Oh Reet, just to add more information to your movie, it states on this website that Shah Jahan's third son, Aurungzeb, seized his father's throne, killed all his brothers and had his poor father locked in a fort."

"How sad," I add sounding dramatically devastated, then grab Natalie's iPad and continue reading, "and the old Shah was forced to spend all of his remaining years locked up in a fort, gazing sadly at his beautiful monument."

"There, you have your movie script," Natalie says proudly.

The door opens and Reet's face is blazing red with anger. Natalie acts like the Shah sitting sadly on the chair staring at me, Mumtaz, lying flat on the floor playing dead.

"You merciless idiots! You are so cruel! You will not spoil the best love story ever. Now if you excuse me, I have some reading to do," as she struts off.

We grab Reet and playfully hug her as she tries to push us off.

We get back to reading when Natalie interrupts, "Pooja, how come when you touched the crystal the lights began to glow? And even when we found the locket, I was playing with it all the time but nothing happened?"

For a second I am speechless. My face turns white. Reet swings around immediately and looks at me nervously, her eyes grow big. She quickly slaps her head with her hand and laughs loudly, "Hare! It's called magic fingers, maybe only India born Indians have it, not NRI."

We all laugh but I try not to look back at Reet. I feel the same tingling sensation again. Thankfully Nats goes back to her reading, "Listen, only after Aurungzeb died did the Mughal Empire disintegrate. This weakened India and the British Empire found it to be the right time to invade and conquer India. As soon as they took control over India, the governors removed the treasures found in these forts and palaces and sold them to rich people in England."

"Now that really annoys me," I say crossly. "The kings or emperors in India spent hundreds of years and crores of rupees building these forts and palaces, and then the British arrive and simply take it as if it all belonged to them."

Reet quickly interjects, "Pooja, my father said all they wanted was to plunder as many countries as they could, steal everything, including natural resources, and become the king of all the countries in the world."

"Yes," adds Natalie passionately, "and what irritates me is that the British didn't own anything in India. These forts were not built by them. But because they conquered the country, they felt it was their right to take everything and make Britain the richest country in the world."

"Ahhhh! If we still had what belonged to India, then maybe we wouldn't have so much poverty and starvation," I add emphatically.

Looking down at all the pages scattered on the floor besides us, I am now even more confused than ever.

"Why don't we give it a break? I'm exhausted and starving," I suggest.

Thankfully they agree, and just as we finish hiding everything away, there is a knock on the door. Fortunately, we hear Kash shouting, "Where are you girls? Come on, we are starving!" Relieved, we all rush for the door.

Chapter 13

Dear Diary,

Something strange is happening. I've hardly eaten my dinner, and I was quiet in the dining hall. Of course, Reet is desperately trying to make eye contact, but I ignore her. I know what's going on in her inquisitive mind, but right now I don't want to think about it.

Thankfully she's sitting with Sanam and Diya, jabbering non-stop about our Sunday Experience Learning Day. Actually, it's another name for a planned activity for boarders, and this term we're visiting a local dam with a beautiful waterfall nearby.

Seriously, this is so lame. And do I look as if I am interested? No thanks!

I stare at my untouched supper – cubes of paneer and peas floating in red gravy. Gross!

My mind is far away. This is all too much for me, but who can I tell? Not my parents.

I haven't spoken to my friends from my old school for ages. Anyway, why would anyone believe me?

I wish I hadn't stolen the red book. Now I have priceless gems in my room *and* a magic crystal lotus. What if the police search my room? Or the FBI?

Suddenly I feel really sick. Looking around, everyone has finished their dinner. Just then Natalie nudges me.

"We're leaving Pooja. And look at your plate, you haven't touched a thing."

"I'm not hungry!" I mumble staring at the blob of strawberry ice-cream that is melting into a soppy mess in my bowl. "Listen, I'm going to make a call," I quickly whisper to Natalie grabbing my tray to leave on the counter.

As soon as I enter the hostel office, I spot roly-poly Mrs. Roy sitting in her massive blue chair. Giving me a huge grin from Kashmir to Kanyakumari, I dial Teja's number.

He answers and I rattle off my story in my deepest, softest, sweetest voice, hoping Mrs. Roy will not hear me.

"What?" he says.

I try to explain again, whispering more to myself because I can feel Mrs. Roy's eyes boring into my back.

"What did you say? Pooja this line is not clear. I have no idea what you're mumbling."

"Teja, this is urgent," I stutter.

"Are you sick?" he suddenly shouts.

"No!" I whisper.

"Then it's not serious."

Exasperated, I roll my eyes up to the ceiling, "Hello! I am having a crisis right now. I have to talk to you, Teja," I begin to sniff loudly, "it's serious."

"Pooja. Calm down. Start from the beginning," he insists, "and for God's sake speak louder!"

"I can't," I whisper agitatedly, looking at Mrs. Roy smiling at me from across her desk. And then like a mirage, she slowly wriggles out of her chair, her massive hips gradually being freed from the tight wedge they have been in. Heaving a great sigh of relief, she smiles at me as she waddles around the desk.

"Oh Pooja, you are so shy. I know you want to tell Teja about your tummy cramps. Don't worry, I'll leave the room to give you more privacy."

For just a second, the world stops and I stare at her in astonishment. I look around mortified. *"Did anyone hear that? My God, which woman speaks about such personal issues publically – especially in front of boys? OK! Maybe not in front literally, but still,"* I think to myself.

My face burning with embarrassment, I watch as Mrs. Roy shakes her fat backside from side to side and disappears through the door. I wish she could be captured by a grotesque alien, put into a giant cannon with tons and tons of foamy bubbles and gooey, smoky gelatin, and ejected to a planet far, far away – never to be seen again.

"Who says 'menses' in front of boys?" Not Indians. Especially in India!

I realise Teja has heard every single word, and suddenly all my other problems disappear.

For a few seconds there's an awkward silence on the phone. I'm sure he's feeling totally uncomfortable as he waits for me to start the conversation.

But of course my voice goes crazy squeaky high. I can't help it! Maybe in my previous life I worked in a circus. This time I sound like Sid from *Ice Age: The Meltdown*.

I hear Teja "Huh!" as I explain the library story. Again he says, "Huh!"

I scream, "Is that all you can say?"

I have to agree with Sid when he tells Mama Rex in the movie, *"Oh, that's your answer to everything. I don't exactly call that communication!"*

"What's with your stupid voice?" he shouts back.

I start to cry. "I can't help it." He knows when I panic my voice goes weird.

Once again I explain my dilemma adding the library story, our discovery of the journal, and the precious stones.

"OMG! OMG!" he whispers in a strong American accent. "Are they real diamonds?"

"Teja, will you get over it and listen seriously."

But the idiot is suddenly deaf.

"We can be rich and famous, Pooja, imagine that!" he shouts excitedly.

By now I am mortified at his stupidity.

"Teja, I called you for advice! Get serious yaar!" I start to cry hysterically. Maybe it's because of everything that has happened, but I now feel homesick.

"I want Mummy! Teja, I wanna go home!"

Suddenly Teja stops, and his voice changes back to his pakka Indian tone as he says gently, "Hey I'm sorry. Really sorry. Why don't I see you tomorrow after breakfast and we can check out the journal together? Will that help?"

Nodding my head, I grunt softly. "I'm scared, Teja."

"Listen, shower and go to bed. I will see you in the morning."

At last I feel some relief. This burden has been lifted off my shoulders. I smile to myself because tonight all I want is sleep.

"Pooja, Pooja! Are you there?" Teja shouts impatiently.

"Yes, you don't have to shout," I grumble annoyingly.

"I asked you a question. Why don't you ask Satya for the answers? Maybe it's time you consulted him."

"What?" I shriek in astonishment. I am now so wide awake!

"You heard me. I was thinking the other day, how come we all ended up in this school at the same time. First we're forced to come here. Then suddenly we have Natalie and Reet. What are the chances of this happening when they could have gone to other schools closer to home? And now, check out what you found, and what Natalie told you."

I grow quiet. My mind races ten to the dozen!

"Then we have Mr. VJS who appears with all this mystery. Maybe it's time, Pooja," Teja speaks tenderly as he senses my foreboding silence. "You know it's been a long time. What did you expect? When you were old and married?" he says jokingly.

"I know," I whisper hesitatingly, taken back by Teja's revelation, "I sensed it too."

"Good! It's time you contacted Satya. I'm sure he's waiting."

"I think Reet also knows," I add, trying so hard not to cry again or sound frightened.

Just then Mrs. Roy arrives, so I quickly say goodnight, put the phone down and thank Mrs. Roy before making my way out of her office.

Totally distracted and overwhelmed with everything that is happening, I stand in the corridor looking out the window. My cheeks burn and my eyes grow large with fear. I'm really scared. It's true, strange things have started to happen since we arrived at this school. I place my hot, flushed face against the cold window pane and stare out into the darkened skies. It is a cloudless night, only the golden silhouette of the moon glimmers in the open sky, and trillions of shimmering stars glow like tiny diamonds.

The opulent garden looks like a picture from a fairy tale with colourful, rambling terraces that sweep across the vast grounds. I wonder what mystery lies beneath this enchanted land. I gaze out dreamily following the dim shadows of tall trees, and my eyes move towards the marble fountain, where night blossoms glow in the dark and tree branches drape themselves with such elegance and beauty set in a mystical paradise.

Suddenly I see a faint glow in the water. Thinking it's the reflection of the golden moon, I stretch myself up to stand on my toes, pressing my face against the cool window pane. It's not just a single glow, but an array of lights that seem to rise from deep within the pond and swell into vivid colours of deep pink, blue and white.

I stand still, and gape in awe as every lotus pedestal rises from the bottom of the pond proudly tall and graceful. The centre case glows like yellow lanterns luring the moon with its enflamed splendour.

The majestic moon dances across the sky radiating its beauty like a huge spotlight from the heavens above, leaving lingering kisses on the sacred flower symbolising purity and wisdom.

In this moment, I realise Teja is right. The time has arrived. The universe has spoken. I have my message.

Not wasting another minute, and with tears running down my cheeks, I turn and race towards my room, passing the common room where Reet and Natalie are playing Scrabble with Kash and Sanam. They see me run past as if a ghost was chasing me.

By the time Natalie gets to our room, Reet is already sitting with me on the floor. What excuse they gave the cousins, I have no idea and didn't even bother to ask. I am too busy rambling to myself like a lunatic.

For a second Natalie looks baffled at the bizarre sight. The floor tiles have been removed, and I am busy rummaging through a black bag. Next to me is my huge trunk I brought from home.

"Now what?" she asks, her eyes shift from Reet to me.

I ignore her, so turning to Reet, she demands crossly, "What's going on? I watch her run for her life down the corridor, and then you ditch me with some silly sinus story." Again her eyes shift from me to Reet.

Both of us still don't bother to answer. Of course, I have my reasons. I am too afraid my voice may go into another weird mode, so I choose to mumble incoherently.

"Shh! Shh!" Reet whispers softly. Her eyes roll like huge saucers as she says, "It's Satya, Satya..."

Then Reet stops, and ignoring the flabbergasted Natalie, shouts excitedly, "Hare! Pooja, you even packed Ladoo," as she grabs my one and only rag doll with one ear and clasps it close to her chest.

I carefully take out a shoebox from inside my black bag and open it. Removing an object wrapped in a blue towel, I carefully place it on my desk.

Reet clamps up immediately as if someone knocked her out cold. Only her eyes follow me as I remove away layers of thick bubble wrap.

"Can someone please tell me what's going on?" shouts Natalie, looking lost and confused at both of us.

"One minute!" I whisper as I undo the last bit of wrapping.

"This, my friend is a snowball!"

"Duh! We all know that. So what's the big deal?" Natalie blurts out rudely looking rather angrily at me.

Reet immediately shouts back defensively, "How many magic snowballs have you seen? Heh! Tell me!" her eyes blazing and her small, mouse-like nose flaring with anger.

Natalie keeps quiet, and continues to look at me mystified.

"Reet! Please give her a chance. She doesn't know what is happening. And for the love of God, stop screaming!"

The snowball is slightly bigger than a tennis ball. Immediately it starts to glow an orangey colour. Reet looks as if she's gone into some meditative pose – dead quiet and still. Natalie stares – more confused than ever.

I gently shake the snowball, and five white swans begin to fly lightly around a cylindrical shaped white pillar similar to a Shiva Lingam. Speckles of gold dust mingled with snowflakes fall softly – just like a picturesque scene from a winter wonderland. The swans look as if they are dancing and gliding as their wings flutter rhythmically to some silent music.

At the base of the snowball is a thick, granite stone with gold calligraphy engraving – Satya, Ahimsa, Prema, Shanti and Dharma.

Natalie looks even more dumbstruck as she watches the ball glow brighter and brighter. "So where's the magic?"

"Why don't you shut up and wait, yaar," Reet shouts impatiently as she excitedly jumps on to the bed.

I grab a chair and sit quietly in front of the snowball, then turning to Natalie I speak in a low serious tone, "What I am about to tell you is my greatest secret, and you have to swear to keep this our secret for the rest of your life. Besides Teja and Reet, no one else knows about this snowball."

Reet quickly jumps up and repeats, "Yes Natalie, you have to swear never to tell anyone, even your parents."

145

I shake my head, "Why are you so melodramatic? I just said that to Natalie!"

"OK!" Natalie replies hesitatingly, "I promise." But somehow she still looks unsure and apprehensive.

"Pooja! That is not good enough," explodes Reet, "that is not a promise."

Shaking her head and looking infuriated, Reet turns to Natalie, her eyes dark with rage as she points her finger directly into her face and says, "This is no joke. This is serious. It's top secret! So please take this very, very seriously and swear never to tell anyone."

I turn to Natalie and smile softly. "Reet is right. This is not a game. If you want to be a part of it, then you have to promise as if you really mean it. Otherwise, we don't tell you the secret. You decide."

"I know!" shouts Reet from behind me, not giving Natalie a chance to consider her options. "Natalie needs to swear on our national anthem!"

"What! That is so crazy!" sniggers Natalie, looking totally fed up.

With a stern, straight face, Reet looks at me. All her stupid playful smiles seem to have disappeared as she adamantly emphasises, "She *must* sing India's national anthem."

"Reet, why are you such a drama queen?" retorts Natalie. "It's just a snowball."

"Is that what you think? Forget it!" Smacking her hand on her head, she turns to me and speaks in Hindi, knowing full well that Natalie cannot understand a word.

"Hare Pooja, this one is really stupid. All these Americans are the same – proud and arrogant. How can we trust her? She will never understand. Forget it! We are wasting our time. Let's go to my room – at least there we can have some privacy."

Natalie, of course, stares at us blankly.

"Natalie, after talking to Teja this evening, I realised that whatever is happening right now is something we were warned about years ago. Reet is correct when she says no one should ever know about it – not even our parents – because we were sworn to secrecy."

Reet stands up, and with both hands firmly on her hips, stares straight ahead.

"So, if you want to be a part of this mystery, just do what this nut tells you. Please sing the national anthem, then we can get on with what we have to do. No need for any more drama!"

Giving Natalie time to decide, I grab Reet by her arm and push her on to my bed and dump Ladoo on her lap. This is one infuriating girl in my life.

The next moment we hear Natalie's deep voice.

Jana-gaṇa-mana adhināyaka jaya he

Bhārata bhāgya vidhātā

Pañjāba Sindh Gujarāṭa Marāṭhā...

Reet and I stand up quickly to join in our national anthem. All three of us look like lunatics, standing to attention, singing away. I mean really!

Poor Natalie looks at us nervously as she trails off, but mad hatter Reet, laughing loudly, hugs her tightly. "Cool! Now you're a proud Indian!" shaking her hips and doing some bhangra jig.

Giving her a high five, I sigh with relief, "Welcome to our mad team!"

"You know Natalie, the only reason I said sing our national anthem is because of the last two lines. They mean..."

"*The saving of all people waits in thy hand, Thou dispenser of India's destiny.*"

"That to me is like swearing an oath."

"We all know you are completely mad, Reet. That's why I still love you and am also a little scared of you," laughs Natalie.

"Hey girls," I shout loudly, "can we get on with our story. Look at the time – the lights will go off just now."

Reet begs me, "Pooja, I am sleeping here tonight. Please!" and jumps into my bed before I can answer.

The snowball sits on the desk, golden speckles glowing warmly from the light from the desk lamp. Natalie is tucked into her bed and I sit next to Reet as I begin my story.

"Reet and I stayed in the same apartment from the time I was four years old. Because our mothers joined the same kitty party, they became friends, and we would meet in the park every day to play."

"I was only nine years old when something strange happened. One rainy afternoon we were playing in the stairway of our apartment. Instead of playing with our dolls, we watched squirrels run up and down the tall coconut trees outside. I remember Reet being her stupid self was climbing the narrow balustrade of our stairway as if she was a squirrel."

"Outside the rain came down harder and the tall coconut trees swayed in the strong wind. As the squirrels chased each other up and down the tree, I felt really sad, watching them scurry around trying to avoid the heavy rain as they searched for food. Tears filled my eyes as I thought of all the birds and animals that get wet in the rain and have nowhere to go."

"'When I grow up, I am going to build a huge shelter in the woods for animals,' I said proudly, 'so they can keep dry especially during the rainy season.'"

"Loud shouts of laughter echoed through the empty stairway as some younger boys from our building appeared."

"'You're totally mad!' screamed Sudir, one of our friends teasing me. We peeped over the balustrade to the street below, watching the auto rickshaws and scooters come to a grinding halt, almost toppling over the poor oxen lying on the roadside. Everyone laughed hysterically. But I pointed out that if the oxen had a home, they wouldn't be sitting on the roadside."

"The boys continued to make fun of me and call me silly names, and Reet giggled with them. I picked up my toys and ran home crying."

"All afternoon I sat at the window watching people rushing around with umbrellas, some standing soaked under shelters waiting for the rain to ease off. The muddy road became a river washing away everything in sight. Tears rolled down my cheeks as I prayed for the animals."

"That night I sat on my bed for a long time. The rain had stopped and it was a very hot night – everything was quiet and still. The crows didn't caw, the trees didn't sway and the auto rickshaws didn't hoot. I remember watching the stars twinkle through the window and as I closed my eyes I could see them play peek-a-boo around the golden moon. I kept counting the stars, until I had fallen into a deep sleep."

Both Reet and Natalie listened quietly as I spoke.

"I can't remember how long I was asleep for, but I got up feeling very cold. I could also hear the wind wailing. Thinking I had forgotten to close my window, I peeped through half-closed eyes... and got the biggest fright of my life! There was Reet lying next to me, staring at me with her big, big eyes."

"I knew I was dreaming. I blinked, then rubbed my eyes but her huge eyes were still glaring at me. Then suddenly we both started screaming."

"But it was no dream," I say softly as my eyes glow with excitement recalling my strange story.

Just then Reet jumps out of the bed, and shuffling her feet as if she is tap dancing, cuts in. "And guess what," she says turning to Natalie, "we were inside the strangest auto rickshaw I had ever seen. It was flying. Cool!"

Natalie stares from one friend to the other in disbelief, then looks at me to confirm this preposterous exaggeration.

But I nod my head, "It's true, yaar. We were actually flying in a magic auto rickshaw. You should have seen us – eyes bulging with fear. At first we screamed till our lungs hurt, then we realised no one could hear us, so we remained quiet and still, too terrified to move."

"It was the brightest orange and purple auto I had ever seen," exclaims Reet.

I interrupt quickly, "We didn't even know who put a blanket over us, but I pushed it aside to sit up. This strange auto was actually flying higher and higher into the sky."

"You mean a real auto rickshaw?" whispers Natalie.

Reet looks at her confused friend, "Yaar! Listen, listen," putting her hand out to interrupt me, "let me explain. You know in India, auto rickshaws have no doors with one small seat? This magic auto had two doors, seat belts, soft leather seats and roll-up windows to keep out the cold air, or rain, or smog or whatever India is full of. How cool is that?"

"Hey!" chuckles Natalie, "that's a cool idea to invent. Doors and seat belts in autos."

"Don't forget," I blurt, "In India, the rickshaw can take about 20 children at the same time, with chickens hanging upside down in front of the driver, including about 50 trays of eggs tied to the back of the vehicle."

All three of us burst out laughing.

"Natalie," Reet continues, "All Pooja could do was scream non-stop. I was scared, but I didn't shout like a baboon. I was so frightened. I really thought we were being abducted by aliens. And as soon as I mentioned 'aliens,' Pooja screamed even louder." Reet slaps her hand on her head as she looks at me.

Ignoring her, I continue with my story.

"This rickshaw was flying like a real plane, soaring high above the clouds, circling around and suddenly gliding down, weaving its way through tall buildings. I was hysterical and my stomach turned topsy-turvy as it flew high up again and then dived down towards the earth."

"Because we were flying so high, I could feel the cold through my pyjamas as the rickshaw whizzed through the wind. Just then Reet caught my arm and screamed into my ear, 'If you don't shut up, I will push you out of this thing! SHUT UP!' She then shoved me so hard that I fell backwards."

"Grabbing the seat behind me to prevent myself from falling, I found myself staring at Teja who was fast asleep on the seat behind us."

Natalie looks at us confused.

"Wait, wait! Pooja, let me explain!" grumbles Reet as if I am not doing a very good job.

"Look Natalie, this rickshaw was far bigger than the usual ones. It had two seats facing each other and two seats behind us. When we saw Teja I was shocked, but quickly jumped over into the back and started to shake him. Hey Pooja, I think it runs in the family. He's another idiot! He simply pulled the blanket over his head and carried on snoring."

"You can imagine my temper by now," Reet continues, "I told Pooja to slap his face. That should wake him up. But of course, besides screaming, the poor sister is useless."

I smile and look at my stupid friend. She's an absolute thriller. I listen to Reet telling us *her* story now.

"We have a crisis," shouts Reet to Natalie, "and all this idiot can do is snore. I wanted to beat him up right there. Of course, I had to keep my temper in check, so I jabbed him hard in his ribs. With a jolt Teja opened his eyes. He thought he was sleeping in his room, you should have seen his face when he saw me glaring at him," laughs Reet.

"Yaar," I laugh with her, "he was so dazed and flabbergasted to see Reet glowering into his face."

"It must have been a fright for Teja to find two idiots screaming at him," laughs Natalie.

"Actually, by now I was howling louder than the wind," Reet shakes with laughter, "with Pooja screaming, sobbing and talking at the same time in her weird high-pitched voice. Teja and I didn't understand a word she said. It was only when he sat up and took in the wide open space above and below him, did he realise that something was truly wrong."

I quickly interrupt Reet, "The only thing he could say was, 'Hey, how cool is this. Wow! Are we really flying in a rickshaw? How cool!' He repeated the same words over and over again. Then Reet screamed into his ear, 'Sorry to interrupt your dream, idiot, we have been kidnapped'."

Reet interrupts me again and turns to Natalie, "At first he didn't believe me. He stared around with his mouth wide open... and slowly realised it was not a dream. Then trying to act brave, he held Pooja's hand lovingly as though he could save her from high above the clouds with some kind of magic. Hehehehehe," she giggles loudly.

Once more I take over with the story.

"Teja looked scared when he saw us flying so close to the clouds. 'Wow, what is this?' he kept saying loudly, staring around him at the flimsy white clouds that looked like net curtains draped across a huge stage. Then casually he asked, 'So who is driving this thing?'"

"'What!' Reet and I screamed together realising we had never even thought about it."

"The next moment, we heard a soft sound coming from the front of the rickshaw."

"Natalie," interrupts Reet, "we were so busy screaming and shouting we didn't bother to check who the driver was. So holding on to the sides of the vehicle, I peeped through the small window between us and the driver. This time I started screaming uncontrollably, far louder than Pooja."

"'What? What?' shouted Teja, pushing me aside to take a look? Without even knowing what I had seen, Pooja was now wailing like a hyena."

"'What?' she kept repeating loudly like a crazy person."

"Oh shut up, Reet." Natalie stares at us in disbelief and whispers, "And so, who was the driver?"

"Teja's head was still stuck through the window when the engine suddenly made a loud droning sound and we dipped towards the ground. All three of us fell back on our seats. Shaking and looking petrified, Teja whispered, 'Giant birds! We have been captured by giant birds!'"

"So who was the driver?" Natalie says impatiently.

Reet ignores her, instead she turns to me and says, "Pooja, I really thought we were going to fall from the sky."

Recalling that night, I have goosebumps. "It was really frightening, yaar."

"Girls!" Natalie cuts in, waving her hands wildly, "I'm waiting! Who was the damn driver? Why were you captured?"

Both Reet and I scream together, "Swans!"

"Suddenly we heard a soft voice from the front of the auto rickshaw, and as we looked at the window, we stared straight into the eyes of a snow white swan. I grabbed Teja hysterically. The next moment it hopped through the window and sat on the seat next to me. Bending its long, graceful neck, it said in the softest voice I have ever heard, 'My name is Satya, I'm sorry if I frightened you!'"

"You mean it was a real swan?" asks Natalie suspiciously.

"Hare, yes man, a real swan," blurts Reet impatiently, "with beautiful white feathers, a black and orange mouth or beak or something."

"I was speechless, just staring at this huge, white bird sitting next to me. He had the gentlest eyes I had ever seen."

Confused, Natalie looks aghast at both of us and asks suspiciously, "A talking bird? I've never heard of that before."

"We hadn't either!" I replied. "I was so scared, but it felt so soft."

"You're exaggerating, aren't you?" Natalie remarks looking at us in total disbelief. "There aren't really any talking swans."

"Hare, wait yaar, let me first tell you what happened then you can make up your mind," interrupts Reet. "Teja, who was feeling nauseous all the time decided to take command and in a gruff voice asked, 'Who are you? What do you want from us?'"

"We were sent to bring you to our master," replied Satya softly.

Pooja continues.

"Then Teja asked, 'Who is we?'"

'For now it's just Ahimsa, the driver, and I,' replied Satya. Immediately Ahimsa, another swan, hopped into the back and with his slender, supple body bowed his long, thin neck. I stared

154

shell-shocked, 'cos I thought some man – a human being – was flying this auto, not a bird.

"Teja, looking more shocked than before, started asking a whole lot of questions. 'What is going on? How did we get here? Where are you taking us? How did you capture us? What do you want from us?'"

"At that moment Reet popped her head through the window and screamed hysterically. 'Guess what, there's no one driving!'"

"'Don't worry, you won't fall,' says Ahimsa. 'It's on autopilot. It knows where it's going.'"

"Please tell us what is happening,' Teja shouts agitatedly looking from Satya to Ahimsa. Satya gracefully hops on to the spare seat in front of us, and turning to Teja says, 'You are Pooja's brother, Teja?'"

"Nervously he asked, 'How do you know my sister? How do you know my name and where are you taking us?'"

Still unconvinced, Natalie stares from Reet to me, listening with some doubt and mistrust. "So what happened?" she screams impatiently.

"Reet pushed herself in front of Satya and asked if we had been kidnapped. And before he could reply, she screamed excitedly, 'Wow, how cool is this?'" Can you believe she then stood on the seat and did some bhangra dancing as if we were celebrating?

"'We have been kidnapped, you idiot! Get serious!'" Teja said. But Reet didn't stop. "'Wait till my friends get to hear about this,' she babbled on incoherently."

Natalie laughs loudly, and Reet joins in as she gives her a high five.

Again Reet takes over with her bright, stupid fantasies.

"I then said to Teja, 'You know Papa is only an engineer and has very little money, but my Aunt Lolly and Aunty Molly are really very, very rich. They won't mind paying ransom for me, crores and crores of rupees. I mean it.'"

"Satya looked at Teja, then at me and in a quiet voice said, 'You are not kidnapped and we don't want your money. Our instruction is to take all of you to our master. You can ask him all your questions when you meet him.'"

"'Poor Mama,'" Reet said sadly before adding, "'I wonder what will happen to her?' shaking her head from side to side."

By now Natalie is hysterical. Looking at Reet, she says, "Reet, you should be an actress. What's with all the drama?"

"Seriously yaar!" she explains, "I wanted them to know that our parents will miss us... and don't have ransom money. Where would Papa find money? That poor man only spends his money on Mama."

"OK! OK! Reet, we get your story," Natalie says hastily, "but who is the master?"

"That is what I asked," replies Reet, "and more importantly, why did they take me as well. What have I done?"

"And?"

"Satya simply said, 'Wait!'"

"I tell you, with the way that rickshaw was flying, I thought I would be dead before meeting the master, whoever he was. Even Teja tried to ask more questions, but the birds said we would be arriving soon. Ahimsa then hopped back into the driver's seat. We couldn't do anything else, like jump out or open the door and escape."

Natalie tries to interrupt but Reet puts her finger to her lips and rolls her eyes in exasperation. "Just listen!" she whispers impatiently, as I continue the strange story.

LEGEND OF THE HIDDEN TEMPLE SERIES

"Do you think he's going to kill us?" I whispered to Teja, grabbing his hand.

"'No!' answered Satya next to me, 'This master is the kindest, gentlest man I have ever known. Don't be afraid.'"

"'But we are frightened!' retorted Teja. 'You kidnapped us and now we're flying somewhere in the darkest night ever without a clue of where we're going.'"

"'I'm sorry, but you will get all your answers shortly. We don't have long to go.'"

"Trying to keep my mind occupied on something else, I looked out the window and watched the clouds slowly moving away. The moon was shining brightly like a spotlight on a darkened stage, and far below us we could see a big lake shining like a mirror for the twinkling stars."

"We were now flying high above rows of houses and buildings, through cities where lights lit the roads like rows of diyas during Deepavalli. We could see miles of green marshy lands and caught glimpses of coconut trees swaying in the soft wind. In between the tall trees, glimmers of lights glowed inside houses. The auto rickshaw flashed streaks of light across the dark sky."

"We knew we would only get some answers when we met the so-called master, so had no choice but to wait. Confused and terrified, I wondered if I would ever see my parents again, or my friends. What if these birds were aliens abducting us for real? To take my mind off these horrible thoughts, I peeped at the stars glittering like tiny dancing lights in the night."

Just then, Reet screams at me, "Please let me tell Natalie this part, please Pooja?"

Nodding my head, I throw my pillow on to the floor to lie down comfortably and listen to Reet.

"Suddenly we felt a bump from underneath the rickshaw and a loud hissing sound as if air was being let out of a balloon. We looked at one another in panic. Ahimsa called out to Satya who disappeared to the front. Then we heard loud, thunderous sounds as if something was banging on the windows. All three of us looked around, eyes filled with fear."

"Look! Cannon balls," I shouted.

"And Pooja screamed, 'No, aliens are attacking us,' as she ducked her head underneath the blanket."

"Of course, even I was scared, but I don't think stupid thoughts like Pooja," says Reet boastfully.

"Even though the windows were locked, we could hear strange jabbing sounds coming from beneath us. Just then Teja whispered, 'Guess what? We're being attacked by monster crows.'"

"I grabbed Pooja and we stared out the window. But Satya quickly shouted to us to stay away from the windows and sit on the floor... and not to move!"

"What is happening?" asked Teja.

"The huge, ugly monster crows were using their beaks to break the windows, while others were shaking the rickshaw vigorously trying to topple it. We were sliding from side to side as the rickshaw came under attack. The huge black birds cawed in unison as they lifted the auto higher into the air. Suddenly we were flipped upside down! They screeched loudly in celebration, and their sharp beaks banged deafeningly against the windows."

Reet shouts loudly, "These are really angry birds! Some even draped themselves against the front window blocking the view for Ahimsa," adds Reet.

"As the auto steadied again, Satya called out loudly, 'Sit back and put on the seat belts. There are oxygen masks above each of your seats. Press the red button on your right.'"

"We looked up and saw three buttons on small pads. Pressing the red button, the oxygen masks fell on to our laps, which we quickly put on and immediately felt the cold air fill our lungs. We could still hear the black monsters screeching loudly as they pushed the vehicle from beneath us."

"Satya popped his neck through the window, 'The tyres are deflated and the first engine damaged. We are going to take another route, which may be slightly longer.'"

"Teja was not very bothered about the danger we were in. He was more interested in asking stupid questions like, 'how many engines does this small thing have?'"

"'It has three,' replied Satya, adding, 'don't remove your masks. We are going to fly at lightning speed now.'"

"A strong wind suddenly appeared, the rickshaw lurched forward, then backwards, and within a split second the engines spluttered loudly and switched off. With our oxygen masks and seat belts on, we stared at each other fearfully. We could hear the key turn several times trying to start the auto, but there was no sound. Just totally dead. Both birds kept whispering to one another, and pressed different buttons on the dashboard. Nothing!"

"Satya then nodded to Ahimsa and both of them took hold of two orange rods that hung against the inside of the door. They pulled them out and beneath them was a green button sealed off by glass bearing the words Emergency Only. With his beak, Ahimsa smashed the glass, pressed the green emergency button, and within seconds the remaining engines ignited, and with tremendous turbo force, the auto jetted up high into the dark sky. In amazement we watched it climb at lightning speed. The crows disappeared as they fell into the darkness below. Slowly the rickshaw slowed down and turned downwards as it finished the last lap of its journey."

Chapter 14

Dear Diary, My Secret!

Sounds unbelievable, doesn't it? Well, even I think so. And now that I'm older, I hope it makes sense to me too!

As I continue to tell my story, the stars twinkle and wink playfully and the bright orange moon smiles in the dark night as if they too are enraptured by my strange and bizarre tale.

I dim the lights as we make ourselves comfy under the quilt, and pray Mrs. Roy doesn't barge in. I imagine her wobbling in like a dragon, her slanted eyes painted black with red and green polka dots speckled on her pointed ears spurting out fire through her thick red lips. And following her is the slimy Mr. VJS with greasy hair and bloodshot eyes smiling triumphantly as he digs up the lost book from my secret hiding place.

A cold shiver runs down my spine but I shake myself quickly as I continue my story.

"The auto rickshaw shook and choked as it made its way downwards. With one headlamp working, it wobbled from side to side, bouncing and bumping through trees and bushes before landing abruptly on some hard ground. Shaken up and petrified, we peeped outside. It was pitch black. Only the stark whiteness of the swans shone in the dark as we jumped off and silently followed them through tall trees and into a huge garden. Suddenly we stopped. In front of us stood a magnificent palatial structure. A massive temple-like building with nine golden domes soaring up like towers."

"Looking windswept and wearing scruffy pyjamas and shivering, we were mesmerised by the exquisite temple built in the middle of nowhere, which was completely sculptured with intricately carved deities, birds and animals so typical of Indian temples. But this was different. It glowed!"

"Lanterns like enormous chandeliers dangled from low ceilings with chimes ringing softly against the cool breeze. Baskets of multi-coloured flowers in their majestic blooms swayed from side to side. It looked like a fairy land."

"It was fairy land!" whispered Reet.

"Two gigantic elephants welcomed us at the entrance by curling their trucks and bending their knees in greeting. We spotted peacocks with their vibrant plumage dotted with hues of blue, green, brown, and speckles of gold happily hop across the moonlit garden and disappear into the darkness. Tall trees cast dark silhouettes across the colourful gardens, and soft flashes of fireflies lit the night to the music of the crickets."

"A heavy silver door towered inside a semi-circular porch. A majestic golden statue of Lord Ganesh stood proudly on the front porch. Clusters of pure white jasmine flowers stringed into rows of garlands draped around his neck."

"Spellbound, we stood rooted to the ground, clutching each other, and terrified out of our wits. The birds pushed us forward across the marble floor into a wide hall. Everything was deadly quiet. Satya whispered for us to sit on the floor. Scared and looking like lost kittens, we linked our arms and sat huddled together. My mind was racing ten to the dozen. Why were we here? Why would talking swans abduct us?"

"Just then Teja whispered in a low, low voice, 'Where can we run to?' His eyes filled with fear. We looked around us, but it was pitch dark everywhere. I started to cry, and Reet pinched me to keep quiet."

Natalie looked at Reet in disbelief as I paused. "Were you not frightened that you could be sold for child trafficking or child labour?"

"Hare! Yaar! Poor Teja was looking for a chance to escape!" interrupts Reet rudely as she glares at me, "but with this idiot crying all the time, we had no chance."

Ignoring her, I quickly explain, "There *was* no way we could escape, Reet, not in the middle of nowhere."

I continued with my story.

"I don't know for how long we sat there. Suddenly, we heard light footsteps approaching. Filled with dread, I stared into the darkness. Everything was quiet, an absolute stillness surrounded us as though the earth had stopped moving. Scented jasmine flowers seemed to waft through the air and spread around us. All of a sudden, I saw dainty feet directly in front of me. A short man seemed to be engulfed in a huge ball of light. We couldn't see his face. I strained my eyes to see where this strange glow was coming from. And then it started to spread out, flowing over us, over the entire temple, gardens and further away from us."

"We turned around to see where it had stopped, but an intense pink light had started to spread like waves across the land. It looked crazy. Weird actually. We were bewildered, staring at some mystery figure inside a dazzling light."

"Strange, tingling sensations seemed to flow through my body. I tried to get up, but I was stuck to the floor – my feet felt like lead, heavy underneath me. I looked across at Reet and Teja. Both looked shocked as if hypnotised. My left eye kept twitching. I was scared, and helplessly looked around me again."

"And then a voice spoke, 'Pooja, at last you have arrived!' whispered the softest, sweetest and most loving voice from within the light. 'I have been waiting a long time to meet you.'"

"All three of us were dumbstruck, and stared blankly like idiots. But thankfully Teja woke up from his trance-like state and asked, 'How do you know my sister? And why did you kidnap us?'"

"Even though he was standing so close to us, we only saw a shadow of a short person in a long yellow robe. He stared at us for a second, then softly said, 'I know all of you, even Teja and Reet.'"

"Reet now jumped up and interrupted him rudely, 'What have I done? Have we been kidnapped?'"

"The Magic Man turned and looked directly at Reet. 'No Reet Sarabji, you have not been kidnapped. I know you. You hate school. You always fight with your mother, making her BP go higher and higher.'"

"'Hare, hare!'" Reet screamed hysterically, and with hands on her hips said, 'Do you have spies watching me?'"

"I pulled her back down on to the floor. She was trembling with fear. Now more confused and alarmed by what he knew, I stammered, 'So how do you know me?'"

"The Magic Man replied, 'You were born on 1 January 2000.'"

"'No, 31 December 1999,' I say defensively."

"'No Pooja,' he says quietly, 'The truth is you were born exactly one minute past midnight. But no one knows that. Doctors thought you were born exactly at midnight on 31 December 1999. There was only one other witness to your birth.'"

"'What?'"I shout incredulously, 'how can that happen?'"

"'Yes, yes,' answered the Magic Man patiently, pointing his middle finger to Satya, who immediately opened his right wing and removed a photograph from somewhere inside his white coat."

"'The doctor recorded my birth as midnight – the last child born before the start of a new millennium,' I argued angrily."

"A picture of my mother in the hospital ward holding me as a new-born baby fell lightly on to my lap, and the Magic Man quietly said, 'There were 108 children born in the world at that exact time.'"

"Looking dumbfounded, I stared at the picture before Teja grabbed it from me."

"'Hare! One minute!'" interrupted Reet. "'Are you saying Pooja was one of the first babies born on 1 January 2000?'"

"'Yes,' was the reply before he turned to me and said, 'You have a birthmark on your right wrist. Is that true?'"

"Automatically my eyes filled with tears, and in shock I turned to Teja, who took hold of my hand to comfort me as he asked, 'How do you know all this?'"

"'I know everything. Each of the 108 children have a special birthmark.' I didn't have to look at my wrist to know he was telling the truth. I hated the lotus flower birthmark with a snake curled around my wrist."

Now Natalie stops the story, grabs my hand to check out the birthmark.

"Wow! How cute!"

"No! I hate it!" I reply as I pull my hand away repulsively hiding it under the quilt.

"Hare! Shut up you idiot! It's not ugly. It looks as if you have a permanent tattoo!" interrupts Reet.

"The Magic Man continued. 'The year you were born is known as the beginning of the Golden Age.'"

"'What's that?' asked Teja."

"'I will explain in a minute, but let me first tell you a little about the Age of Darkness in which we are living. Ancient scriptures state that during this dark period, there will be much hatred on earth, which will lead to bloodshed, violence and suffering. Religious wars and greed for power are some of the reasons why millions of people will die and the world will be destroyed.'"

"'You mean like world wars?' asked Teja."

"'Yes, Teja. War is about power and control of the entire world.'"

"'My father said Britain conquered India, took away all our wealth and that is why we still have so much poverty in this country,' I quickly add."

"'What about the people in Africa who were sold as slaves to America, and Indians sold by the British to other countries to work as labourers?' interrupted Teja."

"'You don't like war?' I asked quietly. He shook his head. 'No one does, it brings too much suffering to innocent people.'"

"'As I was saying,' the Magic Man continued, 'the Golden Age was supposed to start on the first day of the New Millennium – a new beginning and an end to the Age of Darkness so people could live in harmony.'"

"'But that didn't happen,' retorted Teja, 'we still have so much violence in the world.'"

"'Yes, unfortunately man has gone against destiny and created this madness,' replied the Magic Man. 'People thought the world was going to end on 31 December 1999. Some stocked up on food and water, others believed in the Second Coming. Rumours spread that computers were going to crash and there would be havoc on the world stock markets. Millions of people around the world spent days and nights praying. But none of those things happened.'"

"'So how do YOU know about this Golden Age?' I asked."

"'Pooja, India is not only known as the spiritual land, but also the magical land of the world. Some of the greatest saints and sages were born here, and they recorded these findings thousands of years ago.'"

"'But what has all this got to do Pooja?' asked Teja abruptly."

"The Magic Man paused, looked around and said, 'Come with me, I will show you something so that you understand why I brought you here.'"

"Satya and Ahimsa stood up as the Magic Man turned and walked towards a pathway. Hesitatingly, we followed him. The stoned pathway was decorated with colourful rangoli (a form of drawing made on the ground using rice flour/chalk and other coloured powders) and baskets of multi-coloured flowers hung majestically from overhead canopies. Satya and Ahimsa flew low besides us towards a white pillar-shaped building. I bent closer to read the inscription at the base of the pillar. It had the symbols of some of the main religions of the world, and on the top stood a lotus flower with its petals wide open."

"Very softly Ahimsa said, 'There is only one religion, the religion of Love.'"

"Hey Pooja," interrupts Reet excitedly, "our Sarva Dharma stupa! OMG!"

"OMG!" I repeat. "Do you think it's the same pillar?"

"No stupid," she replies irritably, "this one is supposed to be a floating pillar or something."

I stare at her for a second and slowly realise what she is saying is true. I remember Dr. Malhotra explained its meaning to me in his office on the day Teja and I arrived.

"OMG! There must be some link!" I whisper staring at Reet in disbelief. "Why didn't it click when I saw it here?"

For a moment we stare at each other as if the penny has just dropped. And for the second time this evening we rush to the window and push our heads out into the cold night. There sits the lotus on top of the towering Sarva Dharma stupa.

"Come on Pooja, tell me the rest!" exclaims Natalie.

"Well the Magic Man walked through the stupa and disappeared. But his light continued to shine around us. We stood there scared."

"'Teja, where are we going?' I shouted, frightened out of my mind."

"And Reet was shouting to the swans, 'Who is this man? Where is he taking us?'"

"Now more afraid than ever, we held hands and refused to move. But Satya and Ahimsa opened their wings wide and beckoned us towards a silver door saying, 'Don't be afraid.'"

"The door had no handle, but as soon as we stepped on to the mat, the door flung wide open. Inside was a long passage, and tiny lights twinkled from the ceiling like stars in the sky. Hesitantly we followed the birds, and at the far end of the corridor a door opened into an auditorium housing about 20 seats. The hall was dark, but we found our way to the front and sat on a big, comfy lounge suite. A bright orange light glowed on the right side of the suite, showing a small, white pad with silver buttons."

"Satya pressed one button with his beak and my seat extended for my legs. He did the same for Teja and Reet, and for a moment we forgot our fears. Teja kept whispering how cool this was, and Reet, giggling, commented that all we needed now were some snacks and this would be perfect to watch a movie."

"Playfully Reet pressed a few buttons, and almost immediately a tray appeared in front of each of us with mini samoosas, sandwiches, biscuits and hot milk. Speechless we stared at the tray, then at each other, too afraid to touch it."

"Somewhere behind us the soft voice of the Magic Man could be heard, 'Eat some snacks while you watch the big screen. You must be hungry.'"

"I turned around to see where the Magic Man was sitting, but the auditorium seemed empty. Again he spoke, 'What you are about to see will give you an idea of why you are here?'"

"In front of us a huge movie screen lit up. Little African children were sitting on dry, dusty ground outside a hut somewhere in Africa, their undernourished bodies burnt from the strong African sun. Some were crying, others stared blankly into the hot, molten ground as huge black flies stuck to their unwashed faces and snotty noses. Skeletal babies lay on the ground, covered in flies, whimpering from hunger. Their heads were enormous and their bare, small bodies had strange protruding tummies. Just then three little girls aged about eight or nine years old appeared from the hut. They were tiny and thin, their clothes tattered and torn, and they carried small bowls. Picking up the children with tearstained, unwashed faces, they seemed to smile as they fed them watery porridge. Each child was fed five teaspoons only, and as soon as they were put down on the floor, their cries and screams echoed across the empty fields."

"Just then about eight boys came out of one of the huts. Probably aged about six years old, they were carrying a bundle wrapped in a dirty, soiled bed sheet. They pulled it across the yard towards the barren ground at the far end of the land. Looking exhausted and sad, and wearing only faded shorts, their black skin shone with beads of perspiration. Without looking at the crying children, they slowly dragged their feet towards a newly dug grave. They stopped and stared around them, too tired to talk the same story of another parent they have had to bury. They have lost count of the number of people who have died in their village – and this was the last adult. For the past few years, these children had become adults when their parents began dying of HIV/AIDS. They were forced to grow up and learned to survive from the dry, arid land, bringing up another generation of children in poverty and squalor."

"The picture faded out, and only the word, Africa, remained."

"The next story looked like an orphanage somewhere in Europe. Down a dark passage and into a huge room, we saw children lying in cots, staring at the ceiling with frightened eyes, their thin hands tied to the bars of the cots with a dirty cloth. Their heads were rolling from side to side, unaware of saliva that dripped from their mouths. Nurses with masks on their faces walked around, laughing and chatting to each other, oblivious to the cries of the children in pain, and ignoring the smells from soiled sheets. These were unwanted and disabled children, abandoned by society and locked away from the world."

"Then the story changed to somewhere in India where children were working in a fireworks factory. Some didn't have fingers, some had scarred faces, and some were crippled – all caused from explosions in the factory."

"The picture changed yet again to children working in factories, fields and streets in the most atrocious conditions – in rain and snow, under the burning hot sun and in storms. The pictures then changed quickly to China and Japan, Africa and Europe, and places around the world which I had never seen."

"The screen went blank, and my face was wet with tears. We sat in the darkness shocked at the sadness around the world. Then suddenly the Magic Man was sitting in front of us on the auditorium stage – encased in a glow of yellow light."

"'Pooja, what you saw is just a tiny bit of the suffering going on around the world.'"

"'Will it stop?' I asked earnestly."

"He shook his head and said sadly, 'No Pooja! Hatred in the world will get worse.'"

"'But why? Haven't we had enough suffering in the world?" asked Teja abruptly."

"'Yes, the end of darkness was supposed to stop on 31 December 1999. But there's still too much hatred, greed and power in the world.'"

"'So when will it change?' I asked thoughtfully."

"Very slowly he answered, 'When man changes, hatred will disappear. When we practice love in the home, we will see unity in the community. When there is unity in the community, the nation will change and people will start to live a more harmonious life which will lead to a more peaceful world.'"

"'Let me show you something important,' he announced and disappeared into the darkness."

"Immediately the lights went off again and the screen lit up with a map of India, showing rivers and mountains around the country. From somewhere in the background, we heard him talk, 'The Himalaya Mountains is one of the most sacred and revered mountains of the world. It is said it was created directly from the heavens. The Ganges, Sarasvati and Yamuna rivers flow from this mountain and is called the central control box of nature.'"

"'What do you mean?" asked Reet looking confused."

"'Well, it controls the wind, rain, storms, sunshine...'"

"Reet interrupted him again, 'Oh, you mean like the weather and the temperature?'"

"'Yes, something like that, Reet. These rivers are sacred and created to protect mankind. In the beginning man lived in peace and harmony, but later it all changed. Man became greedy for power and hatred rose up. Invasions began, wars broke out, countries were conquered and bloodshed began to spill and flow across the land. At the source of the Himalayan Mountains, something strange and mysterious took place as though there was an omniscient observer silently watching. And then one day the Sarasvati River just suddenly disappeared.'"

"'Scientists tried to unravel the mystery of its disappearance. Researchers said tectonic movement beneath the surface had caused the earth to shift from its axis and so the river disappeared. But saints and sages looked for spiritual answers. They began to pray and meditate and eventually they revealed that the disappearance of this holy river was a sign of impending global disasters and a curse had fallen on man. They claimed man had changed his destiny through his own greed and hatred. The Age of Darkness would continue to reign.'"

"'But this time darkness in the world was not because of wars. This time darkness would reign from natural disasters. The sages warned people that the earth would burn to ash, the land would dry up, glaciers would melt, rivers disappear and animals and plants would be destroyed. And all of this would lead to unaccountable natural catastrophes. When people heard about the curse, they laughed and thought the sages were crazy and chased them away.'"

"The auditorium lights went on again and the screen goes blank. The Magic Man continued to talk softly, 'And so man enjoyed his life and continued to plunder and abuse the earth. The curse continued and after thousands of years of watching and waiting patiently for man to change, nature decided to teach mankind a lesson.'"

"'What do you mean?' I asked curiously."

"'Watch the results, Pooja!' replied the Magic Man."

"The screen lights up again. Loud crashing sounds echoed as we watched huge waves sweeping across the ocean and slamming into the coastline. Small fishing boats disappeared beneath the monstrous waves. Thousands of people on beaches screamed hysterically and helplessly as they were swept away by monstrous killer waves."

"Teja whispered, 'Wow! That was the tsunami.'"

"'Hey, remember Amjith and his parents,' cried Reet reminding us of our neighbours who died in the tsunami while on holiday in Chennai."

"Quietly we stared at the big screen watching the devastation of one of the world's worst natural disasters with horrific images of panic-stricken people screaming as they perished in the vicious and grotesque sea."

"'Earthquakes in New Zealand, Italy and India!' announced the Magic Man as we stared at pictures of bodies being dragged out from beneath rocks and buildings; images of flooding, fires, hurricanes, volcanoes and earthquakes around the world flashed on the screen."

"'Are you saying all these earthquakes and tsunamis were caused to punish man?' asked Teja. 'But why should children suffer and innocent people die in these disasters. They didn't do anything. Kill those people who do wrong?'"

"Then Reet jumped up, 'Yes, punish those who invaded our country.'"

"I simply stared at each of them speechless. 'Yes Teja, that sounds like the right decision, but destiny works according to one's karma.'"

"Teja interrupted impatiently, 'Yes, yes, I know every action has a reaction. OK, let me understand this. If one's action is good, it's good karma, right?'"

"The light around the Magic Man shone brighter as he nodded his head."

"'That means if someone's action is bad, then they are building bad karma,' said Teja angrily, 'so they should pay. Why take innocent lives with them?'"

"The Magic Man sighed softly and paused. 'It is not so simple, Teja. Each person has his own destiny.'"

"Shaking his head in confusion, Teja turned to me, 'This is all too complicated for me. I still don't know why we are here.'"

"Baffled I stared at him. My mind drifted away. This was all too much. Kidnapped by talking swans, flying in a rickshaw, meeting this crazy, faceless man in a strange light and watching scenes about history and geography was all too confusing for me!"

"Now I'm supposed to be some chosen one. For what? Some crazy cult? Do I look like I have magic powers to make a difference to the world, let alone to myself? Fed up, sleepy and puzzled by everything, I said, 'I want to go back home.'"

"'You will go home soon, Pooja. Let me just explain a little more,' said the Magic Man. 'These disasters you've seen are only a few that have happened since the beginning of the millennium. People say the 2004 tsunami was one of the worst natural disasters. But that is not true.'"

"'What do you mean?' I whispered tiredly but curiously."

"'Now we have a new kind of greed and power,' he explained quickly. 'Hundreds of thousands of years ago, kings and powerful leaders invaded poorer countries where they conquered, looted, killed and maimed millions of people, and believed they were richer and stronger. This you have learnt in history, haven't you,' asked the Magic Man."

"Teja nodded his head, while Reet and I shook our heads sleepily. Another history lesson!"

"He continued, 'Now with a newer generation, they are using new tactics to loot and conquer. With the age of technology emerged a modern style of invasion. These days, younger people don't use military tactics to conquer. They are able to hack into the highest state security files and discover anything.

For example, they can now find treasures forgotten beneath the land or seas. They don't want bloodshed. They just want to get rich quickly. They want instant gratification, by making money the quickest way, or by searching for instant get-rich scams and so on.'"

This time Natalie interrupts me with loud giggles, "Hey, that means we don't have to study! We too can surf the net and get rich!"

"Wow!" shouts Reet. "No school! No degree! No Vijay Singh!"

"Can I get on with my story?" They both nod and I continue.

"The Millennium Corporation is the new buzz word in the world of treasure. They are a group of highly professional, intelligent and educated young people who live normal lives, dress elegantly, and holiday in the most exotic places in the world. They explore and investigate the history of every country in the world, hack into security files, research archived documents on computer systems, and bravely put their plan together to loot that treasure. They started small, but have now built an empire with their headquarters in England, and offices all over the world. The Millennium Corporation has five directors and more than one thousand members worldwide."

"The thing is, they don't look like criminals. They look like ordinary, young people, very rich and successful. But, this syndicate is one example of how merciless and powerful people have become."

"'And this is where you are involved, Pooja. I will now explain why I brought you here.'"

"'But this has nothing to do with me!' I added quickly."

"'As strange as this may be, believe me, you are involved,' he replied."

"'I still don't know how? This is toooooo complicated!' I mumbled to myself."

"Ignoring me, he continued, 'The Millennium Corporation had been successful in many raids around the world. Few years ago they started their first project in India.'"

"'Where? How?' Teja asked loudly."

"'Why here?' shouted Reet."

"'Remember during the British rule in India, vast treasures of wealth were found. The British Government looted India and took the treasures back to their country,' I added."

"'What did I tell you guys?' shouted Reet angrily. 'Our Kohinoor Diamond is sitting proudly on the Queen of England's head!'"

"'Reet,' laughed Teja, 'on her crown, you fool, not on her head!'"

"'Same difference,' she replies angrily. 'My Mama says her BP goes up when she thinks how she's stuck in India when she could be sitting in London.'"

"By now these two are annoying me with their side stories, so again I interrupted them and asked that we focus on what the Magic Man has to say."

"The Magic Man calmly continued to explain, 'Many invaluable documents were taken into England during the colonial period and kept in archives. Through years of research, Millennium Corporation have discovered lost treasure buried in many parts of India. Then a few years ago priceless documents were stolen from the archives of a museum in Bristol, England. One of the directors of the Millennium Corporation is the great, great grandson of an archaeologist who helped in the excavation of the hidden forts in India. He heads up this operation and has a wealth of knowledge on Indian history.'"

"'These young people spent years researching the stolen documents and discovered the biggest treasure was buried beneath the land where the Ganges, Yamuna and Sarasvati rivers meet. The location is Prayag, in Gujarat. They began their excavation immediately but quickly this first project had to be aborted. There were major earthquakes and floods, endless problems with machinery, and the most bizarre of all, many archaeologists and geologists mysteriously died or disappeared. This caused a massive setback to their operation.'"

"'Baffled, the directors stopped the project, went into hiding, and no one heard from them for many years. Then two years ago they came out with a different tactic. This time, Millennium Corporation formed a charitable trust in Gujarat to help build schools for the disadvantaged and provide housing for the poor living in rural areas. Not realising this charitable organisation was indeed a front to cover up their secret mission, the Indian Government welcomed their work.'"

"'Get the police,' interrupted Reet. 'That would stop these criminals from stealing our wealth.'"

"Quietly I added, 'You seem to have magic powers, so why don't you help stop them?'"

"'No children,' replied the Magic Man, 'it's not that easy.'"

"'What about the CIA? Let them do their work,' Teja added, 'I have watched programmes where the CIA have solved the biggest crimes. Why bring us here?'"

"The Magic Man listened patiently before quietly saying, 'Teja, Pooja was chosen many lifetimes ago to be born during this period to complete a very special mission.'"

"'But how can a nine-year-old girl save the world?' asked Teja cheekily."

"'Listen to the rest of my story. The Millennium Corporation did not go back to their excavation. Even though they had spent many months at the foothills of the Himalaya Mountains researching the Ganges River, they realised that in order to find their treasure, they would have to change their strategy.'"

"Then for the first time we heard him chuckle softly, 'But once again it is going to cause more disasters for themselves!'"

"'What do you mean?' Teja asked."

"'Teja, these men are highly intelligent people in the material world, but have little understanding of the spiritualism that exists in India. Like most people, these people think the Sarasvati River had vanished. But after four thousand years, the river is still alive beneath the surface of the earth.'"

"'What? You said it had disappeared!' said Teja, looking even more bewildered. All three of us turned to face the screen and watch the Sarasvati River flowing beneath the earth's surface merging with the Ganges and Yamuna rivers."

"'Oh, why does everything sound so complicated,' moaned Teja dejectedly. 'Now tell me again, what do you want from my sister?'"

"The Magic Man replied, 'For thousands of years, people tried to dig up the mountain searching for lost treasure, but they all mysteriously perished. Sages meditating in the foothills of the mountains have revealed that there is volcanic activity under the river and a volcanic fire is slowly burning beneath the Sarasvati River.'"

"'In all of these hundreds of years, this mountain and its surroundings remained safe, but if man interferes with the sanctity of this sacred mountain and plunders this land, then this powerful mountain would erupt, resulting in the greatest disaster ever known in the history of mankind.'"

"'OMG!' interrupted Reet aloud while eating a sandwich, 'I knew the world was coming to an end?'"

"Teja and I stared at this madcap. Ignoring the seriousness around us, Reet turned to us and with eyes wide like saucers and food stuffed into her mouth, and smacking her hand on her head, she exclaimed, 'Pooja, remember last December we went to America on holiday and saw people with placards, *The world is coming to an end.* I told Mama we were all going to die soon, but she just laughed at me.'"

"Reet stood up and looked at me seriously, and forgetting for a second that we were talking about a world crisis said, 'Do you know what she says Pooja? That the end of the world will never happen because she's waiting for me to get married first. Tch! Tch! Cheeky woman!'"

"Teja laughed loudly, adding, 'Who is going to marry you?'"

"Reet glared at Teja and retorted angrily, 'Very funny! Idiot!'"

"Again I quickly interrupted, 'Will you two keep quiet please!' Turning back to the Magic Man, I asked, 'What has all this got to do with me?' I was now fed up and exhausted, and had had enough confusion for one night."

"'I will tell you,' the Magic Man replied, 'There will be a massive earthquake underneath the exact place where the Sarasvati, Ganges and Yamuna rivers meet.'"

"'You mean in Prayag?' I asked softly."

"He nodded, 'It will split the land wide open. Simultaneously the mountain will erupt like a volcano. It will not be lava that spills out, but hot, scalding waves which will rise high above the land and spread across India, travelling at incredible speed and power, flooding everything in sight and forcing its way into the Bay of Bengal and the Arabian Sea.'"

"'It will submerge the entire Asian continent. South America will be torn apart and scattered into little islands floating aimlessly around the world. North America will experience the worst disaster ever forcing the east and west coasts to crumble into fragments of lost cities, tossing them into the hot, fiery waves until they sink to the bottom of the ocean. Africa will break away and drift towards the tip of the southern hemisphere. Unable to survive under those icy conditions, the continent will quickly disintegrate.'"

"'OMG!' we shouted together. By now we were wide awake and terrified out of our wits."

"'When is this going to happen?' shouted Teja."

"'Where? Why?' I cried aloud."

"'When a foreign hand insults the sacred gift of nature.'"

"'What! Hare! Stop confusing me with riddles,' shouted Reet in panic. 'What foreign hand?'"

"'I am just a child! How can I do anything?' I asked anxiously."

"'Pooja,' replied the Magic Man, 'it is destined to happen. That is the reason you were born in the Golden Age. You have been chosen in this lifetime to help avert danger and save mankind from the greatest tragedy in history.'"

"'What can I do? I am only a kid?' I say again quietly, sounding quite dumb and stupid."

"'Where are the other children?' Teja asks. 'Did you also kidnap them?'"

"Suddenly behind him the screen lit up once again, and soft instrumental music played in the background. The silver door opened and girls and boys walked towards us, their faces glowing with the same light as the Magic Man, making it impossible to identify them."

"The Magic Man whispered, 'These are the 108 special children born to serve.'"

"'You kidnapped them,' I said loudly, more scared than ever."

"Teja jumped up shouting, 'All this time you have been lying about some nonsense of saving the world. You also kidnapped us,' and with that he grabbed my hand and marched towards the door."

"'Stop! Look Teja, look!' screamed Reet."

"Both my brother and I turned back, and there on the screen I saw myself with 107 other children standing in a glow of silky pink light until it faded off."

"'So you see Teja, I am not a kidnapper. I only showed you the Truth.'"

"Still holding my hand, Teja led me back to our seats and quietly asked, 'What is Pooja supposed to do? She is only nine years old.'"

"'I know. These special children were born to help lift the curse and bring back the Golden Age,' he replied."

"'And what if Pooja refuses?' asked Teja curtly."

"I listened carefully as he explained, 'As Hindus we believe in reincarnation. You were born in this lifetime to help with this mission.'"

"In other words, my karma! By now my head was throbbing! This talk should be for older people, like my parents. Why me! I am sure this is all nonsense! No one kidnaps a small girl and tells her to save the world. There are kings and leaders who can do that, like Obama, or Modi, or the Chinese or British or the Queen or William and Kate. I like the idea of William and Kate, or Prince Harry... he likes to do charity work. They don't have to study and they have tons of money and time! I am not even sure if I am dreaming all this!"

"Then I heard him say, 'When the time is right, she will realise it is her destiny to complete this important mission. And so will you and Reet.'"

"'What? Why have you included Reet and me?'"

"'We are only children. How can we help save this world?' I asked again."

"He turned and looked at me. 'Pooja, your past life will soon be revealed to you. Each special child has a unique gift to help save the world at different places and different times.'"

"'But all I want to do when I grow up is be a doctor and look after animals,' I replied."

"Her big eyes blazing with anger, Reet shouts, 'Do you know what he just explained? Idiot, you are to help save the world. What is wrong with you?'"

"'Reet, did you understand everything? We are only nine years old. What do we know about natural disasters, and wars, and people dying everywhere? How can I stop all that?'"

"'Hare! I know that. It is not happening right now. This Magic Man said he will tell you when the time is right.'"

"'And what if all 108 children refuse to help you?' asked Teja. 'Life will still go on!'"

"'Yes! I agree, but the question is what Life? Very soon the entire earth will be submerged under the ocean. Nothing will be able to save man. All his weapons, machinery and nuclear power will not help save him.'"

"'So, what you are saying is the world is going to end?' asked Reet, suddenly hysterical as if she now realised how serious the situation was."

By now I was really exhausted and tired, and asked if I could continue the story the next day. "No! I want to hear everything! Please!" begged Natalie folding her hands as if in prayer.

"Pooja," pleaded Reet, "please finish the story. There's not much left to tell about the Magic Man."

"The Magic Man continued, 'Your journey will soon take you to different parts of the world, but Satya and Ahimsa will always be with you, protecting and guiding you throughout your mission. 'Shortly your life is going to change. Remember tonight and what you have learnt. Buried deep in our land lies the vital clue that is far richer than all the wealth of the world.'"

"'Are you telling me to go underground to find clues?' I asked irritably."

"'No Pooja, you will find yourself moving away from your home. In your new place you will meet new people and strange things will begin to happen. Know that your journey has started.'"

"Looking around him, the Magic Man suddenly stood up and quietly said, 'It will soon be sunrise. It is now time for you to leave.' Then talking softly added, 'I have a special gift for you.'"

"Suddenly the light glowed into a deep yellow as if blinding the whole of India. In front of me was a silver tray, and on it a snowball. I sat up in awe, and Teja and Reet bent forward to look closer at this strange snowball surrounded by a golden light."

"'What is this?' I asked."

"'Wow, it's really cool,' whispered Reet, 'can I touch it?'"

"'No,' comes the stern voice, 'it's a magic snowball! All that has happened tonight must *never* be told to anyone, not even your parents. This snowball is sacred yet magical. You can talk to me whenever you want through this magical ball.'"

"Reet chuckled loudly, 'Like Facetime and Skype!'"

"In the snowball speckles of silver and white flowers sprinkled around like dainty snowflakes."

"He continued, 'This chain is for you to always wear.'"

"I looked up, and Satya, using his beak, dropped a chain on to my lap. The Magic Man then whispered softly, 'It is a magic locket, and when opened you will be able to call Satya anytime, anywhere.'"

"'Wow!' shouted Reet, staring at the picture of the swan inside the locket. 'This is so cool! Will I get one too?' she asked excitedly."

"'If I give you one, you will have to stop swearing at your mother and teachers, eat all your food, and stop fighting with the boys.'"

"Reet kept quiet for a second, then quickly said, 'Forget it! I can't help but fight with Mama.'"

"Suddenly a chain is swinging around Reet's neck, leaving her speechless. And next he puts a chain on Teja, who looks up smiling."

"'These chains will protect you always. Sometimes you will find yourselves in dangerous situations. Never fear. A special vial has been placed inside your locket. It is so tiny no one will ever see it besides you. When you rub your finger anti-clockwise on the picture in your locket, the vial will appear which you can drink immediately. Don't ever play with the picture, or believe that you can obtain this potion whenever it suits you. If you do, the magic will disappear from your locket forever.'"

"We remained silent, scared, exhausted and confused. I still wasn't sure if this was real or a dream."

"The Magic Man then said, 'It's time to go home. I will give you some of my magic potion, which will take you home instantly. From the light, a soft hand came forward, and as we stretched our hands out, I felt a warm, thick liquid pour forth.'"

"'Yuk, it's honey!' cried Reet as she licked it, 'I hate honey.'"

"A stern voice butted in, 'Reet Sarabji, drink that now. It's not honey. It's amrit! It has the potency to make you clever, strong and gives you protection.'"

"The light began to change to bright pink, filling the room and all around us like a silvery pink cloud. 'It's time to leave. Go well and stay safe. I will talk to you soon.'"

"The Magic Man disappeared into a flash of light, and before us our magic auto rickshaw waited to take us home."

"Gosh, that was some story!" Natalie says excitedly. "What happened after that?"

"I don't remember anything," I reply, "except the voice of someone shouting in my ear to get up for school."

"Didn't you remember anything?" asks Natalie curiously.

"No, not a thing. It was only when I was in the shower that I felt the chain around my neck. Looking in the mirror I stared at the golden chain. I opened the locket slowly, and staring at me was Satya, the white swan who suddenly winked. Immediately I closed it and stared back in the mirror. This was when I realised it was not a dream! I opened the locket once more, and saw the picture of Satya."

"Later that afternoon, Teja found me sitting under the willow tree feeding the fish in the pond. His face was pale and tired. Behind him was Reet, looking shell-shocked and speechless."

"'Pooja, are you OK?' asked Teja worriedly as he grabbed my hand and held it tight."

"'Why?' I asked irritably, pulling my hand back."

"It was only after each of them had spoken about the night before, did it really sink in that this was real. I had been hoping it was just a dream, but this confirmed that we really had been captured by swans and flown across the sky. I kept asking them if they thought it was true. Maybe we had had similar dreams?"

"'Hare stupid, if it's a dream... what about the chain we all have, heh? How stupid are you?' shouted Reet showing me her chain."

"Teja showed us his chain and quickly said, 'The Magic Man spoke about the three rivers and some disaster and tons and tons of stuff. That can't be a dream! What is wrong with you?'"

"'I don't know. Maybe there was some magic in us having the same dream, but I cannot imagine how we flew out of our windows and far across the land to some strange place, and then landed back on our beds. I'm sure someone is playing a trick on us.'"

"Suddenly we all became suspicious, and looked around to see if anyone was lurking in the gardens ready to jump out and make fun of the fact that they had tricked all three of us. But there was silence. All was quiet. No matter how much we spoke about the strange experience, nothing made sense. For a long time we remained silent, sprawled under the tree staring up at the blue sky. As my heavy eyelids began to sink into slumberland, Reet suddenly jumped up and shouted, 'There's only one way to know for sure if this was real. The snowball.'"

"Both Teja and I sat up immediately and at the same time shouted, 'The snowball.'"

"'Idiots, I just said that,' said Reet, looking at us as if we had gone mad. 'Why are you repeating it?'"

"For a few moments we all fell silent, then again the quiet was broken by Reet's excited voice. 'Pooja! Are you dumb? What did you do with the snowball? Where did you hide it?'"

"'OMG! I stared at them for a second, then turned around and ran towards the entrance of our apartment. The other two followed close behind me. I flung open my door, and started rummaging through my neatly packed drawers, throwing out clothes, shoes and toys, while Teja and Reet searched around the room and on top of my cupboards.'"

"My mother is the neatest person on the planet, and every single item in my cupboard was packed in a colour coordinated way. My clothes were perfectly folded and stacked like one of those designer shops in a mall. The only thing was, I didn't have designer clothes, and at that moment, her perfectly organised cupboard looked like a rubbish bin. But I found it – carefully wrapped in a towel, glowing strangely."

"Teja quickly locked the door while I carefully removed the towel and placed the magic snowball on my desk. The swans flew magically around some elongated marble stone in synchronised movements as if dancing to some acclaimed ballet sequence."

"'Last night was no dream. It really did happen,' whispered Teja. 'We were not dreaming.'"

"'What are we to do?' I asked hysterically. 'What if someone finds this magic snowball? What about our chains?'"

"'Well,' replied Teja, 'wrap the snowball with a towel and hide it in an empty shoebox, and hide it away. As for our chains, silly girls, don't you remember, they are invisible. Only we can see them!'"

"'Hare!' squeaks Reet slapping her hand on her head. 'How stupid! I forgot!'"

And so we locked the snowball away.

As I finish my story, Natalie stares at the snowball glowing in the dark. She is so mesmerised by this strange, magical object that she slowly goes to place her hand on the ball to feel if it is real.

"Don't touch," whispers Reet abruptly. "This snowball can only be touched by Pooja."

Quickly Natalie pulls her hand away. I stare at the snowball for a few moments and then carefully pick it up, shaking it around. The ball glows brighter as if some unknown switch had been put on, and a powerful smell emanates from the ball.

"What is that?" asks Natalie staring at the magic ball.

Sniffing loudly, Reet whispers softly, "It's the same smell we had when we were talking to the Magic Man."

"Hey, I think its jasmine," I reply, inhaling the scent that seems to spread throughout the room. I watch the swans swirling around gracefully when suddenly they disappear. The light softens inside the ball and I read the words, ***Buried deep beneath the Hall of Knowledge lies the untold story of my birth. Truth will soon be unveiled by an ancient painting hidden in the depths of time.***

The words flash brightly as they float around the white pillar.

"Great! What does this mean?" says Reet irritably as she smacks her hand on her head.

"What do you think Hall of Knowledge means?" enquires Natalie. No longer tired or sleepy, both of us stare at the strange words floating inside the ball.

"I know!" shouts Reet underneath the duvet. Excitedly she jumps up and squeezes herself between us. Pulling a piece of paper out of her pocket, she shows us a stained, faded picture.

"It's the library," she shouts elatedly. "What do you see in this picture?"

"Where did you get this picture from?" I ask curiously since we had already packed and hidden the entire folder.

Sheepishly she looks at me, "I took this picture to check if any part of these buildings looked familiar to our school."

"You idiot!" I scream angrily. "What if Mr. VJS caught you with this paper. Both you and I would get expelled."

Natalie quickly interrupts, "Reet, you will get us into big, big trouble if you do what you like without telling us. Do you understand?"

"I'm sorry. Please Pooja! I'm sorry." Tears roll down her cheeks unashamedly as she grabs my hand. I push her aside and grab the paper. Natalie and I stare at the page. It is a faded, old picture of some building and in the background is the dome-shape rooftop of another building.

"Look, look!" murmurs Natalie. "That, my dear, is the building now used as our library."

"OMG!" I whisper faintly. "Look at the rooftop! It is dome-shaped!"

"I told you to look at the rooftop," Reet mumbles softly as she wipes her face.

"Yes, you are right," I whisper in surprise. "That building was part of the ancient fort with the same rooftop built hundreds of years ago."

"Hey, the first floor of the library is called the Oval Gallery which stores only ancient history." I look at Natalie who is staring at the page on her lap.

"Great work Reet," I mumble, "behind that madness of yours, there is some intelligence!"

"Why don't we visit the library tonight and check it out for ourselves," I suggest.

"Cool!" says Reet, ever so ready for some action – or trouble.

"Oh no, you won't!" I say angrily, "You will remain in your room. I can't trust you."

"I'm sorry Pooja, it will never, ever happen again. I promise! Please! I promised the Magic Man I will be part of this project."

And as she starts to cry all over again, Natalie winks at me.

Whimpering softly, Reet looks at me as she wipes her tears and says, "Pooja, we have the answers."

"What do you mean," I whisper.

"I remember the Magic Man said he had hidden a map or something in the snowball which will give us clues when the time is right."

Natalie looks up at her friend in shock, "Reet, you have an amazing memory. Why do you act like a madcap most of the time?"

"Oh shut up!" she laughs excitedly, then boastfully stands up and bows in front of us. "Some of us are born a genius! We are from Chandigarh – land of the brilliant!"

I reach out for the snowball. With the ball upside down, I slowly turn the black base three times clockwise and then two times anti-clockwise. The base opens. I pull out a small square object that looks like a Rubik's Cube – only this cube is very different!

"I love playing with my Rubik's Cube," interrupts Natalie proudly, "but this looks so strange."

This cube is no ordinary Rubik's Cube. It is very small with mixed colours, has both Sanskrit and numerical numbers, and blocks of pictures to fit a puzzle. Each of us has a turn to play with it, turning it around to join the colours or pictures or words – but it seems to be more complicated than we thought.

By now we are all too exhausted. "Listen, let's give it to Teja," I suggest quickly. "He is the Rubik's Cube expert."

I once again wrap the snowball in its towel and place it back inside a beautiful bandini box which I made especially to keep it safe. Removing the tiles from my floor, I hide our secrets, hoping and praying no one will ever find my secret hideaway.

Chapter 15

Dear Diary,

Thank goodness it's Saturday! I didn't mention our annual Kite Festival is in two weeks' time, so let me tell you about it. Even though this tradition was created early in Indian history by kings and royalty who flew kites as a sport, these days it is celebrated all over India and has even become an international event. Our school celebrates this festival in grand style, having competitions and inviting important guests and media to attend. The best part is we have a two-day holiday. How cool is that? My previous school never bothered to observe such festivals, so I'm super excited.

Our Social Studies teacher, Mr. Walters, is in charge of our grade and is the coordinator of the Kite Festival. This year's theme is global warming. We have to create kites with different messages as part of a global awareness campaign.

Every Saturday we have school for half a day. We dress casually and everyone is usually more relaxed. This morning Mr. Walters meets us in class.

"Your names have been divided into different groups and stuck on the board. Once you meet your teams, you will need to work in your hostel common room or the art room. This year we have included several new competitions, and you will find the rules for each of them on your hostel notice board."

Happily, my group leader is Sanam, with Kash, Natalie and myself. Yippee! Thank the Lord I wasn't put into Sonalika's group. I would have intentionally got sick. Who wants that snob?

We all start to talk noisily, checking out groups and planning our winning ideas. Our group decided to work in our common room. Unable to control us, poor Mr. Walters looks around helplessly and decides to dismiss us.

We grab our paints and paper and rush through the corridors, across the gardens towards our hostel. We want to win!

"How cool is this?" beams Kash, jumping for joy as we run down the corridors. Breathless and excited, we dump all our arty stuff on the floor and flop into the cushy chairs.

"Where do we start?" asks Sanam looking at me like a confused, over-dressed Bollywood star in a red Burberry shirt and super skinny jeans with gold bangles glittering from her wrists to her elbows.

Natalie – dressed in black leggings with a pink and lemon paisley-pattern kurti – pulls out her iPad and says, "We don't have these festivals in our country, so what's the first step, Pooja?"

"I heard the tail has to be very, very long and mixed with some glue or glass or something. Why?" asks Kash, pushing her curly locks away from her face and looking at me in bewilderment.

All three of them stare at me as though I have a label on my forehead that says "Miss Know-it-all."

Looking slightly shamefaced, I confess softly, "Sorry to burst your bubble girls, but I don't know how to make a kite. So please don't look at me for answers."

For a second there is absolute silence – shocked, blank faces with mouths wide open stare back at me.

To them I am so un-Indian!

"What!" They shout together.

"Nope! Never made one in my life!"

Then Sanam screams loudly and everyone bursts out laughing, giving high fives to each other. What a bunch of ignorant, stupid fools we are.

Just then Reet dashes in. Looking like a golliwog, she whispers with irritation, "Guess what? I'm in that idiot's group, and they want to work here as well."

With balls of string dangling from under her arms, and eyes bulging with anger, she's muttering every Hindi swear word her mother uses.

Sanam, looking worriedly at our friend, asks innocently, "Which idiot?"

But before she can answer, Sonalika, Indira, Sindu and Mrs. Roy march in. Sonalika, carrying only a flip file, is dressed in a bright purple and pink kurti with designer jeans and strappy pink sandals. Her hair, as usual, is styled to perfection as if she has just spent hours at the hair salon.

With her stuck-up face, she glances at us with disdain, pouting her lips like she's ready to strut on some catwalk. Haughtily she says, "We will definitely be working far away from these imbeciles!"

Her friends drag in tins of paint, huge colourful pieces of cardboard and paper, bags filled with brushes, ribbons, pens, glitter, and tons of other stuff. Reet's face glares angrily as Indira dumps a heavy tin of paint at her feet, and says sweetly, "Reet, please do your share and help."

All four of us stare at them. With strict instructions from their leader, they assemble their stuff neatly on the large table at the far end of the room. Of course, like real imbeciles we listen to Sonalika lecturing to her stooges with Reet fidgeting around like a squirrel whilst the others diligently take down notes.

"I will not have any stupid kite displayed. It has to be the best and the biggest. We have won the competition every year – and we will win this year," she emphasises each word with such articulation that if you didn't see her, you would have thought she was one of the teachers.

"Say it after me now," she shouts loudly, "we will WIN the competition!"

Quietly her stooges repeat, "We will win the competition!"

"Idiots, did you have any breakfast? Say it loudly with some enthusiasm and energy."

Standing like a mannequin she stares at them while they all shout loudly, repeating the words over and over until she's happy with them.

"That's better! Now the universe has heard us and will give us the trophy."

Pulling out a flip-chart and turning towards them, she points out various ideas she has come up with.

Of course, we are staring dumbfounded at our few arty things on the floor. How can we win against this annoyingly, organised, competitive, and confident bully?

Just then my name is called out over the intercom. "Pooja, there is a call for you in the office."

"Hi, Pooja," says Teja, "I have worked on the Rubik's Cube and have a clue."

"What is it?" I ask excitedly.

"Gad! It took me so langggggggggggg!" he grumbles in his wanna-be American voice.

"Huh! Teja, will you please talk like an Indian. I cannot understand a word you're saying," I scream rudely, horrified that my brother tries so hard to be an American.

He keeps quiet for a second, clears his throat and then talks somewhat like an Indian. Not enough effort, I think to myself.

"I don't wanna talk about it over the phone, but meet me outside the library at midnight."

"Do I bring Reet and Natalie with me?" I whisper looking around cautiously.

"Yes! But be verrry careful! Today I found Mr. VJS snooping in my room. Just like what happened to you, he was rummaging through my drawers and cupboards."

"OMG! What shall I do?" I stammer softly, now more scared than ever.

"Right now, you are his only suspect. And he thinks you gave me the book. Just be vigilant. And warn that friend of yours with her big mouth. Reet may get us all into trouble."

"I know!"

"I gotta go. We're busy with our kite," he says quickly. "See you later, and be careful."

I walk into the kitchen and pour myself a glass of water. Sipping it slowly, I stare out the window across the expansive gardens wondering where this is all leading to. I shouldn't be afraid. Last night I couldn't sleep, and for the first time recalled so much about my past. The Magic Man did tell me a mystery would unfold when I changed my surroundings. I wonder how he knew that.

Lost in thought, I suddenly hear a sound behind me. Startled, I turn around to find Sonalika leaning against the kitchen door frame.

"You look worried, Pooja. Anything wrong?" she smirks in her sweet voice.

"No!" I reply quickly, wiping my mouth with the back of my hand. "Not really, just news from home."

Trying not to look nervous, I march towards the door. Quickly she blocks my way, and sneers venomously, "I don't think so! I know you're up to something!"

Hoping to find some trace of guilt on my face, she stares at me. I glance back blankly, as if I have no idea what she is talking about.

Suddenly she hisses angrily, "Beware! Mr. VJS is watching you."

I chuckle softly, "Oh Sona, you have an overly suspicious mind. And guess what, I am not afraid of you."

Roughly I push her aside and march out. My knees turn to jelly, my stomach turns upside down, and I suddenly feel faint. That damn stupid girl is on to me. Just then, out of the blue, Reet appears and pulls me down the stairs towards her room.

Feeling dizzy, I fall on to the bed. My face is as white as a sheet. One look at me, and Reet quickly locks the door and grabs a can of Coke from inside her cupboard. Pudding jumps up on to the bed, licking my fingers and wagging his tail happily.

"Pudding, down!" whispers Reet shoving biscuits into my hand and dropping a few into his bowl. Her large eyes enraged with anger, and with her hands on her tiny hips, she kicks her bed. "Pooja I wanted to tackle her from behind, kick her straight through the kitchen window. That's how mad I was."

Sipping my cool drink slowly, I look up at her. "Please Reet, don't do stupid things that could get you into trouble. You cannot afford to be sent to the office to have Mr. VJS and Dr. Malhotra punish you."

Shamefully, Reet looks down at her fingers and curls each one on top of the other to form a cross, then three fingers on top of the pointer finger. "I know Pooja," she says seriously, "I promised the Magic Man I would be there with you. But that girl simply irritates me!" she argues crossly. "And how come she is suddenly interested in what you're doing?"

"I don't know!" I whisper, looking worried and scared.

With extra sugar inside me, I start to feel much better.

"Teja called. His room was searched. Thankfully he's got the clue to the Rubik's Cube and wants to meet us at midnight."

"Cool!" she shouts excitedly.

"Shut up!" I whisper as I get up. "Why do you have such a small body, but jumbo-size, amplifier voice?"

She giggles softly this time, "Like Mama! What can I do?"

Holding hands I whisper, "Let's tell Natalie our plans. Then go back to our groups and work on our kites."

"I hate that girl!" Reet mumbles irritably, shaking her head in annoyance as we enter the common room.

The secret message of the Rubik's Cube

Late into the night we creep quietly down the stairs. Reet is wearing a black tracksuit and a black cap covers her short hair. Somehow she looks more like a boy than a girl.

Both Natalie and I put on black tights, black T-shirts and black hoodies.

"Cool hoodies," whispers Reet, as we arrive at her room. Pudding is locked in the bathroom, but we can hear him sniffing faintly against the door.

"I hope he doesn't bark," I say with a worried look.

"He's OK. Will settle down as soon as we disappear," whispers Reet.

We tiptoe down the stairs and slowly slip outside. The night looks eerie, and even the stars hide behind thick black clouds, afraid to be an onlooker as the mysterious events begin to unfold.

Shivering with fear, I grab Reet's hand and whisper, "Let's run!"

My heart is pumping fast and loudly. I am petrified in case we get caught. Taking in deep gusts of air, we clutch each other's hand tightly and ran towards a row of trees.

Soft grass beneath our feet makes it easier for us to tread stealthily as we creep through the trees. Leading the way, and avoiding the lit pathway, we manoeuvre ourselves through the shadows along the banks of the beautiful gardens, and down the slopes towards the tall dark walls of the library.

Suddenly I hear a soft rustling sound in front of me. I stop. With my heart almost popping out, I pick up my hand to stop the others, slide slowly down to the cold ground and crawl quickly behind some thick shrubbery. The two girls follow instantly. Fear on our faces and too terrified to move, we sit quietly.

At first we hear soft voices... and then footsteps approaching. Crouching behind the bush, we watch two small lights dancing in the darkness. We wait!

Almost immediately, out of the gloomy shadows appear Neal and Mr. VJS carrying torches – followed by Selina clutching her black hat. Both husband and wife are attired in black trousers and warm jackets, and Neal has a grey backpack over his shoulder. Standing in front of the library, Mr. VJS removes a bunch of keys from his coat pocket. He opens the huge mahogany door and they disappear inside.

We remain hidden as we wait for Teja, and watch the faint lights move up the stairway in the library. The lights fade and then disappear. Everything is pitch black.

I can feel the invisible owls perched in the shadows of the tall trees, watching us with their large, beady eyes as they swivel their small heads from side to side. I shudder.

Just then Teja jumps in front of us, and we screech loudly.

"Shut up!" he whispers putting his finger to his lips.

"Why the hell do you have to give us such a fright? You idiot!" I retort angrily.

"Sorry! I didn't think you'd scream!" he snaps back.

"Did you see Selina walk into the library with Neal and Mr. V?" whispers Natalie softly.

"Yes! Come follow me, quickly!"

Teja leads us down a stony pathway, through tall trees behind the building until we find ourselves inside an alcove. A small wrought iron table and bench sits underneath a tall, ancient tree with a thick woody trunk, and wide branches cascading over dense layers of ferns and glossy green plants. This is such an ideal hideout. We squeeze ourselves on to the bench and Teja pulls out a tiny flashlight, a notepad and the Rubik's Cube from the side pocket of his backpack. Like a teacher, he starts, "We all agree that the secret we are looking for is inside the library, right?"

All three of us nod our heads.

He continues, "Now the usual Rubik's Cube has six sides, each side covered by different coloured squares. To solve the puzzle, we usually turn the sides and mix the colours until each side consists of only one colour. Right?"

Again we nod our heads.

"But our Rubik is slightly different. Firstly it grows bigger as soon as we twist it. Then the first and second side have different colours and pictures. The third side has Roman numerals from zero to nine. Sanskrit numerals are written on the fourth side, and the English alphabet is written on the fifth and sixth sides."

By now our teeth are chattering from the cold, we're confused and brain dead. All three of us stare at him blankly as if he is talking gibberish. Irritated with our dumbness, Teja says brusquely, "OK, so what is the cryptic code again?"

Natalie repeats it slowly, "**Buried deep beneath the Hall of Knowledge lies the untold story of my birth. Truth will soon be unveiled by an ancient painting hidden in the depths of time.**"

"Now look here. As I touch each letter of the alphabet, the cube shifts on its own... and check what happens..."

We watch with bated breath. Like magic the sides of the cube start to turn on their own. We can see pictures and words appearing in bright colours. We stare at it in amazement.

"What is this?" asks Reet bamboozled by everything that's going on.

Natalie peeks at the cube and shakes her head.

"Wait, you fools! Have you ever seen that anywhere else?" Teja asks.

"OMG!" cries Reet. "This is way too confusing for me."

"Shut up, yaar!" yells Teja angrily. "Why don't you just wait until I have finished. This Rubik's Cube drove me mad as well. At one time I wanted to throw it in the dustbin, but then I remembered what the Magic Man said. So I had no choice but to solve the puzzle."

Suddenly the cube stops turning. It clicks... and opens. Teja lifts the side of the cube. It opens up to the left and to the right and becomes a four-sided rectangular block. Suddenly the strange block floats up into the air and glows in the dark. Green lights flicker brightly revealing mysterious patterns.

We push our heads closer, looking in awe at this magic cube. The 3D picture depicts more than one picture, and we watch in amazement as pieces of different pictures are fitted together exactly like a jigsaw puzzle.

"Hey, that is the Sarva Dharma structure," says Natalie, "and the entrance to our school."

"How cool is that?" I add excitedly.

"Look! That picture is of bookshelves against a wall," shouts Reet.

"Shh," mouths Natalie pushing her hand against Reet's mouth, while Teja glares at her annoyingly.

Reet hides her face behind Natalie and remains as quiet as a mouse.

"We know bookshelves represent the library, so that should be where we begin our search," I say quietly.

"But look, there are four columns!" whispers Natalie.

Teja whispers, "No idea where that is – the picture is changing."

The first two pictures slowly fade into the background until we see a faded double painting of Mahatma Gandhi and Jawaharlal Nehru.

"I haven't seen this anywhere!" I whisper softly.

"Now check what happens to the last picture," whispers Teja. A painting of an ancient building glides in front.

"Do you think it's our school building?" asks Natalie looking confused.

"No idea!"

"For a start we know the secret is somewhere in the library, so let's search there tonight," Teja replies as he places his finger on the light of the cube and immediately the light disappears,

200

the rectangular block changes back to its original form and floats back to Teja. He tucks it into his backpack.

"Listen," he interrupts, "we've wasted too much time already. We have to get inside to find the clues."

"I know," I reply, and turning to the others add, "Guys, remember we have to be very careful. Mr. V and his troop are still inside the building."

From the darkness a strange yet small voice answers, "They have just left the library."

For a moment we freeze, too terrified to look up. I feel the hair on my neck stand up as if a ghost just walked by.

"Dr. Malhotra?" the voice inside my head is screaming hysterically. No one moves. We remain transfixed to the ground.

My face white as a ghost – we are now caught! I hold my breath but then the worst thing happens. I need the toilet! This is what happens when I panic! And right now is just NOT a good time.

Of course, Reet doesn't ever seem to have any bladder problems. She simply gets on a high and begins to fidget. Within seconds, she turns around, and letting out a shout, jumps up and rushes off into the darkness.

I stare at this madcap acting like a damn lunatic in the middle of the night, then as she turns to us, I see she's clutching a swan the size of a little pigeon. I choke with joy and relief when I recognise who it is.

"Yes Teja, I do change size," Satya says gently, trying to extricate himself from Reet so that he can breathe.

From the darkness comes Ahimsa, and as the two of them hop on to the table, they very slowly grow into their usual size. With their long, graceful necks and snow white plumage glistening in the dark, the birds bow in front of us.

I am so excited to see them. It's been years. Satya wraps his wings around Teja and in his gentle voice says, "I see you found the first clue. That is excellent work."

"It was such a difficult task," says Teja proudly, "but we somehow got it!"

Ahimsa bends towards me as if wiping my cheeks with his wings, while Satya bends his lengthy neck towards Natalie, "Welcome aboard, Natalie! We have been waiting to meet you."

Natalie shyly lifts her hand to greet him, but is suddenly engulfed by a layer of thick, warm feathers. As tears form in her eyes she feels a strong outpouring of tenderness and affection, and cannot believe a swan is not only holding her, but talking to her as well.

"How amazing is this," she says to herself as he releases her. Ahimsa then spreads his wings around her, hugging her warmly.

Suddenly Teja interrupts, "Guys, we have no time for all this chatter. It's time we went into the library."

"Teja, before we go in, I have a chain for Natalie." says Satya and turning to her, he ruffles his wings slightly and a chain drops onto her palm. Then says quietly, "This chain will protect you at all times, Natalie."

She puts it on excitedly and hugs Satya.

"Neal and his team are somewhere in the building, but not inside the library, so it's safe for you to investigate," interrupts Ahimsa.

"OK, all ready," I say looking around happily. "Let's go, and please be quiet."

Satya gracefully lifts his head and says quietly, "Follow me, I unlocked the door."

He flutters his wings, and slowly glides towards the old building. Anxious and yet excited to start the great mystery of

202

the Magic Man, I follow Teja and the others along the pathway towards the library. I feel the cold night air seep through my body, and pull my warm hat over my ears as I walk fast to keep up with the others.

There is a long stairway up to the entrance of the main library. Holding my breath, I tiptoe nervously, one step at a time. I am petrified in case Selina, her husband or Mr. VJS suddenly appear. Then what? Expulsion? All four of us!

OMG! Can you imagine how my parents will react? But it is too late to panic now – we are already inside.

I didn't realise that at night the library gets really spooky and dark. The glow from our mobile phones seems to cast sinister shadows on the dim stairway. Teja pauses at the entrance, his eyes flash quickly into the unlit and mysterious room.

Signalling for us to follow him, we sneak in, making our way into the massive library. The library is dead quiet... like a graveyard... dark and morbid... cold and eerie... creepy and spooky. My heart begins to throb louder. What if there are ghosts living here? I shudder at my stupid imagination, but seriously, this room is so deathly silent and scary.

Remember, it used to be a fort, and places like this are steeped in history of unsolved murders and spirits roaming around restlessly. If you've ever watched *Unsolved Mysteries* you'd have an idea of how many murders take place in libraries, museums and galleries – and the culprit is never caught? OMG! I'm freaking out...

Just then, I feel something cold on my sweaty cheek, as if someone's cold skeletal hand is touching my face. I quickly grab Natalie's hand and look around neurotically. Thankfully Teja whispers to us to first explore the ground floor, which is the most common area used.

In the dark we move away from the reading lounge and research area, and search quietly through rows of tall wooden shelves. Afraid of Reet's loud voice, Teja decides to keep her with him and I work with Natalie. The swans are slowly circling the massive room hunting for clues high above the bookshelves. The place is dead silent.

"What if we interpreted the code incorrectly?" suggests Natalie.

"I don't think so," I reply softly, "that picture showed us bookshelves. It can only come from the library."

"What if..." replies Natalie, but stops dead in her tracks.

Out of the blue we hear strange noises below us. Suddenly there is a loud crash, as if something exploded. All our mobile lights are switched off. Teja and Reet rush towards us.

"Where did that come from?" he asks in panic looking around the dark, unlit room.

I quickly fall to my knees and place my ear against the cold, hard floor. "Shh! It seems to be coming from below."

Within seconds all four of us lie flat on the floor listening attentively to strange, mysterious sounds beneath us.

"That's the same sound I keep hearing at night," Reet says picking her head up and looking at me.

"Hey, remember this library is massive, and down the corridor, there are many administration offices. Maybe it's coming from one of those rooms," Natalie suggests.

"Why don't I go down the passage and check those rooms," suggests Reet, "perhaps it's just a window that's been left open and is banging in the wind."

"Of course," I smile in the dark and slap my hand on my head imitating Reet, "how stupid of me!"

"OK! Be quick, and don't make any noise."

"I'll follow her," Ahimsa suggests as he flaps his small wings and disappears in the dark.

"Can we get back to work?" asks Teja impatiently. We nod our heads.

We follow Teja silently, making our way towards the far end of the library. He passes the new IT room enclosed with glass windows. As we reach the winding spiral staircase, Teja stops and looks up at the Oval Gallery.

"Hey! That's the room where Mr. VJS found the red book."

"Let's check it out then," suggests Teja.

"This section of the library holds hundreds of faded and forgotten ancient records of Indian history, towering on tall wooden bookshelves. Most of these dusty, tattered palm leaves, foreign scrolls and clay tablets written by ancient scholars are locked away for safekeeping. Other discarded and damaged historical materials, books and journals that were used in later times by past rulers and invaders are kept in steel boxes inside the chambers of this room," explains Satya. "The dome ceiling and architecture on some parts of this gallery still remains unchanged."

The air is musky and stifling as we climb up the stairway. The Oval Gallery opens into a wide space with huge marble columns on four corners of the floor. Large bookshelves stuffed with old, frayed and discoloured historical books line the dark walls. In the dim light we spot ancient painting and murals high on the ceiling with thick, burgundy curtains hanging from tall windows.

"They must be priceless," whispers Natalie.

"Check if our painting is somewhere here," I whisper.

Natalie flashes the light on to each painting as she moves around the room. Just then we hear loud footsteps racing across the wooden floors. We rush to the balustrade and spot Reet running towards us.

"Nothing! Nothing!" she shouts, slapping her hand on her head.

"Doesn't this idiot know she's making so much noise," grumbles Teja watching her in the dark while Ahimsa hovers above her.

"Shh," I say, hoping Reet will take notice, while Natalie heads down the stairs to tell her to be quiet. Just then we hear a strange whirring sound from beneath our feet, and the next moment the entire floor beneath us seems to shudder and shake. We stop dead in our tracks. Teja switches off his mobile, so does Natalie.

Frozen with fear, my fingers curl tightly around the iron railing of the staircase. I cannot see Reet. My heart stops! The humming noise stops. From somewhere in the darkness, a door slowly creaks open.

For a split second I look down at Natalie, then at Teja. Teja grabs my hand and dashes around the dark room searching frantically for a place to hide. I am hysterical as I stuff my fist into my mouth, trying hard to stop myself from screaming for Natalie and Reet.

They have vanished.

Teja pushes me behind the heavy, burgundy curtains. Holding my chest to stop myself from breathing so heavily, my eyes flash in panic as we remain rooted to the floor.

Footsteps! Someone is entering the library. Sensing my fear, Teja grips my hand tightly. The next minute we hear Selina gasp loudly. If Selina is inside the library that means her husband Neal is too.

This place is so huge. Why do they have to come into the library? I could faint right now I'm so scared.

For several seconds it is quiet, then we hear footsteps pacing around the room, her shoes making squeaky sounds on the wooden floors.

"There have been too many unnecessary accidents, Neal," she grumbles loudly in her thick, British accent.

Someone is dragging something heavy across the floor and places it right below us.

"Sit dear!" Neal says softly and then turns to Mr. VJS. "Vijay, that accident was unnecessary. I am worried!"

"OMG! Please don't let me faint," I think to myself as I realise all three of them are sitting in the library right below us.

"Where are the girls?" I wonder. *"Why on earth did I get them involved in this stupid, stupid scam?"*

Who in their right mind wants to wander around in the middle of night believing there is some mystery to be solved? And why risk being thrown out of this school?

Beads of perspiration drip from my brow.

"I don't know what happened," stammers Mr. VJS in his deep, hoarse voice.

"That is not good enough," Selina shouts back harshly. "We paid the doctor a huge amount of money, Mr. Vijay Singh, and I don't need reckless work downstairs. Do you hear me? Fire those men!"

Both men remain silent.

My spasho-attack disappear instantly as I start to tremble with cold and fear. I am more scared of her than an actual earthquake. This woman is merciless!

She screams angrily, "When that kid gets better, get rid of him. I'm not going to be responsible for anyone dying down there."

There is silence in the room for a few minutes, then Selina speaks sternly and coldly, "Neal, I am going back to the house to complete my report. The trucks are arriving in an hour. Both of you make sure the correct documents are sent with this consignment."

She stops abruptly, turns around and in her menacing voice says, "And Mr. VJS, I don't expect any more accidents or problems from you or your men. You have already done enough damage to this project. Firstly, you arrived later than scheduled, then you lost the secret diary, and now this accident. What next Mr. VJS, what next?"

"If the Chairman was not your brother-in-law, I would have thrown you off this project ages ago."

Neal quickly intervenes, "Darling, maybe I could send the delayed cargo first thing in the morning?"

"NO!" screams his wife. "You cannot! We cannot risk anything leaving this place during the day. It's too dangerous. We have a schedule and nothing will change that. Mr. VJS I want that report first thing in the morning."

Sounding terribly exasperated, she stomps off in a huff. Footsteps follow hurriedly as the two men rush behind her.

We remain still in our hiding places, listening to her ranting loudly, "I hate this place, I hate it!"

Her voice echoes in the darkness as she marches downstairs – and a few minutes later we hear a door closing.

The library, once again remains dark and eerie.

I am struggling to stand another second behind these thick, stifling curtains, and with both feet dead, I push the curtain slightly to breathe some fresh air and peep around. Teja holds my hand and drags me down the stairs, as quietly as possible, barely touching the ground. I was hoping to see Natalie or Reet, but the library remains as silent as a graveyard.

We sit quietly at the bottom of the spiral staircase. There is a strange stillness around us. Selina's lingering floral perfume mingled with the strong smell of cigarettes is the only signs of intruders having been here.

Just then Natalie stumbles out from a cupboard, and for the first time, she looks worried.

"Pooja, I don't trust that lady. She is plotting something in this school."

"Yes," agrees Teja, "and I don't think it has anything to do with her research work."

She whispers, "Satya was with me, but he is following the threesome."

"We have to get out of here before the men return," says Teja urgently.

Glancing around bewilderedly, Natalie asks, "Where is Reet?"

"I thought she was with you," turning around in panic.

All three of us tiptoe around the library quickly but quietly, scanning the shadowy room and softly calling, "Reet, Reet."

Ahimsa appears from the darkness. His squeaky white feathers glisten as he hops on to the table. "Check out the IT room, I saw her running that way."

We rush across to the IT room, but everything seems dark and quiet. "Where can she be?" Natalie says alarmingly.

"Shh!" consoles Teja, "she must be hiding somewhere."

From the far end of the room, we hear a squeak coming from a cupboard. Teja quickly opens it, but it is empty. A huge brass vase stands against the bay window, and there, trying to wriggle out of it, is Reet, with hands flailing madly in the air. What an outrageous sight!

Natalie and I giggle loudly. Reet swears under her breath, while Teja grabs her two hands to pull her out.

"How the heck did you get inside?"

"Hare, it's not damn funny, man!" she hisses angrily at us.

Of course, we end up sitting on the floor belly laughing as Reet topples out on to the wooden floor and falls flat on her face.

Poor Teja doesn't see the funny side, "How do you get yourself into these situations?"

"Whew! That was a close call," exclaims Reet in her high-pitched voice, totally ignoring his question.

Looking at me, she explains, "Hare! I nearly died tonight, Pooja. What if Mr. V had caught me?"

"Reet, you are such an idiot," I reply sternly, "it would be your own fault because you keep shouting."

"I couldn't see where you guys had disappeared to. First I thought you had left the room, so I turned to run, but it was too late. They came out of the admin office," she explains dramatically.

"But you went in there earlier, didn't you see another door?" I asked looking puzzled.

"Hare, no! Ask Ahimsa, there were no doors in that room. We checked the windows and cupboards, and didn't find a door. But there was so much noise coming from downstairs."

"What about the other rooms?" asks Natalie.

"There are four offices on this floor. We checked them all," she replied.

Standing at the entrance of the library, with his hands shoved in his pockets, Teja looks even more baffled.

"How did they get here?" he mumbles, mystified at how quickly Selina, Neal and Mr. VJS came from nowhere.

We follow Natalie into the first admin room, flashing torch lights across the walls, photographs and paintings, searching desperately for a secret entrance. Meanwhile, Teja went down the corridor to search the last admin office.

Natalie is mystified. Shining her torch on the wall, she also looks around bewildered and irritated. "Now what?" she says scratching her head as she looks around the neat and tidy room.

"Hare! I was right here," retorts Reet pointing to where she had been standing. "I saw them appear like ghosts in the night."

The next minute Teja rushes into the room shouting excitedly, "Hey come and see this? Quick!"

We stare in front of us in total disbelief. A trap door on the floor – AND it has been left wide open.

"They seemed to be in such a hurry, they forgot to close their secret passage," whispers Teja.

"Should we go down," whispers Natalie staring around the room. Black leather chairs tucked neatly under two mahogany desks sit on opposite sides of the room. There is a huge dark wood bookcase and two steel filing cabinets at the far end of the office. An old, faded, grey Persian carpet placed in the middle of the wooden floor has been folded back.

On the windows, long burgundy curtains are closed. Natalie and I try to pull the drapes aside.

"Wait," Teja calls urgently, "don't! Security can see us through the window."

Satya, sitting on the top of a bookcase, says softly, "There is no window!"

"What?" I ask. "Then why have curtains?"

Shaking his head, Teja strolls across and pulls aside the thick curtains. He stops! For a second he is mesmerised. His mouth is dry! His hands shake slightly as he stares at a massive painting of Jawaharlal Nehru.

All of us stand spellbound, gaping at a life-size portrait – from ceiling to floor – of this great statesman and leader.

Teja pulls the second curtain aside. Mahatma Gandhi is sitting behind his spinning wheel, dressed in his famous white dhoti, in all humility and beauty of a noble man.

We stand to attention saluting India's greatest leaders. Tears fill my eyes as if our famous Indian national anthem is playing softly in the background. I am no artist, but these paintings are exquisite.

"This is the second clue!" Teja murmurs to himself, then turning to me asks excitedly, "Shall we go down?"

"Are you mad, Teja," I shout angrily, "didn't you hear Selina say something about a consignment leaving in an hour. That means they're coming back!"

"Maybe we have some time," interrupts Natalie, "let's check it out, please!"

We are all arguing and talking at the same time when Satya interrupts us, "Why don't the rest of us go down and leave Ahimsa here to guard the place in case they return?"

"That sounds great!" quips Teja.

Call it what you like, but I am too scared. "What if they come in early? We will get caught by the worst criminals ever."

"Pooja, sometimes you are so serious and boring!" grumbles Reet staring at me with irritation. "Why don't you just take a chance and be adventurous for once?"

My face turns crimson as I ogle back horrified. At this moment, I want to punch her.

Ahimsa quickly interjects, "You are wasting time. Go down quickly."

And before I know it, I am following the rest of these fools who think this is an adventure. Meanwhile, I am terrified of what may be hidden beneath this floor.

"There's a shaft inside," says Satya flying back up the stairs, "it seems safe!"

We squeeze into a strange, narrow shaft with a green light blinking brightly. As soon as Teja shuts the door, it starts to make a soft humming sound and descends at a rapid rate into the ground. I think my eyes must have popped out, I couldn't see a thing. I don't know how far we plummeted, but it got darker and scarier as we fell into the dark pit of the earth.

Suddenly we come to a grinding halt. The door opens. I feel the icy cold wind seep through my thick hoodie. Shaken and trembling, Reet grabs my arm tightly as we glance nervously around us.

A lantern with a dim light hangs lopsided from a huge rusty hook on the concrete wall, making the place look ghostly, evil and sinister.

You can imagine how spooked out I am!

Eerie shadows play havoc on the dark walls as if monsters are looming over me creeping closer and closer. I shut my eyes and grab Teja's hand as he shines his torch around.

We seem to be in an old underground tunnel. It is deathly silent and dark. We walk slowly and unsteadily along a long, windy, narrow corridor. Faded paintings of dancing figurines cover the rugged walls.

We follow Satya through dark chambers and vaults, going from one doorway to another until we find ourselves in a long, darkened passageway. Here we notice several huge, wooden doors on either side of the passage. Metal embellishments carved skilfully on the doors make them look very old fashioned.

Teja stands in front of a door and whispers quietly, "Now how does one get inside?" Heavy silver swords embedded across each door seals it, making it impossible to enter.

With her hands on her hips and shaking her head in irritation, Reet mumbles, "What do you think is inside for such stupid doors to be sealed?"

Satya grips the sword with his orange beak and almost instantly it bends backwards.

We are awestruck! How can a teeny-weeny bird lift a heavy sword with its beak? I mean seriously!

Bright spark Teja tries to do the same – but twists his wrist. Teja and Natalie push the door open. It creaks loudly as we step inside. We find ourselves inside a big chamber converted into a brightly lit office.

Excitedly Teja grabs my arm and whispers, "Wow, this is certainly a high tech computer room."

We walk around the room curiously checking it out. It is bare except for a few computers sitting on the three desks, and black leather high back chairs. At the far end of the room there are two tall cabinets, plus a small cupboard filled with crockery, a coffee maker and next to it a small fridge. Loads of papers and files lie around.

"How did they get electricity into this room?" Teja asks curiously, scanning the computer in front of him before picking up documents from the desk.

Natalie quickly interrupts, "Look! There are numbers written on each page. I wonder what they mean.

I grab a few, "This says 027; 261; 423; 225... and so on."

Looking around for answers, there is a white board on the wall above the main desk with dates of consignments, truck numbers and other numbers. Teja tries to use the computer, but they are all locked. We rummage through the cabinets and find loads of files and some ornaments. Natalie grabs a few and shoves them into Teja's backpack.

At that moment, we hear the whirring sound of the shaft going up. Twice in one evening we are scrambling around in panic.

"Quick!" squeals Ahimsa as he flies in. "They're coming! Let's leave!"

We stare in confusion as Teja mumbles anxiously, "Where? What?"

The birds swoop us into the folds of their wings and like magic "POOF" we're gone!

The next moment we find ourselves inside an empty, dark chamber with dust everywhere and cobwebs hanging from the high ceiling. I stare around me.

In the dark, Teja's face is a white as a sheet as he glares at Satya and Ahimsa and demands roughly, "What just happened?"

"What?" asks Satya innocently, without looking at Teja.

"That wall trick. You didn't tell us about it," queried Teja.

"Oh that!" guffaws Satya. "We use it in times of need." Both birds lift their long necks and look at each of us as if they are laughing.

"Where are we?" I whisper.

"In one of the chambers down the passage," replies Ahimsa.

As my eyes grow accustomed to the dark, cold room, I notice a black stain in the centre of the ceiling. I assume a chandelier would have hung there. The walls are covered in grime with faded images of Indian paintings tarnished with time and age. There are large decorative patterns across the filthy stained floor, and on the opposite side of the room is a small lattice window covered with extra thick iron mesh.

Satya and Ahimsa are perched on the windowsill cutting through the iron mesh with their orange beaks as if they were using clippers. Satya turns and looks at us girls, shivering and clutching one another. Teja tries to jump up and peep through the window, but Ahimsa taps him gently with his long neck and says quietly, "Use these binoculars, Teja, and look down at the ground."

Teja quickly grabs the binoculars and peeps through.

"Oh! Oh! Hell!" he swears softly to himself.

"Wow!" he whispers, "so this is where the noise has been coming from!"

"Tell us idiot, instead of muttering to yourself like an old man," says Reet.

Hundreds of metres below us, Teja finds himself staring into a huge courtyard with rows of cages standing next to each other. With lanterns lit around this enclosure, he is able to see big, burly men dressed in dark khaki outfits, black balaclavas and black boots walking around with guns in their hands.

Inside the cages, little children are sleeping on cold floors, curled up like balls to keep themselves warm from the blistery cold that sweeps across in the dark night.

He stares grimly at the sight below him, then without a sound, moves aside and hands the binoculars to me.

At first I can barely see anything because it's too dark and misty. Then I notice rows of cages with children sleeping like animals.

"It's freezing cold," I cry in disbelief.

The sight below me seems to be in some bottomless pit of the earth, mysterious and strange, as if there is actually another land beneath us where people live in some secret hideout.

OMG! It is a real secret hideout!

Everything is dark and gloomy and there is no sky. Suddenly I spot a massive hole in the middle of the ground and I follow a pathway. Hundreds of children are working outside, some pushing trolleys, others carrying crates, some breaking down rocks.

So this is where the noise has been coming from during the night, when everything is dead quiet. Whirring sounds choke loudly from large machines, as small, tired children dressed in tattered shirts and khaki shorts throw broken rocks into the grinder.

I quietly hand the binoculars to Natalie. Devastated and absolutely shocked at the sad sight we have just discovered, we sit for a long time on the dirty floor. Tears roll down my cheeks. This is what the Magic Man meant when he said, "You are born to help children." Maybe one of his plans is for me to rescue these children.

Eventually Satya reminds us that it's time to leave. "This time Ahimsa and I will fly you up and back to your rooms."

Looking at his watch, Teja stands up, "It's going to be morning soon. Let's get out of here, yaar."

We stare despondently at each other before making our way back to our rooms. For once we are all speechless.

Chapter 16

The next morning

Natalie and I sit together for breakfast. Too exhausted after last night's adventure, we stare at the cereal in front of us.

"After last night, I can't eat!" I murmur quietly, ready to cry.

Natalie whispers, "I know, I feel the same..."

Just then Kash and Sanam arrive with plates piled with potato curry and poori and sit opposite us, eating like they never had dinner the night before. Looking at us strangely Kash whispers impatiently, "Girls, girls," snapping her fingers in front of us, "what's going on? Both of you look like someone died."

I look up guiltily, "Sorry yaar, I didn't sleep last night. I'm so tired this morning I just want to crawl back into bed!"

"And you?" Sanam laughs loudly, staring at Natalie already half asleep, her breakfast untouched.

Natalie grunts something inaudible.

"Same with Reet, look at her!" Kash interrupts her cousin. "I nudged Reet to wake her up as I passed her."

I turn to look at Reet – her head slumped on the table, snoring peacefully.

"What punishment has she got this time that could be so exhausting?" giggles Sanam.

Natalie quickly snaps out of her tiredness and laughs with our friends.

"So! Tell me," asks Sanam playfully, "did you all go out chasing ghosts last night?"

Sanam and Kash laugh loudly, while giving each other a high five.

For a second, my face flushes beetroot red. I turn to Natalie whose eyes are like saucers. I quickly elbow her to relax, knowing full well these girls are simply joking. I stare at my invisible ring while my mind wanders off.

How true! It seems we were chasing ghosts last night. And it doesn't make sense. Where did those children come from? How long have they been caged up like animals? After last night, I know Selina, Neal and Mr. VJS are doing something illegal. Whatever it is, they are dangerous people and I am scared.

I quickly change the subject to the Kite Festival.

"I can't wait to see what global warming messages everyone is using on their kites."

Taking the cue from me, Natalie butts in, "I think Dr. Malhotra is a real cool person. This festival is the best ever awareness campaign for the school."

Then she turns excitedly and asks, "Why do people in India throw plastic everywhere? In our country, we have to recycle everything or we get fined."

"Exactly!" agrees Sanam. "Recycling is the way to live!"

"I can't believe how people throw their rubbish on the roadside," adds Kash. "I think billboards and TV should advertise global warming rather than all the glamour movies and celebs."

Natalie chips in, "Did you see how much muck and filth clog the rivers here? You get a beautiful house and right next to it is a dumpsite. Yuck, that's so gross!"

"Hey guys," interrupts Reet pulling a chair from across the floor and plonks it next to me, "Bollywood adverts are good, yaar. Mama cannot live without the latest hot news!"

She's wide awake now as she gives us all high fives.

"Ladies, ladies! I have an announcement," Sanam interrupts excitedly, "Our famous Green for India Organisation has been invited to judge the competitions at the Kite Festival."

"What!" shouts Natalie? "This is the best news ever."

"Wow!" shouts Reet getting up to shake her teeny weeny backside, "How cool!"

"And it gets even better. It's going to be on TV," she says and we clap our hands excitedly.

Students in the dining hall turn to see what the noise is about. Many gather around our table, chatting excitedly about the Kite Festival.

Once again, my mind wanders off! *"Why did Selina say she is doing research work on education? Who is she? And how did Mr. VJS become involved? Where did these children come from? How long have they been locked up?"*

I can hear Reet arguing with someone about traditional kites and theme kites. Her voice rises into a high pitch shrill when suddenly she stops mid-sentence. Her face turns red and immediately she slides next to Natalie and grabs her hand under the table.

I look up to find myself staring into the cruel face of Mr. VJS charging towards us, his eyes smouldering with anger and malice. Natalie and Reet get up to leave, when two large hands grab their shoulders from behind forcing them to sit back down.

The rest of the students quickly disperse leaving Kash and Sanam happily chatting, totally ignorant of the tension around us. They do not fear Mr. VJS like the rest of us, but after a few seconds they realise we have gone very quiet.

Grabbing a chair from the next table, Mr. VJS sits down and turns to Kash and Sanam, giving them a broad smile as he pushes his oily hair away from his thick eyebrows.

"Enjoyed your breakfast, Patels?" he asks loudly. I don't know why, but he addresses all the students by their surname – and this really annoys me. I have my own name, and I'm proud of it.

He places his glasses on the table, and turning to Reet begins to talk in a deep, hoarse voice, "Good morning, Sarabji, did you have a good night's sleep?"

"Yes sir," she mumbles from behind Natalie's shoulder. Her eyes remain downcast, too afraid to look directly into his threatening eyes.

"Good! Good!" comes his response. "This table is making the loudest noise, so what are you girls laughing about?" All five of us remain silent. Reet watches him from under her eyelashes, her thin lips compressed with fear. I look around anxiously, mind racing.

Thankfully Kash speaks, "Sir, the Kite Festival."

Mr. VJS ignores her.

Sanam adds proudly, "Sir, Green for India Organisation is attending our Kite Festival!"

Mr. VJS snubs her rudely and turns to Reet, his only target in life I think! His face turns darker than midnight, "Did you tell your friends I have known YOU for a very, very long time, Sarabji?"

My heart is hammering loudly as I stare back at this lunatic.

"No Sir!" she replies in a feeble voice.

Enjoying this moment, he adds sweetly and innocently, "Then tell your friends why I know you so well, Sarabji."

"I don't know, Sir," she mumbles inaudibly, still not looking up at him.

"But how can you forget all those times you spent sitting in my office? We have a history, you and I, don't we?" he guffaws loudly smacking the table with his fat hand. His face turns impassive and cruel. He curls his moustache and pulls his lips into a sly smile. "You spent more time in my office than your classroom in Bangalore. I see the same is happening here. Dr. Malhotra has told me all about your latest antics."

Reet remains tongue-tied. He continues calmly, "Of course, I had to fill him in with details of all your previous school records." His cold, angry eyes penetrate her small, fearful face as his tone changes to a deep menacing growl. Tears spill down Reet's face.

At that moment, Mrs. Mansoor, the head matron appears, and looks at Mr. VJS in an angry yet strange way. Bending down, she says quietly, "Sorry Sir, male staff are not allowed to sit with female students during meals."

"I know, I know," he replies impatiently, picking up his glasses and pushing the chair back. With his piercing eyes he bends forward and smiles mockingly, "Well, Sarabji, how strange that you and I are in the same school again. Only this time, your parents won't pay the extra to keep you here. I will expel you! Good day ladies!" he says before marching off.

By now breakfast is over and just the five of us remain seated – quiet and still. Natalie is first to break the silence. "Gosh, look at my hand," showing us her palm indented with red welts and fingernail marks.

Reet's face is beetroot red, her eyes bulging with terror and her lips quivering uncontrollably.

Just then Mrs. Jyothi enters the dining hall. "Girls, what is the delay? Your kites must be completed today. You had better get working on them."

Reet bursts into tears. Alarmed, Mrs. Jyothi rushes over to Reet who is now hysterical. Mrs. Jyothi feels her forehead which is burning hot and immediately rushes her to the nurses' station.

Kash speaks quietly and innocently, "We could feel the bad vibe between Mr. VJS and Reet!"

"That man is awful to her," adds Sanam.

I nod my head, now more afraid of Mr. VJS – especially his continuous threat of getting us expelled. He has the power to do just that. I know he will use Reet to harass all of us.

"This man is making her life unbearable," Natalie whispers to me as we walk upstairs.

Later that afternoon Natalie, Teja and I visit the local pizza place. Because we don't go home as often as the other students, we are allowed a friend to join us – as bonding is an important aspect of family life. This weekend, Natalie joins us.

"I couldn't sleep a wink last night... or should I say this morning," sighs Teja.

"Even us," I reply looking miserably sad and exhausted.

Overwhelmed by everything that has happened this morning, as soon as Natalie sits down, she bursts out crying. Teja stares at her, then looks at me confused.

Before I can say anything, Natalie shows Teja her swollen hand, and relates the incident with Mr. VJS. I feel really bad, as both my friends are struggling through my stupid karma! Why should they? If this is my destiny, then let it be just me! Why are both my friends and my brother caught up in this madness? I am so angry I want to stand up and scream.

Hugging Natalie I whisper sadly, "I am so sorry, Nats. You know he is using Reet to catch us out."

"Yes, he's a damn bully when he's alone," retorts Teja angrily, "but did you see how he snivels and shakes like a wimp when he's with Selina and Neal?"

"He is using his power and authority to get to us," mutters Natalie tearfully.

"Well, the quicker we solve this mystery, the better," says Teja thoughtfully.

"Yes! I think so too. That's why I brought those papers we took from the office."

"Cool, Natalie," says Teja excitedly, "let's check them out while we eat." Natalie opens her backpack, selects one page from the pile of folded papers, and as she places it on the empty table mumbles, "I don't know about this one?"

"Hey, this is a spreadsheet with numbers... looks like they're using codes," he answers reading the numbers out aloud.

Natalie checks on the net to find out what these random numbers could possibly mean: 027; 540; 234; 630; 261; 423; 225; 810; 351; 252; 232...

And after a few minutes, Natalie closes her iPad dejectedly. "Nope, nothing here!"

Our pizzas arrive but we're too busy browsing through the other pages to be bothered to eat. And then I look up and ask curiously, "What is Bill of Lading?" pointing to the words at the top of the document.

Natalie immediately searches the net and reads aloud, "It is a document received from a shipping agent. It confirms details of cargo sent from a port of origin to final destination."

"This must be a code, Teja," I say curiously, "but what does 027 mean?"

"It is definitely a code to cover up something!" says Natalie thoughtfully.

"Why don't we try postal code or where a country is located on a map... longitude or latitude... or something like that?" I quickly suggest.

After some time Teja turns to me, looking frustrated, "Nope, that's not the answer."

"Well, at the bottom of all these pages is the same number – 0091. Wonder what that means?"

"Hey, hang on!" exclaims Teja excitedly, "I think I got it!" He quickly types something on the iPad and stares at the screen in deep contemplation.

Grinning as if he had just won the biggest lottery ever, Teja jumps up excitedly, "That my dears, is the international telephone code for India which means...." He stops! Taps on the table lightly, and slowly the tapping gets faster and faster. Like really! A drum roll here, inside a public place! My jaw drops as I stare at my mad brother, before he continues, "They are using each country's own international dialling code as their secret code. Nats!" he whispers breathlessly, "type in 027 and check which country's dialling code this is?"

The next moment she kicks me under the table, "Guess what?" then whispers so softly we can barely hear her, "it's for South Africa."

"OMG!" I put my hand on my mouth. How did we manage to crack this code? I'm shocked! At last someone in the universe is helping us.

Last night I couldn't sleep. I kept seeing those children locked up in cages. And how am I going to rescue them? I'm just a kid myself? Those guards have guns, and I know Selina and Mr. VJS are dangerous people. The Magic Man is crazy to believe children like ourselves can fight these criminals.

Getting back to my story, "Let's try the other numbers and check out the countries," Teja squeaks excitedly and grabs a pen. For each number he calls out, Natalie checks the internet and calls out the country dialling code.

South Africa (027), Argentina (540), Nigeria (234), Philippines (630), Madagascar (261), Liechtenstein (423), Ivory Coast (225), Japan (810), Portugal (351), Somalia (252), Sierra Leone (232), Turkey (900), Denmark (450), Democratic Republic of Congo (243), Slovakia (421), Rwanda (250), Mali (223), Mexico (052), Hungary (036), Honduras (504), and Bermuda (441).

As the last code is called out, Teja sits back in shock. "OMG!" he whispers. "Whoever set this up had a reason for using this type of secret code and for choosing these countries."

I stare at the list of names and numbers. "Teja, check this out. If you add the numbers for each country, it totals seven or nine. I wonder why?"

"Maybe the number nine or seven is their lucky number or something," adds Natalie.

"And I have no idea where some of the countries are," I giggle softly.

"Like Liechtenstein, yaar," laughs Natalie loudly. For a moment we have fun and giggle like kids trying to get our tongues around some of these words to pronounce them correctly.

Natalie pulls out more pages tucked inside her bag. "Maybe we can find information about where the children come from. This is child labour."

I butt in. "I simply hate it! It's illegal!"

"Hey, hang on," Teja interrupts. "There are two signatures at the bottom of this page. The code is 234."

I quickly scan the list of countries. "That is Nigeria, which means Millennium Corporation is sending their cargo through different countries around the world before it reaches the final destination, Bristol."

Teja scrutinises the page closely, "This is a brilliant tactic to avoid border security, but guys I think this first signature is Selina Haskey."

"What!" Natalie and I exclaim simultaneously.

Pushing the plates away, we stare at the beautifully formed calligraphic letters that look like art symbols rather than an ordinary signature. *Selina Haskey*. The second signature is an illegible scribble.

"OMG! We have proof at last!" I cry out.

Natalie whispers excitedly, "Yes, we knew they were involved."

"Pooja, keep these pages very safe," interrupts Teja seriously. "This is a major breakthrough. But we must learn more about Dr. Clanis. Somehow I think he is involved."

I quickly say, "Remember Reet mentioned how she saw him in Dr. Malhotra's office when Selina was insisting she move into house No. 23 and Dr. Malhotra refused. After arguing for some time, Dr. Clanis said the change had to be done, and poor Dr. Malhotra had to agree."

"He is the chairman after all," answers Natalie.

"Or they must be paying him huge sums of money to let them use his school," adds Teja. "I don't think he would do this for charitable reasons."

"Do you think he knows about the children under the fort?" I ask sadly. "We still haven't found out anything about them."

"Have no idea," Teja says shaking his head, "that's the biggest mystery!"

"Maybe we should go back tonight?" suggests Natalie.

"But what if we get caught?"

"Just you and me, Pooja," Teja suggests quietly, then turning to Natalie adds, "you stay with Reet and keep her out of trouble. Remember, Mr. VJS is watching her like a hawk. Also see if you can find out more about Dr. Clanis. I think there's a strange link between him and the Haskeys."

Natalie nods her head.

"Good idea!" I say quickly.

Chuckling loudly, we finish our cold lunch and wait for our school car. As Teja jumps off he whispers, "Meet me same time same place!" and disappears into his hostel.

Natalie and I spend the rest of the afternoon completing our homework.

By late afternoon I couldn't keep my eyes open – and fell asleep on my bed. Natalie had gone down to check how Reet was.

Satya was sitting on my desk when I awoke. His beautiful white wings like soft peaks of snow glowed in the evening sun. He turns his head towards me, and I rub his long neck as I tell him about Reet and Mr. VJS.

Shaking his head from side to side, he says softly, "its good Reet is not coming tonight." Just then Natalie pops in and says Reet is awake, "Even though she is feeling much better, I think she is terrified."

"Thanks for getting Mrs. Roy to agree that she sleeps in our room."

While Natalie chats to Satya, I change into black track pants and a long-sleeved top, and pull on a thick, fleecy hoodie to keep away the evening chill.

Minutes tick by. Reet arrives, and after hugging Satya, tucks herself into my bed and falls asleep almost immediately.

With a feeling of trepidation, I wait for the hostel lights to go off.

Just then Ahimsa arrives through the window. "I've been to Selina's house. There's a meeting of some sort planned for tonight. I heard her ask Dr. Clanis about some 'blue print' of the school."

"Hmmm! I wonder what she's up to?" says Natalie anxiously. "I don't trust that lady!"

"Why don't we spy on their meeting tonight instead of going to the library," suggests Satya, "that way we may get more answers?"

"Brilliant idea! Let me WhatsApp Teja with our new plans," I reply.

At last it is time to leave. Natalie opens the door and peeps into the passage. She notices the passage lights are still on and the dorm parents walking around.

"What's going on, Mrs. Roy?" Natalie calls out softly while making signs with her hand behind her back.

"I hope you girls are feeling OK?" Mrs. Roy calls out as she approaches our room. "We have five girls with a tummy bug." Like a turtle, I dive into bed and pull the duvet over my head.

"Oh, you mean Delhi-belly?" Natalie whispers, "Pooja and I are fine, so far."

"Oh thank heavens," says Mrs. Roy as she peeps through the doorway.

"Pooja is asleep, said she's exhausted, and you know Reet is staying with us," says Natalie.

Tucked in next to Reet and pretending to be asleep, I hear Mrs. Roy talking softly, "I'm so worried about Reet. I have no idea why her temperature suddenly went up."

Natalie says quietly, "I know. Hope she feels better tomorrow."

"Good night Natalie," replies Mrs. Roy. "I don't think we're going to have much sleep tonight."

"OK! Goodnight!" whispers Natalie and closes the door.

Both swans sit on the window sill, Satya turns to me and says quietly, "Pooja, you will fly with me. It's too dangerous to use the corridor. Come, let's go!"

He flutters his wings and immediately grows larger in size. Within seconds I am nestled inside the warmth of his feathers, and we soar out through the window and into the cold night. The wind whistles loudly as Ahimsa leads the way across the sprawling gardens towards the dark alcove where Teja awaits – pacing up and down looking rather worried.

Greeting us quickly, he says, "I just saw Mr. VJS go into the library in his usual frantic state." Rubbing his hands together, he pulls his jacket tighter across his chest to keep out the icy cold breeze.

"Wonder what crisis they have now?" Satya mumbles curiously.

Chapter 17

Just as we sit down on the cold bench, we hear a mobile phone ring loudly from somewhere in the dark. I grab Teja's hand tightly. OMG! Someone is nearby. Staring around with fear, I put my hand over my mouth, and Teja holds me gently around my shoulders.

Satya disappears into the darkness. The nasal, wheezy voice of Mr. VJS suddenly echoes in the wind, "Yes Neal, I've got the folder with the report. Where are they?" He pauses, then responds in his thick, muffled voice, "Yes, I will meet them and come to you." We hear footsteps rushing down the pathway away from the administration building.

Satya flies back to us and sits on the wrought iron table.

"Come, let's follow him quickly!"

I remain seated. Teja glares at me and I begin to cry. "Pooja, what's going on?" he says impatiently. "Come on!"

"It's too dangerous Teja, I'm scared!"

"Oh stop being a baby Pooja," he says angrily. "We don't have time for your drama." Tears roll down my cheeks. Ahimsa hops closer to me, flaps his wings and wraps them around me tenderly whispering, "Pooja, we have to find out what they are up to, and this is the only way. Satya and I are here to protect you. Don't be afraid."

Satya quickly intervenes, "Fly with us! It's much safer, and remember, Selina's house is far beyond the school grounds."

Apprehensively I get up! Teja does not realise that all this mystery and secrecy of my life is now becoming real – and it involves dangerous people. Karma is nonsense! I think destiny is some hogwash story old people or sages talk about. I just want to choose my own life and make my dreams come true. Why am I being put under such pressure to save the world when I can't even save myself? As if reading my mind, Ahimsa wraps me even tighter.

The golden moon shines across the dark skies steering us through tall trees and pathways as we fly over the gigantic grounds. Within minutes, the swans descend into a thick foliage outside the staff village. Security guards are seated inside a small office at the entrance gate.

"I wonder which is Selina's house?" whispers Teja impatiently. Looking as confused as my brother, I spot an enormous mansion with a beautifully manicured garden.

"That must be the house," I say excitedly pointing to the single villa tucked away at the far corner of the driveway.

"No Pooja," interrupts Ahimsa quietly, "that is Dr. Malhotra's villa." Just then we are interrupted by the bright lights of a car approaching. Teja pulls me down, and we hide behind a neatly trimmed hedge with small pink flowers. The car stops at the boom gate, and we notice Mr. VJS in the back seat with two strange men in the front. The guards' salute Mr. VJS, and open the boom gate immediately as if the Minister of India has arrived. They run alongside the car escorting them directly to Selina's house. I stare in shock as they leave their post unattended.

Teja, of course, quick on the uptake, grasps my hand tightly and before I realise what is going on, we are running behind the car along a darkened footpath.

I hate howling winds and cold dark nights - it reminds me of vampires lurking in the dark. Right now I am a nervous, hysterical wreck chasing criminals in the middle of a ghostly night. In the last few months I feel as if my life has gone from craziness to idiotic madness! And where did it all begin? My wonderful, unreasonable parents' decision to exile me! At this moment, who really cares about my problems? No one! Not my parents, nor the Gods, or the universe or even the strange, mystical Magic Man.

All of a sudden, Teja stops and pushes me to the ground. The car stops in the driveway of a huge, white double storey bungalow with a bright red door. Neal steps outside almost instantly, and while shaking hands with the two strangers dressed in black trench coats, he quickly ushers them inside. One is a heavily built man dragging himself on a walking stick. Mr. VJS follows them inside.

Teja takes hold of my hand, guiding me to the periphery of a grassy pathway leading into their back garden. We sit behind a bougainvillea hedge waiting for Satya to find a hideout closest to their house.

"Follow me," he says quietly as he makes his way back. Without rustling their wings, the swans carry us and perch silently on a thick branch of a mango tree. With the cotton curtains drawn aside and the window wide open, we have the perfect view of their dining-room.

Seated around a large mahogany table are six men, all Indians, and on the table are glass tumblers and jugs of water. Neal is addressing the men, while Selina is busy writing notes on her iPad. Her husband is standing in front of a whiteboard speaking slowly, repeating each word a few times as though he is trying hard to make the local men understand his strong foreign accent. Mr. VJS, sitting nearby, repeats the same information in Hindi. Using a laser pen, Neal then reads out a list of country names written in huge, bold writing.

Teja whispers softly, "Hey, that consignment code number 027 is South Africa."

"Gentlemen, as you are aware, we have only recently started sending out consignments to other countries. Through your hard work these deliveries have now reached their destination. Thank you," says Neal looking at the men sitting around the table.

He continues, "At this afternoon's meeting, you heard about the current plans for our organisation. As an NGO, our goal is to help create jobs for unemployed people from your villages, open a medical centre, and provide housing and schools for nine villages around here. You have been selected as managers of your teams and will now be assigned important responsibilities. Most of our work is done at night, and because we work 24 hour shifts underground, we expect you to make sure all work is completed. Tonight you will sign a formal contract of employment with Mr. Vijay Singh, who explained your responsibilities earlier in our meeting."

The men nod their heads silently. Glancing at each other nervously, one young man hesitatingly looks up at Mr. VJS and speaks in Hindi.

Mr. VJS seems to get agitated, and pushing his oily, untidy hair away from his face, turns and looks anxiously at Neal.

"What does he say?" snaps Selina.

Teja is right. Every time Selina screams at him, Mr. VJS becomes a shrivelling, dumbfounded, pathetic weasel. This time he opens his mouth but quickly clamps up. The room goes deathly quiet.

"Mr. V, speak up!" she yells angrily as she gets up and paces the room.

Stammering nervously, he says, "Madame, Jeevan wants to know what is inside the crates. The reason is if they are stopped by police, he should have some information. You also promised to build a hospital for the poor. There are many sick people in his village who need medical treatment urgently, so he wants to know when the hospital will be ready?"

Fearfully the men in the room look at each other as Selina stares at the young man menacingly. She certainly doesn't look pretty now as her nostrils flare, her blue eyes slant dangerously and her face distorts to a sly sneer.

"Oh dear! This is trouble." whispers Teja.

Neal quickly escorts her back to her chair and hands her a glass of water. Then turning around he says quietly, "Mr. Jeevan, let me show you what is inside the crate."

Selina gasps. But Neal ignores her for a moment and disappears from the room. Mr. Vijay Singh stands rooted to the spot, perspiration clearly visible on his forehead. The next moment, Neal returns with a box in his hand, unpacks the tissue paper inside, and removes about six ornaments and places them in the centre of the table. The Indian ornaments are exquisitely carved from black marble stone and studded with gold threading and colourful glass pieces.

Handing the elephant stone to Jeevan, he says, "This is what we are sending out of the country, Mr. Jeevan. Our organisation is promoting the culture and tradition of this country, and these Indian ornaments make beautiful gifts. Western countries are looking to the East for many answers to life.

"Why do you think there are so many westerners in India? Everyone in the world wants to learn yoga, and how to stay healthy, and about Ayurveda medicine and religion. What better way to raise funds for our organisation than to sell these cheap ornaments in western countries? This kind of artwork is not found anywhere else other than in India."

Mr. Jeevan shakes his head quietly.

"Take a look at these ornaments," Neal says smiling confidently as he passes around the beautiful white marble peacock, Taj Mahal, jewellery boxes, hairclips and different animal and bird ornaments. "We are simply taking advantage of your traditional handicraft."

Selina, in her sweetest, gentlest voice, then says, "Mr. Jeevan, don't forget the arrangement we made with the village leaders. We have already started employing men from your village. Besides, we are here to provide a better life for your families."

Placing his hand on Mr. Jeevan's shoulder, Neal smilingly says, "There have been some delays with the hospital project, but we have decided to start a small medical camp every week in each village, starting from next week. I hope this will help you, Mr. Jeevan."

The men nod their heads with relief, and smile at each other, laughing and talking in Hindi as they stare at the cheap, traditional ornaments western people seem so excited about. A few minutes later, after signing their contracts, they are escorted out of the house by Mr. VJS.

Meanwhile the two men who arrived with Mr. VJS remain behind, and within seconds the man with the limp leaves the room and returns with a black duffel bag by which time Selina has spread out a massive sheet of paper on the table.

"Gentlemen," interrupts Neal softly pointing to the paper on the table, "this is a copy of the blueprint of a section of the fort we want you to handle. Bending over the blueprint he picks up a pen and draws red crosses."

Suddenly he stops, turns around and walks to the window. My heart skips a beat. Has he seen or heard us? We remain dead quiet! Neal then shuts the window and returns to the table. Damn, now I have no idea what they are talking about.

Realising we are wasting our time shivering out in the cold, I turn to Teja who is curled up next to me and nudge him quietly.

"Let's go, Teja!"

Yawning softly, he nods his head and murmurs, "Anything I missed?"

"Nope, I think it was a wasted trip," I reply irritably thinking of my warm bed. Just as I snuggle into Ahimsa's wings, I turn around one last time to see what they are up to. There sitting on the table is the black duffel bag, opened and filled with explosives!

I scream, and Teja clamps his hand over my mouth so tightly that for a moment I stop breathing. With eyes bulging and arms swinging around in panic, I push Teja and the swans away from me. Then, like in a slow motion movie, I watch myself topple and fall from the mango tree with poor Teja, Ahimsa and Satya following with a thud.

Hearing the commotion outside, Neal rushes back to the window. Satya and Ahimsa spread their wings to hide us as we lay sprawled on the ground. Neal stares outside for a few minutes before closing the curtains.

Teja shoves me away angrily and limps back towards the overgrown hedge, and before I can get to my feet, Ahimsa disappears into the darkness.

"Where is he off to?" asks Teja.

Almost instantaneously, we hear loud noises coming from inside the house. Satya grabs us into his wings and flies around the garden searching frantically for Ahimsa.

Suddenly we see Ahimsa through the kitchen window causing havoc in the dining-room. He is swinging from a chandelier, sprinkling bits of paper like confetti on to Selina's head. Eyes bulging with shock and fear, Selina is glued to the chair, hands waving about like a mad, hysterical woman, trying to disentangle paper from her wild, blonde tresses. Neal is ranting and swearing in the worst language I ever heard, and at the same time, trying to pacify his wife who is screeching uncontrollably in her squeaky, high-pitched British voice. His face has turned crimson as he jumps up to grab Ahimsa. At that moment, Mr. VJS enters the room and noticing the chaos around him is shrieking vile words in Hindi as he bends down to gather the scattered pages.

There's total pandemonium everywhere!

And then, a loud bang! A gunshot! All I can see is smoke. Ahimsa has been shot... dead!

Amidst the smoke, noise, guns, explosives and criminals, I think I fainted. Well... not sure about that 'cos I've never fainted in my life. But definitely zoned out!

There is absolute silence. Selina appears ghost-like, and Neal is staring at the two strangers. Before I have time to think, Teja clasps my mouth, and quietly but firmly tells me to remain calm and not scream otherwise we will get caught – and expelled.

My brother certainly knows how to put the fear of death into me. I nod my head. I am speechless! Terrified! There is no sign of Ahimsa.

The dining-room window is once again opened and Selina has a cold compress on her forehead and a glass of wine firmly clutched in her hand. Neal is also drinking something from a bottle. A gun lies on the table! Mr. VJS is talking angrily to the men who stare impassively at him.

Trying hard to control myself, I grab Teja's hand and whimper like a lost cat, "Where is Ahimsa?"

"I don't know. Satya says he may have escaped."

Before I can reply, Satya flies through the kitchen window and lands on top of the cupboards – this time deciding to remain invisible.

"OK Mr. Saloojee, let's start again," explains Neal breathlessly and impatiently. "Thank you for agreeing to take on this contract. This mission is very confidential and important to the organisation. As you are aware this school was originally a fort built on hundreds of acres of land. Some sections were completely destroyed due to natural disasters and foreign invasions. Recently researchers believe there are some rare artefacts still buried beneath the fort. We want to retrieve these artefacts and this is where you come in. Our organisation is building the largest, state-of-the-art museum in Delhi and we want to include these artefacts and other priceless treasure we find, so that the children of this country will understand the history of India."

The men listen quietly as Neal turns to the paper in front of him. "Now these areas I have marked is where we want you to plant the explosives. This is a hostel that was built recently, and beneath it lies a section that leads to the sunken fort."

"This is your copy of the blueprint to study the exact location of the fort we want demolished. We cannot reveal anything to Dr. Malhotra because this project is highly confidential, and he is not included in this project. Your job is to infiltrate the school building and plant these explosives in strategic places without making him aware or creating suspicion to any staff member."

The man with the limp looks up at Neal and in a deep, gruff voice says, "When do you want this project to happen?"

Suddenly Selina interrupts them in a firm, demanding voice, "Within two weeks. This means you will have to visit the school without raising any suspicion, become familiar with the building and plan your best strategies."

"Madame," replies the second man, "we are highly experienced military men and have been specially trained in explosives for over 20 years. Our plan will be on your table one week from today, and if you give us the go-ahead, we will execute the plan as agreed," his black eyes cold and calculating as he stares at Selina.

"Please make sure there are no casualties or accidents," Neal says gravely, "there are children at the school."

"Neal," Selina cuts in rudely, "that is not our problem. You cannot have an explosion without casualties. I am not interested in these bloody children. The sooner we complete this project the better."

All four men nod their heads quietly.

Selina pushes a large envelope towards them and announces coldly, "Gentlemen, here is 10 lakh rupees as your first payment. You have two weeks. Get this job done successfully and you will be paid the remaining amount."

With a frosty look at each of the men, she nods, "Good night!"

She turns and walks down the corridor, leaving both Neal and Mr. VJS to escort the men out.

As we fly off towards the hostel, Teja and I remain dead quiet. So much has happened this evening. Teja refuses to talk to me, and jumps out as soon as Satya descends outside his hostel.

Luckily both Natalie and Reet are fast asleep – because I don't want to talk to anyone right now. Even Satya disappears into the night.

Shocked at what has happened to Ahimsa, tears well up in my eyes. Sitting on the bathroom floor I want to scream and shout to the universe, but I muffle my sobs into my towel. Is this my destiny? Is my karma to have Ahimsa die? I know this is my fault.

Eventually I open the door and stare at Reet sleeping squashed next to Natalie. How am I going to tell them about Ahimsa? Where do I start? Tears rolls down my cheeks.

Ahimsa dead!

And my stress right now has shot up way beyond the stars and planets... My spasho-attack descends!

The universe is hurling so many issues at me, and I simply cannot cope right now. How do I rescue the children in the cages? How do I stop dangerous criminals from blowing up our school? Who can I confide in about Mr. VJS, Selina or Neal? These are all impossible things for a 12-year-old girl.

Holding my head tightly with both hands, I pray the pain and confusion I feel right now will go away. I stare helplessly around me. I am certainly heading for a nervous breakdown. What that means, I have no idea. MY KARMA is the worst ever! I now decide I'm not getting involved with whatever the Magic Man told me years ago. I have had enough! I give up!

Chapter 18

The next morning loud banging on the door awakens me. Having just fallen asleep I can barely open my eyes. Natalie jumps up and opens the door. Wobbly Mrs. Roy pushes her roly-poly self into the room. Through bleary, tired eyes, I peep from beneath my duvet – and there behold stands a sight for sore eyes.

Mrs. Roy looks dishevelled and exhausted. Her usual neat and tidy low bun has disappeared, replaced by a long plait with different coloured hairpins to keep her curly hair away from her humongous forehead. This morning she is wearing a long, maxi-style tie-and-dye dress instead of her usual sari.

"Girls! School is closed for today," she whispers hoarsely.

"What? OMG!" cries Natalie. "What happened?"

"Soooooo many children are sick. We don't know if it's food poisoning or some virus. Last night we admitted many children to hospital," she explains, "so Dr. Malhotra has decided to close school today."

I am now wide awake. "OMG! That's serious!"

She squeezes herself into the chair next to Natalie's bed. Shaking her head in sadness and raising her pathetic eyes to Natalie, she whispers, "I am so tired. We did not sleep a single wink last night."

"Why, what happened?" asks Reet waking up, rubbing her eyes as she sits up against the headboard.

"Reet! Don't leave this room," Mrs. Roy interrupts. "As it is you are so thin and unwell now. I don't want you to get the tummy bug. Our hostel has nine girls in hospital. Dr. Malhotra is very worried."

Nodding her head, she continues, "Your meals will be served in the common room. The canteen is closed for the next few days."

"Mrs. Roy, who are the girls from our hostel who are sick?" I ask, sounding concerned.

"Oh! Mm!" for a moment she looks confused.

"Mrs. Roy, you said some of the girls from Meera House were admitted to hospital."

"Oh yes!" and she blurts out names of girls in our hostel. Then, as an afterthought, adds, "Oh, yes, Indira, Sonalika and your friends from England."

"What?" I shout in alarm as I jump out of bed. "I've got to see them."

"Oh no you won't, Pooja!" Mrs. Roy says sternly. "Those girls are in quarantine. No visitors are allowed."

"Yes Pooja!" agrees Natalie looking at me. "It's better they're in hospital."

I glower at Dr. Natalie, who has this annoying habit of confidently giving logical answers in times of crises. And right now, she is a specialist doctor. I jump back into bed and sulk.

Mrs. Roy gets up and waddles towards the door. "There won't be any classes today. Our hostel is quarantined as well, so try and keep yourselves occupied either in your room or use the common room area please," she smiles contentedly. "We have to keep an eye on everyone."

As soon as the door closes, I snap rudely, "For your information Natalie, I wanted to visit Kash and Sanam. They are *my* friends!"

I throw the duvet aside, jump out of bed and march to the bathroom. With the latest crisis, I couldn't be bothered to tell these two idiots what happened last night. Right now I need to be alone.

All morning I remain in my room sulking. Natalie and Reet have disappeared. I attempt some homework but throw it aside as I keep thinking about Ahimsa. The more I think about my foolishness, the more I cry.

Later in the morning, Satya arrives. For a few minutes he watches me quietly, lying slumped over my desk in a paralytic state. Curling his elongated neck towards me, he whispers softly, "Pooja, Teja had these ornaments in his bag." He opens his snowy white wing and drops two ornaments on to my bed. One is a beautiful elephant carved out of black marble and embellished with colourful glass studded pieces. The other is our national bird, the peacock, sculptured in white marble and dotted with glittery stones across its wings.

I look up at him with puffy eyes and utter miserably, "Satya, these are cheap ornaments. What do you want me to do with them?" I burst out crying. Satya wraps his wings around me as I sob uncontrollably. "I am so sorry about last night, Satya, I didn't mean to push you all."

"Pooja, it is not your fault," he says gently. "Why don't you speak to the Magic Man?"

"I don't want to talk to that man," I retort angrily, "I don't want to know anything about him or karma or destiny or whatever!"

I grab a tissue and blow my nose. "After we got back last night I thought about this karmic nonsense and my destiny.

I do not want to get involved. I am too young and this is too complicated for me. Let the police do what they have to. These people have guns and bombs. They shot Ahimsa, remember?"

Satya hops on to the floor and walks across to my hiding place. "Pooja, please talk to the Magic Man," he begs with the gentlest of eyes.

Irritably, I rummage through my secret hiding place and pull out the snow globe. Almost immediately it glows, and grows brighter until I see the shadow of the Magic Man. As usual, I become speechless.

"Pooja, how are you?" comes his gentle, loving voice. He sounds really happy and chilled out – with not a care in the world – purely because he has conveniently dumped all his problems on me!

I am so furious, but before I can respond, he continues, "You have been very busy, Pooja. There's lots happening. Tell me."

I stare back rudely. "Like really!"

Does he know my crisis? Besides everything else that is happening, my voice is playing up again. This time I sound like Olaf from the movie *Frozen,* especially when he says, "*Are you kidding me?*"

So where do I begin? "What happened to Ahimsa? Why are children locked up in cages? Where did they come from? Did you know Selina and her husband are dangerous people plotting to bomb our school... and so on and so on?"

The Magic Man calmly interrupts me, "Pooja, the children will be rescued. But first you have to stop these men from blowing up the school."

"Why me? Get the police!" I shout belligerently. "It is through my foolishness that Ahimsa got killed. So right now, please talk to the hand and *not* to the face! I don't want to be involved in all this stupid karma stuff."

245

Tears roll down my cheeks. Sobbing loudly, I cover my face with both hands. The light in the room grows brighter, and before I know it, I am wrapped warmly into the soft, pearly white wings as Satya hugs me tightly.

I hear the gentle voice of the Magic Man, "Pooja, you didn't kill Ahimsa! He is hurt, but not dead. Look!"

Slowly I look up at the Magic Man, only to see Ahimsa comforting me.

"Are you really here?" I whisper in disbelief, touching his long, graceful neck gently.

"Yes Pooja, I was only hurt."

I am so relieved and ecstatic that I grab him tightly to make sure I am not dreaming.

He strokes me lovingly, "I am safe and well Pooja. Yes, I was shot but the Magic Man mended me. Turning to the snow globe I whisper softly, "Thank you for saving Ahimsa."

The Magic Man nods his head explaining softly, "The birds also have their own magic to keep them safe, just like you have been given your own magic. If you had looked into your locket last night, you would have seen Ahimsa flying back to me."

"I am very confused. I don't know where to start," I whisper. "Why didn't Ahimsa go into the house invisible? Why did he allow himself to get shot?"

"That is all part of this play," the Magic Man responds. "Sometimes certain things have to look real to test your faith in what I have said about your destiny."

"Is that why my parents sent us here?" I utter in bewilderment.

The light spreads brighter around the room.

"Your journey to usher in the Golden Age started when you were born. This is a very important part of the process."

Then I quickly add, "We found a diary and gem stones inside the book. Selina, her husband and Mr. V had been searching for it. Are they criminals wanting the treasure buried beneath this fort?"

"Yes Pooja. Selina and Neal are members of the Millennium Corporation I told you about. If they bomb the school, many people will get hurt. You have to stop them!"

"And how am I supposed to do that?" I reply angrily. "These people are dangerous."

The Magic Man whispers, "Pooja, you have the magic and we will help you."

Not convinced with all this mumbo-jumbo story and with tears rolling down my cheeks, I ask cheekily, "Why don't *you* stop them? Why are there so many things happening that you want me to solve, yet you are sitting happily in your temple, or ashram or monastery or whatever you call it?"

The Magic Man chuckles. "Not really, Pooja!" he replies in a more serious tone. "Selina and Neal have already found treasure beneath this fort, but there is one sacred jewel – an oval-shaped yellow diamond– they are desperate to find. That jewel is a divine stone... and will never be touched by a foreign hand. Millennium Corporation are only pretending to work as a charitable organisation."

I grab one of the ornaments from my desk and ask curiously, "So tell me, what is so secretive about these stupid, common ornaments?"

The light inside the snow globe grows into a bright pink light dazzling me until my eyes hurt. I cover my eyes and in doing so, accidently push Satya aside. His wings brush against the ornaments lying on my desk and the elephant falls over with a loud thud onto the tiled floor.

Startled, I stare down at the shattered pieces of black stone. Of course, once again I start to cry as I pick up a few broken pieces and place them on my desk.

"Why are you upset, Pooja?" says the Magic Man.

Tears well up as I blubber nervously, "I've messed up again. We found these ornaments in the office beneath the fort, and then last night Neal showed similar ones to the men at the meeting. And now I have broken it." I weep softly.

"Pooja, your clue is right in front of you."

Through my tears I stare at the pieces of stone on my desk. Against the black marble, a few specks of coloured stones flash brightly like tiny rainbows floating in the air.

Mesmerised, I gape.

"OMG!" I cry softly, glaring at the sparkling gems. I look up at the Magic Man as the light in the snow globe begins to glow brighter again. I place a red gem stone on the palm of my hand, and whisper almost inaudibly. "Are these for real?"

The ruby stone glistens on my palm, and I select a large emerald, sapphire and diamond from the debris of broken pieces of the elephant.

The Magic Man explains, "Pooja, do you really think Selina and her team are exporting these cheap ornaments? Go back to the diary again and find out about the Tree of Enlightenment."

"What kind of a name is that?" I snap petulantly. Didn't I just tell this man I am not getting involved? Why don't adults sometimes listen to young people? He is still giving me instructions. So much pressure and tension again in my life. The pink light recedes to a soft glow until I see just a shadow of the Magic Man disappearing once again.

"Great," I stare crossly at the fading light, "that was some help!"

It seems karma or destiny, or whatever craziness is going on right now in my life, is certainly out of my control. I stare dumbfounded at the gemstones as Ahimsa picks up each one with his long beak, and places them separately on my desk.

"Let me text Teja!" I mumble softly turning to the birds who are sitting patiently besides me.

"Pooja, why don't you call him?" suggests Satya.

"Oh no, he's so angry with me right now, I'm sure he won't answer my call."

"Why don't I bring him here instead?" suggests Satya. "It will be easier for him to see exactly what we have found."

I nod my head.

"And no one will see him," he continues. Turning to Ahimsa he says gently, "Ahimsa, please leave, you have to rest."

I hug Ahimsa sadly, then watch them disappear through the window.

I recap what I know, which is still very confusing to me:

1. Magic Man – diary and Tree of Enlightenment.
2. Gemstones inside ornaments.
3. Confirmed – Selina and Neal belong to the Millennium Corporation.

"Where are these two girls?" I think to myself. I quickly put away the snow globe and hide the gemstones. Just then Satya arrives, and at that very moment, there is a loud rattling of the door knob. Satya hides behind the curtain.

"Who's there?" I whisper.

"It's us," shouts Reet frantically, "open the door!"

I unlock the door and the two beauties march in – still looking a wee bit annoyed with me. But at this moment, I don't care. I bolt the door again.

Without looking at them, I push the curtain aside, Satya hops out and Teja jumps off.

"Hi!" he smiles at the girls.

You should see their faces, I smile to myself smugly. I watch their eyes mirroring disbelief as to why and how Teja got into the room. I continue to ignore them. Turning to Teja, I explain what had just happened with the Magic Man and how we found the precious gem stones. Feeling left out, the girls quickly gather around. As I place the hanky on the desk and carefully open it, the gems glitter brightly. All I can hear from Reet is, "OMG, OMG!"

"What about the other ornament I sent you?" enquires Teja staring at the broken elephant.

"It's here!" I reply taking it from my box. "I was too frightened when the elephant broke. That's why I called you straight away."

"Let's break the peacock!" suggests Satya.

"Yes!" both girls say in unison.

Teja bangs it hard against the desk. Nothing. He bends down and knocks it on the tiles. Nothing.

"Be careful Teja, it is marble, so we may break a floor tile!" I say.

"Now what?" exclaims Reet.

"I think we need a hammer or something," suggests Natalie.

"Where do we get one from?" I ask irritably.

"At least we now know Selina and Neal have found some treasure," suggests Teja thoughtfully.

"And they're certainly not researchers of education!" laughs Natalie.

I reply quietly, "I don't think Dr. Malhotra even knows they are not researchers. Maybe these people got the children to dig out gem stones from beneath this fort?"

"Remember, these forts had palaces, temples, hallways and grand rooms where kings hid their treasures, and Millennium Corporation have found some of them," explains Satya.

"Give me the peacock, please Natalie," asks Satya. Holding it in his beak, he flies up to the ceiling and flings it down with a bang. The ornament shatters. Amidst the white marble and tiny colourful glass lay a handful of precious gemstones. We all gasp.

There are nine pieces of glittering precious stones in each ornament. Teja examines the largest emerald stone I have ever seen, and the huge diamond nestled in Natalie's palm glitters in the sun.

"But why would Neal show the ornaments to those men last night?" enquires Teja staring from me to Satya.

"No idea, but did you notice how Selina started to panic. She couldn't breathe!" I quickly add. "And Mr. V was fidgety and sweating."

Satya in his gentle voice says, "I thought he was having a heart attack. He kept gulping tumblers of water."

"OMG!" A light bulb moment! Teja jumps up, his eyes light up excitedly, "I think Neal took a chance. No one would suspect that the gems would be hidden inside those ornaments."

Both Natalie and Reet looked very confused, but right now I don't have the time to explain – they'll have to wait.

Then I tell them what the Magic Man had said about these ornaments being able to go through security checks quite easily because the gems are covered in some kind of opaque chemical gel before being packed inside the ornament. In this way they are not tarnished nor are the stones detected through any form of security.

"Wow! Clever thinking!" exclaims Teja thoughtfully.

Satya interrupts, "The Magic Man said we must first save the school before it is destroyed... and all the rest will fall into place. So let's work on that for now."

Reet is hysterical! As usual her voice echoes, "We are going to die," she shouts crazily, "I don't want to die with Mr. V."

Teja hits her on her head to shut up. I ignore her and Natalie gasps in shock, "Guys, this is really serious. How do we stop them? First we found the gemstones and now the bomb blast."

"OMG!" Reet whispers in alarm. "I hope it's not during our Kite Festival. Everyone is so excited for this event!"

"This is disastrous!" Teja adds gravely concerned.

"Now we will all be killed!" cries Reet anxiously.

Satya interrupts quietly, "Pooja, let's read the diary to find the answers."

"Yes, yes," I say quickly, "the Magic Man said the children will continue working here until we solve this mystery."

"Why?" cries Reet aloud, "it's not fair."

"I know, but right now we have to find the missing link," I explain.

"Pooja, bring out the diary. Let's read it," Teja calls out impatiently. I quickly open the velvet book box and we gather around Teja.

He scans the pages quickly until he reads, **"He who seeks the Truth shall find my resting place beneath the Tree of Enlightenment."**

"Hey, there it is," he chuckles amusingly, "Tree of Enlightenment."

"Nats," he calls out, "queen of Google, check what it says about the 'Tree of Enlightenment'."

Teja continues to scans the pages quickly and stops to explain, "He talks about messages written on the leaves of the peepal tree. Well, it seems they received many symbols and cryptic clues from this tree which helped them enter the fort to find treasure."

Natalie interrupts us, "Hey, hang on and listen. The tree is a very old, sacred tree under which Lord Buddha meditated."

"Anything else?" asks Satya softly.

"It is believed that for hundreds of years, wise old men and sages meditated under these trees and received messages from Gods. To impart this knowledge to the people, they wrote the information on the leaves of the peepal tree. That is why this tree is called the Tree of Knowledge."

Teja continues to read, "OK, so let's see what else Mr. Ealdwinne has to say about this tree.

"It became very frustrating that after months of digging around this site, we couldn't find a single entrance into this disused fort. It was as if an invisible shield was placed around this abandoned derelict building. Instead of finding a way into the fort, we found strange cryptic clues on the leaves of the peepal tree.

Finding no success, our team decided to give up our search and go back to our original site. The morning of our departure, I decided to take my bath in the nearby river where the sun was already shining on the tall tree tops mirroring sparkly bright lights on to the shimmery water. Nearby, my friends splashed under the sapphire-blue burbling water as it cascaded down the mountainside. I was sad, disheartened and wanted to be alone. I could feel the warm water soothingly caress me as it gently passed through the forest. I sat on a small rock in the water disillusioned that we failed to uncover the mystery of this fort. There was a strange stillness in the air with only the melodious sounds of birds

*as if a divine orchestra played from high above. I succumbed
to the tranquillity around me and closed my eyes.*

*Suddenly I could hear a soft hum pulsating around me.
Startled I opened my eyes and I looked around. It was not my
meditation! Not sure if this was a dream, I looked around,
confused and disorientated until I felt the water beneath
my feet swirl and become rapid and strong. As I arose to get
out of the water, my heart sank. My right foot was wedged
between two rocks. I pulled and pushed against the hard
rock, but it remained stuck. The babbling water around my
feet rose and heaved. I look around for help but there was
no one. Everyone must be waiting for me at camp! I slipped
down into the water to remove the rock with both hands,
but found myself staring at a conical shape conch pressing
my feet down forcefully. The water around it was vibrating
like a whirlpool. As soon as I touched the conch my foot was
released, the strange sound started to grow louder and was
soon reverberating through the vast forests resonating in
every leaf and tree. Curiously, I picked up this shiny white
shell turning it around to find out where the loud sound
was emanating from.*

*Thinking maybe there was a stone stuck inside the
conch, I tipped it over. Out fell a faded green peepal leaf. I
almost dropped it because immediately the humming sound
stopped. This time there was a colourful drawing of a small
brass pot which tapered at the neck and on it sat a huge
jewel. Below were the words,* "To step into my abode, seek a
brass pot concealed by time."

"This is so confusing!" grumbles Reet irritably, "how more
crazy can this story get?"

We all agree. It was way over our heads. None of us knew
what this man was writing about.

But Teja continued to read slowly.

"We searched everywhere in the jungle for a brass pot, from dried-up streams and rivers to hilltops and mountain sides, but we failed. Few weeks later, our local guides spotted something shiny sticking out from the sand near our campsite. At the foot of the tree trunk, was a tarnished brass pot with a sealed cover. Being very superstitious, these locals told us to immerse the pot in turmeric water and place it in the sun.

Inside the pot was a golden lotus and a peepal leaf with message, "The sound of the conch will lead the way to the Abode of Truth." Of course, we looked confused and frustrated. But almost immediately we heard the soft humming sound coming from the conch again. As we carried it through the forests, searching for the entrance to the fort, the sound grew louder. This sacred Tree of Enlightenment showed us the miracles of some Higher Power through its own mystery, and once again we found the answers we sought.

Concealed for thousands of years this mysterious and unknown fort was about to be unveiled by a team of British scientists. At last we stood at the entrance of this long, forgotten fort. Tightly sealed and locked were two massive metal doors embossed with exquisitely carved elephants embellished in delicate silver and gold designs. At first we were mystified as to how we were going to open the door as there was no latch or keyhole. Each door had unique metal carvings of an elephant with a raised trunk. When we placed the golden lotus flower on to the raised trunk, we found it fitted perfectly and the doors slowly creaked opened."

"Wow!" I exclaimed in wonder, "what an amazing story!"

"Don't talk nonsense, Pooja," shouts Reet angrily, "I would go crazy if I had to keep decoding strange codes for months in a forest."

Natalie looks at me thoughtfully and says, "So what are we to find?"

"What did I tell you?" complains Reet angrily. "This Magic Man is stupid. He gives us too many confusing problems to solve."

I can't help but agree with Reet. Just then Ahimsa flies in the window and everyone is delighted to see him.

Turning to me, Ahimsa says, "Pooja, I forgot to give you these papers I grabbed from the table last night."

Satya and Teja take them from him, and within minutes Teja exclaims, "OMG, you brought us the blueprint of their plans!"

"What!" we all chorus as if we know how to read blueprints. Actually it's the first time I've ever heard of such a word.

Looking stupidly at everyone, I ask, "OK, you all look like experts. What is a blueprint?"

You should see their faces – a Kodak moment!

So Natalie Googles it quickly and in her so-called authoritarian voice says, "It's a design of a building or something."

"This page has a design of a massive house. How weird?" Reet quips in.

"What?" We all stare at her. We just said design of a building, so why would she talk her usual nonsense. But when we look at the page, it is a design of many buildings around our school.

"Look! There are the staff quarters...," Teja explains, "...and here are the maintenance sheds." He stops suddenly at a large red cross. "Hey what is this?" He pauses... looks closely and keeps quiet.

"What yaar?" shouts Reet, staring at Teja's startled face.

"What?" we all scream.

"There is only one cross and it is on Dr. Malhotra's office."

Just then there's a knock on the door.

"Are you girls OK?" shouts Mrs. Roy. "There's so much noise coming from this room."

We stare at each other with terrified eyes. I rush to open the door and Mrs. Roy walks in quickly, looking around suspiciously. Amazingly, the room looks neat and tidy. Not a crease on the bed nor a book out of place. The gemstones, blueprints, Teja and the swans have disappeared. Poof! Gone!

Natalie, Reet and I sit quietly as we get a lecture on rowdy behaviour and how to behave like ladies.

"It doesn't mean that because there is no school, you should be making so much noise," explains Mrs. Roy crossly. Then in her deep, angry voice she says, "All three of you will help in the hostel kitchen this afternoon. There is a chef there who is supervising our meals, so you girls will help him prepare the afternoon tea."

Reet jumps up, "Mrs. Roy, we didn't mean to be noisy, please don't punish us. We want to study this afternoon."

"Oh no, Reet," she answers sweetly, "that is the last thing on your mind. If left unattended, you will get into trouble. So take your friends and show them how to work in the kitchen."

Nodding our heads silently, Mrs. Roy looks at us sternly and says, "Listen carefully, I am going to the hospital to visit our students. I want to see all your homework completed by the time I get back."

Natalie and I nod our heads. As soon as she leaves, we hastily lock the door. The swans appear and Teja pops out from the cupboard carrying the diary and papers found in the red box.

All three of us are grumbling about our punishment when Teja says, "You deserve it. When I tell you to be quiet, you never listen."

I sit on the floor staring at the pages on the bed. *What are we going to do about Dr. Malhotra's office?* I think to myself. Looking totally freaked out, the girls gather around me on the floor.

"For now we know only one location," replies Teja, "and I don't have a clue about the Tree of Enlightenment."

Ahimsa interrupts us quietly, "Let's see if the Rubik gives us some answers."

"Of course, why didn't I think of that," Teja jumps up excitedly. "But before we do that, please keep your mouths shut, and if you have to talk, talk quietly."

He pulls out the Rubik's Cube and turns it around. Once again a painting of an ancient fort glides in front. It grows brighter and bigger. It is hanging on a massive marble wall, surrounded by tall pillars and ancient furniture. But there is something different about the painting, and before I have a chance to react, it fades quickly into the background.

Reet shouts quickly, "Hey, this is the same painting we saw earlier. Do you think it is somewhere in the library? Look at the marble ceiling... it has the lotus flower design on it."

"Must be important, yaar. Shall we check it out?" asks Teja. "What do you think guys?"

"Such a waste of time," Reet grumbles.

"Teja, it must be very important because it's come up again," I say.

Satya nods her long neck, "I agree Pooja, and perhaps it has clues to save the school."

As the pictures slide away, an ancient statue of Lord Ganesh in a coppery colour stone comes into view. Of course, I am now busy humming my favourite Ganesh mantra, *"Vakratunda Mahakaaya, Suryakoti Samaprabha..."*

Teja pushes me, "Why are you becoming like Reet? Stop your meditation and concentrate."

Irritably I glower at him, "Do you know where that statue is?"

He shakes his head and brusquely says, "There is a temple in every street in India, so how would I know!"

The picture fades away almost immediately and is followed by a picture of our school with hostels, playground and an auditorium.

Reet shouts excitedly, "Hey, check that out! Stop that picture!"

We cannot stop it, and slowly it fades off on its own.

"Hare, she babbles, "I saw the huge metal door!"

"What door?" retorts Teja irritably.

Natalie interrupts, "Teja, check it again!"

"What? Where?" we all shout in unison.

Teja touches the Rubik's Cube again – nothing! It remains blank! The green light disappears and glides back on to Teja's palm.

"Do you think Neal is planning to use explosives in the auditorium or school grounds?" Natalie murmurs softly, looking at us with horror.

"OMG! We saw most of the school... anything can be a target," I squeak in my high-pitched Minnie Mouse voice, "and there are students everywhere."

We all stare at each other, not having the faintest idea of what we are meant to do.

Standing up, Natalie looks frightened. "Now what?"

Looking at his watch, Teja replies, "I don't have any ideas right now. It's almost lunchtime and we will get into trouble if we don't show up for lunch."

Natalie continues, "But Pooja, we have to check this out. We don't have enough time."

"I know, but we are not allowed out of our hostel," I reply angrily.

"Well why don't we at least find the painting?" she asks tartly, "that way we may get some answers."

"I don't know where to start," I say emphatically, "and we have to prepare for exams and there's so much homework. Sorry, but I don't have any answers."

"But we have to find some answers before they blow up the school," Reet butts in.

I stare back at my friends. Teja quickly intervenes, "Natalie, we have one weekend left, so perhaps we can search on Saturday?"

"Yes," I agree nodding my head.

Teja walks to the window where Satya is waiting, "Guys, I'm leaving," he says, "I have tons of homework to catch up with."

At that moment, Natalie says quietly, "Don't you think all this is really too big a problem for us?"

"What do you mean?" Teja says as he walks back.

"Perhaps we should get the police involved..." she suggests, "... Dr. Malhotra, or my mother. She is a human rights lawyer. We came to stay in India because she is investigating something about violations of children's rights."

"I thought she was working for a children's charity or something?" retorts Reet inquisitively.

"Her assignment is very secretive. Maybe I can talk to her?" replies Natalie.

"Yes! Good idea!" I quickly say, relieved that good old Natalie can help resolve our problem. Right now I am scared and confused.

"What?" says Teja staring at me angrily. "And what happened to your stupid story about saving the world and children?"

"I know, Teja, but let the police come in and capture these people," I cry softly. "This is a real crime with real dangerous criminals."

"Oh, shut up! Pooja! We have a job to do and it's urgent, so let's get that done!" he glares at me, looking outraged at my suggestion.

"But why does it become my problem?" I snap back.

Reet jumps up and shouts belligerently, "If the Magic Man wanted us to get help, he would send the help, Pooja. Listen to Teja!"

Can you imagine a 12-year-old girl, playing detective with people like Selina and Neal, and now we have evidence that our school is going to be blown up. I've never heard of other adventure stories for young people that have been as dangerous as this one.

Come to think of it, even Harry Potter and his friends were not given such crazy deadlines to save the world. What pressure and tension! And now even my best friends are scared. Personally I am terrified. My knees cave in when I think about Selina, Mr. VJS, ghosts, being expelled, my parents, explosives and guns!

OMG! Can you imagine what my father would say? My normal life was so easy and uncomplicated. Movies, eating chaat or pizza, mango festivals, Holi and simply fooling around with my friends. That is what I called LIFE! TOTALLY SIMPLE!

Do you see any complications? Nope! No talking swans. No flying auto rickshaws. No boarding schools. No caves or forts or tunnels. No diamonds and gem stones. No Magic Man. No criminals.

Just then my stupid brother nudges me and glowers at me with dagger eyes.

"Stop your stupid day-dreaming," he growls furiously, "and let's do what we promised."

Without waiting for me, he disappears out the window with Satya.

Chapter 19

Dear Diary,

BREAKING NEWS: DATE FOR KITE FESTIVAL CHANGED!

"The Kite Festival will be held this Saturday!" Dr. Malhotra announced this morning during assembly. "And with so many students taken ill in the last week, your exams will begin later next week.

All hell broke loose after assembly – teachers rushing around anxiously trying to re-confirm arrangements for Saturday, and students everywhere making last minute changes to their kites.

Natalie comes over and whispers, "This probably means we can't go out on Saturday."

"OMG! I haven't even thought that far!" I answer quickly. Licking my lips, I take a deep breath to calm myself, *"With so much going on at school, I don't have time to go searching for clues. That can wait!"*

Of course, Reet, the manic arrives.

"Pooja, what are we going to do? Hare! Do we need this stress right now?" she says slapping her hand on her head as she stares at me anxiously.

From behind her, we hear the familiar thunderous voice of Mr. Vijay Singh, "Sarabji, before you get detention, get out of this class now. Your class teacher is looking for you."

Before I can blink, Reet has disappeared. Mr. VJS turns to the class and announces loudly, "There's been a change of school programme for today. For the rest of the day, you will join Mrs. Jyothi and Mr. Walters in the library. Please pack your bags and go now."

Before we can even react, he stares at us angrily and shouts impatiently, "Go, go, go now!"

Grabbing our bags and with books bundled under our arms, we run quickly down the stairs and across the long pathway towards the library building. The last thing we want right now is to get into any sort of trouble with this sleazy criminal.

Terrified out of her wits, Natalie sits quietly next to me at a desk right at the back of the library. Avoiding any eye contact with this slimy, ugly man who is waiting to be relieved by Mr. Walters, we pretend to be doing some work.

Rubbing my locket anti-clockwise I try to make contact with Satya. On a piece of paper I write, **Change of school plan for this weekend – find out what is going on.** I drop it underneath my desk. Within minutes, I hear the flutter of his wings and the soft, warm feathers nestle near my feet.

Then the strangest thing ever happens. I see Mr. VJS striding towards me, holding his mobile phone in one hand. My eyes go fuzzy, my head is pounding, and my face is burning – I'm sure Natalie can feel the heat shooting out of my ears as we watch him get closer.

"Dear God, if you are here right now, please help me!" I mumble frantically to myself, as I chant another of my ever-famous mantras through tight lips, *"Om Namah Shivaya, Om Namah Shivaya, Om Namah...."*

Under the desk Satya gets smaller and smaller. Mr. VJS suddenly stops in front of me.

Do you think the Gods ever show any mercy when I need it the most? Nope! Never! No Ganesh, no Shiva, no Buddha, no one! Just my karma!

Mr. VJS is staring at me, while Nats and I are pretending to work. Our eyes glued to our books, hands trembling, lips quivering, legs jerking with fear.

"Narayan," he says in a slow, croaky voice. I look up uneasily.

"I have been meaning to meet with you," he sneers contemptuously. "There are strange things happening in this school and Sarabji's name always comes up. I'm sure her best friend knows more than she's letting on. Don't you think so?"

"I don't know what you mean, Sir," I mumble in terror, holding my breath. Just then his phone rings and he moves back, slowly stepping away from my desk.

I hear him whispering, "Hello Neal..." and his voice fades away. I remain fixed to my seat, my neck stiff bent over with fear. Natalie sighs softly and holds my hand tightly.

Minutes pass by, then Natalie pinches me and I look up to see him running out the door. I disappear into the reading room with Satya in tow.

Sitting on the floor, I listen as he recalls the conversation he overheard between Mr. VJS and Neal. Mr. VJS told Neal everything had gone according to plan, and he had already sent him details of the change of plans for Saturday. He added that there would be no interruptions from students for the remainder of the week. He went on to say how difficult it was to convince Dr. Malhotra to change the date for the Kite Festival and only when he mentioned how many students were admitted into hospital and it would be to their disadvantage if exams were to be written as planned, did Dr.. Malhotra agree to the change.

He paused as he listened to Neal, then said, "Brilliant. No one suspected. Oh yes, India is famous for food poisoning. Delhi Belly! Ha-ha!"

I am flabbergasted... shocked... outraged! "Are you saying Mr. VJS and Neal caused the food poisoning problem here at school?" Satya nods his long neck.

"OMG, Satya, students got sick!" I squeak in my high-pitched Alvin the Chipmunk voice, "So this is why our exam and Kite Festival dates have changed."

"I think we should search the library tonight," suggests Satya.

"Yes, but why rush," I frown with confusion, "we still have Sunday."

"Pooja, I don't trust these people. Why did Neal insist that the Kite Festival date be changed?" asks Satya.

"Do you think they have other plans?" I say looking startled and scared.

Satya nods his head, "Let's not take any chances. This morning, Ahimsa and I will go down to the forest to see if we can find those clues we saw in the Rubik's Cube."

"Great! That sounds like a good idea," I sigh with relief knowing full well that the search is still going ahead.

Guess what – my karma is changing. This afternoon we are having dance rehearsal in the auditorium for our end of term dance production. I'm sure I pleased at least one of our hundreds of Hindu deities. This is now my chance to check the silver doors or steel doors we saw in the Rubik's cube. I tell Natalie and Reet about my plan at our afternoon tea break. Let's see if my karma remains positive – for today at least.

All afternoon we dance, try out costumes, practice in groups, put on stage make-up and help out with curtains and lighting.

And every chance we get, we look around for secret doors. But there is nothing! Reet, Natalie and I are looking stressed. Supper will be soon and yet I am standing here clueless, confused, exhausted, brain dead, and totally puzzled. All I need is a shower, food and sleep.

Reet is on stage with her class. She's got the beat, the moves and the style as she shakes and swings her hips to the melodious upbeat songs of Bollywood. Reet is having the best time ever – no love for sports, no love for animals, no love for food, no hobbies, no reading, only music and dance. She is on a high.

Once more, Natalie and I sneak to the back of the stage, and for the 84th time search the four dressing rooms. There are no hidden doors or cupboards, only the usual mirrors with bright stage lights and a few wooden cupboards.

Suddenly we hear screams – and the music stops! We rush on to the stage, and there lying on the floor is Diya. Miss Hegde sprints across the stage, while teachers and students gather around, all talking at the same time. No one really knows what just happened. Reet edges over to me and mumbles softly, "Something fell from the top and hit Diya on her head."

I look up alarmed, and there sits Ahimsa on a high beam just below the ceiling, looking small and innocent straining his long neck towards a window. Reet slips something into my hand and goes back to her friends.

I turn white as a sheet, staring in horror at Ahimsa and then at the contents of my hand. With Natalie standing next to me, we watch as staff carry Diya off the stage.

Few minutes later, Miss Hegde announces, "Students, Diya is not seriously injured. I think she may have slipped on stage, and when she fell, bumped her head. Rehearsals are over for today, so please return to your rooms, have a quick shower and get ready for dinner."

Turning around, she spots Natalie and me standing near the curtain, white-faced and petrified as if we committed the crime.

"Pooja and Natalie," she calls out sweetly, "please check all stage lights are switched off, curtains drawn, and dressing room doors are locked before you leave."

Of course, I am suddenly wide awake and immediately we spring into action. Natalie and Reet usher the kids out of the hall as quickly as possible, while Ahimsa still sits high above the stage with a bird's eye view of everything going on.

Sitting behind the closed curtain, I look at the red stress ball in my hand. *"Why did he take the red stress ball from my desk and throw it on to the stage during rehearsal?"* I think to myself.

Ahimsa glides down softly and sits on the floor next to me. The hall is now darkened, curtains drawn, doors locked, lights off and Reet and Natalie join us. I am sure he can sense we're not exactly impressed with him, so he quickly says, "Sorry girls, but this was the only way I could get you alone to show you where the doors are!"

"What? Where? Why?" I mumble incoherently, spinning around on the dark stage.

"But Ahimsa, Diya could have gotten hurt," says Reet.

"No, Reet. A stress ball is not harmful and I wouldn't hurt anyone. It was meant to distract the rehearsal, not for her to fall in shock and sprain her ankle," he chuckles softly, "plus the rehearsal was going on for far too long!"

We all smile in the dark. From the time Ahimsa got shot, he has become strange!

"OK Ahimsa," whispers Natalie softly and gently, "show us the doors."

"You are sitting on it!" he whispers casually.

"What?" grumbles Reet crossly, "you are worse than the Magic Man."

He stands up and spreads his wings wide, growing larger than his usual size.

"Where? I can't see any latch or keyhole here," I say softly looking at this snowy white bird in confusion. His eyes grow bigger and begin to shine a bright white light on to the wooden floor. He bends his long neck to the floor and says quietly, "Look, when the wooden planks were fitted into the floor, they were not just cut and knocked in. Each row is staggered into different sizes or colours."

Looking totally disinterested and confused, we stare at this crazy swan. Why is he giving us a lecture on carpentry?

But Ahimsa takes his time to explain the entire process. He looks us momentarily and continues, "If you look at this exact spot where the trapdoor is located, the wooden planks are arranged differently."

We quickly fall to our knees and bend forward to see what he's talking about. Small dark and light wooden planks can be seen in a criss-cross pattern. With his beak, he loosens two planks of dark and light wood. In the empty gap is a symbol of a parasol.

"Pooja, place your ring finger inside this gap. As soon as it fits into the parasol, the invisible ring will turn green and you'll hear a click. Remove your hand immediately," he says gently.

I place right ring finger on top of the symbol. A green light shines brightly as it clicks. I remove my hand and almost immediately the symbol starts to rotate. Suddenly the wooden panelling shifts aside and we peep inside.

Natalie flashes the light from her mobile phone and we notice black marble steps leading downstairs. It is dark and empty.

Ahimsa whispers softly, "Quick, get inside." He immediately changes his size again and as we enter, the door closes behind him.

We can barely see anything, and again Natalie's mobile gives us enough light to show that we are inside a narrow passageway. Nestled inside Ahimsa's wings, we seem to be gliding through a long, windy, dark tunnel. Suddenly we stop. It is a dead end! The granite stone wall in front of us is black, unlike the discoloured ancient walls around us. Thick wooden beams criss-cross against the impenetrable granite wall.

"What is this?" asks Reet, "another trick?"

"No Reet," replies Ahimsa, "we all know there is a secret that lies beneath this fort and that is why it remained impregnable for hundreds of years. It is believed that ancient sages prayed in the Ganges River that this divine secret be protected from all evil. Ealdwinne mentioned in his journal, there was something more powerful than man protecting this fort. It was only after most of his men had mysteriously died, did Ealdwinne realise that maybe this unnatural misfortune that fell upon them was a result of that curse. Before he could abandon this project, he decided to build this wall and seal it off permanently to avoid further catastrophic tragedies to ever happen again."

"So what's on the other side?" I ask quietly. "I'm sure this passage doesn't end here."

"No, Pooja," replies Ahimsa. "There was a massive steel blast door built specially to protect and preserve the legacy of this king. Whenever the fort was under siege, the king and his family were smuggled underground and escaped through these steel blast doors to hidden chambers beneath the fort where they were kept safe."

"Wow!" whispers Reet so captivated by the story that she doesn't realise she is actually whispering.

"Girls," says Ahimsa, "directly above us is Dr. Malhotra's office.

I look up in total disbelief, "What? Is this for real?"

The ceiling stretches high up and in the darkness we can barely see the top. Natalie is aghast, "Why would Neal want the explosives to be planted in Dr. Malhotra's office?"

"Let me show you what they want, but first I want you to take out your lockets and drink the magic potion," Ahimsa replies. "This nectar will allow you to enter this forbidden palace."

As instructed by Ahimsa, I open the locket and rub the picture anti-clockwise. Magically, a tiny vial of amrit falls on to my palm. I break the seal and drink the contents. Both Natalie and Reet do the same.

"Pooja, place both your hands on the centre of the wall," instructs Ahimsa.

Without flinching, I push my hands against the wall.

Natalie, standing with Reet whispers, "Look, it's moving!" The thick granite wall creaks softly, moving slightly away from the sealed wall. Through a miniscule gap, I stare stupefied at the largest steel doors I have ever seen.

"Hare!" cries Reet, "how are we going to get through that door?"

Ahimsa shakes his long neck then looks up at us and says quietly, "That is why I told you to drink the amrit. Besides protection, it also gives you special powers to fly with me. The door is sealed, and the amrit will allow you to fly through steel and concrete without harming yourself."

"OMG! OMG!" cries Natalie.

"Come, we don't have much time," says Ahimsa.

I hear a faint whirring sound and within a blink of an eye we are swallowed up by the metal door. We find ourselves

271

inside a large, sparsely decorated room. "This was the king's secret room where weapons were stored for impending invasion. There are two concealed panels at the far corner of the room. Come, follow me!" announces Ahimsa as he flies towards the hidden panel on the left.

Alongside the panel I notice faded engravings. Ahimsa turns to me, "Pooja, look inside your locket, you will find a Sanskrit code that lights up. Press those numbers onto this hidden tablet." Looking very confused, I removed the chain from my neck and open the locket. I didn't know what Ahimsa was talking about but suddenly four numbers shone brightly - I press the numbers onto the small, clay tablet – the size of a mobile phone which glistened amidst the 3D engravings.

A door on the panel unlocks, and we find ourselves inside a lift surrounded by a thick metal wall. This lift is different however, it is round and has seats covered in animal fur. The door closes instantly. It is cold and dark, but a single green light flashes brightly at the top of the wall. Slowly the floor begins to swivel, and before we know it, we are moving downwards as if we're inside a mine shaft plummeting towards the abyss of the earth.

We scream as this strange machine descends like lightning into the mysterious darkness – going on forever and ever until suddenly the lift shudders slightly and stops. The green light now turns to red. The door opens. We remain seated, light-headed and woozy. Icy cold air hits us, and I clutch Reet's hand even tighter. There is an eerie, chilly silence, as if the ghosts from the past have come out to scrutinise us.

Ahimsa disappears into the darkness. Petrified, we rush after him into another dark corridor. And suddenly we find ourselves standing inside a magnificent, large circular hall with exquisite carvings and sculptures that seem to stand still with time – beautiful, pristine and elegant. Priceless paintings remain untouched on the faded wall, displaying the beauty and splendour of ancient times.

"This is one of the secret palaces which the King had built to safeguard his family." says Ahimsa.

Elevated pillars decked with intricate drawings, gem and gold paper are seen around the large hall. Walking through an archway we enter numerous chambers where gold and silver ornaments and richly adorned jewellery remain tucked away in old, dusty drawers and inside silver embellished boxes.

Ahimsa explains, "Millennium Corporation have information that these hidden palaces still exist with millions of dollars' worth of treasure. They have reached the sealed wall, but now realise that the only way to gain access into this forbidden palace is through Dr. Malhotra's office and into the passage."

"So this is the reason for the explosives," exclaims Natalie, touching an ivory and gold hairbrush delicately as she walks by.

Alongside the dark marble wall are colourfully carved wooden chest cupboards with curled handles. I stare at these weird handles that look like two brass stems of a light fitting. At the end of each stem is an intricately designed flower made of brass and bronze. It's really old and stained but has beautifully curled leaves embedded on either side of the flower.

"Wow, this is strange looking," I say curiously.

Reet, pushing me aside, grabs the handles and opens the door. "Yuck, it's so old fashioned. Look, who has those ugly handles inside the cupboard!"

"Reet, stop pushing me," I grumble as I move to the next cupboard. All six cupboards, covered in dust, have these strange handles inside.

Suddenly Natalie shouts from inside a cupboard, "Hey Pooja, my finger is stuck!"

I rush over to her, and of course stupid Reet is sitting inside the cupboard floor with Natalie trying to do some kind of acrobatic trick with the handles... and got her finger stuck inside a brass leaf.

Irritated with both of them, I push Reet aside and grab the handle which is old, rusty and firmly stuck into the metal. I try to bend the flower to the left and to the right to free Natalie's finger when suddenly both flower handles move simultaneously around like sunflowers bending towards the sun.

The back panel of the cupboard moves slightly and slides to one side. Instantly all six cupboards glide sideways. We all jump aside, our mouths drop open in shock.

"OMG!" cries Reet, "Check this out!"

On the marble wall in front of us is a huge, ancient, oil painting.

"OMG! This is the missing painting!" We stare in awe. This is the exact picture we had seen in the Rubik's Cube – the gigantic oil painting of an ancient fort the Magic Man wanted us to find. It is so huge that we step backwards to get a better look at the entire painting.

"Do you think this is how the original fort looked?" Natalie questions immediately.

"No idea, maybe... Look, it is built on many hills!" I say pointing towards mountainous ravines, rivers and hilltops.

"How big do you think this fort is?" asks Reet.

"It crosses through acres of land and goes all the way up to the mountains," I whisper in fascination as I stare up at the canvas.

"And there are different entrances," interrupts Natalie excitedly, and quickly adds, "ah, another entrance. That's two, let's see if we can find any more."

Ahimsa quickly interjects from behind, "Yes, I can see two more – and two huge gateways."

"Wow! This is a massive fort. So far we've counted six entrances..." replies Natalie.

"That must be the assembly hall, and there are... five different gardens..." I count quietly. "Generally the king meets all his people here, holds all royal meetings, and it's also a place where festivals of music and dance are held to entertain the royal family."

"Wow, how awesome!" cries Reet excitedly. "Pooja, I am sure it's like in the movie, *Jodha Akbar*. Do you remember where Hrithik addressed all his men..." and so she goes on until suddenly I shout, "Miss Aishwarya, (actress in the movie) stop being an idiot! We have no time for your Bollywood love story right now."

Poor Reet shuts up immediately. I do regret it, but at the moment I'm too stressed and this girl irritates me sometimes that I lose my temper. "Now that we have found the painting, what happens next?" I enquire turning to Ahimsa.

Natalie is taking photos with her camera from all angles, and I turn back to check if I can see anything different. After all the Magic Man said, find the ancient painting.

Then I hear a soft whisper next to me, "Pooja I can see Lord Ganesh next to a huge tree!"

"What?" I swing round to find Reet standing next to me, her huge, frightened eyes staring at the painting.

Reet stretches herself, but Ahimsa decides it's better if he carries her up. Using a pen from her pocket, she points to a place far away from the buildings towards the river. She is right... it is Lord Ganesh... way down the mountain near the riverside?

"Why was this statue built so far away from the fort? Is this the one we keep seeing in the cube?" I wander.

These unanswered questions baffle me even more, but we don't have time to work out another puzzle. Looking at my watch I quickly suggest, "Listen we are already late. Let's go before someone notices we are missing."

Ahimsa touches the handle with his beak. Immediately the painting disappears and the cupboards are back in their places.

"Pooja, we will have to come back to check this out," Natalie says excitedly."

And once again the ancient painting remains hidden.

I do have great news though! In exactly nine days, five hours and 43 seconds my school holidays begin. Yippee! I can't wait!

Chapter 20

Dear Diary,

Today is our annual Kite Festival. It is still dark and cold outside, and the golden sun hasn't yet emerged from its deep slumber, but we are already on the rooftop of our school building. Everyone is rushing around in warm hooded jackets and track pants. Colourful kites in different shapes and sizes flash pass me.

Kites unpacked, strings checked and few last minute touch-ups are hastily completed. Bloody hell! Who thought kite flying could be this competitive and intense? I thought it was about having fun.

Well let me tell you how serious this particular festival, in our school, actually is. The competition has three main categories: first are the teams that hijack the most number of kites; second is staying afloat in the air for the longest period of time; and third is the most creatively designed kite. I love the team names too – Google, Yahoo, Hotmail, Facebook, Twitter, Instagram and WhatsApp. Now that is what I call real COOL!

Already there are hundreds of kites flying from nearby villages and peals of laughter echo across to the valley whenever a kite is cut down. It seems everyone in the village also decided to fly kites with us today.

"Thank heavens tomorrow is Sunday!" screams Reet loudly.

I am having so much fun that I've completely forgotten about explosives, criminals or paintings. We begin our competition as soon as the deep red glow of the wintry sun peers over the horizon. Immediately the ochre sky turns into a vista of colours as bright messages of global warming flutter majestically. Messages of forestation, solar heating, pollution and recycling wave triumphantly. Endangered animals like polar bears, humpback whales, penguins, and rhinos are lifted gracefully by the icy winds. Shouts of laughter sweep across the terrace as students gaze up into the majestic, cloudless skies, screaming with joy or sadness whenever strings are cut. Long tails flutter and sway in the breeze as they dip their way towards the ground and disappear between tall trees and buildings. Some kites float aimlessly without tails and after a few minutes vanish into the nearby forests.

Just then Natalie nudges me and points across to the terrace of Gandhi Hostel. Selina is walking towards Mr. VJS. With the noise around them, he bends his head closer to hear what she is saying.

"She doesn't look like a happy lady," whispers Natalie.

With huge black sunglasses and a black duffel bag slung over her shoulder, she storms off hurriedly. Mr. VJS hesitates momentarily, and looks around him casually before following her.

Just then Kash grabs me. "Hey girls, chill and stop looking so serious. You're missing the best."

I turn my head to see the dazzling colours of kites launched from the boys' hostel. Large bold messages like Trees for India, strange and vibrant shapes of motor vehicles, trucks, large signs saying Cut off Emission, and It's Cool to be Green fly majestically against the amber skies.

We laugh, clap and scream at the top of our voices as we read the different messages aloud. The humpback whale floats proudly avoiding the hijackers who are trying to nip it. Some kites come down even before taking off, while others struggle for a short while before being cut down by their opponents.

I watch the sky glow in a rainbow of colours when Reet comes storming towards us mumbling under her breath.

"Guess what! I hope our team loses this year," she curses angrily. "Our Miss Perfect leader, Sonalika, and her mates think they know it all. What nonsense yaar!"

"What happened Reet?" enquires Kash caringly. Of course, Reet can't stop ranting, "She just won't give me a chance to fly the kite, yet all the others in our team have had a chance."

Reet smacks her head with her hand as she stares up at the sky. "That idiot, Indira, the Miss-second-in-charge leader is too damn bossy." Staring at us with her frightfully large and angry eyes, she shouts furiously, "Do you know what she did? She pushed me away and said I am too short to fly a kite!"

Kash, Natalie and I try to keep a serious face as our friend goes berserk with rage.

"Idiots! They are just idiots. This is all I can say. I rest my case!"

"You should have insisted Reet," comments Natalie, just to irritate her even more.

"What?" Reet whispers indignantly. With her two hands on her hips just like Aunty Jolly, and her eyes rolling upwards in anger, she shakes her head from side to side, "Do you think they will ever give me a chance to contribute to anything?"

"No! We have everything under control," she mimics Sonalika.

"Reet, don't stress," interrupts Kash, "just calm down and have some fun."

Reet stares at her as if she's mad.

"I think Indians here are toooooo serious," laughs Kash, "it's not only a competition, you know!"

Laughing loudly, Natalie nods in agreement, "Exactly!"

Reet glowers at us for a second, mumbles in Hindi about what crazy people these foreigners are, then turns and storms off in a huff.

Ignoring her, I giggle loudly, "Poor Reet. With her temper, she's definitely going to miss the yummiest breakfast!"

Giving everyone a high five, we move over to the tables laden with sandwiches and hot milk, idly, vada, chutneys and sambar, fruit and lots of savoury snacks.

"This school rocks!" shouts Natalie and Kash. Kites decorate the blue sky with vibrant colours dancing in the cool breeze like coloured powder during Holi Festival.

Sanam rushes over to us with a huge grin on her face, "OMG! The TV reporters have arrived!" Just then the loudspeaker crackles announcing our team, Yahoo. I clap eagerly. At last it's our turn. You should see us. Breakfast discarded, we sprint across the terrace to grab our kite. We have been waiting patiently – and now can't wait to show off our message.

"*Let's see what the judges think?*" I think to myself proudly as I open the box. It is empty! The box is empty! OUR KITE IS MISSING! Kash, Sanam, Natalie and I stare in aghast.

We have spent hours designing our Food for India kite, showing poverty in rural areas. In panic I screech in a high-pitched voice, "Where is our kite?"

"I don't know," both Natalie and Sanam cry, looking around confused.

Kash is shouting hysterically, "Where's our kite! This can't be happening!" Her whole body begins to tremble. Her eyes go all funny and large, her hands shake in a strange panic rhythm as if she's about to start break dancing. Sanam grabs her quickly whilst teachers nearby rush to see what the problem is.

Nats and I are rummaging under tables, pushing away kites lying on the terrace. By now everyone has joined in the search. Where could the kite mysteriously have disappeared to?

"Yahoo team, we are waiting for your kite," calls the announcer.

All I can do is stand there, ready to have a nervous breakdown. My eyes begin to fill with tears. One look at me and Natalie rushes to inform Mr. Walters about our missing kite. Chaos suddenly reigns in our team! Nurse Geeta arrives to check on Kash.

Through my tears, I watch Sanam talking quickly to the teachers, "Kash is having an anxiety attack! She needs something cold to drink and to be somewhere quiet." They all nod their heads. Nurse Geeta escorts Kash down the stairs and away from the noise.

As for me, I stare stupidly around. My brain is in overdrive, but my body is rooted to the ground. Minutes tick by. Dead in my tracks. Frozen still!

OK! Kash is having a panic attack. Understood!

What do you call my ridiculous problem! I'm definitely abnormal! Or weird! Or strange or peculiar!

Whatever bizarre word you want to describe me right now, please use it! It will be so appropriate!

Focus, Pooja, focus! Right now there are bigger problems.

Our kite is missing-

Thank the Lord, my loyal friend Reet appears amidst this confusion, takes one look at me, grabs my elbow and walks me to a chair. Ignoring everyone's strange looks, she shouts loudly as if I am deaf and stupid, "Pooja, look up at the sky and check if someone is flying your kite. Do that while I will get you some lemonade. Do you understand?"

Before I can react, she disappears into the crowd while I glare at the blue sky. Our kite was larger than most with a massive Food for India sign across the entire kite. Gulping the sweet lemonade is definitely the answer to my crisis! Whenever I get into a stupid state, Reet is always there to rescue me with five spoons of sugar in a glass of lemonade! I think she sneaks in another three spoonful's just for sugar overload!

Just then Mrs. Roy arrives with Natalie. "I'm sure someone may have accidently taken it."

"I can't see it anywhere," says Sanam scrutinising the kites in the air.

Miss Hegde arrives and one look at our hysterical team, says calmly, "Listen girls, don't panic, we will give you a chance to participate when you find the kite."

Still looking confused and dazed, we simply nod our heads.

Natalie storms across to Sonalika's group. She has a sneaky feeling their team may have sabotaged the kite. Reet – like a true detective – follows her discreetly, a few paces behind, dodging between students and teachers. Anjali and Sonalika screech with laughter, listening to Indira dramatizing Kash's panic attack.

As for me, the sugar has kicked in. I am back! Diya arrives, limping but happy to join in our search, checking every nook and corner and going through empty boxes lying around. "Pooja, I know it's Sonalika. No one else can be so nasty," she says crossly.

"I remember her giggling like mad when we discovered our kite was missing," I reply calmly, refusing to panic or have one of my crazy, weird attacks again.

Meanwhile, Reet is lurking around Sonalika, having remembered her whispering something about saving the best for last. Whatever that means!

Like a true Chandigarh detective, Reet follows the girls around. Just then Sonalika's phone rings. Reet tries to get closer to hear the conversation, but of course with Mrs. Roy munching on a plateful of pakodas in front of her, what chance does she have of hearing anything?

Reet watches Sonalika whisper something to Indira and Anjali, and both girls nod their heads and rush towards the stairs. Reet tails them back to our hostel, and like two thieves they enter the common room. Standing quietly in the passage, she hears cupboard doors opening and closing. She quickly hides behind a sofa, and a few minutes later the girls emerge carrying two big black, plastic bags.

"What idiots! Why are they carrying dirt bags?" Reet thinks to herself stealing a glance from her hiding place. This doesn't make sense... so she follows them through the corridors, down the stairs towards the administration building and into the management offices. They stop in front of Mr. VJS office, knock once and enter.

Looking around fearfully, "OMG! I have to hide." She dives under the secretary's desk. Everything is quiet.

"If I get caught, my life will be over!" she whispers to herself as she presses her palms together in prayer. "Lord Ganesh, I can't close my eyes. I'm on guard. I don't know the words of any mantra, but whatever it is, I ditto that!" She pauses, looks up again and quickly mumbles, "Just to let you know... I'm really scared."

Suddenly the thundering voice of the one and only enemy, Mr. VJS rings loudly across the empty office. Reet shivers uncontrollably!

She thinks quickly. Does she phone Natalie or do something by herself? Too nervous to fumble with her mobile, she slides on her tummy towards his door and hears the shuffling sound of the bin bags. Then Mr. VJS laughs in his wheezy, unpleasant voice, "Good, put the stupid kite into that corner locker. That should teach those girls a lesson." The girls giggle awkwardly, sounding ever so chuffed with themselves.

"What about my folder?" he asks in all seriousness.

"Sir, we searched Reet's room and found nothing. We think it may be in Pooja's room," replies Indira.

Reet is now fuming with anger, and her big eyes grow even larger. "Those girls stole the kite! OMG! Damn crooks, rogues!" she swears softly.

"Yes, yes, I know that, but I thought you were going to check her room while the girls were busy flying their kites?"

"We will definitely search tonight, Sir," replies Anjali.

"Girls, listen carefully," his voice turns into a deep menacing threat, "I want the folder now. Do you understand?"

Both girls remain silent. Seeing their reaction, Mr. V's voice quickly softens and laughs lightly, "What I mean is, Sonalika will get the Student of the Year prize if she works with me. She promised to get the folder."

"Yes Sir, we will get it immediately!" quivers their frightened voices. Anjali then adds softly, "Sir, we also found something else Reet is hiding."

"Yes, yes, what is it?" he shouts impatiently.

Reet hears the shuffling of plastic again and the next minute Mr. VJS laughs loudly, "Ah! Good work ladies, this will help build my case against Sarabji. Lock it inside that cupboard. I will sort it out later. Now go!"

Reet rushes down the passage and into the reception room. Incensed with rage and every possible form of anger, she dives behind a large sofa. Within seconds she hears them scurry down the passage and leave the building.

Reet remains frozen, too afraid to move in case VJS appears. Terrified and fuming mad, she moves her hand in the form of a cross and whispers desperately, "Please God, help me get out of here alive! The last thing I need right now is to get caught," she mumbles to herself. The next moment, as predicted, she hears a door close, a key turns and footsteps coming in her direction. Holding her breath, eyes shut, she shoves herself flat against the sofa. Luck is on her side as he quickly rushes past and out the building.

For a full five minutes Reet remains frozen behind the sofa before jumping up and bolting down the corridor at the speed of lightning and out of the administration building as if the devil is after her.

Oops! Actually, out of nowhere, the devil appears. This time he is accompanied by a stranger in a black trench coat, holding a walking stick. Reet stops, stares for a full second, then makes a U-turn into the garden where the sprinkler is on. Terrified of Mr. VJS and his scrooge, Reet sprints across the wet grass, over the fence and past the auditorium. Abruptly she stops, then slips through the door and sits in between the chairs to catch her breath. Just then a large hand clamps over her mouth. Reet tries to wrestle herself free, but her wrists are pulled behind her back and tied.

Meanwhile, back on the rooftop, the biggest miracle has just happened!

Mrs. Roy found a spare kite in her office and gave it to us. "Well Pooja, tell me you now believe in good karma," says Sanam.

Once again our team breaks into another dance move, hugging and swaying together!

"Where's the kite?" Kash calls out happily as she joins us.

"We haven't seen it yet. Mrs. Roy is keeping it safe," Natalie shouts happily. "Actually, we don't care what it looks like, as long we fly a kite."

"Hey girls," I shout loudly looking around, "has anyone see Reet?"

"OMG! Where is she?" replies Nats standing on her toes and scanning the terrace. Then looks at me and says quietly, "Let me send her a text."

Knowing Reet is always so inquisitive and loves hanging around where the action is, I didn't bother much about finding her.

Throughout the day, colourful kites dot the sky, and each time a kite falls, shouts echo amidst loud music and chatting. The TV crew are everywhere, joining in the spirit of such a grand and colourful festival.

The school building – as a backdrop to the festival – is also decorated beautifully, with vibrant-coloured marigolds and chrysanthemum garlands hanging gracefully from doorways and hallways.

At the centre of the Sarva Dharma, a rangoli competition is going on. Students play artistically with an array of bright, multi-coloured powders and fresh flowers, creatively shaping the most unique designs ever, while judges walk around each piece of artwork admiring the talent.

On the open field, a stage has been set up for the junior dance team competition. And to keep everyone sustained, tables around the school are kept filled with special festival sweets of sesame and jaggery rolled into balls, and trays of milkshakes and fresh fruit juices, all prepared by the school catering team.

By late afternoon, hundreds and hundreds of colourful kites dot the clear, blue sky as the wind carries them high above the clouds. At last our team is called – again. Natalie and I carry the sealed box to the front of the terrace, followed by all our friends. As I remove the kite, I stop for a second and stare in shock. It is in the shape of a giant fan.

"Who did this painting," whispers Miss Hegde coming closer.

"I don't know," I whisper softly. There are gasps of surprise and disbelief around us. The entire fan is a painting of a scene from the tsunami tragedy. The background is deep blue, and trees, vehicles, houses, boats and animals painted in dramatic, vibrant colours are being carried away by the sea. People and children crying and filled with fear look so alive yet tragic. How did the painter capture such a horrific moment from one of the worst natural disasters in the history of the world?

I quickly explain, "Mrs. Roy found this box lying on the kitchen counter this morning. She checked with team leaders to see if all their kites were in, then decided to bring it here in case something went wrong with a kite belonging to one of our teams."

"Wow! Thank heavens! This is a stunning piece of artwork," says Dr. Malhotra who joins the judges for the kite poster competition. The judges stand around the mystery kite commenting on the graphic details... the expressions of fear and helplessness on the faces of the people in the water... the colours that blend with the background of the massive wave on the brink of swallowing everything.

"I wonder who painted this?" says Mr. Vikram, the Maths teacher. "It looks so real."

"Look at the tail?" says Miss Davis. "There are bows of material shaped like an arrow. How very strange."

Waiting impatiently for the judges to finish, we quickly grab the kite. Just then the wind picks up and the kite immediately rises up into the early evening sky. Even the fading sun seems to pause for a moment to share in the beauty of this giant fan majestically floating on to the golden, magical platform. As it glides up higher, the kite spreads out like a gigantic screen over the expansive, orange sky. Teachers and students stand gazing in wonder, recalling events they remembered on that dark day. Its long, colourful tail waves from side to side, cutting off kites gliding nearby.

Strangely the sky becomes a battlefield as more kites go down as they face the challenge of the intruder fan kite. Kash, Sanam, Natalie and I take turns to hold the rod which seems to demand more string as it soars proudly into the evening sky.

I notice Sonalika talking to Mr. VJS, as they gaze angrily towards the sky.

The gigantic fan kite dominates the amber sky, gracefully rising higher and higher as if reaching out to the stars. Suddenly it begins to glow with magical lights, and everyone stares in bewilderment.

In the darkness amidst twinkling stars there are only two kites left. The fan and Sonalika's kite.

Dr. Malhotra looks at his watch, walks over to where Mr. Vikram and Mr. Walters are standing and whispers, "This should be over now. Are the fireworks ready, Mr. Vikram?"

"Yes, Sir," nods Mr. Vikram.

A grand fireworks display is about to take place to mark the end of a beautiful Kite Festival. But, the fan kite is in no hurry, swaying and dancing amongst the glittering stars that slowly emerge to peek at this mystical scene.

Sonalika and her friends cheer loudly as she pulls and tugs the string to get closer to the fan kite. I take the reins from Natalie and watch the fan kite play hide and seek, as it eludes, bends and sways, rising up and then gliding down away from its opponent. Shouts of frustration from the far end of the terrace are heard as Sonalika forcefully pulls the string forward and then backwards, hoping to tangle the opponent.

All the boys from their hostel join us on the terrace. Teja stands proudly with his friends cheering me on.

Just then Sonalika's kite dangles limply as the tail gets cut. Everyone screams with joy, even the teachers are applauding. From far below us, the villagers are whistling, clapping and drums beat loudly and rhythmically.

But Sonalika's voice screeches, "Look! It's not down yet! My kite is still flying!" staring at me furiously with angry dark eyes. "I will win this competition!"

Suddenly a huge white bird appears in the sky, and flies closer and closer towards the kite. It soars high into the sky and touches the fan kite. The kite slowly closes up – just like a real fan – and becomes an arrow. Even though I am still holding the string, I don't seem to have any control... the kite seems to be doing its own thing!

Everyone is speechless! And then, as if in slow motion, the fan kite with the strange white bird guiding it, heads directly towards Sonalika's kite. It flies through her kite tearing it into small pieces of coloured paper that fall like tiny broken rainbows. Fireworks light up the sky.

With incensed rage, Sonalika screams hysterically, waving her arms around madly and stomping her feet furiously. Teachers and students clap and cheer as once again the last remaining kite soars up into the sky. And then it stops – and as if paying homage to the thousands of people who died so tragically that fateful morning – it unfolds once again and with stars sparkling in the dark sky, takes its final bow.

Just then Dr. Malhotra announces over the microphone, "Pooja, Sanam, Kash and Natalie from Yahoo team are this year's winners. Give them a round of applause, ladies and gentleman. A beautiful kite ends this amazing Kite Festival."

As is tradition, the winners cut the string and we watch our magical kite soar away into the cloudless dark night.

The firework display officially begins. Thunderous crackers burst into a frenzy of deafening noise with explosive and glittering lights brightening up the darkened sky. The terrace is over-crowded and as we move downstairs to the large open ground, I search for Reet's golliwog hair amidst the crowd.

"*This is so strange.*" I think to myself, "*I hope she is not sleeping in her room. Reet is famous for staying in bed whenever she is angry or sulking.*"

A huge white tent has been set up with tables of delicious vegetable rice, noodles, salads and manchurians.

I am exhausted, but the thrill of winning is the best thing ever! I am so excited. All our friends sit on the grass talking excitedly about our amazing day as we tuck into our favourite foods.

"I don't think I will ever forget this day," says Sanam, looking proudly at her friends.

"Our kite was the best," quips Kash, "but where did it come from?"

Still confused, Natalie shakes her head, "No idea. And did you see the size of it when it opened up in the sky. It was the size of a movie screen!"

Suddenly Sanam looks at me and asks in alarm, "Hey, where's Reet?"

I stop eating, "I haven't seen her all afternoon." I look around anxiously! Kash quickly interrupts, "Don't stress, Pooja, she was so angry with her team, I'm sure she's helping the teachers in the junior classes."

"Not helping, thrilling them with her antics, of course!" laughs Natalie.

"As long as she doesn't teach those kids how to swear and she stays out of trouble, I am happy." I smile.

Just then Teja appears with his friends bearing bottles of 7UP and bowls of fruit salad with my favourite kulfi ice-cream. Smiling happily, they shout in unison, "For the winning team, dessert is served," and they plonk themselves down on to the grass next to us.

Sitting next to me, Teja quietly says, "Listen to *our* story. Our kite was shredded to pieces and left inside our box. We didn't even know until our team was called."

All of us shout aloud, "OMG!"

"What a dirty trick!" cries Sanam in alarm, "but why sabotage our kites?"

"I think they forget it's not only about competing, but also about having fun," chips in Colin.

"So true!" Kash and Natalie say together as they give the boys a high five.

We thought we had problems when our kite disappeared. We remain silent, seething as we listen to Teja talking.

I am beginning to worry about Reet. I haven't seen her since we discovered our kite was missing, and she's missed out on the best part of the day. I have an uneasy feeling about this.

Suddenly we hear a loud sound like thunder... and the ground rumbles and begins to shake. Students are suddenly quiet, then in the distance someone shouts, "Earthquake!" The ground trembles once again! Students begin to scream in panic.

Jumping up, we stare at the confusion as students are running away from Nehru Hostel.

Just then we hear the voice of Dr. Malhotra over the intercom. "Students, please remain seated on the ground. This is an emergency. Do not leave without the permission of a staff member."

Dark smoke can be seen rising from one of the buildings. Mr. Walters takes the microphone and very calmly but firmly states, "All staff, there has been an accident. Please come and stand in front of this podium. Students, please form a line in front of your class teacher so we can check that every student is present."

"OMG!" we shout, leaving our dinner on the ground as we head towards the podium.

Kash shouts, "Teja look, smoke coming from Nehru House! I wonder if there's a fire!" We stare in shock! Black smoke billows in the dark.

Teja and his friends rush across the grounds to help some of the children. And then we hear the final announcement that makes me want to faint!

"Students, there has been a blast of some kind in Nehru House. It's very dangerous to go anywhere near it right now. Remain in this ground and get into your classes so staff can take register. Please check that all your class friends are with you. All senior students, both boys and girls, please report to Mr. VJS and Mr. Walters immediately!"

Tears roll down my cheeks as I stare at Natalie. That was an explosion! These criminals bombed the hostel while the firework display was on.

Natalie holds my hand tightly, as we hear the sounds of police sirens approaching.

Sanam whispers behind me, "Pooja, don't cry! Dr. M said 'blast'. It may just be a gas cylinder that exploded."

Unable to tell them the truth, I blurt out in panic, "I have no idea where Reet is! Let's look for her!"

We scatter quickly and search the grounds amidst the chaos, smoke and people. She is nowhere. Usually she would be coming to tell us the latest breaking news she had heard from the staff. But she is nowhere to be found!

"Something has happened to Reet!" I weep loudly as I turn to my friends.

OMG! SHE IS MISSING!

From somewhere in the darkness, Teja grabs my hand, "What's going on?"

"Reet is missing. She hasn't been seen since early this afternoon," I cry hysterically, "what if something has happened to her?"

"Get Satya quickly, he will know!" he whispers calmly. "Let me tell Colin I am with you."

At that moment I spot Mrs. Roy wobbling towards us holding a few children's hands. Kash and I sprint across, and breathlessly tell her my story.

"No, no! Not that child! Kash, take these children to their teacher, and stay with them. They are frightened."

Turning to me, she says urgently, "Come with me Pooja, let's look in her room."

I am shaking like a leaf, my lips tremble with fear, and my legs are weak and wobbly!

Sniffling quietly, I follow Mrs. Roy. Already the school grounds are buzzing with security guards, policemen and firemen! There's pandemonium everywhere! Students are screaming, and teachers and staff are moving the students to safety.

Our hostel is deathly silent! As soon as Mrs. Roy opens Reet's room door, we stand aghast! Books are scattered all over the floor, her mattress is lying against the wall, and the bedlinen, shoes and clothing are thrown inside her bathroom.

"Oh baap re!" cries Mrs. Roy, "someone has broken into this room!"

Mrs. Roy gets on her phone and quickly calls security. I know in my heart something is wrong. Reet is in danger. I start to cry... no... sob hysterically. Tears spill down my face as I stare around the messy room.

Where is Pudding? Has he been taken as well? This is all my fault. This is because of my stupid karma. My best friend has gone. Where have they taken her to?

I know it is Mr. VJS. He's the only man capable of doing something as cruel as this. But where do I start searching for her? I hold my face with both hands as tears flow unashamedly, and I slowly fall down to the floor.

"Pooja, beta, don't cry! We will find her!"

My sobs grow louder. I am hysterical. "*If only you knew what I know!*" I messed up!

Why didn't I tell an adult? How was I to know that Selina would plan this explosion today?

Mrs. Roy holds me tightly against her huge bosom, "Pooja, even I am worried. I hope security comes quickly. They are all so busy with the bomb blast in Nehru House."

I push her aside and stutter in panic, "What? How? When?"

Tears stop! Sobs disappear! I am alert! Sitting bolt upright, I stare at her in astonishment.

"Please don't tell anyone I told you, Pooja," she whispers softly as if the walls have ears. "Yes, someone tried to bomb Nehru House, but it didn't go off properly! It fizzled out and there was just a lot of smoke."

"Is anyone hurt?" I ask anxiously. The last thing I want now is to feel even guiltier.

"No, the strangest thing happened. Police have now found a cellar inside the basement of Nehru House. Apparently the blast shattered a portion of the floor. How strange! No damage to the hostel."

"Is that where the smoke is coming from?" I ask anxiously.

Mrs. Roy nods her head and gently explains, "Pooja, that hostel has been part of this fort for hundreds of years, and in all this time we have worked here, no one has ever found a cellar."

As soon as she pauses, I quickly interrupt, "Mrs. Roy, why don't we check our room. Maybe Reet is there."

"Good idea Pooja, let's go," as she takes my hand.

As if things can't get any worse.

As soon as we enter my room, we find drawers all over the floor, clothes strewn all over the place, and our laundry basket upside down in the shower. Shoes, books and toiletries are everywhere! Once again, from the doorway, we stare around in horror. From the corner of my eye, I suddenly see a slight movement behind the curtain. Mrs. Roy calls security again.

Too terrified to move, I glance around praying my things hidden beneath the tiles have not been stolen.

"Pooja, security will be here soon. I'm going to check that the other rooms have not been broken into. You quickly tidy up the room and go back to the grounds. Don't worry about Reet, I have already informed Dr. Malhotra. OK?"

I nod my head – couldn't ask for anything better right now.

As soon as she leaves, I lock the door and rush to the window. Satya and Ahimsa hop on to my desk. Before I can say a word, Satya says quickly, "Pooja, Reet is abducted. She went to investigate the missing kite and was caught. Let's meet Teja, he has the Rubik's Cube."

Tears roll down my cheeks as I blubber furiously, "OMG! How did this happen? Criminals, kidnappers, date changing. What's going on?"

Satya replies softly, "Pooja, the Magic Man said these people are dangerous, and remember Selina doesn't care about who gets hurt. For now Reet is safe, but we have to rescue her. Millennium Corporation discovered a cellar below Nehru House. Inside the cellar was a trapdoor, leading to an underground tunnel to hidden chambers beneath the auditorium. When the blast occurred, Ahimsa and I managed to defuse the bomb, so only the floor of the cellar fell apart and not the entire building. Mr. VJS's men found the trapdoor and are heading towards the auditorium.

"Can you imagine how many students would have been hurt if that bomb had gone off in Nehru House," I exclaim in shock! "OMG! This is all too much."

I call Teja and tell him to meet us at our usual meeting place. Nestled inside Satya, we swoop up and fly across the huge grounds and down towards the fountain. Inside the dark alcove Teja is waiting, pacing the floor as he looks around nervously.

We sit behind the thick, overgrown hedge while Satya updates him. Teja takes out the Rubik's Cube and immediately the green light begins to glow as it glides up and starts to rotate. The first picture is Lord Ganesh. Next a flashing sign fills the screen like a bunting hanging from the clouds with the cryptic words, "***Beneath the tail that fell from the dark blue sky lies the secret!***"

"Not another code!" I say aloud, angry that even in times of a crisis, we have to still find stupid answers from these stupid codes.

Teja is so incensed he blurts out, "What bloody tail? Does this Magic Man think we have nothing else to do but play games?"

"Teja, from the beginning I said this destiny thing was all nonsense! And now Reet's life is in danger!" Tears roll down my cheeks shamelessly.

At this moment, all I want to do is stand on a mountain top and scream until my lungs hurt. I cannot even describe the fear and pain I feel knowing that Reet is missing.

Just then Natalie arrives and Teja blurts out the latest. Satya interrupts us, "Look, that picture is where the forest is. We flew over there this morning! Right Ahimsa?"

Ahimsa lifts his head and says quietly, "Yes but now we have two big problems. One is the auditorium, and the other is finding Reet. What shall we do? Both are urgent!"

"We have to find Reet," I butt in crossly, "let the police sort out the explosives. I really don't care."

Teja and Nats nod their heads. The green light continues to flash on the floating cube. "I suppose we have to decode this cryptic code to find Reet," mumbles Nats looking upset and frustrated.

"What can fall from the sky besides birds or planes?" I ask.

Natalie stares at the cube before whispering, "Teja, make it bigger please. Don't you think it could be another type of tail – for example, a kite tail?"

"What?" both Teja and I exclaim in unison. Teja touches the cube again and it flickers brighter, but this time it looks like a virtual tour on a geographical TV channel. We stare at images of broken ruins lying discarded across the vast land. Buildings like temples with broken statues lay abandoned and forgotten inside the thick, dark forest. And then we see a long tail hanging from a huge tree.

Suddenly Natalie shouts, "Look, there's a kite flying across that tree!"

"OMG! OMG! What if this is true? We could find Reet!"

"It is the same kite and same tail, Pooja," says Satya quietly, "I flew with the kite, remember? The kite fell somewhere near the forest. It could have landed on that tree."

I suddenly jump up and hug him tightly, "I knew it was you! Thank you for making us win that competition."

Natalie chuckles softly, "That was just awesome!"

"Guys, can you finish that later," grumbles Teja, "we have to find Reet."

Ahimsa looks at Satya, "You take them in the Ojas. It's quicker and faster. I'm going to check out the auditorium.

"Who is Ojas?" Nats asks in bewilderment.

Satya answers quickly, "The name of the auto rickshaw, Natalie!"

"Great, can we go now pleasssssse!" I cry impatiently. The swans nod their heads, and as if by some strange, unexplainable magic, Auto Ojas suddenly appears inside the alcove. We jump inside our famous purple and orange auto rickshaw and within seconds are airborne flying across the expansive land far away from school.

Soon we find ourselves staring at a beautiful waterfall with its white, foamy waters tumbling down a mountainside over the rocks and into a river. And then we enter a dark, shadowy forest, as thick mist slowly seeps around us obscuring our vision. Ojas wobbles dangerously as it descends slowly on to a deserted grassy field.

Teja, shining a torch in front of us, leads the way through the silent, dark woods, pushing away thorny branches that swept across our path. I can hear the rustling sound of the wind on the swaying treetops, and am terrified out of my wits. But right now I don't have time to think about my fears. I have to rescue Reet.

Satya flies next to me, "It's not far, Pooja! The kite is just after we climb that little hill."

"Thank God," I mumble, trying not to look at the dark, spooky surroundings. And soon enough, we reach the top and land on the soft ground.

Surrounded by wild forests, we look down the steep cliff covered by dense groves of tall trees and thick vegetation. Satya hovers over us, his wings flapping against the strong wind. "Look down to those trees at the bottom of that valley," he says, "the kite is hanging on one of those trees. Let me go and check and then you can follow."

Teja quickly hops on to a boulder and stares intently as Satya disappears into the darkness shrouded by mist and thick, lush trees. Both Natalie and I strain our eyes searching for Satya or any sign of the kite. Suddenly we hear the flapping of wings, and almost immediately we spot the long tail dangling from a tall tree.

"Let's follow Satya," shouts Teja, as we jump down and head towards the trees.

We stop and stare at the largest, most massive tree I have ever seen. The thick, woody trunk of this humongous tree is monstrous. Our kite is draped over the top of the tree like a tablecloth, with its long tail dangling out of sight. As we follow the tail that snakes its way down, we are shocked to find it resting at the foot of a Ganesh statue. My jaw drops! Natalie jumps forward to push the thick shrubbery away from the coppery metal statue. I burst into tears. Lightning flashes across the sky. For hundreds of years, this sacred statue had been hidden. But now, I am so hysterical I cannot stop the tears from rolling down my already wet face.

"Teja do you know what this means?" I cry loudly. "The Magic Man is right! This is my destiny!"

The snowball, the Rubik's Cube, the journal and all the cryptic codes are real, not some mumbo-jumbo fantasy tale. Teja holds me as the silvery rain showers down from the dark skies mingling with my hot, salty tears.

"Pooja, look at these leaves. This is the peepal tree!" says Natalie.

Startled, Teja and I sit next to her and stare at the thick, leathery, heart-shaped leaves. "This is the Tree of Enlightenment!" she whispers as she picks up a leaf lying on the statue and hands it to me.

As I turn the shiny leaf over, my ring begins to glow and gold writing becomes visible on the leaf, "***The sound of my conch will lead you to the missing link.**"*

"This is just like the journal," says Teja excitedly looking at both of us. "Do you think it is telling us to use the conch to find Reet?"

Natalie and I stare blankly – utterly confused!

Satya nods his long neck! "Yes Teja, Pooja was destined to find this Tree first. This is where her journey begins and a place where information will be imparted to her."

"Hang on a second!" I say looking around the tree, "and where is the conch?"

Bewildered Natalie and Teja jump up.

I grin in the dark as I shout happily, "Silly fools! It's here!"

As I place my finger on the metal conch firmly fixed on to Ganesh's hand, it magically changes to a pale white porcelain shell. Once again as history repeats itself, we hear the soft hum from inside the conch.

With trepidation, I carry it carefully in both hands, the soft sound wafting through the forest as we make our way back to Ojas.

As soon as Ojas lands inside the alcove, leaves and trees begin to reverberate with the sound. Satya then carries us under his wings and as we fly through the grounds to the hostels and canteen, the sound grows louder. Brightly lit lights everywhere – sirens blast and blue lights flash all over the school grounds while the students are still seated inside the big white tent.

"That means she is somewhere here," whispers Natalie nervously hoping we will find Reet on time.

Just as we arrive at the auditorium, the conch begins to vibrate, making the most deafening sound. Satya flies around the large auditorium but everything seems quiet and still. There is no sign of Mr. VJS or his men or Reet.

"I don't like this," says Satya, and immediately we fly through the trapdoor and into the narrow passageway. Satya stops at the sealed wall, red lights are blinking brightly. "What is happening?" I whisper to Teja, "There's no one around."

But there on the wall, are four explosives attached to a timer ominously ticking away.

"OMG!" I grab Teja's hand. This is the first time I am actually staring at real explosives! Besides my spasho attack, I think I am heading for any other attack right now which medical science has never even heard of.

"The men must have come through the trap door and into the tunnel to plant these explosives," says Satya.

"We have to tell Dr. M," cries Natalie urgently, "this is serious!"

"Yes we will, Nats, but first let's check if we can find Reet," replies Teja, no longer arguing about outside help.

My mind is racing, "*Like really! Would that help? We are stuck in a passageway going nowhere WITH A BOMB TICKING AWAY!*" *Every part of my body is shaking with fear. I can't think straight.*

And then I hear voices! Someone is coming back into this passage!

As usual in a crisis, I can't talk. Can't think. Can't do anything. I stare furiously at my brother pacing the narrow floor scratching his head hoping to come up with a plan.

The next moment Satya sweeps all three of us into his wings and we disappear into an empty, dark chamber. Does anyone else realise that right now we could have a bomb going off, and we're locked up in some dungeon... and no one knows our whereabouts!

"Put your mobile light on, Teja, what's wrong with you?" I hiss angrily staring at both these idiots sitting like shadows against the dark wall.

"Who's there?" the voice of Mr. VJS booms from behind the wall, sending shudders down my spine. Teja grabs my hand tightly.

"Listen Mr. V, we don't have time for you to investigate any noise. This place is going to blow up in 20 minutes! So let's get out of here now!" a strange voice echoes arrogantly.

"This will certainly get rid of your problem anyway!" laughs another deep voice as their footsteps fade away.

The next moment Ahimsa arrives.

"Did you find Reet?" I ask quickly.

"No Pooja," he replies, "she is locked up somewhere here but before we search, let me explain what has just happened. I was in the garden outside the auditorium when one of Mr. VJS's men caught me – they tied me up and left me inside his office. It was there that I found Pudding barking inside a cupboard. By the time

I got back here, the explosives were already planted. I decided to inform Dr. Malhotra about the explosives in the passage. The police are already downstairs, and all the students are being evacuated from the school. So we need to find Reet fast."

We nod our heads in unison. This is just too serious for me! We are tired, confused and want to find our friend.

Ahimsa and Satya stare at the conch which is now glowing brightly. Satya carries it in his beak and Natalie and I cuddle up inside his wings. Ahimsa follows with Teja. We seem to fly through thick walls, steel doors and archways until we find ourselves inside a large hallway leading into dark, dusty corridors. Terrified out of our wits, each of us run from room to room searching for Reet.

Suddenly I hear a noise in my head – not the conch, but rather a soft cry. Standing in one of the darkest chambers at the far end of the hallway, I stare around in terror. "What is that noise? Is there a mouse somewhere? What if there are ghosts?" I softly whisper to myself. Ghosts! An icy cold shiver runs down my spine. What am I doing lurking in dark, dilapidated, cold, blood-curdling haunted places!

OMG! My brain is in overdrive! I run out of the room as if all the ghosts of Shraddha International School are chasing me. Looking totally gobsmacked, Teja watches me disappear past him down the corridor and into the darkness. He and Satya chase after me, but I have gone wild, screaming like a lunatic and flapping my arms. Before I know it, I trip on one of the broken pillars and go flying across the floor, hitting my head hard as I fall. I end up sprawled, unmoving, and half dead with piercing pains running up and down my right leg. Stars float above me as I stare at the high ceiling.

Teja grabs me tightly and shouts angrily, "Are you bloody mad? Why the hell are you running like a mad person?" Ignoring him, I watch in fascination as tiny beaded mirrors in the ceiling twinkle and rotate around the large room like stars dancing in the dark night.

Teja shakes me vigorously, "Get up Pooja, you are becoming a drama queen like Reet. I don't need that right now."

"But look," I say dreamily, "the stars are with Reet. Look! She's inside the stars."

"What damn nonsense are you talking about?" shouts my brother anxiously. "Have you gone crazy?"

"There, look! There she is!"

Natalie rushes over, falls to her knee and holds my hand, "Pooja does your head hurt? How many fingers am I holding up?"

As usual she is now the doctor. I ignore her and smile again. As Teja lifts me up, I point to a broken table lying in the corner of the room.

"Look everyone, Reet is inside the stars. She's sleeping!"

Satya starts to flap his wings, louder and louder, and Ahimsa joins in as they hop across the room towards the broken table. Teja follows them wondering if they too have gone mad.

But there beneath the broken table lies Reet, curled and tied up, lying unconscious. Explosives, criminals, ticking bombs – all is forgotten. We stare at our friend, eyes shut and looking deathly pale. Natalie runs across and cradles Reet in her lap. Tears roll down my cheeks as I watch my crazy, mad friend lying unconscious.

"Pooja," Natalie shouts angrily, "whoever left her here knew that the building would blow up soon."

"These people are criminals," Teja exclaims angrily staring at Satya, "can they be so desperate to even kill. Let me inform Dr. Malhotra."

Just then we hear footsteps coming towards us.

OMG! What if it is those thugs with Mr. VJS! We are doomed!

Teja whispers for us to be quiet. And then we hear a familiar deep voice. My eyes grow large, and Teja looks as if he has seen a ghost. Through the door enters Dr. Malhotra, followed by the entire police team and paramedics. Rushing in, he goes straight over to Reet.

"Is she OK?" he asks watching the paramedics attend to her.

"I got a message on my phone from a strange number, telling me to get here quickly. How did you get below my office?"

All of us are dumbstruck! How *did* we get here? Satya and Ahimsa have disappeared!

"Are you all alright," he asks again, looking at me lying on the floor?

"Yes, thank you, Sir," I reply softly, "I think I sprained my ankle."

"Sir, I think she also hurt her head," interrupts my brother.

"Seriously, does he have to exaggerate everything?" I think to myself.

Dr. Malhotra speaks quickly, "Look, we have to get you all out of here immediately. There's an ambulance waiting outside. Teja and Natalie, you come with me. The paramedics will carry Reet and Pooja. There are already policemen trying to defuse the explosives so the quicker we get out, the safer we will be."

Reet and I are admitted to hospital. Satya and Ahimsa never left our hospital room, and each of them wrapped their warm wings around us as we slept soundly through the night. Thankfully, by the next morning my friend was awake and bouncing about like her usual self.

Teja and Natalie arrived to visit, followed by Mrs. Roy. Poor Teja looks so pale, as if he hadn't slept a wink. Trying hard to smile and be cheerful, he says, "Guess what guys, all the students had to stay in local hotels last night. How's that for a treat!"

I hug my brother tightly and tears, once again, roll down my cheeks. "I love you Teja! You are the best!"

Taken back, he guffaws in embarrassment trying to make light of my sudden bout of affection. He then looks at Reet, "Sorry guys, we just heard that both of you are discharged. There's nothing wrong with you besides your brain!"

Mrs. Roy chuckles loudly as she holds Reet tightly and lovingly. The nurse walks in and smiles, "Pooja, your leg should be better within the next few days, but for now you will have to wear a special 'boot' that will help it heal without putting too much pressure on it. Just keep the leg elevated for the next 24 hours."

She then turns to Reet and says in concerning loving way, "Reet, if you feel dizzy or have headaches, you must come back for some tests!"

Teja laughs loudly, "She is a headache already without having a headache! I'm sure she's going to want to stay with Pooja and Natalie for the next week, Mrs. Roy."

Reet shouts excitedly, "Yes please, Mrs. Roy, please!"

Wobbly Mrs. Roy smiles and is just relieved we are all safe, "Girls, you are all going home. Dr. Malhotra has contacted every parent about what happened at school, and a decision has been made to close the school until next term. Kash, Sanam and Diya are staying with family until they fly out to England for the holidays."

"Yippee!" shouts Reet excitedly! "Extra holidays!"

Our parents are on their way, but until they arrive we're staying at the local hotel with Mrs. Roy, Natalie and Teja.

We're so excited to check into the hotel – Reet sharing a room with Mrs. Roy while Natalie and I share a room together. Mrs. Roy couldn't wait to tell us about the headlines we made in the newspaper and how the police, with the help of the Deputy Head, Mr. Vijay Singh caught a man trying to escape.

"What?" we shout together.

Poor Mrs Roy proudly says, "He is our local hero, you know! Today they're checking all the classrooms and buildings to ensure they are safe.

We are dumbfounded! Speechless!

As soon as Mrs. Roy leaves, Natalie shout angrily, "What just happened? How did that sleazy criminal become a national hero?"

"And I prayed he must die in that bomb blast. I am so mad!" replies Reet furiously, slapping her hand on her head.

"Ouch, you hurting your head, Reet," I say quietly.

Teja interrupts us and says softly, "Ladies, we will ask the Magic Man, but for now listen to my story. We have a secret!"

"What are you talking about? Everything we have done so far is a secret – from the Magic Man to the explosives," I giggle nervously. As if on cue, we hear the soft flapping and swishing of wings as Satya and Ahimsa arrive to join our conversation.

"Listen to what happened yesterday, and you will realise how huge this secret is!" Teja continues, looking at me seriously.

He explains. "Dr. Malhotra called me to his office this morning. He said he had received a message from an unknown person telling him where to find the explosives in the auditorium, but the only way he could get there was through a hidden trapdoor in his office. He didn't understand what it meant, because there was no trapdoor nor hidden passageway below his office. He frantically searched his walls and cupboards, checked underneath the carpet and everywhere. There was no hidden door. Then he received a second message that the painting was in front of him. He was shocked. How did the person know he hadn't found the hidden trapdoor? Was there someone hiding in his office?

"He quickly locked the office door and walked towards the famous painting, *Talking to the Swan*. Moving it to one side he found a small blank pad embedded into the wall. He tried to twist and move it around, but it didn't move. Then another message came. This time it was a question – what year was Raja Ravi Varma born? Find the answer on the painting and press the four buttons on the pad. Scanning the painting meticulously, he found the year 1848 with the signature of the artist. As soon as he entered the numbers the pad beeped and the trapdoor opened.

"He found a stairway leading him down and along a long passage until he found the sealed wall with the explosives and the chamber where he found us. He was very grateful that we had found Reet before the explosives went off.

"Sorry Reet!" Natalie exclaims sadly. Reet is oblivious as to what has happened, and stares at each of us unbelievingly.

I look at Ahimsa and smile playfully, "So did you enjoy sending those text messages to Dr. Malhotra?"

"What?" Natalie and Reet shout together.

Teja interrupts, "Wow! Ahimsa. I'm sure you chuckled loudly as you hid in his office playing games with him? How cool was that detective work!"

Ahimsa raises his long neck, and looking at me with his gentle eyes, winks and replies, "Yes Teja, besides rescuing Pudding and playing hide-and-seek with Mr. VJS and his stooges."

"Why don't we check out the snowball?" says Satya.

"OMG! That is the best thing I've heard today." I jump up, but the pain shoots up my foot, and I topple back into the chair.

"OK, Miss super-fit sister," says my brother mischievously lifting the bag on to the bed. "Can I at least take it out for you?"

Silently we watch as the snowball begins to shine brightly. Before I can blink, the Magic Man appears.

"Pooja," he says gently, "I hope you and Reet are feeling much better."

I must be drugged or delirious because I don't have an answer.

The Magic Man continues, "Reet, you are a very brave person to have followed those girls, and didn't think about yourself when you put yourself in danger. Pudding is safe and Mrs. Roy has arranged for him to stay with a staff member."

"Wow! Thank you," she says. This time she cannot jump or dance around. I smile to myself but refuse to make eye contact with the Magic Man. He has put us through such danger with criminals, explosives, guns, and people getting hurt. It's not right.

"Pooja, are you still angry with me?"

Again I refuse to communicate! I am an Indian and like things simple and practical. But in the last few months, I have had no control of my life. However, after hurting my head, something has definitely shifted. I am learning to accept that this is my destiny and crazy things are going to happen.

The Magic Man says lovingly, "Pooja, I have to thank you for handling this mission so well. Even though you fought and argued with me, you still managed to complete this first mission. You, Teja, Natalie, and Reet saved the school."

Everyone jumps up excitedly, "Yes, we did! Yippee."

Reet interrupts, "But please Mr. Magic Man, for our next project, don't confuse us with such difficult codes and messages."

We all laugh, even the Magic Man chuckles softly.

"What happened to Selina and Neal," asks Natalie guardedly, "have they been caught?"

"No, the Millennium Corporation haven't finished looting our treasures. They will be back. To avoid getting implicated, they were on a flight back to England yesterday afternoon."

"What about Mr. VJS?" whispers Reet fearfully, "Please tell me why he didn't die?"

He laughs softly, "No, Reet, until the children are rescued, we need Mr. VJS at this school.

"And you made him the national hero?" I snigger angrily.

"Pooja, that is to give him added confidence and arrogance. Then watch how it will destroy him. Millennium Corporation has no idea that everything beneath that auditorium has been sealed again. Dr. Malhotra cannot open the trapdoor again unless an entry code is given to him. There's no evidence of palaces, children, treasures or guards or anything. It will never open again until the time is right and you unlock those doors."

"What? Why?" asks Teja curiously.

"Remember, Teja, I told you years ago that a curse had fallen unto man through his greed for power. That Age of Darkness continues to reign," whispers the Magic Man, "the hidden temple that lies buried far beneath the fort is part of your mission to discover. It is Pooja's destiny to help unravel this mystery. No man nor machine can stop this mission. Now the time has come for each of you to play a valuable part in this mission so that the Golden Age can be ushered into this world. It is only then, will all of humanity live in harmony."

As he speaks, the light spreads across the room and slowly it disappears as the Magic Man fades away.

The next afternoon our parents arrive to take us home. I'm ecstatic to go home, but why do I have a strange feeling something more is about to happen! I have just finished packing and security have carried our bags out to the cars. Natalie has gone down to help Reet. Thankfully our precious documents and gems are safely stored away with Satya. Inside my backpack I have the snowball and Rubik's Cube carefully packed. Standing at the open door, I smile as I stare at the empty room. I have grown up in the last few months. I fought with my parents for sending me here, but today I can proudly say, I am so happy to be a student at Shraddha International School. Maybe my mother was right after all!

I walk back to check my cupboard one last time when suddenly the door shuts. I turn around quickly. A cold shiver runs down my spine. I yank the door open and peep down the corridor. Everything is dead quiet. Trying not to think anything sinister, I dash out of the room and down the corridor towards the car park where my parents are waiting.

Still shaken and frightened, I hug my mother tightly, and from the corner of my eye, I see a shadow move behind a glass window at the very top of the library building. Who is that? There is no attic or room at the top! But there is someone watching me! My face turns deathly white!

Shaking off this uneasy feeling, I smile and turn towards my friends. I cannot wait to get back home – Emerald Cascades, here we come!

Inside a hidden, dark room at the very top of the library, a man with beady, black eyes stares menacingly as the last car leaves the school. He limps back to his desk, switches on the lamp and glares at the photographs he has pasted on the wall in front of him. He picks up an intricately carved silver letter opener, and from his seat, throws it angrily at the pictures. The sharp, pointed tip hits Pooja's forehead. He laughs to himself as he slowly removes his false leg!

THE END